DS 2/23
→ NOVt

KT-549-546

9030 00007 5997 9

## PRAISE FOR *BLACK REED BAY*

'Urgent, thrilling and richly imagined. Without doubt his best yet' Chris Whitaker

'Reynolds captures the claustrophobic feel of a small town ... a tense slice of American noir' Vaseem Khan

'Brilliant ... if you love Harlen Coben and Lee Child, you will love this ... the sense of place is absolutely startling ... cinematic, epic, you will forget to breathe, everything you want from a thriller' Miranda Dickinson

'Compelling and stylish, with devious twists and a cleverly crafted ending. Very, very impressive' G J Minnett

'If you were hooked on *Mare of Easttown*, this will be right up your street ... I read this obsessively' Nina Pottell, *Prima*

'Beautifully written, deeply atmospheric and cleverly plotted, with a brilliant new protagonist' Andrea Carter

'Rod Reynolds has done it again with his superb new thriller! *Black Reed Bay* is a twisty, high-stakes, high-voltage murder mystery featuring a serial killer, sickening police corruption, and a badass but vulnerable protagonist who can't be bought and won't give up: a must read!' Tim Baker

'Tough, determined and full of heart, Casey Wray's a legend in the making. *Black Reed Bay* is utterly gripping and packs one hell of an emotional punch. Perfect for fans of *Bosch*' Steph Broadribb

'There's something particularly special about *Black Reed Bay*, and it's Detective Casey Wray ... I felt like I'd known her all my life' Joy Kluver

'A showpiece that clearly demonstrates Reynolds' command of the American thriller genre. No mean feat' Jenny O'Brien

'Awesome read. A turn of the screw in every chapter' Oscar de Muriel

'Addictive and intelligent, with its inspiration in the dark unknown of the Long Island Serial Killer and with an enduring cast of characters, including protagonist Casey, who hopefully we will meet again' Liz Loves Books

'This is a cinematic read I can see on the big screen. I have never been to Long Island, but I feel I have now. The attention to detail and the clarity with which Rod evokes the setting and time is quite impressive' The Book Trail

'A very clever and unputdownable read ... *Black Reed Bay* will pull you in ... I'm sure I've found another one of my top ten reads of the year. Brilliant stuff' Hooked from Page One

'With slow, building tension, an understated element of threat and an overwhelming sense of mystery, fans of the author really will enjoy this book' Jen Med's Book Reviews

'It's another cracking crime thriller from one of my favourite authors, and I'm delighted to see that it's just the first in a new series. I can't wait to see what he's got in store for Casey Wray next' Espresso Coco

'An intelligent and super-addictive high-octane action thriller / crime novel / police procedural – call it what you want, but call it excellent, because that is what it is ... Impressive writing, well-rounded characters, oodles of atmosphere, tons of suspense until the riveting end'
From Belgium with Booklove

'Rod Reynolds is a marvellous writer. He isn't flash, or showy, but what he writes is immaculately crafted, beautifully plotted and so well thought through that his characters blaze with authenticity ... Pitch perfect, stylish and beautifully rendered' Live and Deadly

## WHAT THE READERS ARE SAYING
★★★★★

'The first book I have read by Rod Reynolds but it won't be my last'

'Tense from the very beginning and had me turning pages late into the night'

'Crackling with pace and life'

'A British author who manages to set books in America ... and still makes them come alive!'

'A really tense crime read'

'Flows superbly and has the reader gripped'

'A gripping read from start to end'

'Very thrilling and plenty of twists'

'I loved this taut, tense thriller'

## PRAISE FOR *BLOOD RED CITY*

'A searing, white-hot journey through the dark underbelly of modern London. Bristling with tension, danger and seamed with the constant threat of violence, *Blood Red City* is both crime fiction at its gripping best and an all-too-believable portrait of a city under the sinister control of the oligarchs ... confirms Rod Reynolds' status as one of the greatest crime talents of his generation' Tim Baker

'Echoes of the fears and worries of a modern world abound in this pacy and subtle novel' *Sun*

'They say that London is the money-laundering capital of the world. Rod Reynolds shows how that is possible in this complex thriller. His London is fast, busy and full of threats ... Reynolds is a great scene setter and he is as good at action as he is at the development of Lydia's character. She is brave, clever, sometimes silly and absolutely credible'
*Literary Review*

'A well-researched, complex and fully realised story with three-dimensional lead characters. The creeping tension and mistrust is palpable' *Shots Mag*

'You are in for a treat with this whip-smart contemporary thriller. Strikingly realistic with an exciting, serpentine plot. I couldn't put it down!' Hair Past a Freckle

'Wow! If you love a tense, tight thriller which must immediately be made into a film, look no further! ... it's another stunner!' Phillipa's Quick Book Review

'Brilliant read from start to finish ... couldn't put it down' Dawn W

'Packs the pages with tension and thrills ... This is a wonderfully twisty story and I was totally hooked from the outset' Grab This Book

'An exciting thriller – the chase across London to find answers, witnesses and a body is full on ...Fans of Holly Watt will love this tale' Booksplainer

'Reynolds has given us a glorious, compelling story, a fast-moving, heart-in-the-mouth chase set against the magnificent background of London in all its pomp, all its grim and shabbiness' David Harris

'A complex string of events that the author masterfully weaves in to a kicker of an ending' The Twist and Turn Book Blog

'A combination of darkness, gritty reality and an insight into the murky world that surrounds those people with billions of pounds at their disposal. It's fast paced, paranoia-riddled ... A punchy, taut, gripping read' Books behind the Title

'The intricate plot is expertly planned and satisfyingly developed ... at breakneck pace ... Rod Reynolds has a background in advertising and media, and this is strongly reflected in his writing' Paterson Loarn

# BLACK REED BAY

## ABOUT THE AUTHOR

Rod Reynolds is the author of four novels, including the Charlie Yates series. His 2015 debut, *The Dark Inside*, was longlisted for the CWA New Blood Dagger, and was followed by *Black Night Falling* (2016) and *Cold Desert Sky* (2018); the *Guardian* has called the books 'pitch-perfect American noir'. A lifelong Londoner, in 2020 Orenda Books published *Blood Red City*, his first novel set in his hometown.

Rod previously worked in advertising as a media buyer, and holds an MA in novel writing from City University London. He lives with his wife and family and spends most of his time trying to keep up with his two young daughters. Follow him on Twitter @Rod_WR, and his website: www.rodreynolds.com.

**Also by Rod Reynolds and available**
**from Orenda Books**
*Blood Red City*

# BLACK REED BAY

### ROD REYNOLDS

**ORENDA
BOOKS**

Orenda Books
16 Carson Road
West Dulwich
London SE21 8HU
www.orendabooks.co.uk

First published in the United Kingdom by Orenda Books, 2021
Copyright © Rod Reynolds, 2021

Rod Reynolds has asserted his moral right to be identified as the author of this work in accordance with the Copyright, Designs and Patents Act, 1988.

All Rights Reserved. No part of this publication may be reproduced in any form or by any means without the written permission of the publishers.

*This is a work of fiction. Names, characters, places and incidents are either products of the author's imagination or are used fictitiously. Any resemblance to actual events, locales or persons, living or dead, is entirely coincidental.*

A catalogue record for this book is available from the British Library.

ISBN 978-1-913193-67-6
eISBN 978-1-913193-68-3

Typeset in Garamond by www.typesetter.org.uk
Nature Vectors by Vecteezy.com

Printed and bound by CPI Group (UK) Ltd, Croydon CR0 4YY

For sales and distribution, please contact info@orendabooks.co.uk

*For Izzy*

| LONDON BOROUGH OF WANDSWORTH | |
| --- | --- |
| 9030 00007 5997 9 | |
| **Askews & Holts** | |
| AF CRI | |
| | WW21004137 |

# PROLOGUE

Casey staggered across the beach towards the access tunnel, Maggie's arm draped over her shoulder. She could feel McTeague's eyes on her back, no need to turn to see it, his rebuke as unnerving as the stolen gun bulging her waistband.

Maggie had fallen silent now, shock and exhaustion overpowering even her heartache. The dump site where they'd found the bodies was a half-mile away, tracking north, on the far side of Ramona Boulevard. Six weeks since their discovery; a chance find, nothing like what they'd expected. A rotting wasteland that embraced death, lifting its veil to reveal a depravity none of them were prepared for at the time.

A plane came in low overhead, on its way to JFK or Newark, its lights blinking against the coming darkness. Casey's feet sank deeper into the sand with every step, bearing Maggie's weight like it was her own grief and sense of loss made human. The waves washed over the beach behind them, what was usually a calming sound now grinding in the face of hopelessness. Because that was the truth of the situation; so many dead already, the pain and sorrow inflicted on so many lives, and still they were no closer to an answer. The lies like the dunes that backstopped the beach, mounting over time, until one day you realised you couldn't see past them.

McTeague overtook them and went into the access tunnel, heavy footfalls echoing off the concrete. As they approached the entrance, Casey looked up at the graffiti sprayed above the tunnel mouth:

*You live in my* ♥

Red letters, cramped together in a childlike script. The paint had run in places, the heart shape smeared and faded. Everything about it almost impossibly sad.

# CHAPTER 1

*Six Weeks Earlier*

Cullen was waiting by the car, two Starbucks take-out cups on the roof. He pushed one to Casey's side as she came over. 'How's your head?'

She took it from him, mouthing 'thanks', with a grimace to demonstrate how bad she felt. Alcohol messed with her caffeine dependency – usually coffee was the first thing on her mind in the mornings, but after a night out drinking, the next day was all about a breakfast burrito and a chocolate milkshake. A weakness she'd never admit to Cullen. 'I'm good.'

They climbed into the car. Cullen started the engine, looking over. 'Heard you were dancing last night?'

'You've seen me dance.' Casey jacked the heater to full and held her hands over the vent, one after the other.

'When?'

'At Mickey Capel's wedding.'

'That was dancing? I thought you were having a breakdown.'

She flipped him off, grinning.

He backed the car out of the space and steered them out of the Third Precinct parking lot. 'So?' He looked over again.

'They played Beyoncé, what do you want me to say? You play Beyoncé, I'm gonna dance—'

'No, not the dancing.' Cullen snorted as he said it. 'Who was there?'

'I'm not your snitch.'

'The hell you aren't.'

'You wanna know the dirt, you bring your own ass to

Shakey's. I stayed up until two o'clock in the goddamn morning, I earned my secrets.'

'You want to know what I was doing at 2am? Changing a diaper.'

Casey said the words along with him. 'Is that, like, your catchphrase now? You said the same thing last month.' She let go of a yawn. 'You knew what you were signing up for.'

Cullen watched the road, pretending to sulk.

Casey took a drink from her coffee, but it was watery, her taste buds annihilated by too many mojitos, needing salt, sugar, grease to jolt them back to life.

Cullen touched his nose, the way he did when he had something to say but wanted her to ask first. She ignored him, knowing he'd spill it eventually.

Sure enough...

'I heard Billy D was getting tight with someone.'

Casey shot him her best knowing smile, although he always told her it looked like a leer. Billy Drocker was the youngest detective in the office, with a reputation as a player – in his own mind, at least. This was the first she'd heard of him on the prowl the night before – but she wasn't going to dent her rep as the gossip queen by letting Cullen know that.

He opened his hands on the wheel. 'Come on...'

'I told you. You get your ass to the bar and you won't need me to help you catch up.'

'Was it you?'

She nearly spit coffee. 'No!'

He thought about it, then nodded to himself. 'I'm gonna tell people it was you.'

'Son of a—' She couldn't get the last word out, laughing too hard. 'You're a dick.'

'What's wrong with Billy? He's young, he's fun, he says he's hung...'

'Jesus Chr— ... Are you trying to make me throw up here? You really think that's the image I need in my head right now?'

Cullen went quiet, but he was giggling to himself – a tell there was more coming. After a few seconds: 'So there must be someone else then. That's why you're being coy.'

'Well actually...' she angled herself towards him, fluttering her eyelids and putting on her best Marilyn Monroe voice '...I'm forever holding out for you, David.' She purred at him until he couldn't keep a straight face any longer.

He turned back to the road, shaking his head. 'I'll find out, you know. I'm a detective.'

'You couldn't detect a fart in a paper bag.'

'I taught you everything you know, Big.'

'No, you taught me everything *you* know. And I never forgot that morning.'

'I'll crash this car, you hurt my feelings like that. Swear to God.'

'It'd be a goddamn relief.'

She looked at him again, and he winked at her, breaking into his infectious little chuckle, which took her along with him.

She only stopped when her head started to protest, her hangover reasserting itself. Payday drinking was a tradition in the department, the same venue, mostly the same faces every month. Cullen got smart and called time on his attendance when his wife Luisa gave birth to their second kid, and now they went through this routine each time, as he tried to live vicariously through Casey.

The needling about her personal life came up like clockwork too, more a running joke than a serious enquiry these days. It was over a year since Luisa made her last attempt to set Casey up on a blind date, sending Cullen to work with a picture of 'Brad she knew from college' and an offer to have them both over for dinner sometime. Casey's polite but firm rejection got the message across, and the game around the department went on: who could get Casey Wray to drop a crumb about her home life? Different rumours reached her over time – frequently at first, but less so since she made sergeant: that she had a boyfriend serving overseas, that she was a lesbian, that she'd had her heart broken before she joined the department and quit men as a result.

She never commented on them; it amused her some to keep people guessing, but mostly because the truth just wasn't that interesting. She worked eighty-hour weeks in a job that left her physically and emotionally drained, and the only folk she spoke to were cops and perps; stable relationships did not arise from that scenario.

But thinking about the blind-date offer now reminded her how much she'd secretly appreciated the gesture, and she decided to throw Cullen a bone. 'You know who did show up last night?'

'Who?'

'McTeague.'

He glanced over. 'Seriously?'

She nodded her head. The one face that wasn't a regular: Robbie McTeague. The name alone inspired a cautious reverence. Among the older hands in the department, he was known as The Hat, on account of how many different ones he wore: major-case lead detective; ethics enforcer; the chief's strong arm; spy for the DA.

'What's that about?'

She shrugged, her eyes bugged out to show she was genuine this time. 'Maybe the chief sent him to make sure no one's having too much fun.'

'Was he drinking?'

'Couple beers. He didn't stay all that long.'

Cullen contemplated that as if he could divine some significance from it.

Casey cupped her hands around her coffee, still trying to warm them up. 'I always think he pulls those moves when he wants to rattle someone.'

'Who?'

'I don't—'

'No, for real now, you can't keep that kinda shit to yourself.' His expression turned serious for the first time.

'Honestly, I'm just spitballing. I don't know why he was there.' She saw him stealing glances at her. 'Swear to God. Now would you watch the road?'

It was true she didn't know why McTeague had come. It wasn't the case that he never showed up for drinks, but it was rare. And more than that, he never did anything without a purpose. She rubbed her head and looked out the window, the bay coming into view in the distance under a sky so cold and hard it could've been blue ice. 'Where is this place anyhow?'

'Ramona Villas. It's in the centre of the island.'

She knew the name but not the locale. A hundred miles of barrier islands ran parallel to Long Island's south shore, and the section that fell under Hampstead County's jurisdiction was twenty miles long but less than a half-mile wide on average – and in places, barely wider than the highway; looking at a map, it was like a long, thin stick caught in the surf just off the shore. But even their small stretch was made up of more than a dozen beach communities, many of them affluent enough to employ private-security companies – limiting their contact with HCPD.

'You get a chance to listen to the 911 call yet?' Cullen said.

'Not yet.'

He took one hand off the wheel and dug into his pocket, pulling out his cell phone and passing it to her. 'Here.'

Casey took it from him, looking at the screen. 'You got a message from Luisa here. Says she's divorcing you because you're a deadbeat.'

'Yeah, yeah.'

'How's she doing?'

'Tired. Same as always.' Cullen and Luisa had two daughters – four-year-old Sienna, and Shauna, who was just three months. Casey had been waging a light-hearted campaign for years, telling him Lu was too good for him, but truth was, they were the best-suited couple she knew. A teacher before she had the kids, Luisa was smart, practical and matter-of-fact, in a way that grounded a man who was prone to spells lost in his own head.

He reached over and tapped the screen, one eye on the road. 'There. Hit play.'

Casey started the recording and held the iPhone's speaker to her ear.

'Hampstead County 911, what's your emergency please?'

'He said ... Oh, fuck he's...'

'Ma'am?'

'He's gonna kill me.'

'Ma'am? Who's...?'

'I just fucking told you, he's gonna...'

'Okay, ma'am, can you give me your name please?'

'Tina Grace.'

'I see you're on a cell phone. The system has you on the beaches by Ocean Road. Can I get your location?'

'I don't ... Fuck, I think he's coming.'

'Ma'am, can you tell me where you're at?'

'I don't ... Barton Beach, somewhere in there. Please, you need to send someone, I need...'

'Can you give me an exact location? Can you see an address anywhere around you?'

'No. No, I...'

The call became unintelligible for a few seconds, a rustling on the line as if the woman was holding it to her body or was running.

'Ma'am?'

'Fuck, fuck, fuck...'

'Ma'am I want you to stay on the line, I have a unit headed for you now. I need you to move to somewhere they can track you down. Is there a highway near you or any kind of ... anything the officers can use to locate you?'

'I'm looking at ... It's all houses. 214, there's one back there with 214 on it...'

'If you're in immediate danger can you try to seek shelter in one of the houses?'

'I tried, I ... I already knocked on this motherfucker's door but they won't open it.'

'And there's a man pursuing you?'

'He's gonna fucking kill me. Where are the cops?'

'Tina, can you tell me the man's name?'

A sharp crack made Casey jerk the phone away from her ear. She waited but the recording came to an end in silence. 'There anything more?'

Cullen shook his head, taking his phone back. 'That's all of it.'

'Figure she dropped her cell?'

'Could be.'

'What time was this?'

'A quarter after four this morning.'

*Tina Grace.* Casey said the name to herself as she looked at the time on the dash; a little over five hours ago. 'We have anything on her beyond the name?'

'Home number – no answer. We're trying to work it back to an address.'

'Anyone try calling the cell back?'

'It's dead.'

Casey pulled her seatbelt slack so she could stretch her shoulders. 'Maybe when she dropped it.'

'I guess.'

'What? What're you thinking?'

'If someone took it outta her hand...'

Casey nodded as he spoke, shook by the terror in the girl's voice. The words she'd used. 'She sounds young.'

'And strung out.'

Cullen made a right onto Fifteenth Street, took them down to the causeway that connected the beaches to the mainland. They cruised out over Black Reed Bay, the car jolting as it crossed each join between the concrete slabs that made up the roadway. At more than a mile long, by the midpoint it always felt to Casey like they were in the middle of the ocean; up ahead, the islands were still a thin line of green and brown dividing the water from the sky, the only marker they hadn't left dry land for good. A clear day, the winter sun still climbing, white light reflecting off the bay all around them, flooding through the windshield – but carrying no warmth. Casey fumbled in the door compartment for her shades.

She brought up the maps app on her phone, studied the area around Barton Beach. 'Ramona Villas isn't in Barton Beach.' She used her fingers to estimate the distance on the screen. 'They're different places, must be two miles from there.'

'Uh-huh.'

'So did we track her to Ramona Villas?'

'Her boyfriend lives there, he called 911 too. And half his neighbourhood.'

'They had a fight?'

'Sounds that way. She was tearing the place up, spooking the residents. Half the homes'll be empty for the winter, probably sounded like she's raising holy hell.'

'So the boyfriend was the one trying to kill her?'

'Not according to patrol.'

'No?'

'Nope. Regular square.'

'Then who?'

'Said he didn't know. He's talking like she just flipped out.'

Casey gazed at the water, playing it out in her mind. Imagining this woman going house to house, looking for help against whoever the hell had her terrified. Domestic call-outs were a lose-lose in her experience; patrol dealt with most of them and it was rare for one to require detective bureau involvement. The few that did come their way usually involved one party or the other having disappeared, only to show up a day or two later when tempers had calmed and everyone's time had been wasted. Sometimes it was a matter of hours, just long enough for the misper to sober up or come down. But the other kind – the kind that came along maybe once a year – was the one where a body was waiting for them at the scene.

'You're chewing on something,' Cullen said.

Casey kept her eyes on the water, always so ominous in the winter months, no matter how calm. The reeds that gave the bay its name were coming into view in the distance. 'I can't figure why she'd say she was in Barton Beach.'

Cullen shook his head. 'Let's see what the boyfriend's got to say.'

Ramona Villas was a small neighbourhood in Ramona Beach, a seafront township dotted over more than two miles until it came up against neighbouring Barton Beach. The Villas was a one-street community that branched off of the only highway, Ocean Road, before looping round to rejoin it further along. Ocean Road itself ran east-west for more than twenty miles across the length of the island, and then on over water to link it to the rest of the chain. Two crossing points moored the island to the mainland – the western route via the causeway they'd just taken, and the shorter bridge across Black Reed Bay's narrower eastern expanse.

Headed east on Ramona Boulevard, Casey watched the houses as they passed. Big lots, facing the ocean; every one of them had to run well north of a million dollars. Pristine whitewashed exteriors, tidy yards, the majority with boats on their drives, trailered and tarped for the winter. She thought about the payments on her car, manageable on a detective's salary, but not comfortable, and wondered for the hundredth time in her life how anyone made enough money to afford a vacation home.

'This is our boy,' Cullen said, pulling up to the kerb outside a two-storey clapboard house straight from the same cookie-cutter as all the others. A patrol car was parked on the driveway. 'Jon Parker, aged forty-six. No record, never been in any trouble at all.'

'Forty-six? That's gotta make for an age gap with the girlfriend.'

Cullen pushed his door open. 'You all lust after us older men. Be honest.'

Casey smacked him on the arm – because he was asking for it and because, at forty-one, he had barely two years on her.

The uniforms climbed out at the same time as them, and Casey recognised Frank Kidman coming round from the passenger side of the cruiser, stamping his feet as he walked to warm them up. He touched his temple with one finger as a greeting.

'Morning, Big. If I'd known they were sending you I'd have brought flowers.'

'Why? You wanna fuck with my allergies, Frankie? '

Kidman smiled. 'You guys know Underhill?' He gestured to his partner and nods passed all around.

'What do we got?' Casey said.

Kidman hooked his thumb at the house. 'Jon Parker, he's the owner, called it in last night. You listened to the 911?'

Casey and Cullen nodded.

'Sounds like bad shit, but Mr Parker says he wasn't the one chasing her, and there was no one else out there. Way he tells it, she just freaked out and took off.'

'You take a statement?'

Kidman nodded. 'Not much more than what I just told you.'

The front door opened, and a man stood in the doorway. He looked like he wanted to come over but couldn't decide if he was allowed.

'You searched the house?' Cullen said.

Kidman shook his head. 'He wouldn't consent to it.'

Casey glanced at the man watching them, his breath fogging the second it met the freezing air. 'We'll revisit that. What about along the street?'

Kidman pointed west. 'The last ping on her cell placed her within a half-mile radius of here – there's only one tower, so they couldn't pinpoint it any tighter than that. She mentioned the address 214, so we went up that far, but neither of us saw shit. Right?'

Underhill nodded.

'Any sign of her phone?'

Kidman was shaking his head. 'We looked around outside 214 – the front yard, both sides of the road; if it's there, we didn't find it – but I'm pretty sure. Spoke to the owner, Mr Stadler – he saw the girl, said she woke them up banging on the door, but they didn't talk to her. They called 911 because they were worried for her. He couldn't say if she still had her phone when she was outside, didn't know anything about it. Haven't come across it on their property so far.'

'Did he see anybody chasing her?'

He shook his head, eyes closed.

Casey looked along the road. 'How far is 214?'

Kidman pointed. 'Four houses along. Few hundred yards, maybe.'

'So what about these other properties in between?'

'Mr Sandford lives next door to Mr Parker, he saw her...' He pointed to the neighbouring house. 'Another 911 caller. Didn't see where she went, didn't see anyone else on the street with her. Except Mr Parker. We didn't get to the rest yet.'

Parker stepped down from the doorway at hearing his name.

Casey saw him coming but she looked along the road, then back at Kidman. 'So that leaves the two in between. Go try them now, let me know what you get from the residents.'

Kidman and Underhill slipped away as the man approached, aiming for Cullen, his hand out to shake. 'I'm Jon Parker, this is my place.'

'Detective David Cullen, and this is Detective Sergeant Casey Wray.'

Parker shook Cullen's hand, could only spare Casey a nod. 'How you doing today, detectives?'

Parker was trim and lean, wearing a black turtleneck sweater and grey dress pants. He had the deep tan of a man who lived at the beach year-round, and his hair was a chestnut brown, worn short. She would've made him for younger than he was if not for the receding hairline around his temples. 'You made a 911 call this morning concerning your girlfriend?'

'Yeah, but I already told these guys, she's not my girlfriend.' He nodded to indicate the uniforms.

Casey took out her pocketbook, wrote down *girlfriend?*, wondering why that would be the first point he wanted to clarify. 'Tina Grace, that's her name?'

'Yes, ma'am.'

'So what is your relationship to Miss Grace?'

Parker wrapped one fist inside the other, pursing his lips. 'It's ... we're casual, you know?'

'Uh-huh. And you're aware she told the dispatcher someone was trying to kill her?'

'Yeah, I know. Wasn't me though. I told the patrol officers that too. I don't have a clue what was going on with her.'

'She'd been at your property?' Cullen said.

'Yeah. Yes, sir. But she completely lost her...' He glanced from one to the other. 'She freaked out and said she had to go. I asked her why and she says someone's coming for her, so I tried to calm her down, said I'd call her a cab, and that worked at first because she sat down on the couch. So I went to get her a glass of water, and she just took off. Gone. The first thing I knew was when I heard the front door slam. After that she's running down the street, shouting about someone coming to kill her.'

'Did you go after her?' Casey said.

'Sure, I mean, at first. But anytime I got close she spun out worse, so I quit. I didn't know she was calling the cops.'

'Was there anyone else with you?'

He shook his head, eyes closed.

'Anyone else on the street?'

He shook it again.

'You have any idea at all what could've spooked her that way?'

'No, ma'am, none.'

He looked at her and then at Cullen, taking his hands out of his pockets and folding his arms. His expression was neutral but he came off jittery, riffling his fingers against his bicep. Or it could just be that he was cold.

They were standing in the shadow of the house, and even though the morning was bright, Casey could feel the chill penetrating the soles of her shoes and through her coat. She rubbed her hands and clasped them together, making use of it. 'You think we could talk inside?'

Parker glanced back at the house, then said, 'Uh, sure, okay.' He turned to show them in.

The front door opened onto a spacious living room that Parker had obviously spent money on. The furnishings were high-end European style, right out of a magazine shoot, centred on an L-shaped sofa suite around a square glass coffee table the size of a football field. 'Can I get you something to drink?'

Casey nodded. 'I'll take a water. Thanks.'

Parker disappeared into the kitchen, and Casey made a tour of the room. To their left the wall was lined with artwork, modern pieces that were all about colour and form, at odds with the restored wooden ship's wheel mounted above the front door. Straight ahead of them, two steps led up to a wide den lined with bookcases, a cracked leather sofa tucked away to one side; large folding doors framed the beach and the ocean beyond.

She moved slowly towards the steps, then paused by the coffee table; there were indentations in the carpet indicating it'd been recently moved. She looked at Cullen, pointing them out with her foot. He nodded as she moved on.

She'd just made it to the den when Parker came back. 'Beautiful view.'

He handed her a glass. 'Thank you.'

'Mr Parker, when did you last see Miss Grace?'

He planted one hand under his chin, balling his fingers. 'I guess when she was heading down the street.'

'What time would that be?'

'After four.'

'Can you describe what she was wearing, please?'

'Lemme see ... I guess a black top and jeans. Black jeans too, I mean.'

'Can you be any more specific? Any logos or distinguishing marks on them?'

He shook his head. 'Her top was one of those strapless ones. But just plain, no designs on it.'

'What about a coat?' Cullen said.

He screwed his eyes shut. 'That was black too. Thin, though, not a winter coat. Didn't come past her waist. She had the collar turned up.' He motioned with his hands, as if it needed a demonstration.

Casey baulked at the description; Tina Grace running scared in the dark, and completely unprepared for the cold. 'And have you had any contact with her since?'

'No. Her cell's dead and there's no answer at her place.'

'What's her address?'

Parker held his hands out as if he was powerless. 'I don't know it. I don't know where she lives. I just have her numbers and ... I tried messaging her, but...'

Cullen came over to join them, his notepad and pen ready, prompting Parker to reel off the details he did have from his cell. When he finished, Cullen said, 'She live out here or on the mainland?'

'Mainland. She lives somewhere in town.'

'Family, friends?'

'Look, it's like I told you, we're real casual. It's not like we're...' He made the same gesture.

'Understood,' Casey said. 'How long have you been seeing each other? Casually.'

'Maybe, like, a month.'

'Is this the first time she's been over here?'

Parker hesitated, as if he was trying to remember. 'No. She's been two or three times now.'

Casey was making notes too, so Cullen jumped in again. 'Has Miss Grace ever done anything like this before?'

'Not with me.' Parker perched on the arm of the sofa.

'But with someone else?'

'No – I mean, not so far as I know.'

'Does she have any history of erratic behaviour? Any mental-health issues?'

'I don't think that I'd know, even if she did. It's not the kind of thing we talked about.'

'Were you guys drinking last night?'

'Yeah, some. We had a couple beers.'

'Anything else?'

'I had some wine with dinner but that was before she came over—'

'Narcotics, Mr Parker. He's asking if either of you were getting high.'

'What? No. No.'

'Okay. You understand, it's a question we have to ask given the circumstances. Does Tina use drugs? Could she have taken something before she came over?'

He rubbed his forehead with the heel of his hand. 'I mean, it's possible, but I never saw her take anything when she was with me. She seemed fine when she arrived.'

Casey held his stare a moment, then went on. 'Okay. So talk me through what happened last night.'

'Well ... Tina came over around eleven, we had some drinks and then, uh...'

'You guys were intimate?'

Parker looked away, embarrassed. 'Yeah.'

'And then?'

He spread his hands. 'I fell asleep. We were in the bedroom and the lights were on, and I guess I woke up sometime later and, we ... uh, we had sex again, and it was after that she went crazy.'

'Right after, or did something happen?'

'Not right after. Like, a few minutes after. She was putting her clothes on.'

'Did she get a phone call or a text, anything like that?'

'I didn't see her with her phone, but I was in the bathroom for a minute, so...'

'So it's possible,' Casey said.

Parker scratched his cheek and opened his hand – *who knows?*

Cullen pointed with his pen. 'Where did you guys meet?'

'What?'

'You and Tina. Where'd you first hook up?'

He squinted, as if he was trying to remember. 'A bar in town.'

'Which one?'

'I think Skunk, it's on Riddell.'

'You think?'

He made a kind of half-shrug. 'I was partying a lot at the time.'

'How come?'

'How come I was partying?'

'Yeah.'

'I'm sorry, but what? Do I need a reason?'

'No, of course not,' Casey said. 'The patrol officers say you refused consent to search your property?'

Parker looked off to the side. 'That's right.'

'Any reason why?'

His expression turned incredulous. 'You think she's hiding under the bed or something? I told you, she ran off. Go ask the rest of the neighbourhood, they saw her.'

'We will. But you have to see that with what she said on her 911 call and the fact you were the last person to speak to her, we need to take a look around.'

'You can't seriously think ... I called you guys in, for God's sake.'

'I understand, Mr Parker. It's not an accusation. It's possible she left some clue to her disappearance – intentionally or otherwise – in your property. That could really help us out.'

Parker looked at them.

Cullen stepped forward. 'The alternative is we go get a warrant. That's a process – not always a quick one. So while we're waiting, we'll need to have officers stay with you. Couple cruisers parked up on your property. The neighbourhood will see, that's for sure. And a place like this, story like this, good chance the media gets a tip-off too. Maybe send a TV truck to sit outside and keep an eye on things while we wait. Catch that footage of a team of investigators coming back with their warrant to pick this place apart—'

'Or...' Casey held her hand up. 'Or, we take a quick walk around your house right now, and no one has to know anything about it.'

Parker didn't move for a few seconds. Then he glanced towards the staircase, then the window, and then he nodded. 'Okay.'

But the search provided no answers. Aside from the living room and den, there was a large kitchen on the ground floor, and a small room looking out on the ocean that Parker had set up as an office. Upstairs, the house had three bedrooms – the master with an en suite, and two smaller guestrooms, either side of a separate bathroom.

The guestrooms were at the front of the house and looked untouched, little in the way of furniture in either. The master was a grander room, overlooking the ocean and flooded with light as they looked around. The bed was unmade, brilliant white bed sheets crumpled at the foot end; cologne and alcohol mingled in the stale air. They poked around the en suite, and a walk-in closet lined with an array of suits still in the dry cleaner's plastic, but there was nothing that grabbed Casey's attention.

Finished in the bedrooms, they went downstairs again and had Parker show them the garage, accessed through a side door off the kitchen. Like the rest of the house, it was neat, ordered and minimalist. A black Lexus hybrid took centre stage, a full MAC toolset that looked like it had never been touched standing against the back wall. Two sets of golf clubs, some cardboard packing boxes, taped shut and stacked in even piles in the corner; a plastic crate full of oily rags and assorted junk the only sign of disorder.

There were no other outbuildings, so they walked around to the rear of the property, but there was nothing to see. No fences, no yard to speak of, just a deck leading off the French doors from the den, then a stretch of uneven turf that ended in the tufts of beach grass that marked the top of the dunes the house backed on to. The wind whipped Casey's hair across her face as she walked to the lip of the dunes and looked down on the beach fifteen feet below.

Back inside, Parker was waiting for them by the steps. 'All set?'

Casey nodded. 'Thank you for your co-operation. We have a duty to establish Miss Grace's whereabouts and her safety, so anything you can do to help with that would be appreciated.' She passed him her card. 'You hear from her, or think of any other way we can get in contact with her or anyone close to her, please give me a call.'

'Of course.' Parker took it, already moving to see them out the door. 'You think she's okay? I mean you see this kinda thing all the time, right?' He looked at Cullen as he asked it, still taking his lead from him.

Casey offered her hand. 'Thanks for your help, Mr Parker. We'll be in touch.'

They went outside, and Casey slapped her shades on, the low sun in her eyes, tweaking her headache. She looked each way along the road, houses at intervals all along the ocean side, facing open country on the other, thick scrub and overgrown salt grass, with Ocean Road cutting across it in the distance. The stunted groundsel trees and marsh elders that grew there had been stripped bare by the Atlantic winter, branches frozen stiff and sharp as ice picks. Beyond the highway, scrub gave way to salt marsh and pockets of standing water that eventually merged into the far-off bay. The reeds that covered the marshes swayed in unison in the breeze; from the mainland, looking into the sun on days like today, they stood in silhouette – the 'black' reeds that gave the bay its name. It was picturesque in the bright light, but Casey could only think how desolate a place it was for a woman to find herself alone in the dead of night.

Cullen followed her down the driveway, waiting until they were almost at the car before he spoke. 'So you think he's lying about something specific, or...?'

Casey stopped and took one more look back at the house. 'I think that motherfucker's lying about everything.'

# CHAPTER 2

Casey was first into the car. Cullen slid into his seat and she put her hand on his arm to stop him starting the engine. 'Just hold on a second.' She was looking past him, towards Parker's house. There was no sign of him at the windows, but she had the feeling he was watching. Same for the whole neighbourhood. 'Lemme hear the 911 again.'

Cullen passed his phone over. 'You think he's gonna crack and come on out here to confess?'

'Worth a shot.' Casey fired him a dead-eyed stare to emphasise the sarcasm. She let Tina Grace's call play out again, the scared woman's voice filling the car.

'Seriously, what're you thinking about? The coffee table?' Cullen said, as the playback ended.

She gave the cell back to him and stared straight ahead through the windshield. The breeze coming off the ocean was whipping around the shrubs and bushes along the roadside. 'I think they were getting high all night on whatever was cleaned off of that table, and then something happened to send her haywire.'

'Something he did?'

'Maybe, maybe not.'

'Bringing all your detective smarts to this one, huh, Big?'

'You wanna dazzle me with your theory?'

He took his hands off the wheel and held them open. 'Hey, I'm with you. She showed up at eleven, bolted at four – booze plus whatever for that amount of time? Easily enough to mess with her head. But my guess is she made a soft landing at a friend's place and she's still asleep now.'

Casey took out her cell. 'Read out her contact numbers to me, would you? Landline first.'

Casey typed the number into her phone as he called it out. It rang but there was no answer. She dialled the cell phone, but it was dead.

Casey sent a text message to the cell phone for Tina to contact her urgently, watching the next house along the street as she spoke. A man was making slow work of checking his mailbox at the end of his drive.

Cullen followed her stare and saw what she was looking at. 'Check this guy out. He's just dying for us to notice him.'

'That the guy Kidman spoke to?'

Cullen pressed the ignition. 'I think so. Half the street must've seen her last night.'

The man was openly looking their way now, the mailbox pretence dropped. Casey gestured for Cullen to pull up to his property. 'Let's give him his two minutes.'

Cullen pulled the car forward fifty yards, stopping near to where the man was standing. He had on a wide-brimmed sunhat and shades, and it was only coming close that Casey realised he was older than she thought – sixty-plus. 'Morning.'

'Morning. You folks with the police?'

'Yes, sir – Detectives Wray and Cullen, Hampstead County PD. Understand there was a commotion out here last night?'

'That's the word for it. Young woman woke up half the beach.'

'Did you see her?' Cullen said.

'Not like I could miss her. She came hammering on my door.'

'You speak with her any?'

'No, I called 911 and I shouted out to her to sit tight, the police were coming. But she was beyond making any sense.'

'What was she saying?'

The man's forehead creased. 'I don't know, talking about someone coming to kill her, all kinds of profanity.'

'And you didn't open up?' Casey said.

'I'm not about to let a stranger into my house at 4am, I have my wife upstairs. I didn't know she was Jon's friend at the time, that might've made things different. But there was no one around, whatever she was talking about, she was all twisted up. We kept an eye on her through the window, for as long as we could see her.'

'Did you see anyone else on the street?'

'No.'

'What about Mr Parker? Jon.'

'Oh sure, but not when she first came knocking.'

'No? You mean he was along after?'

'Yes. A few minutes or so.'

Casey glanced at Cullen and then back at the man. 'What's your name, sir?'

'Ellis Sandford. I spoke to the other officers earlier, they should've told you that.'

'Do you have any idea who she was running away from, Mr Sandford?'

He let his hand rest on top of the mailbox. 'Herself, I'd say.'

Cullen held the double doors open for Casey and then followed her inside. HCPD was made up of five precincts, theirs based in Rockport and the largest of the five – though politics meant the department was headquartered way out at Harrison, in the east of the county. The Third was home to a six-strong detective bureau, under the command of Lieutenant Ray Carletti.

Casey had been partnered with Cullen shortly after she joined the squad; he had three years under his belt already by then, but he'd never shown any resentment to her making rank before him. In fact, he'd had her back as she cleared the department of dead wood – two twenty-year men pensioned off, another vet transferred out – and filtered in her own team. They'd talked about it once, way deep into a night at Shakey's, and he'd explained it like this: 'I figured out I'm Robin a long time ago, and I'm good with it. Batman's an asshole.'

The irony was, Casey would've placed herself in the same bracket – until Ray Carletti made it plain he saw leadership qualities she never knew she had.

She made for the staircase, hitting the button for the elevator as they passed, but without stopping. Cullen shot her a sidelong questioning look.

'What? I thought you'd need the elevator, old man.'

Cullen jabbed her in the shoulder with his finger. 'I went to the gym last week. You know that?'

'What for? Hide out from the kids?'

'Of course,' Cullen smiled, opening the stairway door. 'But it's a start, right?'

The team worked out of an open-plan office on the second floor; the room was long and narrow, the desks arranged in pairs, facing each other. Carletti was in his glass cubicle at the far end, half hidden behind his computer screen. He looked up when they walked in and waved Casey over.

She knocked once on the glass door and opened it to stand in the doorway. 'Morning, Boss.'

'What's up, Big. Heard you were dancing last night.'

She rolled her eyes. 'You sound like Cullen.'

'I knew I left too early.'

'I'm a good dancer, goddammit.'

'And no one in my office will say otherwise.' He sat back in his chair. 'Without my say-so.'

'You through with me? Can I go back to Cullen giving me shit so I can at least give some back?'

Carletti broke a thin smile. 'How was the beach?' He said it with an eye-roll in his voice, as if he was expecting a comeback that it was a waste of time – but that wasn't how she was feeling about it.

'Weird.'

'Weird how?'

'You know anything about this one?'

'Not really. Some kind of a domestic.'

Casey squinted. 'I'm not so sure. The boyfriend – actually scratch that, I think they're fuckbuddies at most – he's lying his ass off.'

'About what?'

'Most probably the fact they were getting high together, but I don't know. There's a 911 call, the girl sounds really fucking scared. And she said she was in Barton Beach, but she was nowhere near there. Mr Liar says she'd been to his place before, so why would she say that?'

He picked up a pen and propped it under his chin. 'If they *were* high or whatever – she's all confused...'

She tilted her head from one side to the other. 'Maybe. He was real uncomfortable when we got inside the house.'

'What're you telling me – you think he did something to her?'

'No, I'm not ready to go that far. I just don't think the night ended well for this girl.'

'How old?'

'The girl? Early twenties, he told patrol.'

'Any witnesses?'

'Some of the neighbours saw her pass by. Uniform canvassed the neighbourhood but they didn't get anything useful. The place is remote.'

Ray rubbed his face. 'Check with her family and friends – if she hasn't shown up, we'll escalate it.' His eyes strayed back to his monitor.

'Sure. Anyway, you wanted me?'

'Yeah, shut the door.'

Casey stepped inside and pulled the door behind her.

'I got word McTeague's gonna be in the building today.' He looked up at her again. 'You have any idea why?'

The heat between Carletti and Robbie McTeague was an open secret. Rumours about its origins were easy to come by, but Ray had never spoken about it with her, even with a head full of whiskey, so Casey took that to mean the topic was off-limits. Although his Special Investigations unit worked out of Harrison, Captain McTeague's juice with the chief of police and the DA meant he, in effect, operated outside the chain of command. In polite conversations he was referred to as the chief's troubleshooter; it gave him the latitude to get into Carletti's business seemingly at will, and kept the bureau under the microscope.

Casey shook her head. 'Why would I?'

'Come on, Big, everyone talks to you, you know everything. He was at Shakey's last night, huh?'

'Yeah.'

'You speak to him?'

She made a face. 'You're kidding, right?'

'No.'

She held her hands up. 'No.'

'Okay, who did then?'

'Honestly, I wasn't paying him all that much attention.'

Carletti ran his finger and thumb over the corners of his mouth. 'I do not need him up my ass right now.'

'Maybe he doesn't show up – you don't know. Why meet trouble more than halfway?' It was one of Carletti's favourite sayings.

He breathed out hard, then held up his hand to wave her off. 'Whatever. Go clear every outstanding case before lunch. Tell the others the same. That's one less thing he can come at me with.'

Casey laughed, opening the door again.

Heading out across the office, she stopped at Billy Drocker's desk and stood over him until he couldn't pretend she wasn't there any longer.

'What?' he said.

'Heard about you last night...'

'Heard what?'

'You know.'

He was blushing now, avoiding the looks Jill Hart, his partner sitting opposite, was shooting him. Casey winked at her. Of the three detectives she'd brought onto the team, Jill was the one that needed the most nurturing. She was part of the new breed of cop the county wanted to push: book-smart, computer-literate, and a damn hard worker. But it worried Casey she might've plucked her out of uniform too soon, before she could develop a hard enough edge.

'Was it that new girl in Public Information?' Casey said. 'Blonde bob, nice ass. What's her name – Christina?'

'I got nothing to say, Big.'

'Yeah, I knew it. You're so predictable...'

'Hey, I never said a word. And if you knew anything you wouldn't be over here fishing right now.'

Casey glanced at Jill again, who nodded in confirmation and mouthed, 'Christina.'

'Jesus, you are a piece of work. She hasn't even been here five minutes.'

Drocker slumped lower in his chair, his face on fire now but grinning, pretending to busy himself with his keyboard. 'Haven't you got any work to do?' He raised his voice, fake-grandstanding. 'Is there no crime in this motherfucking precinct anymore?'

Jill was laughing, and Cullen had turned his chair around and wheeled himself over. 'Don't ever get your ass arrested, Bill. You're a walking guilty plea.'

Casey patted his shoulder and kept on to her desk, still enjoying the Billy D show. As the greenhorn, Billy had the role of squad clown put on him, and he took all the shit that came his way with good humour. An extrovert by nature, he was also a blue-chipper, and everyone could see it – so the ribbing carried no heft. It hadn't been that way for her, starting out. Four years since she made detective, but seeing Billy fly and feeling like it was yesterday; the difference to her own experience so stark. Getting clowned just as much as he did, but taking it all to heart back then. The only woman on the squad when she joined, and pegged as a career uniform officer prior to that point, back then every joke, every offhand remark, seemed to confirm that she didn't belong. Her first week on the job she'd picked up the nickname 'Big'; 'Big Case' Wray as it started out – a play on her name, but also on the fact that she was only ever assigned the cases no one else wanted – and told to her face it would always be that way.

Two things brought about the change in her standing: winning over Ray Carletti, and years of busting her ass harder than anyone else in there. Not that she'd started out trying to make a name for herself, but the same addictive personality that'd seen her throw herself into everything from online poker to running found its most potent fulfilment in outworking her colleagues. Passing the sergeant's exam eighteen months back was just the icing on the cake.

Cullen was still smiling as he wheeled himself back around. Casey sat down to collect the messages on her desk phone, but he held his hand up to get her attention first. 'Had a call from dispatch – missing person report for one Tina Grace.'

Casey pressed the receiver to her shoulder. 'Who called it in?'

'Name of Brian Walton. And get this: says he's her boyfriend.'

'Boyfriend.' Casey stretched the phone cord, untangling it. 'Huh. Get his address, we'll go see him.'

'Sure thing.'

She hit the button for voicemail and the machine said she had one new message. She pressed two to skip the preamble and waited for it to start...

A woman screamed down the line. Then ten, then a thousand. So many it became a wall of sound. Casey whipped the phone away from her ear.

Cullen caught the sudden movement and looked over.

Casey stared at the receiver. 'What the fuck?'

# CHAPTER 3

Brian Walton gave an address in the north of Rockport, but asked to meet at a Dunkin' Donuts a couple blocks away. He didn't say why, but it wasn't hard to guess – keep the cops away from mom and dad's place.

Casey got out of the car to see Cullen watching her over the hood.

'Why you staring at me that way?' she said.

'You okay?'

'Sure, why?'

Casey had played the message for Cullen before they left the office. She'd listened to it again herself to check there was nothing more at the end, but the screams died away after a few seconds and the playback cut off. No surprise, when she checked, that the call had come from a blocked number.

'Just asking,' he said.

'Get outta here, it's some asshole screwing around.'

'I know. You pissed anyone off lately?'

'Me? You mean apart from the hundreds of perps we've locked up? No.'

'Smartass. I'm just saying it's weird, that's all. I never heard of anything like that.'

Casey shut her door and walked around the car, heading for the entrance. 'It's probably the collective conscious of every poor woman Billy D talked into his bed, screaming at the realisation he isn't the marrying kind after all.'

Cullen shook his head in disbelief as she passed him. 'Where do you come up with this shit?'

Casey pushed through the doors and looked around. The smell of hot donuts made her stomach stand to attention. Brian

Walton was at a table across the room, by a window that overlooked the expressway and a Motel 6 beyond it. He was wearing the black-and-green checked shirt he'd told her to look out for. Casey nodded when he made eye contact.

'I'll get coffee,' Cullen said, coming in after her.

'Thanks. Sugar mine, huh?'

Casey went over and hovered by the edge of the table. 'Mr Walton?'

'Hey.' He started to stand up then seemed to change his mind, indecision leaving him caught in a crouch. Nervous, hesitant – definitely not cop-wise.

'I'm Detective Sergeant Wray, HCPD.' She pointed to the counter. 'That's my partner, Detective Cullen. May I sit?' Casey took the chair opposite him before he answered, to signal it was okay to sit his ass down again. 'You made a missing-person report about Tina Grace, that correct?'

'Yeah, she's been gone since yesterday.'

'Okay. Yesterday what time?'

'I left her in the morning and then she called me at like one or something.'

'In the afternoon?'

'Yeah. Afternoon. That's the last time we talked. I been trying her cell since, but it's dead. She always carries one of those battery packs in her purse, keeps it charged, so...'

Cullen came over and set two coffees down, nodded at Walton. 'Detective Cullen. You want something?'

Walton shook his head. 'I'm good.'

Casey looked him over. He had dark hair with blonde tints at the tips, worn long enough that he had to push it behind his ears every time he dipped his head. He had a scar running through one eyebrow, and a nose ring fit snug through his left nostril. Couldn't be older than twenty-five. His work shirt was clean and unmarked, but worn in. He had a tattered leather bracelet on his wrist that he picked at while he talked. The line connecting this guy and the man in the million-dollar beach house wasn't an easy one to see.

'Is it unusual for her to be out of touch for this long?'

'Yeah, she's always on her cell, texting mostly. First thing she does in the morning is hit me up.'

'And you guys don't live together?'

'No, she's got her own apartment. It's on Belmont and twenty-third, behind the Dollar Tree.'

'Have you been by today?'

He nodded. 'She's not there. That's when I called you guys.'

'Does she live alone?' Cullen said.

'Yeah.'

'To be clear, did you go into her apartment?' Casey said. 'Do you have a key?'

He nodded again. 'She gave it to me a couple months ago.'

'Was there anything out of place inside? Anything that seemed unusual?'

'No. It looked pretty much the same way it always does.'

'What about friends? Family?'

'I sent texts to a couple people, but only one got back to me. She said the same as me, haven't heard from her.'

'And her family?'

'I don't speak to her mom.'

He looked from Casey to Cullen and back as if he had more to say, and she gave him time, tilting her head to prompt him, but then he looked down at the band on his wrist again.

'Does Tina have a job?' Cullen said finally. 'So we can try her place of work?'

He shook his head. 'She quit last month. She's been trying to find something new since then.'

Casey blew on her coffee and took a mouthful, only realising now her hangover had died down. She glanced at Cullen to see if he had another question lined up, but he'd gone back to watching Walton. 'What do you know about her movements yesterday?' she asked.

'What do you mean?'

'Where did you see her last? In the morning.'

'At her place. I stayed over.'

'And after that?'

'I had to work.'

'No, I mean where was she when you spoke to her at 1pm?'

'Going to her mom's. She was picking up groceries for her.'

'You know where her mom lives?'

'Yeah, like ten blocks from Tina.'

'What's the address?'

'It's on Fairfax, thirty-five hundred or something...'

Also in town, not over the causeway. Casey wrote it down, lingering over the last letter as she decided how much to tell him about the beach house. Her instinct was that this was becoming something more serious than a domestic call-out, but if Tina Grace was flaked out on a sofa somewhere – maybe even at the mom's place – it wasn't her business to let poor Brian Walton know his girlfriend was seeing someone behind his back. 'Is there a chance she would've gone there?'

He shook his head. 'I called her brother, Tommy.'

'Can I get his number, please?'

Walton read it out, then laid his cell on the tabletop.

'Has Tina ever done anything like this before?'

'No, nothing.'

'Does she have any medical conditions? She on any meds?'

'Only Tylenol for a hangover. She takes them with chocolate ice cream, that's her cure.'

Casey glanced at her hands, half a smile at the image – a woman she could relate to. 'What about narcotics?'

Walton tugged at the band on his wrist.

'Brian?'

He glanced away at the counter.

'Brian, it's important you tell us this stuff now. You won't get her in trouble, but it could help us in a big way.'

He took a breath and let it out. 'Not really, sometimes a line every now and then. Just at parties or whatever, not, like, most of the time.'

'She use a regular dealer?'

'No way, she'd never buy the stuff herself. It's just if someone's offering, like that.'

Casey nodded. 'Was she using yesterday? Or the night before, when she was with you?'

He shook his head. 'It's not my deal, she knows that. They test at my work if they think you're getting high.'

'Okay. Thank you, I appreciate your honesty.' Casey clasped her hands. 'You said she quit her job – does she have any savings or credit cards? How's she supporting herself?'

He spun his cell around in circles. 'She saved a bunch of money so she could quit. She had it all figured out – she told me she had enough to live off of for three months.'

'So what's she been doing with her time?'

'Looking for work, mostly. With the interviews and stuff, it all takes time. The rest ... I don't know. Watches TV. She visits her mom a lot, she stays over at her place like once or twice a week.'

Casey wrote it down, wondering about Tina slipping off to Ramona Beach and if sleepovers at the mom's could be a cover story. The more she learned about Tina, the more she struggled to get a handle on her, the fragments they knew about her life nowhere close to fitting together. She looked at Cullen again, raised her eyebrows to see if he had anything else he wanted to ask.

'How long have you guys been together?' he said.

Walton had his elbows on the table and was pressing his mouth into his hands, his head dipped low. 'Two years. It was our anniversary a couple months ago, right before Christmas.'

Casey clicked her pen off and on again. She passed it to Brian with a sheet of paper. 'Write down the names and numbers of her friends – the ones she's closest to. Also, do you have the key to her apartment with you right now?'

Walton nodded. 'Yeah, why?'

She jutted her chin at the pen to signal him to get writing the contact list. 'Do you have to get back to work or can you take us there now?'

'Uh ... sure, my shift doesn't start till later. But you gotta get people looking for her, K? She wouldn't just ghost me.'

'We'll do everything we can.'

Tina Grace lived in a stubby 1950s apartment building that ran to five or six storeys, a black fire escape zig-zagging down its front. Walton led them up to the fourth floor, where the stairway opened onto a tired but clean landing, two apartments facing each other across grey linoleum. He pointed to the one on their left, and Casey banged on the door. 'Tina Grace?'

She waited a few seconds, then directed Walton to open up.

As he turned the key, the doorway opposite opened and a man in a Lynyrd Skynyrd tee came out. 'Brian? Everything okay?'

Casey badged him. 'HCPD. We're looking for your neighbour, sir. Have you seen her?'

Walton glanced back over his shoulder, looking at the man like a puppy hoping for scraps.

'Tina? I don't think she's home.'

'When did you see her last?'

He stared at the floor, running his hand through his hair. 'I'm not sure. She's in and out all the time. Tina ... I don't know. Is she in trouble?'

'We just need to find her. We're gonna take a look inside, see if you can remember the last time you saw her for me while we do, huh?'

The man kept looking at Casey, something more to say but holding it back. She waited a beat, but he seemed to lose his nerve, looking over at Brian instead. 'Hey, sorry, man.'

Walton nodded and went to go inside, but Cullen put a hand on his shoulder. 'Better if we go first.'

Casey drew her gun and toed the door open. 'Tina Grace?'

She stepped into a short hallway, Cullen at her shoulder. The apartment was dark, daylight coming through a window in the kitchenette to her left but barely penetrating. On the other side was a bedroom, and the door at the end of the hallway was closed. She poked her head into the bedroom without touching anything. It looked like Tina had just left it, the faint smell of citrus perfume lingering. The bed was unmade, a black nightgown and some other clothing strewn over the foot of it, and one of the closet drawers had been left open. She beckoned

Walton to come take a look. 'Was it like this when you came by earlier?'

He nodded. 'Yeah.'

Casey backed out and carried on down the hallway. A second door on her left opened into the bathroom, barely big enough to hold its components: a shower stall with a watermarked plastic door, flanked by a toilet and a pedestal sink.

She moved to the end of the hallway and nudged the last door open with her elbow.

'She's not there, right?' Walton called from behind them.

She didn't answer, went into the living room. It was long and thin, stretching the width of the apartment to either side of her, a window at either end letting in a milky-grey light that gave it an ethereal quality. A big flatscreen was the centrepiece, mounted on the wall across from her. The furniture was right out of IKEA, but tastefully accessorised with an oversized anglepoise lamp, console tables made from wood that was so distressed it had to be expensive, and a matching credenza. Above it was a collage of pictures, the same girl featuring in most of the shots; some showed her with friends, some solo, flashing the peace sign or sticking her tongue out. Casey pointed her out to Walton. 'Is that Tina?'

He nodded.

'How recent?'

He twisted his head. 'That picture? Like five or six years, maybe? It all goes on Instagram now.'

Casey turned around slowly, taking in the little that was on display. No signs of distress, of someone who didn't think they'd be coming back. No obvious sign of drug use, or medication – anything that might've impaired her judgement.

She went back to the kitchenette, looking for signs of alcohol use – checking the sink for a dirty glass, the trashcan for an empty. Nothing. She opened the refrigerator, found it was stocked up – plastic trays with leftovers, fresh milk and juice, a produce compartment filled with vegetables. No alcohol on display there either.

She holstered her gun and faced Walton in the hallway. 'Does Tina have a laptop or tablet?'

He shook his head. 'She uses her phone for everything.'

'Do you have access to her emails?'

Walton shook his head, his face screwed up like the suggestion was ridiculous.

Casey put her hands on her hips and looked around, thinking. Trying to get a feel for this woman's state of mind, leaving her apartment to visit her rich hook-up out on the beaches. Her gaze fell on the bedroom one more time. 'Bag that nightgown, please?' she said to Cullen. He went across the hall and took the discarded clothing from the bed, slipped it into a paper bag. Then she led them all out of the apartment and directed Walton to lock it shut.

The brother, Tommy Grace, didn't answer his phone but Records turned up an address for him and a Margaret Grace at 3550 Fairfax Avenue. They dropped Brian Walton back at the Dunkin' Donuts, and it was a twenty-minute drive from there, towards the edge of town, the county line a few miles beyond that.

'Where are we with this?' Cullen said.

'In what sense?'

'Is this starting to feel like a priority situation?'

Casey stared at her cell phone screen in her lap. 'Sounds like she's close to the mom, so if she's in the dark too, then yeah, I think so. Tina refused to take Jon Parker's cab, it looks like she had no cell phone after she called 911, so unless she'd already ordered an Uber or something ... But I can't see her doing that, the distressed state she was in. So how else does she get back to town? And it's a hell of a place to be stranded alone at night.'

Cullen nodded, shifting lanes to make the turn onto Fairfax. 'Brings us back to Jon Parker, then. If she was stuck out there, she'd have every reason to go back to his place, even if it was just to make a call. She'd have to be real scared of him to think running off in the dark was a better move.'

'Depends on what was in her head, though, doesn't it? If he's telling the truth about her blowing up over nothing, could be she was just paranoid.'

'Then it's still on him for juicing her up on coke or whatever.'

'She's a twenty-something-year-old woman, there's just as much chance she juiced him up.'

'He's a middle-aged man, he should know better.'

'Why? Because he's "the adult in the room"? She's a woman, not a child.'

'What? Slow down, Big, I meant he should know better than trying to act like he's twenty himself.'

Casey looked at him sidelong, eventually creasing her eyes when she realised she'd taken him wrong.

The silence stretched as they drove, Casey pissed at herself for jumping on her high horse too soon. For her first two years in the department, she'd laughed at every sexist joke, pretended not to hear every misogynistic comment, in an effort to be *one of the guys*. So when she made sergeant, knowing she'd won Ray over, she promised herself she was gonna stamp on it hard, to make sure the likes of Dana Torres and Jill Hart, coming up after her, didn't have to put up with the same shit. But Cullen was the wrong target. The guy lived for his wife and two girls; he had a knowledge of Disney Princesses that would put Walt himself to shame, and she'd never heard him disparage a woman in all the time they'd been partners. 'My bad.'

Cullen glanced at her. Then he broke into a grin. 'Jackass.'

She threw up the peace sign and blew him a kiss.

He glanced out of the corner of his eye as if he was going to say something else, but then he focused on the road in silence. She saw him disappearing inside himself, the way he did from time to time.

'Hey, I said I'm sorry...'

'No, no, I was just ... You think there's something going on between Billy D and Jill?'

'What? Dave, no. Are you crazy?'

'I don't mean, like ... y'know, live. But you think she likes him maybe? She looked super invested when you were getting on him earlier.'

'No way.' She looked across at him, questioning herself momentarily before rejecting it again. 'No. Definitely not.'

'I'm just saying...' He pulled an innocent face. 'She couldn't take her eyes off of him.'

'She's got a boyfriend, you doofus. They're high-school sweethearts.'

'So what? When's that ever stopped anyone?'

She turned all the way to face him. 'Are you projecting? Is this your way of trying to tell me something?'

'No, idiot.' He mimed banging his head on the steering wheel in frustration. 'I'm too old and too tired for that.'

She rubbed his arm, laughing. 'No argument from me on the old and tired.'

'Seriously, though. Luisa says Billy's cute.'

Casey waved her hand down Cullen's profile. 'Sure, but it's not like she's got much to compare against.'

'Hilarious.' He lowered his window and nodded his head towards it. 'Just gonna let some of the sexual tension outta here.'

Casey rolled her eyes. 'It's like minus one thousand outside, would you close that?'

He hit the switch again. 'Seriously, though, you don't think he's hot?'

'Who? Billy?'

'Uh-huh?'

She turned her mouth down. 'I never went for jocks.'

'Ohhhh, right, I remember ... because your type is...?'

Casey smiled. 'Nice try.'

The houses became more rundown the further they went along Fairfax, and once they crossed 12th Street, the chain stores petered out until the only commercial units they saw were liquor stores and a pawn shop. It was one of the first suburbs built after the war, at the time an aspirational neighbourhood for families. But when the Hazeldene chemical works shut down in seventy-three, it was the beginning of the end for Rockport's manufacturing base. One by one the other factories took tax breaks to move out of state, and by the time the eighties rolled in, the well-paid blue-collar jobs were all but gone, sending the town and the inland suburbs into decline. Any new money since had been sucked into the construction of vacation homes and condos along the shoreline, the pull of bay-front gentrification like gravity.

They came to a stop sign, the Grace residence on the opposite corner of the intersection. Casey turned her head, the house next to them was abandoned. The windows and doors had once been boarded up, but thieves had torn away the plywood, looking for copper plumbing or any other metal to strip away and sell as scrap. Neighbourhoods like this one lost one to two manhole covers a week, to scrappers looking for easy cash.

Margaret Grace's bungalow had beige stucco walls that were peeling all over, the property separated from its neighbour by a chain-link fence. Bare tyre tracks cut through a hardscrabble front yard, a makeshift driveway, but there was no car in sight.

They rang the doorbell, Cullen glancing at the tyre tracks. 'Nobody home?' A loud clap behind made them both wheel around; a screen door, hanging off one hinge at an angle, flapping in the wind.

They turned back as a woman in blue jeans and an Islanders jersey opened up. 'Yes?'

'Margaret Grace?'

'Yeah?'

'Detectives Wray and Cullen—'

'Uh-huh.' She pointed to the shield clipped to Casey's pants, underlining that she'd worked that much out. 'You're making me nervous, what's this about?'

'We're looking for your daughter Tina, Mrs Grace, have you spoken to her?'

'What for?'

'We had a call she was present at a disturbance in the early hours, and this morning she's been reported missing. We're trying to establish her whereabouts.'

'Tina?' The woman raised her arm to lean on the doorframe. 'I saw her yesterday.'

'What time was that?'

'She was over here in the afternoon. She'd went to the store for me.'

'When did she leave here, ma'am?'

Mrs Grace squinted. 'I don't know, maybe three?'

'Have you talked to her since then?'

'No. I don't...' She pulled out an iPhone in a dented pink case and studied it a second. 'No, there's nothing on here since yesterday. What disturbance?'

'There was an argument at a property on Ramona Beach, officers were called out there in the early hours...'

'What was she doing at the beach?'

'It seems like she was visiting a friend,' Cullen said.

'She don't have any friends live on the beach.'

'Do you know a Brian Walton, Mrs Grace?'

'It's Maggie. Haven't been a Mrs in a long time. And yeah, Brian's her boyfriend, he don't live at the beach.'

Casey nodded. 'Mr Walton reported Tina missing this morning, he hasn't heard from her since yesterday either.'

'Have you tried her apartment? She lives on Belmont—'

'We've been by but she's not there. Is there someplace she'd normally be at this time? I understand she's not working right now.'

'Yeah, she quit because they were screwing her over.' She scratched the side of her neck. 'I don't know where the hell she'd be at.'

'Mr Walton mentioned Tina has a brother – Tommy, is it?'

'Yeah. He's not home, he...' The name seemed to spark her into action; she brought her cell out again and tapped the screen. 'Lemme call him...'

She waited as it rang, then: 'Yeah, it's me. Have you talked to your sister? ... Uh-huh ... No, since then ... Yeah, the police are here ... Yeah, yeah, right now. Call me back.'

She hung up and leaned against the doorframe again. 'He's gonna ask her friends and let me know. Jesus...'

'Is there anywhere else she might go, ma'am? Does she ever travel out of town, anything like that?'

'No, where's she gonna go? She's lived here her whole life.'

'Is her father...?'

The woman wrinkled her face. 'He left us ten years ago. The last time he walked out this door is the last time any of us spoke to him, Christ knows where he is now. If he's still alive. No way.'

Casey nodded in understanding. 'Look, I'm ... I'm sorry to have to worry you this way. Can we come inside for a minute, so we can take down some details?'

'What kinda details?'

'Name, date of birth, that kind of thing. Just basic information.'

She thought about it a second and then swung the door open for them to come in.

They followed her into a small living room. It was cramped but tidy, a table and two chairs against one wall, a small couch and two mismatched armchairs arranged to face an old-style dark-wood TV cabinet with doors to close it away. A radio was playing Motown in another room, and there was a strong smell of perfume, the heavy floral scent Maggie Grace wore, as if she'd spritzed the walls with it when she put it on. But after a few seconds inside, Casey picked up an undercurrent: a pervasive smell of alcohol the fragrance was supposed to mask. Cullen shot her a look that said he'd noticed it too.

Maggie Grace sat down at the table. 'So what should I tell you?'

'Let's start with Tina's full name.'

Casey spoke and Cullen wrote, taking down Tina's personal information. She was twenty-four years old, five-two and around 105 pounds. In her mother's words, 'There's nothing to her, but you'd never guess it the way she talks about the size of her butt.'

'Do you have a recent photograph?'

The woman started to get up, then thought again. 'On my phone?'

'Sure.'

She pulled one up and turned the screen to Casey. It was badly shattered, jagged fractures running across Tina's face. 'She sent me this a week ago.'

The selfie showed a smiling Tina standing in front of a full-length mirror in what looked like her bedroom. She was dressed to hit the clubs, wearing a close-fitting black top that showed off her midriff, and tight black jeans with a carefully placed rip in one knee. Her face was heavily made up, but with the kind of skill the Instagram generation seemed to be born with, and Casey could only marvel at. Her hair was a dark auburn, worn in a centre-parting and to shoulder length, curled at the ends. Her expression was hard to judge, neither smiling nor pouting, not as posed as these shots usually were, an assuredness about the woman that spoke to a level of self-confidence that made her look more mature than twenty-four.

'Can you send that to me please?' She took her business card out and laid it on the table, then wrote down her cell number in pen. 'Here.'

Maggie picked it up and turned it end-over-end on the tabletop. 'What you talked about before – who was she arguing with? What happened?'

Casey put her phone in her pocket to buy a moment, then looked up again. 'We're still establishing the facts. Ma'am, does the name Jon Parker mean anything to you?'

Maggie looked blank, shaking her head. 'He beat her up or what?'

Casey hesitated, thrown by how direct the question was. 'We don't know for sure what happened yet. The reports were just about a disturbance.'

Maggie chewed her bottom lip, taking it in. 'Tina wouldn't stand for no crap, she'd give as good as she got, someone tried to hurt her.'

'Has your daughter been involved in this kind of disturbance before?'

'No. I just told you, she wouldn't stand for that crap. I never taught her much, but I taught her that.' She looked about to say something more, but then her phone came alive – Tommy's name on the screen.

Maggie snatched it to her ear. 'Yeah? ... Neither of them? ... All right, where you at? ... Yeah, well can you come back here now? ... Okay.'

She hung up. 'Nothing. He talked to her two best friends.' She stared at Casey, her eyes slipping out of focus.

Casey started talking again to keep her in the moment. 'Ma'am, does your daughter have any medical conditions?'

They went through the same roster of background questions, but the answers were consistent with Brian Walton's – except on the subject of narcotics; Maggie Grace said Tina never touched drugs to her knowledge.

'How often do you see her?' Casey said.

'She comes over about once a week. Sometimes more than that, since she quit her job.'

'Does she ever stay with you?'

Maggie waved a finger over the tabletop. 'No, she's got no need to. Easier to go back to her place.'

Casey glanced at Cullen, her theory maybe confirmed, but opening up more questions. She stood up to go. 'If it proves the case that your daughter's missing, we'll do everything to figure out where she is. In the meantime, let me know immediately if she contacts you...' Casey pointed to the card in her hands. She offered a brittle smile as a goodbye.

Maggie Grace folded her arms but then unfolded them again immediately as if she'd forgotten something. She grabbed her phone up.

'You know I got this message earlier. I didn't think anything about it...' She trailed off, pressing the voicemail icon. 'I thought it was just someone messing with me, but listen.'

She stood up and put the phone to Casey's ear. A woman started to scream.

Then ten, then a thousand...

## CHAPTER 4

Carletti's glass door was propped open, but Casey knocked anyway. 'Something I need you to hear.' She started back to her desk before he could say anything.

When he caught up to her, she lifted the handset and pressed the button for speakerphone, Cullen already waiting there for them. She played the message. The screaming kicked in and

Carletti stared at her. Even Dana looked up from her desk at the far end of the office.

'What the hell was that?' Carletti said.

'Picked it up this morning,' Casey said. 'Tina Grace's mom got the exact same message.'

Carletti smoothed his tie. 'We don't know who from?'

She shook her head. 'Blocked number. I have no idea what to make of it.'

'I don't … Before you met her or after?'

'Before. But after I went to the beach.'

'Could it be the girl? Is that even possible?'

'No fucking clue.'

'The mom says not,' Cullen said, 'but I don't think she can be sure either way.'

'Or someone taunting her?' Carletti reached for the handset from Casey and hit the button to play it again, off speakerphone. 'And why you?'

Casey waited while he listened, then took the receiver back and put it down.

'It's the same scream, right? Overlaid?'

Casey nodded along.

He stared at her, ran his hand over his mouth. Dana drifted over in the silence, pad in hand, drawn by the sense something serious was going on.

When Carletti spoke again, his voice was quiet, deliberate. 'What time did the 911 come in?'

'Just past 4am,' Cullen said.

Carletti looked at his watch. 'It's two-thirty now, so that's ten hours. Can we establish if she made it off the island?'

'I asked the mom about accessing Tina's Uber account, but she didn't know the password. The brother the same, according to her. We think her cell might've been put out of commission, so I don't know if that would've been an option anyhow.'

Carletti turned around. 'Billy, check the Uber police portal and see if Tina Grace's account shows any activity – then or since. If there's nothing, call them and find out if they made any pickups at all on Ramona Beach around four the night of – can't be much going on out there that time of the morning. That comes up empty, try the local cab companies.'

Billy nodded, reaching for his mouse.

'Do we have a picture to work with?' Ray said.

'Her mom gave us this.' Casey held up her iPhone to show the photo Maggie Grace had sent her. It was only looking at it again that she noticed the resemblance between Maggie and Tina. Tina's hair was a couple shades darker, but they both had the same milky skin tone and rounded facial features, accentuated by teardrop-shaped eyes that angled down at the corners.

Carletti twisted the phone towards him to see better. When he looked up again, Casey continued. 'Her mom put us onto her social-media profiles too.'

Cullen took over. 'No activity on Facebook or Instagram since yesterday, early afternoon. A little earlier than that for Twitter and TikTok. I scanned back through the last few weeks on all of them, and going quiet like that seems pretty unusual – she's a frequent user. From what I saw, it's rare that she goes more than a few hours without posting somewhere.'

'Where are you at with this?' Carletti said.

'Jill checked hospitals and jails, nada.'

Jill looked over her monitor. 'I called the women's refuge at St Peter & Paul's too, but they haven't had anyone new show up this week.'

Casey went on. 'We've got her set up on NCIC, and we've put an alert with a description on the website and all the department social feeds. We'll get an appeal out to local media too. Her boyfriend let us into her apartment, but there's nothing there to suggest she was in distress or she wasn't planning on coming back.'

'Okay. And what do you need?'

'Bodies. I want to go back to Ramona Beach, I need some bodies to knock on doors – the guys I had got reassigned. We track Tina down and these messages are just some asshole getting his kicks. But if not...'

'I'll speak to patrol to shake some uniforms loose.'

Casey threw her jacket on. 'Thanks. We'll head back out there now.' She made for the stairs.

Cullen caught up to her as she pushed through the double doors leading out of the office. 'You wanna start in the same place?'

She nodded. 'Jon Parker.'

A sheet of clouds had blown in off the Atlantic by the time they made it to Ramona Beach, masking the sun and making the ocean a drab green-grey colour. It felt like a different place to the one they'd visited just a few hours before, its sheen dulled a notch, the cold more depressive.

Cullen rang Parker's doorbell, waited and rang again, but there was no answer. Casey tracked around the side of the house, battling the wind, to peep through the French doors, but the living room and den were empty. She went over to the edge of the dunes that led down to the beach, scanning east and west to see if he was on the sand somewhere, but there was only one person in sight, a woman walking a dog in the distance. The waves were a white froth, crashing in off the ocean.

She came back around to find Cullen sheltering in the car, reading something on his cell. 'Got the list of 911 calls from last night,' he said. 'Six total, including Parker's and Tina's. I've sent it to you.'

Casey was marching on the spot looking past him, and nodded to indicate the next house along the street. 'Ellis Sandford was another of them?'

'Yeah, he was first up.' He looked around, consulting his phone between glances, trying to pick out the addresses listed on the screen. 'Then the next three houses in order.'

'I'm not about to freeze my ass off out here waiting for Parker. Let's talk to Sandford, then – we'll follow her route. Maybe he knows where Parker's at and how long until he's back.'

They walked across to Ellis Sandford's place, scanning the road and the grass verges for anything out of place. There were no fences between the properties, spaced far enough apart that a row of gristly shrubs was all that served to demarcate the line between them. Sandford's was a similar build to Parker's, only wider and with a boat trailer holding a sailboat under a grey tarpaulin parked in front of the garage.

Sandford opened the door before Casey even got there.

'Detectives?'

'Mr Sandford, could we have a moment of your time? You happen to know where your neighbour's gone to?' Casey pointed to Parker's house.

'No, miss, I didn't see him leave.'

'Do you know if he works? We need to speak to him urgently.'

Sandford shook his head. 'He's retired.' As he said it, a woman appeared down the hallway behind him, looking out at Casey but making no move to come over. 'This is about last night again?'

Casey held up the picture of Tina Grace on her phone. 'Is this the young woman who came to your door?'

Sandford took her wrist to bring the phone closer to his face, and Casey had to quash the impulse to snatch her arm free. He studied the image on the screen. 'Yes.'

Now she withdrew her arm. 'She hasn't been seen since and we need to locate her. You called 911 at 4.03am, can you tell me exactly when was the last time you saw her?'

He shifted his weight, holding on to the door. 'I couldn't say. She was out here for a minute or two, then we watched her head that way' – he pointed west – 'towards the Van Heusens' place. It couldn't be more than five minutes after I made the call, so what does that make it? Four-ten, just before?'

Cullen glanced towards the house Sandford had indicated. 'Was she walking? Running?'

'A bit of both. She was clearly agitated but she wasn't getting anywhere fast – she kept doubling back and swerving across the road. She was acting as if she was scared, but as I told you, there was no one else out there that I could see. I thought she was drunk – it was quite frightening the way she was carrying on.'

'For her too, I guess,' Casey said softly. If the bite in her tone came across, Sandford's expression didn't register it. 'Did you see where she went after that?'

Sandford shook his head. 'We were watching from upstairs. I lost sight of her when she went beyond the trees.'

Casey looked over and saw a small stand of firs clustered around the front of the next house, blocking the sightline to their porch. It crossed her mind they were for exactly that purpose. She turned back to Sandford. 'Do you have any security cameras on your property?'

He shook his head. 'We're pretty isolated out here, it's a waste of money. I keep a loaded Ruger next to my bed, that's always served me just fine.'

Casey glanced away to stop herself from saying something stupid.

'Did this woman give you any indication at all of what happened between her and Mr Parker?' Cullen asked.

Sandford thought about the question before he gave an answer. 'No, she was mostly talking nonsense. But look, Jon's a wealthy man, good-looking guy, has a lot of free time to fill. She's not the first young woman he's had over there. You understand me?'

Casey glanced towards Parker's house, then back at Sandford. 'We may need to speak to you again, Mr Sandford. Thanks for your help.' She headed back to the road, then made a right towards the Van Heusen's property.

Cullen walked at her shoulder. 'So: playboy Jon Parker.'

'Yeah, that's a real shock.'

'Sandford wants to be him so bad it hurts.'

'That's what bugs me.'

Cullen pulled out his phone and looked at the screen, carrying on as he read. 'I coulda been considered a playboy, you know.'

Casey looked around at him, one eyebrow raised. 'Uh-huh.'

'All I was missing was money. And looks.'

'And charm. Don't forget charm.'

'Luisa used to say I'm charming. I charmed her, once upon a time.'

'Right. And what does she say now?'

He squinted, wrinkling his nose. 'That she used to drink too much.' He swallowed a smile, pleased with his own joke.

They came around the fir trees and followed a short path to the porch. Cullen looked up from his phone. 'Uniform reported no one home here when they tried this morning.' A wooden carving next to the door carried the name *Four Winds*, the property number below it. Cullen rang the bell and stepped back while a tune played out on chimes inside.

A blonde woman with newsreader teeth opened the door, looking like she'd been expecting them. 'Hi, Ellis said you'd most probably come by. I'm Greta Van Heusen.'

Casey introduced them both. 'You made a 911 call last night about a disturbance?'

'That's right, there was a girl coming along the street making all kinds of noise and shouting and – Ellis said he already told you the details.'

'When did Mr Sandford speak to you, ma'am?'

'He came over this morning, I think after you were at his house the first time. He explained the police were investigating and he was co-ordinating with you.'

Casey sensed Cullen bristling even before she looked. His tongue was poking out the corner of his mouth, and he raised his eyebrows.

Casey turned back to the woman. 'Can you talk me through what you saw, please?'

'Of course, but I don't know that I can be ... I guess I heard the shouting, that's what woke me up. We couldn't see what was going on, but it sounded like it was coming from Ellis's place, so Jerry – my husband – he went outside to see what it was. I think he made it about halfway to Ellis's when the girl saw him and started to come over.'

'Is your husband home, Mrs Van Heusen?'

'No, he won't be back till late. He commutes to the city, that's why he was furious, because he has to leave by five-thirty in the mornings, so you can imagine … Anyway, he went out there and that just brought her this way.'

'Did they talk?' Cullen said.

'I think he tried to ask what was the matter, but he couldn't get any sense out of her. She kept saying someone was coming to kill her, that she had to get away, over and over.'

Van Heusen's eyes flicked to something behind them, and Casey looked around and saw a HCPD cruiser pull up at the end of the drive. Kidman and Underhill again. She signalled to them she'd be over soon as they were done. 'So what did your husband do?'

'He couldn't get her to listen so he invited her into the house – I couldn't believe it. I think he felt sorry for her. She came as far as the path, about where that car is…' She nodded to indicate the cruiser. 'Then she started up again. I'd come downstairs by that point, I wanted Jerry to come back inside, but he was still trying to talk her down. A few seconds later she walked off.'

'Which direction?'

'That way.' She pointed west; Tina Grace continuing to head away from Jon Parker's house.

'Was that when you called 911?' Casey said.

'Yes … I mean no, I called from the bedroom, before I came downstairs.'

'Did you or your husband go after her?'

She shook her head firmly. 'I didn't leave the house. Jerry kinda half followed her, but I told him to let her go, I thought it was better for the police to deal with it. She was obviously upset about something and she seemed real unpredictable, I was worried about...' She trailed off, deflating a little. 'I just didn't want to get involved.'

'I understand, ma'am. Did you see her talk to anybody else? Or anyone following her?'

'No. Well, Jon came by, we saw him catch up with her, but that was only for a few seconds, then it looked like he gave up and walked back towards his place.'

'Did either of you speak to him?'

'No, we didn't want ... I thought he'd be embarrassed enough anyway, so I said to let him go by. Jerry just wanted to get back to bed to try to catch some more sleep before the alarm so he went along with it. But he couldn't sleep after all that, he ended up going to the office early.'

Cullen was making notes as the woman spoke. Casey glanced back at the cruiser, eager to turn them loose. 'Are you friendly with Jon Parker, Mrs Van Heusen?'

She flopped her head to one side and then the other. 'Sure, some. He came over for one of our barbecues last summer – we always invite him, but he only made it that one time. We mostly see him walking on the beach and he always stops to say hello, but he's kinda private. He doesn't get involved in any of the neighbourhood associations.'

'Do you know where he is now?'

'I don't, I'm sorry. He doesn't keep a regular schedule, I guess being retired and all. There was someone stopped by his place this morning, after you guys left.'

Cullen looked up, his expression like he was trying to determine the significance. 'Is that unusual?'

'I don't ... I mean I guess not, I don't usually watch who comes and goes, I'm not like—' She cut herself off, shifting her gaze towards Sandford's house but not quite landing it. 'I don't want to come off as a busybody or anything, I was just a little on edge after last night. Makes you more watchful, you know?'

Casey nodded again and looked at the house and the doorbell – the regular type, not a video model. 'Do you happen to have any security cameras on your property? A video doorbell or anything like that?'

She shook her head. 'I'm sorry. This is a very safe neighbourhood, we never...' The sentence dissolved into a shrug.

Casey forked over her card. 'I'm gonna leave this with you, can you pass it on to Mr Van Heusen and have him call me first chance he gets?'

'Of course. Did something happen to the girl?'

Her face was stitched with concern. Casey laced her hands together in front of her. 'We're trying to find her, that's all I can say at this stage. Appreciate your help.'

They stepped off the porch and followed the path to where the cruiser was idling. The passenger-side window came down as they approached, and Kidman looked out. 'Hey, Big, back again.' He nodded at Cullen too.

'What's up, Frankie, you warm enough in there?' Casey stuffed her hands into her pockets.

Kidman grinned. 'Plenty, thanks. You can climb in the back if you wanna defrost, but I gotta cuff you first.'

Casey shot him an acid smile. 'That's your wife you're confusing me for, Frank, I'm not into that shit.'

He grinned. 'Lieutenant Ray got us detached to you guys again, said you couldn't handle your own investigation so you needed us to take care of it?'

Cullen patted the hood. 'You're the cavalry? Shit, we're in worse shape than I thought.'

'Yeah, yeah,' Kidman said. 'So what's going on?'

Casey brought up the list of 911s from the night before on her phone. 'I need you to canvass the rest of the neighbourhood. We'll talk to the 911 callers, I want you guys to speak to everyone else. Concentrate on the houses to the west of this point – that's the way she was headed – then try a couple to the east. See if anyone who didn't call it in saw anything – it's the biggest news around here since electricity so they all want to talk. Take any gossip comes your way, but most of all I want to know where Tina Grace went. Walk the route, take your time – keep a lookout for the cell phone in particular. We've got a description of what she was wearing, ask about that in case anyone needs prompting. So far the only people we can place on the street at the same time she was are residents – but she was talking about someone trying to kill her, and on her 911 call she cuts herself off at one point and says, "I think he's coming". Best bet is she was referring to the guy she spent the night with, Jon Parker, but if there was someone else out here I want to know who. If not, I want to know how she left the vicinity. I can't see her walking back to Rockport.'

'You sure about that?' Kidman said.

'What?'

'That she left the vicinity? I mean, I don't wanna be morbid, but—'

Casey straightened up to cut him off. 'I know.'

Casey crossed Ramona Boulevard and stood on a small mound on the verge that gave her a view over the first line of scrub and out as far as Ocean Road and the reed beds beyond it. The wind was strong enough that there were whitecaps on the bay; behind her, the Atlantic battered the empty beaches. Her hands and toes were going numb from the cold.

Cullen came over, a mug of coffee held out for her.

'Where'd you get that?'

'Mrs Van Heusen brought them out. She had a whole care package with her, but Frank and his boy scarfed the cookies.'

'Son of a bitch. I'm gonna kick him in the balls.'

'He'd only enjoy it.'

Casey took a mouthful of coffee, could've wept when she realised it was already lukewarm. She and Cullen had spoken to the two other residents to make 911 calls: Hilary Dunning, an older woman who lived alone, one along from the Van Heusens; and Christopher Stadler, next door to her at 214 – the address mentioned on the 911. They'd interviewed him on his doorstep – a mid-fifties, WASP-y Rotarian who expressed concern for the 'young lady in distress' – just not enough to open up when she'd come hammering. From his and Dunning's accounts, it sounded as if Tina was getting more worked up the further along the road she got. According to Stadler, when she left his place she carried on going west, still heading away from Jon Parker's. 'What did they get from the rest of the residents?'

Cullen was already shaking his head, his gaze turned out to the bay. 'Nothing new. Parker's neighbour to the east saw Tina Grace walking up the road, towards Ellis Sandford's place, but could only see her from behind and went back to bed; the house one along from that is empty – they're snowbirds that winter in Fort Lauderdale, apparently. They called at a few more places east of that but got "didn't hear a thing" or no one home.'

'What about to the west?'

'Nothing. There's a gap between the Stadlers at 214 and the

next house, something like six hundred yards, no residences in between. Beyond that, no reports of any sightings, no reports of strangers banging on doors in the middle of the night. First the residents that far along heard about it was this morning – sounds like Ellis Sandford was calling around to spread the news. There's a couple places have security devices – it'll take longer to review the whole night, but there's no sign of her in the time window we're looking at in that vicinity.' Cullen turned to face her, the wind tugging at his overcoat. 'Case, Frank Kidman went knocking more than a mile along the road to the west.' He jutted his chin at the acres of wilderness spread in front of them, the dark water beyond it in the distance. 'There's no other way out.'

Casey dipped her head. 'It's possible she calmed down. Passed the rest of the way without the residents further along noticing. If she made it back to Ocean Road she maybe could've hitched a ride.'

'You think? From what we heard, sounds like she was getting more worked up, not less.'

'Because she was getting more and more desperate.'

'Yeah.'

Casey took a deep breath at the same time as Cullen. 'Any chance she could've doubled back, headed east?'

'And not been noticed by Ellis Sandford? Or one of the others? Anyway, that eventually loops back to Ocean Road too, so unless she did flag down a ride … in the dead of night…' Cullen peered out over the scrub at the windswept highway – mid-afternoon and not a car in sight.

'I know,' Casey said, looking down at her feet. 'I know. I'm reaching.' She tipped the cold coffee onto the grass and gripped the mug with two hands. 'We need a proper search crew out here. And where's Jon Parker at? That's what I wanna know right now.'

Cullen glanced down at his watch. More than ninety minutes since they'd arrived there. Two calls to Parker's cell had gone unanswered, the messages they'd left not returned. 'There's no way he could be making a run for it – is there?'

Casey weighed the chances. 'My gut says no, but I want to know what he was lying about before this goes any further.'

'I don't know if I believe these other guys, either,' Cullen said. He turned his gaze towards Ellis Sandford's residence. 'I get the feeling he'd lie for his hero Parker.'

'Sure.' Casey's cell phone rang; she checked the screen before she answered, but didn't recognise the number. 'Casey Wray.'

'Detective?'

'Yeah, who's this?'

'My name's Jerry Van Heusen, my wife said you wanted to speak with me.'

Casey looked over, the Van Heusen's house, a hundred yards down the road from where she stood. 'Yeah, that's right. Thank you for calling me, sir. About the disturbance last night—'

'Yeah, I think my wife told you what was happening. That girl was whacked out of her mind on something.'

'Your wife said you talked to the woman in question?' Casey couldn't help emphasising the word woman.

'I spoke at her, and she spoke at me, wasn't a lot of communication – she was way gone. Lord knows what she'd taken.' He coughed away from the phone. 'Look, the thing is, I saw something ... I mean, I maybe should've said something last night, but I was tired and my wake-up time is brutal, so...'

Cullen had taken the mug from her hand and gone to cross

the road again, but Casey clicked her fingers to get his attention and waved him back over. 'Go on.'

'I don't even ... I mean, I half saw it, I guess. I didn't think much of it but in case it matters to you...'

'What did you see, sir?'

Cullen raised his eyebrows at hearing the question.

'There was a car, in the distance. It was up on the shoulder, quite a way off, and it had to be parked half in the bushes because I could only make out one tail light.'

Casey made a motion for Cullen to take out his pad. 'What kind of car was it?'

'I honestly couldn't tell you, like I said, it was only really the light I saw. This one, red spot.'

'What about the colour or type – light, dark? SUV, a sedan?'

'Sorry.'

'Did you see the woman you spoke with approach it?'

'She was heading that way when I went back inside, but I don't know if she even saw it or not. It was pretty far away and she was walking kinda stop-start, you know?'

Casey turned around, scanning west along Ramona Boulevard. The road was dead straight, stretching to its vanishing point in the murky distance. 'Approximately where would you say the vehicle was parked, Mr Van Heusen?'

He blew out a breath, sounded like he was thinking it through. 'Three, four hundred yards off. Somewhere past the Stadlers' place. They're at 214.'

Casey started walking hard that way.

'Detective?'

# CHAPTER 5

Casey sensed something was off as soon as they set foot in the office. It was quiet, tension smothering the room like a wet sack. The source of it became clear as she approached her desk, and she slowed to assess the scene. In Carletti's office, visible through the glass: Captain Robbie McTeague, leaning against the wall in the corner of the room. He was looking on while Ray spoke from his chair.

Cullen was ahead of her and glanced back. 'Bad day to be Lieutenant Ray.'

Casey kept watching as she sat down. It looked like Carletti was protesting or defending himself, throwing his arms about as he spoke. For McTeague's part, he had his hands in his pockets and one leg crossed in front of the other. He wasn't saying anything, letting Carletti jaw. The other detectives in the office watched on openly, their way of showing they had their boy's back. Only Jilly had her head buried in a file, still nervous enough around the brass to have divided loyalties.

Ray Carletti was the closest thing to a mentor Casey ever had. Before he took her under his wing, she was maybe a month from quitting the department altogether. The ribbing, the ingrained sexism – she could've dealt with those in isolation, accustomed to both from her time in patrol. But what was new was the impostor syndrome that came with making detective; she'd anticipated the feeling, but not its ferocity, nor how much it would magnify the impact of the other two.

She'd stopped eating; after three months on the squad she'd dropped ten pounds – her appetite shot by stress. She lived on coffee, exacerbating the problems she was already having sleeping. After any downtime, even just a weekend, she felt like she wanted to throw up the night before going back on duty.

The first case she'd been assigned was a robbery from a business downtown. Her partner cried off going with her at the last minute, blaming a sudden illness; the fact she didn't pick up on that as a red flag was cited later as proof she'd never be worth shit as a detective. When she pulled up to the address, she found it was a sex store run by a six-foot-eight drag queen who went by the name of Rolo. He took her inside and stood her next to a counter full of ball gags to explain that he'd had his anal virginity stolen the night before, and she simply had to arrest the asshole who did it. Rolo could barely get the words out, he was laughing so hard. When Casey got back to her desk, it was covered in lurid pink dildos, more spilling out of her top drawer.

Her clearest memory of that day was being in a bathroom stall afterwards, tears in her eyes at the humiliation, ready to quit on the spot. It was only the anger raging underneath that kept her from doing it – the fuck-you determination she'd built up during her years in patrol.

Now the memory kept her strong. A reminder of how far she'd come. The squad was nothing like how it used to be, and she couldn't imagine life outside of it. She thought about that sometimes: whether she'd changed the job or the job had changed her. She liked to think it was the former, but then she'd consider how long it was since she'd spoken to her hometown friends – ten months and counting – or the last time she went to a bar with someone who wasn't a cop, and she wasn't so sure.

Carletti was still talking but McTeague had dipped his head to stare at the floor, as if everything he was hearing was old news. Casey walked over to Jill Hart and leaned on the back of her chair. 'How long they been going at it?'

'Ten minutes or so.'

Billy D twisted his neck to talk over his shoulder. 'Loot's getting his ass kicked.'

'What's it about?'

Billy shrugged, turning back to watch again.

Dana Torres had the desk closest to Carletti's office. Casey's first recruit, the two went back years; they'd served in patrol together, even working the same downtown beat, albeit eighteen months apart. Casey went to stand by her, a sheet of paper in her hand as flimsy pretence. 'You hear anything from in there?'

Dana fiddled with the small cross she wore on her necklace. 'Not really. Not enough.'

Casey watched a few seconds longer, just until she caught Carletti's eye. He gave the slightest nod, without breaking his verbal stride, but McTeague picked up on it and looked around.

Slowly he uncrossed his arms and held up one finger to signal Carletti should pause.

He pulled the office door open and stood in the doorway, almost filling it. 'Something you need, Detective Wray?'

Casey folded her arms. 'No, sir.'

He kept eye contact with her for a second or two, then went back inside. When she turned around, Cullen looked spooked.

Dana glanced up from her seat. 'He's such an asshole.'

She said it loud enough that Casey had to swallow a laugh. 'Do you even remember the last time you gave a fuck about getting in trouble, D?'

Dana kept her eyes on McTeague, who was back on the other side of the glass wall, watching Ray defend himself. 'Nope. Smoked way too much grass as a teenager to remember that far back.'

This time Casey couldn't hold the laugh in. She patted the back of Dana's chair, turning away. 'Keep your ears open for me, huh?'

Dana gave her a thumbs-up without looking around, holding it up in the air for all to see.

Casey had thought long and hard about bringing Dana onto the team. Even though she'd known her for years, they'd never been close, running in different circles within the department. Brash and outspoken, Dana had always seemed to Casey everything she wasn't: confident, loud and popular. But those same traits made her a natural on the street – a cop who took no bullshit, but didn't rub you up the wrong way doing so. Casey's concern had been whether she'd have enough command presence to harness that kind of strong personality – but Dana had bought into Casey's vision for the department from day one, making it easy for her.

Cullen was looking at Casey expectantly when she got back to her desk.

'Don't know,' she said, before he could ask the question.

He ran his hand over his mouth, back and forth. 'Who you think would win in a fight?' He nodded towards the office.

'Those two?' McTeague was six foot three of muscle-going-soft, and a full head taller than Carletti; but Carletti was a street fighter who came out of the Ronson Heights neighbourhood at a time when a shared allegiance to the pope did nothing to stop the Irish kids going at the Italians. 'Never happen. McTeague's the type would shoot you in the back the night before.'

Cullen nodded, picking up a printout to read. 'Motherfucker's cold as penguin shit.'

Casey sat down, organising a timeline in her thoughts. She

looked at the clock on the wall behind her – already more than twelve hours since Tina Grace's last known contact. She skimmed through her notes, the list of 911 calls on the desk next to her. The Stadlers at 214 were the last to report seeing Tina on Ramona Boulevard. Their call was timed at 4.12am. Casey cross-checked it against the list. They were the last to see her, but not the last to call 911…

She stood up so she could see Cullen over his computer. 'Jon Parker didn't call 911 till 4.21am. That's a full eighteen minutes after Sandford made the first call – so at least that long since Tina left his house.'

Cullen stuck his bottom lip out. 'So? We already established he's not big on compassion.'

'Yeah, but doesn't that seem strange to you?'

'Depends. He's got less cause to be alarmed, right? He knows who the girl is banging on doors around the neighbourhood, so he's got less reason to call. Especially if he knows she's high or whatever.'

Casey circled around her desk. 'Call Parker again, would you, see if he's home yet?'

She moved past Cullen as he picked up his phone to dial, and went over to the next set of desks. 'Hey, Billy, you get anywhere with Uber about the woman disappeared from the beach?'

Drocker had his phone cradled to his ear but was obviously on hold for someone. 'Yeah. There was nothing on the portal, but I spoke to one of the girls over there and she said they didn't have any pickups on the beach between 1am and 7am yesterday.'

Casey cocked her head at him. 'Billy…?'

'What?'

'I know that tone.'

Billy blushed. '*What*?'

'"One of the girls" – were you flirting with her?'

'No.' He slumped low again, eyes on the ceiling, muttering to himself. But when Casey wouldn't look away he finally said, 'What? She sounded hot.'

'You're unbelievable.'

'She likes cops, she gave me her Instagram, that's all. You want the rest or don't you?'

Casey made a face of fake outrage. 'Hit me.'

'I checked Lyft too, they had nothing out there that time, and I tried the local cab services – same deal.'

'Okay. So if Tina Grace made it off the beach, it wasn't in a cab. Unless it was off-meter.'

'I checked that – there's only two companies serve Ramona Villas and they both use GPS to keep track of their guys. Stop them taking cash fares on company time.'

Casey raised her eyebrows, impressed. 'Okay, good. So?'

He looked at her, uncertain. 'There something else?'

'Is she hot or isn't she? The Uber girl?'

He sighed but was already unlocking his cell phone. He held up his screen to show a picture of a brunette airbrushed with a cat filter and cartoon spectacles.

Casey steadied the phone to examine it, already shaking her head. 'Way out of your league.'

Billy rolled his eyes, and Casey fought to keep a straight face. When she looked up from his cell, Jill was watching them over her computer.

'Why do the kids do that?' Casey said. 'With the whiskers and the glasses and stuff?'

'Uh ... it's cute, I guess?' Billy said.

'When I was a kid, I used to walk around half-blind so as not to have anyone see me in my glasses. Now you wanna airbrush them on.'

'Oh wow, Big,' Billy said, his tone all fake amazement, 'they had glasses when you were a kid?'

'What, back in the Stone Age?' Casey smiled at Jill, inviting some backup, but she was wincing. It made her want to put her arm around her, suddenly wondering if Cullen was on to something after all.

She clapped Billy on the shoulder playfully and mouthed 'thanks' as she moved off.

She dropped into her chair again, took a mouthful of water and started transposing the timeline onto paper. She visualised the stretch of Ramona Boulevard where the last known sightings of Tina Grace took place: five houses, all facing the ocean on the same side of the road, spaced between fifty and a hundred yards apart.

Tina left Jon Parker's heading west; the first place she tried was Parker's neighbour, Ellis Sandford, and his 911 call was timed at 4.03am. When Sandford wouldn't open up, she carried on to the Van Heusens'. Mrs VH – Greta – called 911 at 4.06am, which was when her husband Jerry was outside trying to talk to Tina – and when he claimed to notice the car parked further along the road in the bushes.

By 4.12am, according to the time of their 911 call, Tina had made it as far as the Stadler property at 214, the last house of the five. Christopher Stadler, the WASP-y Rotarian who made the last reported sighting, said when he'd turned her away, Tina carried on heading west and that he lost sight of her shortly after. He claimed not to have seen the stationary vehicle Jerry Van Heusen reported seeing further along

Ramona Boulevard, then or earlier in the night – and none of the other residents had mentioned it either. Which left a question in Casey's mind as to whether Jerry Van Heusen could be mistaken – or lying.

Casey had walked the stretch of road Van Heusen indicated, the break between properties past the Stadlers' just as Frank Kidman had described to Cullen – a gap of more than six hundred yards, uninterrupted views of the ocean on one side, thick scrubland and salt-marsh on the other, until it merged into the bay. She noted tyre markings all along the roadside there, but the street was narrow enough that anytime two cars met, one would have to drive on the dirt to get by. It was a good place to idle for someone who didn't want to be seen by the residents – but why would anyone need to? The best reason she could come up with was a B&E on one of the empty houses. She made a note to check for reports of known crews working the area – and another to check Jerry Van Heusen's background and movements; he wouldn't be the first perp to try to divert them with a phantom suspect.

'Bingo.' Cullen ducked his head around his monitor. 'Parker's home. Says he's been golfing all day.'

Casey bug-eyed him. 'Golfing? Son of a—' She stood up, one last look at Carletti's office as she grabbed her jacket. McTeague was doing the talking now, standing over Ray, who had his hands gripped in front of him on the desk and was staring at them. Pick up the pieces later maybe, but nothing she could do to help him now. 'Let's go.'

They made their third ride out to the beach in darkness. Crossing the causeway, the bay was a black mass all around them, the wind barrelling in from the sea and buffeting the car off course.

Cullen had already touched his nose twice by the time he spoke his mind. 'You know what the brass will say about this.'

'What?'

'"What if she just took off?"'

Casey had an empty gaze pointed at the highway, thinking. The lights from the barrier island were ahead, studs of white and yellow the only thing between them and the Atlantic beyond, a lone pair of headlights moving along Ocean Road in the far distance. She could hear the wind whipping across the bay, and in the darkness it was easy to mistake it for the ocean's roar. 'Took off where?'

'Wherever they go. The ones that just fall off the earth.'

Casey looked at him sidelong. 'You can't seriously—'

'I'm just playing devil's advocate. They're gonna say, "You spent all day on this, to the exclusion of the rest of your caseload. Looking for an adult who might just've left of her own free will."'

Casey pointed ahead through the windshield. 'Not the most promising place to strike out from.'

'Hey, I don't need convincing.'

'You really think Ray would come at us on this? Tina Grace has a boyfriend – or two – and a mom she was picking up groceries for. You're telling me she suddenly decided to leave for Hollywood in the middle of the night?'

Cullen tapped the wheel. 'I'm not talking about Ray...'

'Anyone wants to argue it, they can listen to the 911 and then come tell me that's a woman making rational choices.' Her cell buzzed and she went to pick it up from her lap but then realised what he was really saying. 'Fuck – McTeague's got you spooked. That's it.'

The causeway split where it met the land, curving gently through ninety degrees in either direction to become Ocean Road. Cullen took the exit towards Ramona Beach. 'I'm not obsessed with him the way you are.'

'That's called deflecting.'

'Whatever he's piling onto Ray for, shit only rolls downhill. Means anything he – or they – can prod at, they will.'

She brought her phone up again, attention wandering. 'So they can prod. Who cares?' She read the message on screen:

*This is Brian. Called friends like u asked no one seen or spoke to her. What u got?*

Took a second to place it as Brian Walton – Tina Grace's boyfriend. 'Jesus.'

'What?'

'That Brian guy just messaged me like we're classmates.'

'Only way kids communicate these days.'

'He's a grown-ass man. Anyway, you can add it to the Casey and Dave justification file: her friends are still reporting radio silence.'

'We should check him out. Just to be sure.'

Casey nodded to herself, sending a note to Billy D to do exactly that.

Cullen glanced out of his window, endless acres of salt marsh hidden behind a pitch-black veil. Casey looked back at her phone and began scrolling through the backlog of emails – lab results, a decision from the DA's office not to press charges in one of her cases – not registering at first that he'd gone quiet. When she did, she looked up and saw his eyes were damp.

'Hey, you okay?' She turned towards him.

He huffed, half-ass trying to mask it. 'Yeah.'

'What's wrong?'

He shook his head, already retreating from it. 'Don't worry about it.'

'I was only busting your balls about McTeague...'

'Christ, it's not...' He let out a breath, a nervous laugh. 'Look at it. Makes me think about the girls. What the fuck would I do if it was Shauna or Sienna?'

Casey looked out his window and saw it through his eyes this time. He'd joked more than once before now that being a dad was making him soft. She reached over and squeezed his shoulder. 'Hate to tell you, but those girls are just gonna keep kicking your ass. Believe me, I know.'

He grunted, almost a laugh, swiping his eyes with the back of his hand. 'You remember last year when Sienna had that eye infection and we had to take her to St Mark's?'

Casey nodded, remembering the picture he'd shown her of the toddler with her eye the size of an apple.

'They wanted me to hold her still so the nurse could give her a shot. Tiny little needle, nothing, right? I mean, it's gonna hurt her, I know that, but only for a second, and I also know it's gonna make her better.'

Casey knew the story; he'd told her about it at the time, but he clearly needed to get this off his chest.

'And I couldn't do it. Couldn't even do that, because it cut me up so bad to see her bawling. They had to get Lu to pin her down, five months pregnant with a bump out to here.' He gestured with his hand, glancing over.

'Don't give yourself a hard time...'

'I'm just saying, you and me, we know what's out there,

what's waiting for these kids in the world. How fucking bad it can get. And when you know that ... I'm telling you, there's nights I can't sleep for thinking about it.'

She reached over and gripped his shoulder, wondering where this was coming from. 'At least your girls got you looking out for them. You and Lu ... there's not every kid has a start like that.'

He sniffed, wiping his hand over his eyes again.

'It's the dumbest things set me off. You tell anybody about this and I'll kill you.'

Casey kept the smile on her face but he'd made her think about her own choices – the day a twenty-two-year-old Casey Wray broke the news to her mother that her only child was moving across New York State to join the Hampstead County Police Department. Even now she'd call her decision a no-brainer: a starting salary in excess of forty thousand dollars a year for a high-school goof-off who'd graduated 'more by luck than judgement', in the words of one of her teachers. She'd spent the intervening years working for minimum wage in dead-end jobs in K-Mart, Claire's Accessories and the 24-hour gas station on Route 9, until the aimless years of partying and living one day to the next got to feel like a waste of a life. Back then HCPD was famous for its progression plan, which would almost double her salary after six years – an unimaginable amount of money to her at the time, and the reason more than half the applicants to HCPD were serving officers from nearby forces.

Still her mom couldn't understand why she wanted to do it; Angela Wray had been born fifty miles from the town where Casey grew up, just over the Pennsylvania border, and she considered New York City a foreign country. She offered to let

Casey stay at home rent free, and no matter how many times she asked the question, never could grasp why Casey wanted to leave Jasper, NY. Or why holding out for a promotion to manager at the K-Mart wasn't enough.

Casey understood a successful application would mean moving to Long Island, to Rockport, a town she had no connection to and, in her mom's eyes, embodied the urban decay she heard all about on the news. But against competition from so many experienced cops, it seemed such a longshot she'd get in, she didn't waste time thinking about the reality of it until it was too late.

'It's gonna get worse before it gets better, y'know? The crap I put my mom through...'

Cullen waved it off. 'Take it down the street. She thought you were an angel.'

He'd met Angela a handful of times before she died, and she'd warmed to him the same way everyone did. The first time, at a dinner at Casey's place, she'd noticed her mom smiling at him the way a kid would at Superman – almost wonderment – and she'd asked her about it after.

'Well, he's a cop,' her mom shot back.

'And? So am I,' Casey had said, bemused.

'No, a real cop I mean. A policeman.'

It'd felt like a slight at the time, but she came to understand that it had nothing to do with Casey, and everything to do with how her mom saw the world; a product of small-town Pennsylvania, with a husband fifteen years her senior – killed by a heart attack before Casey was old enough to remember him – both of whom shared the view that a woman's place was at home raising a family. Betraying an assumption that one day Casey would grow out of the police thing and settle down to do just that. The idea almost made her laugh now; Cullen had said to her once that the job was so far under her skin, she'd need an exorcism to be free of it.

They made the turning off Ocean Road onto Ramona Boulevard. It was still more than two miles to Jon Parker's house and they drove in silence, passing two of the short underpasses that acted as pedestrian access tunnels through to the public beaches. The high beams lit up the bleak roadway ahead, the blacktop slick in their glare, no streetlights now they'd left Ocean. Casey thought again about the chances Tina Grace would've walked out of here in the dead of night. How scared she must've been even to try.

## CHAPTER 6

The porch light accentuated the bruise.

Not quite a black eye, the welt curved around Jon Parker's orbital bone to where it met his temple, creeping down as far as his cheekbone. The skin wasn't broken, but it was prominent enough to be the first thing Casey saw when he opened the door.

'Detectives. Is there any news?'

'Can we talk inside, Mr Parker?'

He stepped back, pulling the door wide. 'Of course, come in.'

Casey led the way, circling around the sofa to stand by the coffee table. A little callback to her suspicions, see if it made him uncomfortable.

'Can I get you guys a drink?'

Casey shook her head before he'd even finished asking. 'Have you heard from Tina today at all, Mr Parker?'

He held his hands open. 'No, I'm afraid...' He took his cell out and glanced at the screen, as if it was just occurring to him to check. 'I guess Detective Cullen told you I've been golfing this afternoon, so ... I did try calling her but it's always dead.'

'We can't find anyone who's heard from her today,' Casey said. 'Speaking frankly, I now have serious concerns for Tina's wellbeing, so we need you to walk us through what happened last night in more detail.'

Parker glanced behind him at the sofa, thinking to sit, but then staying on his feet. 'Of course, anything I can do.'

'You said she arrived here around eleven last night?'

'Yes.'

'Do you know where she'd been before that?'

He shook his head, giving a small shrug. 'I don't think we talked about it.'

'Did she seem troubled at all when she arrived?'

'I think ... No, she just seemed herself.'

'Had she been drinking?'

'Sure, some, I think. But she wasn't drunk or even close to it. I'd had some wine, so it's hard to tell. It's not like I'd ask, you know? I've got no right to interrogate her on how she spends her time.'

Cullen stared at him. 'We're just trying to get a handle on where her head was at.'

'Yeah, I get it.' Parker made another little meek gesture with his hands – seemed to be his fallback, but it was hollow and it was starting to piss Casey off.

'Where'd you get the bruise, Mr Parker?' Casey stared at it for emphasis.

'Ha, yeah, I kinda hoped it wasn't that noticeable. I do

boxing training at the gym, couple days a week – just for fitness, I'm not a fighter or anything. I bobbed late.'

'The Sweet Science.' Cullen said it with a rising lilt, hinting at sarcasm.

'Busy day,' Casey said.

'Excuse me?'

'Boxing, golf.'

Parker smiled. 'I'm a lucky man, I have a lot of free time.'

'We were told you're retired?' Cullen said.

'Yeah, going on ten years now. I did my time on Wall Street, so – sounds selfish, but the crash came at the right time for me. I took a nice package to walk, enough to let me move out here. I wanted out anyway, so it wasn't a hard decision. People cling on, they burn out, end up with a lifestyle they can't give up and they can't afford. I wasn't about to go that route.'

He was pleased to tell it; not quite arrogant, but enough to give the lie to the meek act he was trying to pull off before. 'Where did you golf today?'

'Sentona Hills. You know it?'

'Uh-huh,' Casey said. Knew it in the way most people did – as a fifty-grand-a-year country club she wasn't likely to be joining anytime soon. The kind of place only the top brass would ever see the inside of. 'When Tina left here last night – talk me through that again.'

Parker glanced behind himself again and decided to sit this time. 'Well, okay. Like I said, she started saying she had to go – this was totally out of nowhere.'

'This was after you'd had sex the second time?'

'Uh, right.' Casey nodded for him to carry on. 'So she ... I guess she was putting her clothes on when I went to the bathroom, and when I came back she said she had to leave. She looked kind of panicked. I asked her why, is everything okay, and she said someone was coming to get her. I asked who, obviously, but I was kind of in a daze at this point, I wasn't sure if she was kidding around or something. But when she finished getting dressed she went right downstairs, so I put my sweats on and went down too, tried to get her to just sit down and talk. I was just saying, "slow down a minute", you know? But she was getting more and more worked up – over and over again, "I gotta go, I gotta go". So I offered to call her a cab and then … Then it's like I told you earlier. I went to get her some water and she just bolted.'

'Did you follow her immediately?'

'Yes.'

Cullen looked down. 'You stop to put some shoes on?'

'Uh, sure. Yeah.'

'Because your neighbour Ellis Sandford called 911 at 4.03am.' Cullen flipped the page on his notepad, working from Parker's statement and their own notes from earlier. 'He stated Tina Grace was at his door a few minutes, but he didn't see you till after. The Van Heusens made their call at 4.06am, and Mrs Van Heusen said she saw you catch up to Tina sometime after that. So that's at least a four-to-five-minute gap from when she left your house, probably more. How long's it take you to put your shoes on?'

Parker rubbed his forehead with his knuckles. 'It's a little hazy, I need to think here. Yeah, I put my sneakers on, then I stood on my porch a while because I assumed she'd come back. I could see her the whole time, I was calling out to her to come inside.'

Casey glanced around the living room, her gaze landing on a standing walnut cabinet in the corner by the steps to the den. 'Do you own a firearm, Mr Parker?'

He shook his head. 'No.'

If true, it spiked one theory they'd batted about on the ride over: an argument that got out of hand, and when Tina ran, Parker delayed following while he went to find his gun. Casey wasn't ready to rule it out yet.

Cullen slipped right back into the same groove. 'And where was Miss Grace when you got outside?'

'At Ellis's door, knocking.'

'And you didn't go to her at that point?'

'No, I was ... I thought I should give her a chance to cool off.'

'And then?'

'She moved on down the street. Listen, detectives, I'm not an idiot, I know why you're asking me these questions, but you can drop the accusatory tone, okay? I'm here to help, we want the same thing. I didn't go to her right away because I was embarrassed what Ellis and the others would think – it looks bad on me, her going crazy.'

Casey watched him losing his cool for the first time that evening, trying to decide if he was being disingenuous. If Ellis Sandford would more likely be impressed Parker had a girl half his age over, or be pissed she was disturbing his little kingdom. 'So how long did you wait?'

Parker checked his watch, as if it held the answers. 'I'm not sure. When she was past the Van Heusens' I went after her, maybe a couple minutes. By then I thought I'd have a shot at talking her back inside.'

'You told us this morning you didn't see anyone else out on the street.'

'That's right.'

'Jerry Van Heusen came out to see what was happening.'

'What? Yeah, of course, I saw Jerry. I thought you meant, y'know, apart from the neighbours. Strangers.'

His voice was level still, but his eyes were flaring now.

'So to be clear, who exactly did you see on the street last night?'

He closed his eyes, making sure this time. 'Just Jerry. But I didn't speak to him. Wait, there's no way Jerry would've done something to ... Christ, he's pulling in eight figures a year.'

'That's not what we're suggesting. But you can see how recollections change, it's important we get this straight.'

'Nothing's changed, you didn't ask me in detail earlier—'

Casey spoke over him. 'Mr Van Heusen reported seeing a car parked some ways down the street to the west. Did you see anything like that?'

Parker stopped breathing. Couldn't decide where to put his eyes.

Casey relaxed her face, waiting. The sudden silence like a mic drop. 'Mr Parker?'

'No.'

'Did you call a cab for Tina in the end?'

He turned his head slightly before he answered. 'No. She was gone before I had a chance.'

'So that couldn't be the car Jerry Van H saw?'

'Unless she called her own,' Parker said, so quick, it was as if he had it prepared.

Casey nodded, his readiness sparking something now. 'We're looking into that. How did Tina arrive out here, Mr Parker?'

'A cab, I think. I ... I know I keep saying this, but I don't think we spoke about it. I assumed.'

Casey watched his face as he lied to her, remembering every tic. No fluttering eyelids or other obvious tells, but she'd be able to refer back to his expression right now. 'Have you noticed any unusual cars parked out there at night in recent days?'

'I don't really keep watch.' He glanced towards the den and the picture windows, too dark outside to even make out the ocean; unsettling to think of its immense power, so close, lurking unseen in the darkness. 'If I'm looking out, it's usually in that direction.'

'Can you think of anyone not from the neighbourhood would have had a reason to be parked out there last night?'

He shook his head. 'It's a very quiet place, you've seen what it's like.'

Cullen had glanced at her twice, trying to play catch-up. She ignored him, dipping her head and taking a step back, signalling they were wrapping up. 'There's just one other thing I wanted to ask – have you had any strange messages or calls in the last twenty-four hours? Anything unusual at all?'

'No.' He shook his head, spreading his arms across the sofa back. 'What sort of thing did you mean?'

Casey waved it off. 'Doesn't matter. Just notify us immediately if you do – or if you see anyone hanging around your house.'

He uncrossed his legs and sat forward. 'What do you mean hanging around? Is there something I don't know here?'

'No, but it pays to be vigilant.'

Parker squinted at her, saying nothing.

Casey opened the front door. 'We'll be in touch.'

'Wanna tell me where you were going back there?' Cullen looked over at her, steering with one hand in his lap.

'Motherfucker deserved it.'

'Someone "hanging around"?'

'Yeah. He wants to lie to my face, I'm gonna leave him with something to worry about.'

'What did I miss?'

'Nothing. It only came to me when he said about Tina maybe calling her own cab. He was too quick – he had his answer all ready to go.'

'Yeah, I got that, but ... Yo, you listening to me?'

They were on Ocean Road, approaching the causeway, Casey distracted, looking back across the other side of the freeway...

There. 'Slow down a second.'

Cullen braked, and she craned her neck to read the traffic sign they'd just passed. 'Barton Beach. That's all of them.'

'The highway sign?'

'Every sign we passed says Barton Beach. Tina Grace told 911 she was in Barton Beach. Ramona Beach isn't listed on any of them.'

Cullen looked at her and sped up again. 'So...?'

'How's she gonna take a cab to Parker's house if she doesn't even know where he lives?'

Cullen stared through the windshield, processing it. 'So what are you saying?'

'She didn't take a cab out to Parker's – someone gave her a ride. And they were still waiting for her at four in the morning.'

## CHAPTER 7

Cullen parked in a space by the precinct entrance, sensing her urgency. 'You sure you don't need me?'

Casey shook her head, already reaching for her door. 'Go home, pops. Family's more important.'

'You planning another run at Parker in the morning?'

'Let's see what shakes out tonight.'

Cullen smiled. 'Just keep inviting yourself in, he craps himself every time you open your mouth.'

Casey pulled the handle and jumped out.

'Hey, Big? Don't stay too late, huh? There's still a chance she shows up somewhere.'

'C'mon...'

He took his hands off the wheel in surrender. 'I know. But you can come at it again in the morning. Fresh. When's the last time you ate dinner at home?'

'Have you seen my refrigerator?' She flashed a weak smile. 'Quit stalling, get out of here.'

'Why don't you come over Saturday night? I'll make tacos, Luisa would love some better company.'

'You can't use me to prop up your marriage forever, you know.'

'What? I promise to play Beyoncé if it seals the deal.'

She closed her eyes, not feeling it right then but not wanting to offend. 'Sure. That'd be nice.' She shoved the door closed and waved him off.

Inside, she ran up the stairs with her mind racing. The conclusion felt solid: somebody gave Tina a ride and was still waiting for her five hours later. Why the hell else would anyone sit there otherwise? At four in the morning on a bitter winter night? That went way beyond friendship. A working theory: Parker has a private car service he uses. Ellis Sandford said the man had girls coming over on the reg, and it wouldn't be out of character if he impressed his dates by sending a driver to collect them.

She came to her desk and slumped down into her seat, the

2am finish the night before catching up with her again. Dana was still working but she was the only one, the place otherwise deserted.

Casey searched out Maggie Grace's number in her notebook and then dialled.

'Yeah?'

'Mrs Grace, it's Casey Wray with HCPD, we met earlier.'

'Wray. The lady detective, yeah, okay. What's going on?'

'I just wanted to check in with you. Have you heard from your daughter by any chance, Mrs Grace?'

'No, not a goddamn word.'

'Well, I'm sorry to say we're no clearer as to her whereabouts, but I wanted to let you know that my colleagues and I are working on it, and we're evaluating a lot of different pieces of information.'

'Okay. What does that mean, exactly?'

She said it flat, no edge to the question, but it still managed to nail Casey; if she was going to call this woman, at least talk straight. 'I, uh, just thought you'd want to hear something from us rather than nothing.'

'So you called to tell me nothing instead?'

Casey smiled in spite of herself. It was the kind of thing her own mom might've said. 'Look, I just—'

'No, hold on, I'm sorry. It's … Shit, what do you do with a day like this?'

'I understand. Totally. I'm sorry if I'm disturbing—'

'You're not disturbing me. I'm sat on my ass with a Miller Lite, wondering what the hell they got into now.'

'Ma'am?'

'You got kids, detective?'

'No.'

'So maybe you won't understand, but from the minute they're born, you spend your time worrying. All the bad shit could happen to them. And then it does, and it dawns on you that all that worrying didn't do nothing to stop it. It still happened.' There was a sound like she took a drink from her beer. 'Christ, listen to me.'

'You said earlier Tina's never done anything like this before, Mrs Grace?'

'Unless I'm mistaken I asked you to call me Maggie. My taxes pay your salary, don't you have to do what I say?' She scoffed at the end of it though, skewering herself as fast as she'd pumped herself up. 'No, not Tina, she's the good kid. Girls normally are – present company excluded. Tommy's the one. You got brothers, you'll know.'

Casey wrote *Tommy Grace – check* on the pad in front of her. 'What are we talking about here, Maggie?'

'Christ knows. I'm scared and I'm on the way to drunk, I don't even know myself.'

'But you mentioned your son, is he involved in some kind of trouble? That might relate to...?'

'No, no, hold on, don't go messing with what I'm saying. Tommy's a screwup but...'

Casey waited, but the pause was more like someone reconsidering their own words than hesitating. 'But what, ma'am?'

'Tommy's had some problems with the law. Nothing you ain't seen before; you probably know already, so what the hell – drugs, fights, been going on a few years. He's a smartass so he likes to blame it on his dad ditching out, but he was fine the first six years after he went, so he's full of shit.'

'Does Tina get dragged into it? Is that what you're saying?'

'No, no, and that's what I wanted to get straight. Tina's got a good brain in her head, she set herself up right after high school – thought about college but decided it wasn't for her, got a job, worked her ass off so she could get her own apartment. I was just ... You can't help sitting here thinking how messed up it is you worry about one and then this happens.' She let out a breath. 'I thought beer was supposed to help you quit thinking?'

If only. 'Listen, is Tommy there? You think I could speak with him?'

'He's out, he's gone looking for her. He came back like I asked earlier – don't get the wrong impression of him, detective, he's got a big heart. That's half his problem. But he left again a while back.'

'I understand. If Tina doesn't show up tonight, I think it'd be good to speak to him anyway – kids talk to each other in different ways to parents. Could you have him call me if I don't catch up with him first? Or I can come by tomorrow?'

'Yeah, he'll talk to you. He tries to bottle it up like a tough guy, but he's worried about his sister. I'll tell him.'

'Thanks. And, hey, you didn't get any more of those messages, did you?'

'The screaming? No. You figure that out yet? You can trace calls right?'

'The number's blocked but we'll look at it.'

'I ask you something, detective?'

'Ma'am?'

'How often do they show up again?'

Casey took a silent breath. The figures were astronomical. An estimated six hundred thousand reported missing in the US each year, a hundred thousand active cases at any given time. A good proportion were eventually accounted for – dead or alive – but even that could take years; and Tina's circumstance wasn't promising. 'I couldn't say offhand. People do strange things – was Tina under any kind of pressure, anything she might want to get away from? Brian Walton told me she left her job with some savings, but did she have money worries?' It only occurred to her as she said it, playboy Jon Parker's possible appeal suddenly more obvious.

The line was quiet a moment, Maggie wrestling with something. 'I don't think so. She brought me a week's worth of groceries yesterday, she's been doing that since she stopped working 'cus she says she has the time, and she won't ever take any money off of me. She didn't seem any different, just herself.'

Casey slipped down in her chair, letting her head loll back. Her stomach was starting to fritz, appetite coming back with a vengeance. 'Thanks for your time, ma'am, I'll keep in touch. Talk to Tommy for me, okay?'

'Detective – thank you. I'm sorry I got at you. I appreciate you taking the trouble.'

'Sure.'

She hung up and prowled over to Dana's desk, made a pistol with her fingers. 'This is a bust, hand over your snacks.'

Dana showed empty hands without looking up. 'Too late, Big. I ate my last bag of chips at lunch. Actually, that was lunch.'

'You want something from the machine?'

'No, I'm good. You staying late?'

Casey looked at the stack of files on her desk, untouched since yesterday. An inbox she'd barely glanced at. 'Just catching up some.' She nodded at Carletti's office. 'How'd it finish up with the boss and McTeague?'

'Bad. McTeague kept up that silent but violent shit he pulls, but at the end he was tearing strips off of the lieutenant. Soon as he left, the boss stormed out. His car's still in the lot though. You know anything?'

Casey shook her head. 'Nuh-uh.'

'You need to check in with him, Big. Didn't feel like a regular McTeague drive-by to me.'

Casey nodded, staring at the empty office in front of her. 'Ray was worried about it this morning.'

'There you go.'

'I'll talk to him when he's ready. I'm gonna go get some food.'

'Hey, Big, before you go – Billy asked me to give this to you. It's the check you asked for on that guy, Brian Walton?'

Tina's boyfriend. Casey took the folder from her, skimming the text.

'He's got priors for marijuana possession, and a domestic complaint a few years back.'

Casey jumped to the second page. A domestic disturbance call-out, the complainant a woman named Adaline Twomey. Officers took a statement he'd struck her with an open hand and been threatening her with more; he denied all of it, said she was drunk and abusive, and she'd called HCPD out of spite. The woman later decided not to press charges, and the file was closed.

Interesting. Not the same as Tina's situation, but a red flag for sure.

'Thanks for this.' She started to move off but stopped and turned back. 'Hey, you think there's a chance Jill's got a thing for Billy?'

Dana screwed her face up. 'What? Where're you getting that from?'

'Not me, it's Cullen's dumb theory.'

Dana shook her head. 'Something wrong with that boy. No way.'

'That's what I said.'

'Dave's messing with you, that's all. Can you imagine a worse couple than those two?'

'He'd break her heart in about five minutes flat.'

Dana nodded, then smiled to herself. 'Be a hell of a five minutes, though.'

'Ewww...' Casey walked off laughing. She went to the vending machine and bought a candy bar and three bags of Lays, dropped two of them on Dana's desk as she passed. 'For tomorrow's lunch.'

The tap on the shoulder made her jump, Casey working alone, even Dana gone for the night.

'Jesus, Boss.'

'Bar's open.' Carletti pointed to his office.

Casey rubbed her eyes, her vision blurring from staring at her screen too long. Another department tradition, the lieutenant turning his office into an impromptu speakeasy after hours. 'I shouldn't. I can still taste last night's mojitos.'

'There's a cure for that.'

She stood up, mimicking duress but already moving off. 'How come you're still here?'

'Lost half my goddamn afternoon to McTeague. The rest of it to meetings. Some point I gotta do my actual job.' Ray overtook her to hold his door open.

Casey went inside. 'Wanna talk about it?'

'Robbie? Nah.' He produced a bottle of Bushmills and two smudged tumblers. 'What's your excuse?'

She took the glass he offered and they clinked. 'For working late? Same as you, catching up. I been on the missing woman all day.' She took a sip of the whiskey, almost gagged it down. She'd never acquired the taste, despite Grandpa Owen's best efforts when she was younger. But it was part of the deal when it came to drinking with Ray.

'You should go home,' he said.

'People keep telling me that. Do I look that bad?'

He smiled. 'You work too hard. You need to have a life too.'

'What's that look like? Sit on the sofa by myself and watch cop shows?'

He looked faraway for a second. 'No, not your style, I'll give you that. But trust me, it goes by fast, and it takes and it takes. Turn around at the end and it's left you with nothing.'

It was rare for him to come over melancholy so fast – usually his end-of-the-night setting; maybe the after-effects of his run-in with McTeague.

'You sure you don't wanna talk?'

He swilled his drink gently. 'I'm just saying there's a balance to be struck. You proved yourself a long time ago.'

'I know.' She stared at him, nodding. 'But I like what I do. I like the buzz.'

'I get that. Believe me, I get that.' He curled his mouth down, as if disappointed in her – or himself? Then he fluttered his fingers, suddenly light again, dismissing it. 'Any progress on your misper?'

She told him about the car Jerry Van Heusen reported seeing and her theory it was someone waiting for Tina Grace. Ray stared at the picture of his kids on the cupboard behind him as she spoke; there was one of each of them, clipped from the same original and placed next to each other inside the frame – his ex-wife, Vanessa, who'd been in the middle, removed in crude fashion.

Ray titled his chair back when she finished, his tumbler held in front of his face. 'If she knew the car was there, why wouldn't she go right to it? Why run around the neighbourhood, knocking doors?'

'If Parker sent the driver though ... either she didn't know it was still waiting for her, or she did and she was scared enough of Parker not to get back in a car with his guy.'

'You told me earlier you weren't sure about him. Parker.'

'I'm not – in either direction.'

'We have anything on him we can leverage? Traffic tickets, anything?'

'He's clean. Guy's rich and retired and lives on the beach. Even you couldn't get in trouble in those circumstances.'

Ray raised his eyebrows, as if to say *try me*. 'Bored, though. If he's chasing girls half his age...'

Casey put her glass down, covering it with her hand when Ray offered a top-up. 'Someone punched him in the eye. Since this morning. Says it was a boxing accident.'

'Tell me it wasn't you...' He poured himself a refill.

'C'mon, he'd still be in the emergency room.'

Ray was already laughing at his own joke and he doubled-down on hers. 'So what do you want to do? You're not here drinking my whiskey for the company.'

'What I *want* is a full search team with choppers and boats on the bay and a hundred men on foot. I'll settle for a dog unit – run a sweep along Ramona Boulevard from where she was last seen.'

'How big of an area are we talking?'

'It's five hundred yards from Parker's house to the address she was last seen outside. She left there headed west, but it's another six hundred yards to the next property after that, nothing in between, on a road that's dark and remote as hell. We spoke to residents right along the beach, no additional reported sightings beyond what we already had. The island's only half a mile wide at Ramona Beach, and all she had on either side of her is freezing water and those little bastard trees made to poke your eyes out. Add to that, it's fully two miles back to Ocean Road, which is empty anyway because it's four in the morning, and she was wearing a lightweight coat in thirty-degree weather.'

He puffed out his cheeks, staring at a point on the ceiling, eyes already two-drinks glazed. But he could see it, as clearly as she could; she could tell. 'She hasn't shown up by morning, then okay.'

'Thanks.'

'I hope to hell she didn't walk out into those marshes.'

Casey put her hands together, stifling a yawn – the whiskey making the office feel airless. 'Me too.' She gulped the last of her drink, readying to go, but Ray looked like he was working up to something so she kept her seat.

He rubbed his face. 'You know what that piece of shit laid on me?'

'McTeague?'

He tipped his chair forward, like a full-body nod. 'Fucking civil-rights violation. You believe that?'

'Over what?'

He opened one of his desk drawers as if he was looking for something, but closed it again just as quickly. 'Zoltan fucking Kuresev.'

It was an incident everyone in the bureau knew about, and it divided opinion. To some of the brass, it was emblematic of Ray Carletti's status as a cowboy cop, one who didn't neatly fit into a modern police department; to the rank and file who worked for him, it made him a hero.

'The Crackhead from Crimea', Zoltan Kuresev was an addict wanted for a series of residential burglaries around Rockport. On the day in question, one of Cullen's CIs had come up with a location for him, and he'd ridden out with a patrol unit to bring him in. They found him in the flop as advertised and picked him up without incident, but the patrol unit was called away on an urgent response, so Cullen had to bring him back by himself. It ran smoothly until they arrived at the precinct, and that was when all hell broke loose. Transferring him from the car to the holding cells, Kuresev went from placid to raging in a heartbeat, landing a kick in Cullen's balls and then trying to bite his face and neck. Cullen dropped to his knees, in too much pain to fight him off, and the only thing that prevented a seriously bad outcome was that Ray Carletti was coming in from the parking lot at the same moment, and ran over to intervene. Kuresev was out of control by that point, maybe high, maybe scared about the looming comedown, and it took four of Ray's best right hands just to slow him down. Even then Kuresev had kept kicking and bucking; Ray tried to lock him up in a choke, but in the process he ended up bouncing Kuresev's head off the asphalt. That, and the arrival of two uniforms from inside the office, finally brought matters to an end.

Casey hadn't been there that afternoon, detailed to a training seminar at Harrison; she'd never given it a lot of thought, but she wondered now if it might've gone down differently if she'd been present.

Ray dropped his gaze to the desk. 'I'm telling you. Dumb crackhead's found himself a lawyer, and they're bringing a suit. McTeague says it warrants an internal inquiry.'

'Into what? Why you subdued a suspect who kicked a cop?'

'Departmental failings.' Ray held his hands up in a *what can I do?* gesture. 'That holier-than-thou asshole's been after me for years, and now he's got a tiny little screw he thinks he can turn.'

He was looking at her and for a second she thought about asking the question that seemed to linger between them – where'd the bad blood start? But he broke off before she could work up the front.

'So you ride it out,' she said instead. 'Just ride it out. It'll pass.'

Ray swirled his drink again. Then he shook his head, seemed to snap out of it. 'Anyway. You don't need to sit here listening to me gripe. Go home.'

Casey stood up, checking her pockets for her phone and keys.

'And hey, don't say anything about McTeague to the others,' Ray said. 'Not for now.'

'Sure.' She tucked her chair under the desk. 'Anything you need, you know to holler.'

He looked at her, nodding. 'Always.'

Casey parked on the street outside her house but didn't get out right away.

She'd driven a longer route home, skirting the shore so she could look out across Black Reed Bay. Alone with her thoughts but not lost in them; a dark reverie, seeing Tina Grace staggering into the marshes across the water less than twenty-four hours earlier. Lost and disorientated, finding herself in reed beds that grew above head height, her skin and clothes torn by groundsel trees sharpened by the Atlantic winter. Water underfoot, dragging her down, sudden depths that you couldn't see in daylight, much less in pitch darkness. Maybe thinking it was a viable shortcut to Ocean Road, the highway lights tantalising her in the distance. She didn't know where she was, didn't know the terrain. Soldiering through it, more afraid of whoever she believed was pursuing her, only to find herself trapped by the marsh. Realising it when she was too far gone – no fight left, no way out, just exhaustion and panic.

Casey ran her fingers along the dash to bring herself back into the present. The image too raw to hold on to for long. On its heels, another thought she was trying to suppress: if that wasn't how it went down, it was only because it was something worse.

Home. Safety. All the things people took for granted until life ripped those certainties from them.

Casey dragged herself out of the car, dog tired now. Her bungalow was in Rockport Gables, a quiet neighbourhood on the south side of town, the street dead at that time of night. For years she'd lived in a rental apartment in the centre of Rockport, the kind of building where an argument three floors down could sound as loud as your own TV, all the while dreading ending up in a place like this. She used to rib the older hands in the department about their *Desperate Housewives* setups in planned communities and pristine subdivisions, but somewhere along the line, the appeal snuck up on her. So two years ago, she'd put her detective's salary to work and mortgaged herself to the eyeballs for her own slice of the cliché. Moving in had been bittersweet; defying her own expectations, she'd felt as if she belonged right away, but the sense of missed opportunity hit at the same time. All that extra space, a room she could've given over to her mom, a backyard Angela Wray would've revelled in making her own, in a neighbourhood she just might've considered safe enough to move to. The realisation having dawned a year too late.

She dropped her bags and keys on the couch and went to close the drapes. From her living room she could see the intersection at the end of the street. There was a figure standing on the far side of it. He was leaning against a car, dressed in a dark coat and with a hoodie pulled over his head, shielding most of his face from view. He wasn't looking in any particular direction, but he turned his head her way twice as she watched, like he knew she was there. She stayed like that a few seconds more, but the guy just stood there, glancing her way and then staring down the street.

She pulled the drape over and thought it through, only realising in the darkness that she hadn't even turned a light on yet. Burglaries were common in the Gables – it was just middle class enough to attract people with money for Apple and Sonos gear, but most of the properties had nothing more than basic security. Slinging drugs was another possibility – but even though she knew for a fact some of her neighbours would get high once they'd put the kids to bed, picking up on the street corner wasn't their style. Especially when everyone knew there was a cop living on the block.

She stood back and pulled her ponytail out, her own hypocrisy suddenly apparent. Clowning on the likes of Ellis Sandford by day, and at night peering out her own window like his fucking apprentice. She went to the refrigerator, took out a pack of turkey breast, ate four slices and went to get ready for bed.

She opened her eyes with a start, not sure if she'd dreamt it. She blinked, roused from a sleep so deep she couldn't even bring the green digits on her alarm clock into focus.

Then it sounded again. Definitely real this time – the front doorbell.

She rubbed her face and tried the clock one more time – just past midnight. She'd been asleep less than an hour. She got up without turning on the light and snatched her holster from the dresser.

She padded silently down the hallway and looked through the spyhole. No one on the other side. She stepped back, drew her gun. 'Who's out there?'

Silence came back, a suffocating wave.

She checked the spyhole again and then crept into the living room and split the drapes to look out onto the street. The sidewalks were empty. She looked along at the intersection but the figure from earlier was gone, the sedan he'd been resting on still parked in the same place.

She circled back around and opened the front door with her gun in the compressed ready position, blasted by cold air as she did. Barefoot onto the stone porch, wrapping her free arm around herself. Scanning the block, the sycamore across the street the only thing that moved, swaying in the wind.

She looked around a moment longer before she gave up and shut the door. She went back to the bedroom, holstered her gun again and left it on the nightstand, then sat on the edge of the bed, listening.

A sudden buzzing sound made her heart cut out. Her cell

phone was next to the bed, set to silent vibrate – and now someone was calling. A blocked number.

She picked it up and accepted the call. 'Who is it?'

The other end was quiet – not silent, a noise that could be someone breathing or could be just background hum. She counted off three seconds...

A woman screaming. Then ten, then a thousand. The silence and the darkness magnifying it all, filling the room, filling her head.

She ripped the phone away from her ear and went to hang up but heard the cacophony stop. The call timer kept ticking, showing it was still connected. Slowly, she brought it back to her ear. 'Who the fuck is this?'

That first sound again – breathing, or faint movement, almost intimate, as if it was someone sitting right next to her, unseen in the dark, just out of reach.

Then a voice, distorted, inhuman...

'Tina Grace is dead.'

## CHAPTER 8

It was almost 7am when Casey walked up to the main doorway of Tina Grace's apartment building, the buzzer panel on the wall made redundant by a broken catch that was keeping the door ajar. She went inside and up the stairs, running on caffeine and the jittery adrenaline that came with two hours' broken sleep.

All night thinking about who was fucking with her. She'd spent a half-hour driving around her neighbourhood, looking for the man she'd seen or anyone else she could beat some answers out of. No certainty he was involved, but better than doing nothing. But it'd proved to be wasted time; the sidewalks were empty.

The call felt even more invasive than the doorbell. Even now, in daylight, she could hear the voice in her head. She'd realised pretty soon after that it was a recording, not someone speaking live on the line, whoever made it disguising himself with a vocoder or editing software. Stripping away the theatrics had helped dissipate the shock, but did nothing to lessen the sense of violation.

She came out onto Tina's landing and knocked on her door – no real hope she was there but wanting to be sure. When no one answered, she knocked on the neighbour's door – the guy in the Lynyrd Skynyrd tee from the day before.

He opened up looking half asleep. 'What's ... oh, Detective, hey.'

'Sorry to disturb you early, sir, but I need to nail down Tina's movements the day before yesterday.'

'Sure, uh – she's still missing?'

She nodded. 'Are you friendly with her?'

He folded his arms and leaned against the doorframe. 'Yeah, she's cool. I mean, we don't really hang out, but she's a good neighbour to have – quiet, just a regular person. We've been here eight years, the last guy in there smoked so much weed it was coming through the walls.'

'You said she's in and out a lot of the time?'

'Uh-huh. She keeps a weird schedule, goes out late a lot of nights. I'm not judging her, just saying.'

'You ever ask her where she goes?'

'To her boyfriend's place, I guess. Brian.'

The boyfriend who still lived at home with mom and pop,

and who thought she stayed with her own mom twice a week – nope. 'Did you recall the last time you saw her?'

'Yeah, I thought about that. I didn't see her, but I heard her come home, so that would've been after six, when I got back from work. Then I heard her go out again around ten-thirty.' He went rigid. 'I don't want you to think I'm watching her or something – the walls in this place are like paper, that's all.'

Casey put her hands in her pockets, turning it over. Another assumption busted: Tina wasn't out partying before she went to Jon Parker's; she'd been at home. 'How often does Brian Walton stay over?'

He puffed his cheeks. 'Maybe a couple nights a week? I don't know, it's hard to say for sure.'

'You ever hear them arguing? Any shouting, anything like that?'

He screwed up one side of his face. 'No, not really.'

'Not really?'

He shook his head. 'I mean, every now and then you might hear raised voices, stuff like that, but nothing that ever made me worry about what was going on.'

'You ever hear what they're fighting about?'

He shrugged. 'You can't make out the words, just voices. Him and her. Why, did Brian do something wrong?'

'No, not to my knowledge, we're just looking at all the angles. What about Tina's brother, he ever come around?'

'Brother? I didn't know she had one.'

'Tommy Grace.'

He shook his head. 'Sorry.'

Casey nodded, fishing in her pocket for her card. 'Thanks for your help.' She found one and handed it to him. 'Do me a favour, call me right away if Tina shows up, please?'

'Sure.'

She hesitated. 'Hey, what's the rent on a place like this?'

The man stopped in the doorway. 'We pay eighteen hundred a month.'

'How about Tina's?'

'Hers is a one bed so it's less, but not by much. Like, fifteen hundred, I think?'

Casey held up her hand in thanks. He went inside and she was left alone. She crossed the landing to the window and looked out; the glass was grimy and the view was nothing more than the dollar store and the redbrick fifties apartment building over the street. Again she was hit by the sharp contrast with Ramona Beach. Looking out, she felt that dirty rush that came whenever something didn't add up.

Casey set the Starbucks cup down in front of Cullen and he grabbed it up with a smile. 'Thanks.' His face soured when he saw the name she'd given the barista to scrawl on it – *Asshat*. 'Christ, would you grow up?'

'I'm in a bad mood, you get the flak.'

'Why, what's up?'

She told him about the night before, Cullen snapping out of his chair when he heard someone had been at her door. 'Are you serious?'

She shot him a dead stare.

'That's crossing the line, Big. Way over.'

'Yeah, tell me about it.'

'We have to come down hard on that shit. Speak to patrol, they can put a car on the street tonight to—'

'Slow down, I don't need uniform all over my block, freaking out my neighbours. I'll watch my own ass.'

He pressed the takeout cup to his chest, shaking his head in disbelief. 'What the hell is going on here? Jon Parker?'

She came around to his desk and perched on the edge, facing him. 'I don't know. Dumb move if it is.'

'Something's not right with him.'

'Yeah. But that doesn't mean ... Ah, fuck that guy.' Casey looked up across the office. 'Ray been in yet this morning?'

Cullen shook his head. 'He'll be pissed, he hears about this. Especially being you.'

'What does that mean?'

'You know how protective he is.'

'You say it like it's only me.'

'No, I said *especially*.'

'Is there a difference?'

He held his hands up, two fingers wrapped around his coffee cup, hampering his surrender gesture. 'I didn't mean anything by it.'

Casey gave him a look, then dropped it when she stood up again. 'He promised me a dog team if Tina hadn't shown up this morning.'

'You checked in with the family?'

'Not yet. I spoke to her mom again last night and I went by her apartment this morning to talk to the neighbour.'

'You want me to call them now?'

She shook her head, saying 'thanks' to acknowledge the peace offering. 'I want to talk to the brother, supposedly he was out looking for Tina last night. He's been in some minor trouble too.'

'Define trouble.'

'There's a bust for weed on his record – possession, not supply – and Maggie said he gets into fights—'

'*Maggie?*'

Casey frowned. 'Yeah. Mrs Grace?'

'I know who she is. You're on first-name terms with her?'

'And? You heard her yesterday.'

He backed away from it, hiding behind a sip from his coffee. 'Anyway.'

She circled back to her own desk and picked up Brian Walton's background check, tossed it across to Cullen. 'Brian Walton's got a domestic disturbance call-out on his sheet.'

'The boyfriend? From the Dunkin' Donuts?'

'Yeah, I know. Looks can be deceiving, right? Tina's neighbour said he hears them arguing from time to time.'

'They're practically teenagers, that doesn't mean anything. Once they start popping out kids they'll be too tired to fight, like the rest of us.'

'The only reason you guys don't fight is because Lu would kick your ass. Rhetorically and physically.'

'I know how the chain of command works.' He tossed the paperwork back to Casey. 'So you wanna go talk to him again or what?'

'Not yet.' She tapped her pad with her pen. 'This guy takes priority.'

She picked up her phone and dialled Tommy Grace.

A watery sun was trying to break through the clouds when they pulled up to the Grace property, but it carried no warmth; the kind of weather that would always inspire Angela Wray to predict snow was coming, no matter how many times it turned out not to be the case. One of those tics that run in families; at first annoying, then routine, and finally missed when it was lost.

Maggie met them on the doorstep. She led them into the living room, the perfume smell even stronger – their visit anticipated this time. Tommy Grace was sitting cross-legged on the couch; Casey was expecting someone cut from the same cloth as Brian Walton – a lazy assumption that was way off. Tommy wore his hair clipped short in a high and tight, and he had on a fitted white tee and blue jeans, with a gold chain hanging loose around his neck. It sat wrong on him, as if he'd borrowed it from someone older and heavier set. His arms were muscular, much more so than the rest of him; a man who spent time with weights, but focused on the parts for show. No tattoos, but a definite wannabe tough-guy aesthetic.

Maggie stationed herself next to him, a hand on his shoulder. 'This is my son, Tommy.' She was nervous, nothing about the situation comfortable for her, that was evident; but so was her pride in him.

Casey introduced them both and looked at Maggie. 'May we sit?'

She waved her hand at two mismatched armchairs behind them. 'We called everyone. Everyone. No one's heard from her.'

They sat down, and Tommy watched her and Cullen in turn, rapidly flicking his finger against his left thumb. 'They know, mom.' His voice was soft and reedy when he spoke, almost hesitant in the delivery; made him sound younger than he looked.

'It's useful to know,' Cullen said, defusing it. 'Thank you.'

'Are you running searches yet?' Tommy said.

'We're hoping to get a canine unit deployed today.'

'At the guy's house?'

Casey hesitated. 'What do you know about that?'

'It's what you told my mom. She was at some guy's house on the beach, right? They got into it over something?'

She glanced at Cullen, caught off-guard by whether Tommy knew something or was just making an educated guess. 'There were reports of a disturbance.'

'Yeah. So it was a guy, right? She didn't go all the way out there to watch TV. You picked him up yet?'

'We're still establishing the facts of what's going on here. Tina's an adult, and it's been barely twenty-four hours since—'

Tommy snorted and looked away. 'She got into a fight with some douchebag on the beach and vanished, and you wanna act like she took off?' Maggie put a hand on his shoulder to signal him to cool down, and he looked around at her. 'Goddamn waste of time.'

Casey leaned forward in her seat. 'Trust me, no one, and least of all me, is underestimating the seriousness of the situation. But we have to establish the facts to determine the best course of action. Otherwise we're relying on guesswork, and that doesn't get us anywhere.'

'Gotta protect the rich boy, huh?'

'Until there's evidence—'

'How you gonna find any evidence you don't get inside his house?'

'We searched his property, Tina wasn't there. Is there a reason you're so certain what happened? Did your sister contact you that night?'

'I got a brain in my head is all. What do the numbers say about what happened? They look good for her?' He half turned to look at his mom, maybe regretting how harsh his words

were. Or maybe he'd been sounding off that way all night –
Maggie's expression was unchanged.

'Lemme ask that again: did your sister contact you on the
night in question?'

'No.'

'Is there anywhere you can think she might've gone to? Any
friend or family member you haven't gotten to yet, maybe a co-
worker?'

'You're asking for a list of everyone in her life,' Maggie said.

Tommy waved it all away. 'I've been anywhere she'd be at, I
was out all night. Y'all know where she went. Starts and ends
at the beach.'

'Just think along a different track for me a minute. Did Tina
talk as if she was scared of anyone at all? Anyone you can think
of might've wanted to harm her?'

Tommy stared at the floor, scratching his throat with one
hand. 'Who knows? She got her new life. That's what her
friends told me when I asked around. Dropped them like a bad
habit when she started making bank.'

'Can you expand on that?' Cullen said.

'Is what it is. Set herself up in a new apartment and moved
on.' There was a rawness to the way he said it, clear it wasn't just
her friends felt rejected and hurt.

Maggie laid a hand on his arm. 'Tommy, knock it off. It's just
life. Things change, she never meant to make anyone feel bad.'
She looked up. 'He always felt like she was rubbing his face in
it, but that's not Tina's way.'

'Mom—'

'It's the truth.' She looked up again. 'He's more sensitive than
he looks.'

He shrugged her hand off and stood up, almost a physical

rebuttal. 'What is it you think, Detective? You looking for some mysterious dude in her life who wanted to hurt her? How about the guy she had a fight with in the middle of the night. Lives on millionaire beach, somewhere she got no reason to be, ain't no one in her life knows who the fuck he is. He fit the bill? Or we all just gonna sit here asking stupid-ass questions and pretending it's something less obvious?' He stormed out of the room.

'Tommy...' Maggie jumped up but stopped in the doorway when she heard the front door slam.

She drifted back inside slowly. She looked at Casey. 'Should I go after him?'

Casey held her hand up. 'It's okay, let him cool off.'

Maggie pushed up the sleeves of her sweater, looking hollow. 'He's been angry forever, it feels like. Years now. He just ... I gave up trying to figure out how to handle it. I'm scared this is gonna push him over the edge.'

'It's a difficult situation for all of you. How old is Tommy?'

'Just turned twenty-two. Don't listen to what he says about Tina, it's his way of beating up on himself.'

'He feels left behind?'

She nodded. 'That's what I think. He feels like he's got to be the man of the house, look out for her, but she never wanted it. Tina's smart and confident, she doesn't need a protector – especially not her little brother. She just doesn't see him that way, and it makes him feel inadequate.'

'Who does Tommy think she needs protecting from?' Cullen said.

'Just, y'know ... from life. Since their dad ain't around, he feels like he's gotta step up. But Tina's...' She shook her head, reaching for an explanation. 'Tina doesn't look at life like

Tommy does. Like it's a fight. You talk to her for five minutes, she'll tell you the world's one big opportunity, if you got the heart to chase it.' She glanced around the dreary room, looking humbled. 'Christ knows where she got that idea.'

Casey crossed her legs. 'Maggie, where did Tina work last?'

'This place on fifth, Bronsons. They took her on in their accounting department. She gets mad at me because I never get it right – finance assistant or something.'

'Why did she leave? You said they were screwing her around?'

Her embarrassment showed. 'I didn't mean it like that. She wanted something better. She'd been there going on two years, and they'd trained her up, but they weren't paying her for the role she was doing so she said she had to go somewhere else to earn right.'

'Pretty brave to quit without anything else to go to.'

She scratched the back of her hand – the skin already red. 'That's Tina though. But I mean headstrong, not impulsive. She won't say anything to me or anyone till she's fixed on a decision already, but she'll have been turning it over for a long time. Makes people think she's rash, but really, she just knows her own mind. She gets the stubborn part from me.' She flashed a quicksilver smile when she said it, gone just as quick as it appeared. 'The rest is her dad.'

'You mentioned he left some time ago?'

'Ten years. We was both...' She looked down, bulging one cheek with her tongue. 'I decided it was time to quit drinking, he wasn't ready. In the end, I told him it was get sober or get out.' She looked at Casey, eyes hooded. 'He made his choice, and, uh ... Seems ironic now, I guess...'

It felt like an admission and an apology, all in one, an

acknowledgement that, despite the perfume, the smell of liquor was too ingrained to miss.

'Did he ever make an attempt to contact Tina? Or Tommy?'

She was already shaking her head. 'He barely cared about them when he was here. He went out the door and he never looked back. Way he looked at it, I was giving him his freedom.'

'I'm sorry.'

'It is what it is. Tommy hated him for it, still boils his piss thinking about it now, but Tina ... I don't know, she just found a way to let it go. Not straightaway ... in time.' She shrugged. 'But things kinda fell apart for me after he went. My, uh ... My seat on the wagon wasn't so secure as I thought.'

Casey nodded. 'I understand. Can I ask about Tina's relationship with Brian Walton?'

Maggie wrinkled her nose. 'It's a kiddie romance, she outgrew him a long time ago. She just doesn't have the heart to break it to him. They've known each other for years.'

'Does that mean they argue a lot?'

'No, he's too scared of losing her to speak out, he's like a little lost puppy. Deep down he's probably got it figured out, but he doesn't want to face facts. He ain't gonna get another girl like her and he knows it.'

Casey looked down at her hands, feeling like all the indications were Tommy Grace was right – there was Jon Parker's house, and everything else was incidental. She stood up. 'We shouldn't take up any more of your time. Thank you for seeing us again, I hope Tommy'll be okay.'

Maggie followed them to the door. 'You said you're bringing in search dogs?'

'Hopefully.'

'Should I ... What do I do?'

Casey looked past her, wishing she had a lifeline to offer. 'Keep your phone with you. I'll call you myself as soon as there's anything more I can tell you.'

Maggie nodded silently. Then she came forward, and Casey held her hand out as if she was going to shake it, but instead Maggie passed her a torn slip of paper. 'This is her email password. Just in case it's useful. I already checked, she hasn't sent any emails since before yesterday but ... maybe you can do something with it.'

But the dogs were delayed. Two frustrated calls to the office, Carletti not there the first time and sounding distracted when she got hold of him an hour later.

Cullen leaned against the car as she hung up. 'What did he say?'

'He's working on it. There's a training exercise over in Harrison that's sucked up all the manpower.' They were standing outside Jon Parker's house, Casey taking them back there in anticipation.

'How long are we talking?'

'Another hour maybe.'

Cullen turned around on the spot, looking along the houses. 'Incoming. The mayor of Ramona Beach just spotted us.'

Ellis Sandford stepped off his porch and started towards them, one arm held up as a greeting. 'Morning, Detectives. What's the news?'

'Nothing to share at the moment, sir.' Casey reached for the car door.

'You spoke with the other residents?'

'We did.'

'I understand there's talk of a car parked somewhere further along the road?'

Casey had her door open but stopped. 'That's right. Did you see it?'

'No, but I wouldn't be entirely surprised. Anytime a driver comes over here by GPS, it directs them to that spot past the Stadlers'. You see them stop for a minute and then crawling along here, trying to figure out where they're actually headed for.'

'Okay. That's good to know.'

'Is that the current thinking, then? That the young lady went off in the car Jerry saw?'

'We really don't have enough information to say at this point. I want to keep away from speculation.'

'Yes, of course. But I can't imagine any other explanation; Jon's a stand-up guy, I don't think he can be blamed for that young woman losing her mind.'

Casey sensed Cullen looking at her sidelong. 'Yeah. Well, we'll see. We'll be back in a little while, excuse us.' She jumped into the car before Sandford could say anything else.

Cullen slid behind the wheel, looking over at her. 'Where now?'

She watched Sandford back away. 'Head west. I just had to get him out of my face.'

'He just can't wait to go into bat for Parker, can he?'

Casey stared out the window, scanning the brush along the verge. Wondering how a dog team would be able to work in that, even if they did pick up something. 'I think he just wants to move the problem out of his little kingdom. He's certain Tina Grace took off in a car he didn't even see. She's at fault, no blame on one of his residents, go look elsewhere.'

'You think that's all it is?'

Casey shrugged.

Cullen glanced over in her direction, squinting – seemingly as much at the bleakness of it all as at the grey light. 'What are you looking for?'

Casey shook her head absently. In her nightmares, a scrap of clothing snagged on a branch. Still caught between hoping Tina Grace was someplace far off, and, if not, that she'd left some marker to where she went.

The canine unit was waiting for them outside by the time they got back to Jon Parker's house.

They'd driven all the way to the end of Ramona Boulevard and then looped back, Casey having Cullen drop her off early so she could walk the last half-mile again, looking for any disturbance in the vegetation that might indicate Tina Grace heading into the scrubland. But the groundsel trees and bushes that lined the verge met and overlapped, like a five-foot-tall mesh of barbed wire, a landscape that couldn't have been better designed to cover any trace of a human passing through. There was no chance of picking out a broken branch or a footprint beyond the brown wall that sat unmoving, appearing impenetrable.

The K9 officer climbed out of his car the same time as Jon Parker came out of his house. Casey glanced at him but carried on over to introduce herself.

'Bob Titus,' he said, shaking hands. 'And this is Silver.' He pointed to the collie at his side, already pulling gently at its lead. 'Silver's all ready to go, if you've got the scent sample for us?'

'Great,' Casey said. Cullen produced the bag with Tina Grace's nightgown and handed it over. 'This one right here is the house the misper was visiting.' She briefed him on Tina Grace's known movements, pointing out each house in turn. 'The resident's name is Jon Parker, he can take you to her last known point, if you need?'

Titus made a hand signal to the dog. 'She's alerting, so she's already picked up something. Better to see what she's got by herself first, then we can always make another pass from the LKP.' He looked along the road, taking in the brush over the street. 'Gonna be tough if we have to head in there, though.'

Casey nodded. 'Understood.'

Titus let the dog start to move off, keeping the lead short. As soon as they were clear, Jon Parker crossed towards them. 'Don't I get a head's up on something like this, Detective? I've had police cars showing up outside my property all morning, a courtesy call would go a long way.'

'You called us in to find Tina, sir. That's what we're doing.'

He glanced over towards Ellis Sandford, watching proceedings from his porch, the first of several of the residents now on the street to see what was happening. 'Look, I'm getting a little tired of this attitude. I've answered every question you've asked and busted my ass to be helpful.'

'Is that a fact?'

Parker looked at Cullen, a kind of appeal for help.

Casey put her hands on her hips. 'Actually I had some more questions I wanted to ask you. You have a couple minutes?'

'I have to be somewhere at twelve, but...' He held his hands out and let them drop to his side – the helpless victim again.

'I was looking over the logs again, and I wondered why you waited so long to call 911?'

'I didn't.'

'Ellis Sandford made the first call eighteen minutes before you.'

'Really?' He shifted his weight from one foot to the other. 'I guess I didn't know that at the time.'

'So it was at least that long since Tina left your house.'

'Yeah, I understand the implication. I told you what I was doing – I went outside to try to help her, and then ... I was trying to keep a lid on the situation.'

'Okay, so what changed? What made you decide to call after all?'

'Jesus, was I wrong to call or not to call? Which is it?'

'It's a question of trying to understand how events unfolded.'

He set his jaw, the muscles in his cheeks bulging.

'Is this an inconvenience to you, Mr Parker?' Cullen said.

'You're putting words in my mouth, Detective. I'm trying to answer—'

'Did something change? Did Tina Grace do something to prompt it?'

'No, it was just ... I guess seeing Jerry Van Heusen come out, all the disturbance, I figured I should do something more. I don't know.'

'You caught up to her somewhere along the street, right? The last time?'

He nodded, rubbing the stubble on his throat.

'Where exactly were you?'

He looked west shaking his head, his lips moving but forming no words at first. 'I wasn't really paying attention. Somewhere between Mrs Dunning's and the Stadlers'. I couldn't pick out the exact spot.'

'And you're sure you didn't notice the car Jerry Van Heusen

reported seeing? That far along, you would've been closer to it than he was.'

'I was concentrating on Tina.'

'Is that a no?'

'I didn't see it. I'm not discrediting what Jerry told you, but I didn't see it.'

Cullen peeled off and went back towards the road, walking slowly as if he was surveying it.

'Where's he going?' Parker asked.

Casey shook her head as if it wasn't important. 'Where was Tina the last time you saw her? Can you be exact about that?'

'Same place. Where I left her.'

'You didn't watch her carry on walking?'

'I was trying to help her, and she started up again and ... Look, it pissed me off, okay? It's a small place, I like to keep my business private. Nothing I said was getting through, so I turned around and I came back here.' He checked his watch. 'I need to get going.'

'Of course. Is it golf again today?'

'Sadly not.'

'Will you be at home later? We might need you to show us Tina's last-known point.'

He stepped back towards his house. 'I already told you. I can't be more exact than what I said. And I can't change my schedule today.'

Casey nodded as he retreated. 'Understood. I guess we'll come back tomorrow if we need to.'

She left him on the doorstep and made her way to where Cullen was standing.

'What's up?' He was looking towards Titus and Silver, the

pair moving slowly along the verge between Ellis Sandford's and the Van Heusens'.

'I wanted to see what he would've seen. Straight road, clear night, if the car was still there, I can't see how he would've missed it, even that far off.'

'Still there?'

'Yeah, I was thinking about it, and there's a few minutes between when Jerry Van Heusen reported seeing it and when Parker caught up with Tina. Say whoever it was drove off in between?'

'Convenient timing.'

'Yeah, it would be. But what about if they turned the lights off once they saw people on the street? Or drove off and waited further along.'

'Maybe.'

'That's your way of saying "bullshit".'

'You ever known me to shy away from saying "bullshit" when that's what I mean?'

He cracked a grin as he shook his head.

'But I'll take any odds you're offering he's lying,' Casey said.

'There a chance Jerry Van Heusen was mistaken about what he saw?'

'Sure. But...' She pushed her hair out of her face. 'There are traffic cams on the causeway lift bridge. Call Billy and get him to get hold of the footage, would you?'

'Sure, but we don't know what we're looking for.'

'How many cars coming off the island that time of night?'

'*If* it came off the island. *If* it came off via the causeway and not the bridge at the other end. *If* she got into that car. *If*—'

'Okay, okay, point taken.'

They looked over when Jon Parker's garage door opened. He

pulled out in his Lex and turned left, then took off down the street.

They were trailing a short distance behind the K9 unit as they worked when Christopher Stadler, the resident from 214, came along the street to intercept them. There was a woman a half-pace behind him.

Casey held her hand up to greet them. 'Mr Stadler?'

'Detective, this is my wife, Marie.'

The woman had her phone in her hands and she looked at it as she spoke. 'Detective, I ... Actually, this is a little embarrassing.' She brought it up to eye level. 'I took a video of that young woman the other night. I didn't think to say anything to Christopher before I left for work yesterday morning, and then – honestly, it just slipped my mind until I saw your officers out here searching...'

Casey stepped closer. 'That's okay, ma'am. May I take a look?'

Stadler put his hands in his pockets, spoke off to the side. 'I told her I don't know what she was thinking. Taking videos – it's juvenile.'

'It's helpful to us, sir.'

Stadler kept looking away.

The woman pressed play, Casey and Cullen crowding round to watch. They were looking down on the street from the upstairs window of the Stadlers' place, Tina already in shot when it started. She came towards their house from the direction of Jon Parker's, walking fast but in a ragged path, checking over her shoulder. From her gait, it was obvious she was scared of something, but there was an uncertainty to her movements too, a sloppiness to the way she swerved across the street and back that suggested some kind of chemical intake. Her mouth was moving, but she was way too distant for the recording to catch her words. Her cell phone was in her hand but it wasn't clear if she was talking into it or to herself.

A few seconds in, Jon Parker appeared in shot from the same direction. Tina stopped and spun around as if she'd just realised he was there, shooting her free hand out to signal him to back off. He kept coming a few more paces and then stopped five yards short of her. She was clearly distressed, backing away and yelling something at him.

Parker looked shook up himself, saying something back to her, his body language betraying a man who looked angry and rattled. He pointed to the west, stabbing the air as if he was instructing her to keep going that way. Marie Stadler's voice cut in at this point on the recording. 'Christopher? Are you seeing this?' Christopher Stadler's voice came back, but his words were inaudible, coming from another room.

On the screen Tina kept backing away from Parker, now glancing towards the house next to her, its light just enough to give form to her face for the first time. She held her phone up, shaking it as if threatening to call someone. Parker threw his arm in the air, apparently in frustration, pointed to the west one more time and then wheeled around to march back the way he came, bringing his cell phone to his ear as he left the shot. Tina darted onto the path to the Stadlers' front door, and Marie could again be heard saying, 'Christopher?' Then the video cut out.

'Is that all of it?' Cullen said.

Marie Stadler nodded. 'That's when I ran downstairs to find Christopher, and he called 911. The girl was knocking on our door – really hammering. I tried to shout out to her that the police were coming, but she just walked off again.'

'And you told the patrol officers she was heading west when you saw her last.'

'Yes, that way.' She pointed up the road.

'Did you see her again after that?'

'No, not at all. I was worried for her, because of the cold and because – well, if a car came along...'

'A car?' Christopher Stadler said. 'No one drives along here in the dead of night.'

'But if one *did* come along – it's so dark out there, I didn't think they'd see her in time to stop. Even so, I know I shouldn't say it, it was a relief when she moved on.'

'Marie...' Christopher Stadler shot her a look.

'What? It's the truth. You said the same thing.'

Christopher made a sour face.

Casey gestured to the phone. 'Did you happen to hear any of what they were saying to each other?'

She had her hands up, a gesture of helplessness. 'I'm sorry, I couldn't make it out. They were shouting though, I can tell you that.'

'We're not uncaring, you understand,' Christopher said, 'but that kind of drama ... This isn't the city, this is a quiet neighbourhood. I called our pastor this morning to ask his advice, and we'll be holding a prayer session for the young lady later on.'

Casey looked at him, haunted by Tina's expression when she'd looked towards the camera. Even in the dark, the footage grainy, she couldn't fail to recognise the terror. She brought up her own phone, turning to Marie. 'Can you AirDrop that video onto my cell please?'

She looked confused, and Cullen stepped over to help her do it. The file arrived and Casey shot her a smile.

'Thank you both for your help. We should check in with the canine units.'

The Stadlers took the hint, Christopher reluctant to go at first, as if he wanted another shot at redeeming himself, Marie following suit when he finally turned. Christopher started jawing at her again as soon as they were out of earshot.

'Domineering asshole,' Cullen said. 'Imagine being stuck out here with him all your life.'

Casey was already playing the video again, scrolling to the point in the footage where Parker was shouting and pointing down the road.

Cullen watched on over her shoulder. 'What do you make of that?'

She was staring a hole through the screen. 'Lying son of a bitch.'

It was almost an hour before the K9 officer signalled to Casey and Cullen that something was happening.

Bob Titus was past the Stadler property when they caught up to him, Casey hopeful she was about to have her theory confirmed. But as they approached, he held his hand up for them to wait. Silver was pulling at her leash and pawing the grass along the left shoulder of the road, and Titus was saying something to her. A few seconds later, he let her off and issued a command Casey didn't catch.

Then he beckoned them to come close.

'What've we got?'

'Not sure I can answer that just yet.' Titus watched Silver sniffing along the brush as he spoke. 'So, Silver followed the scent sample to right around there.' He pointed to a patch of dirt on the roadside near where they were standing, Casey's eye drawn immediately to a set of tyre tracks running through it. 'And that seems to be where it ends.'

'Okay. But there's something more?'

'Possibly. Something's got her attention, but she's not working from the scent sample now.'

'What does that indicate?'

'Well, I don't want to speculate, but if there are fresh remains in the area, it could be she's picking up on them.'

Casey closed her eyes. The first image that came into her mind was of Jon Parker speeding away in his Lex. 'Shit.'

Cullen was on the same wavelength, spinning around to look towards Parker's house in the distance.

Titus saw where they were looking and held his hand up. 'Let's don't get ahead of ourselves. Like I said, whatever she's picked up, it isn't from the scent sample. Now, it could be a false alert, but she's a pro, and I can't remember the last time she made a mistake, so I doubt it.'

'Then what is she telling us?' Casey said.

'We need to let her do her work,' Titus said. 'It's possible she'll pick up the trail again, but I'd be surprised.'

'But you just said she might've picked up on fresh remains?'

Titus nodded. 'That'd be my guess.'

'But how can that be if it's not Tina's scent?' Cullen said.

Titus opened his hands. 'If there is a body out there, it might not be your misper.'

# CHAPTER 9

Darkness was closing in when they hit. It'd been a painstaking process, Silver roaming along the roadside and then doubling back to Titus periodically, her way of signalling she was still scenting something. Then, a quarter-mile along the road from where they'd started, she plunged into the bushes and disappeared for more than ten minutes, the intermittent sounds of a branch creaking or snapping the only sign she was still moving.

They waited, Casey checking her watch: 5.30pm, maybe a half-hour until the last of the light was gone. The cold had become so pervasive, Casey dispatched Cullen to bring the car up to shelter inside. But just as they climbed in, Silver started barking. Two sharp bursts, a pause, then again. Repeated at short intervals. Coming from the same point, indicating she was stationary. As soon as he heard it, Titus started picking his way into the brush, without a word. Casey followed, grabbing her flashlight and signalling Cullen to wait behind.

The terrain was murderous. Eye-level branches came at her from every direction, tangles of brambles and spike grass underfoot, some part of her snagging with every step. In the half-light, her mind warped anything that brushed her face into the touch of a snake or leech. The ground ranged from waterlogged to flooded; at one point her foot came out of her boot and she had to use both hands to wrench it free from the mud. It came up full of dirty water.

Then suddenly it opened up. A tiny clearing, the ground just that much firmer. Silver, soaking wet and mud-spattered, sitting rigid, sounding her alarm like a rifle salute for the fallen.

Next to her, a body, submerged in a pool standing of water. Casey shone her flashlight.

One look told her it wasn't Tina Grace. The woman was naked, her corpse greying and bloated. There was no sign of her clothing.

Casey stood next to Titus, neither of them getting within fifteen feet, neither of them speaking. She looked over the corpse: a life cast aside like trash. A black abyss of humanity.

It took her more than five minutes to get back to the road. Cullen saw her emerge and he looked up at her in alarm, as if she was being pursued, her urgency evident even before she spoke. 'Get on the radio. We got something.'

## CHAPTER 10

At first light, they came in numbers.

Casey and Cullen arrived at the same time as the medical examiner, pulling up behind their truck. Bob Titus was already present, briefing a new K9 unit of cadaver dogs. Forensic investigators in dark-blue HCPD coveralls and gloves were gearing up to comb the surrounding area. At the centre of it all, standing next to an arc light that seemed only to illuminate the road, Pete Lyman and Winston DeFray – two of the better dicks from the Homicide department at Harrison.

Lyman spotted them coming over and broke off from his conversation with a patrol officer. 'What's up, Big? Shoulda known it'd be you causing trouble.'

'For you? Always. You screwing with my crime scene?'

'That fucking jungle? If it was up to me you could have it.'
He tilted his head to examine her cheek, a deep scratch running
all the way from her temple to the corner of her mouth. 'See it
beat up on you already.'

Casey feathered it with her fingers, the skin raised and angry.
It'd stung like hell overnight, but she'd come off lightly; Bob
Titus had caught himself on poison ivy, and Silver had come out
covered in ticks. 'Hadn't noticed. You're taking over already?'

'Of course. Can't let you amateurs make any more of a mess.'
He said it with a wink – only partial insult intended.

'You're gonna bring us in though, right? We got a misper
that's tied up with this.'

'Yeah, I heard something about that. But that's not your girl
in there, right?'

'She was last seen less than a half-mile from here.'

'Even so...'

Casey took a breath, straightening her spine. 'Okay. I'll talk
to Carletti.'

'Be my guest. Honestly, this one screams dead end. You can
swing it with the brass, I got no problem with you tagging
along.'

DeFray shot him a *what about me?* look, but it bounced off.

It took less than two hours for Lyman's assessment to fall apart.

It was one of the cadaver dogs, Bolt, that made the find. As
they were zeroing in, her handler cautioned that in those
conditions, there was always the chance of a false alert, but one
look at what they found shattered that notion too.

About the same distance from the road, this time partially buried in a shallow grave. There were animal scratchings all over the site – scavengers having carried away whatever they could uncover. The ME's techs taped off the area before Casey could look for long, Pete Lyman standing next to her, making a small whistling sound.

By 11am it was a frenzy. With Bolt back in her wagon on enforced rest, her partner, Arrow, was working solo when she found the third. The corpse was on its side, wedged into a waterlogged natural ditch. It was possible to identify it as a woman by sight. She was naked, the parts of her that were visible as grey and lifeless as the sky overhead. There was a patch of skin gone from her shoulder, missing or torn away. Her face was turned into the ditch, a small mercy according to Lyman – missing eyeballs or lips the image he said always haunted him the most. For Casey, it meant no answer to the immediate question.

She grabbed a tech. 'Best guess for how long she's been there?'

The tech started to shrug—

'Is less than thirty-six hours a possibility?'

The tech rubbed her forehead with the sleeve of her coverall. 'Can't know for sure until we get her out, but I think that's extremely unlikely.'

Casey nodded her thanks and fought her way back to the road, any relief that it wasn't Tina cut with the knowledge that it just passed the pain on, another family about to have their lives ripped up.

Cullen was waiting for her by the car. He handed her a coffee from a takeout tray someone had brought by. 'What the fuck have we walked into?'

Before she could answer, an unmarked edged its way past the ME's truck and the row of cruisers, and came to a stop. Robbie McTeague climbed out, hulking in his greatcoat. He glanced in her direction, but only as he scanned the crowd for the senior officer. Lyman, eager, already crossing towards him.

'Should've expected him to show,' Casey said.

Cullen rested his coffee on the car roof and rubbed his face, looking tired.

'You okay?'

He nodded. 'Shauna was awake most of the night. Luisa's pissed because it was me woke her up when I came home. She wouldn't settle after.'

They'd been on the island until almost ten the night before, and back at six-thirty that morning. Casey hadn't slept much either, adrenaline running too high, pushing her to drag herself to the window every few hours to check for the guy in the hoodie from the previous night. But there'd been no sign of him, and her cell phone and doorbell had stayed silent.

'How the hell did you make enough noise to wake up a sleeping baby?'

'I snuck in to give her a kiss. I've hardly seen her in a week. I didn't think it'd disturb her.'

'Gonna get worse before it gets better.' Casey took in the vehicles scattered along the street.

'I know. Lu carries the load as it is, and she never complains, but when shit gets crazy like this ... It's just hard. Sleep's precious with kids. Sometimes I think...'

Casey waited for him to go on, but he fell silent. 'What?'

'Nothing. Six years to my twenty, then...' he slid his hands apart, like a jet taking off '...I'm gone.'

Casey screwed her face up. 'Seriously?'

'Uh-huh. If I get my way.'

That one caught her off-guard. 'The hell else you gonna do for money?'

'Lu wants to go back to teaching. And she doesn't even want to wait six years...'

'Doesn't answer my question.'

He shrugged. 'I got options.'

She leaned against the car, reeling a little. Just words, the prospect years off; but hitting hard this morning, her emotions already rinsed. 'I thought ... I kinda figured we'd end up running the place. Together.'

He glanced at her. 'The department?'

'Sure.'

He let go of a dejected laugh. 'You need to think bigger, Case. The brass gonna shoot you to the stars – you'll be long gone by the time I drag my ass home for good.'

A compliment, but one that fractured the cosy future she'd imagined for herself.

She swivelled to face him, but he spread his hands on the car roof and stood looking out at the ocean, a vacant stare that seemed to take in the whole world. Then he turned to her again. 'You think we're gonna find our girl in there?' He nodded across the street towards the marshland.

Casey's stomach knotted at the thought. 'I hope not.' When she looked back, she saw McTeague staring at her. He swirled his finger in a tight arc to beckon her over.

She moved off before she could think about it. 'Watch yourself, Big,' Cullen said as she went. 'Don't run your mouth.'

Lyman turned as she approached, looking put out when he saw why he'd lost McTeague's attention.

'Sir?'

McTeague had his head bent low, speaking to his feet. 'Detective Wray. Understand this started with an investigation of yours?'

'That's correct, sir. A woman named Tina Grace disappeared not far from here two nights ago.'

'She's not one of our vics so far, then?'

'Doesn't look that way.'

'Open leads?'

'There's not a lot to go on.' She told him about the scent trail ending in the vicinity of where Jerry Van Heusen reported seeing the parked car.

He nodded, as if it was the answer he was looking for. 'The chief wants a handle on this in the worst way. Scale's important.' He glanced at his watch. 'How long since you found the third one?' This directed to Lyman.

'Almost an hour. There's another dog team on the way so we can expand the search area. We're already a half-mile along from the first vic, there's a shitload of ground to cover, and it's nasty as hell in there.'

McTeague ran his knuckle over his mouth. 'So there could be three or there could be six. More.' He closed his eyes. 'Jesus Christ.'

He was quiet a moment, scanning the personnel along the street and then looking west along the road to its vanishing point. Then he pointed at Lyman. 'You liaise with me directly on this, understand? Everything comes to me, you don't scratch your ass without checking first.'

Lyman looked ashen. 'Yes, sir.'

He turned to Casey. 'Same for you. What do we know about this car with your misper?'

'Next to nothing, sir. We've only turned up one witness who saw it so far, and all he saw was a taillight.'

'Get an ID on it. Traffic cams, private security cams, whatever you have to do. The first sign your girl's dead, that car becomes the priority lead for the whole thing. You work your case but you run it through me.'

Casey rocked back on her heels. 'I'll have to clear that with Lieutenant Carletti.'

McTeague stared at her. 'I just said it. So no, you don't.' Then he took his phone out and focused on the screen, Casey and Lyman already invisible to him.

Casey drifted back to Cullen, feeling like she'd just stood in front of an airplane engine.

'What'd he say?'

'He's such a dick...' Before she could finish, she was distracted by a bright light behind Cullen. It went off then on again, and she realised it was a camera crew, the first on scene, buzzing from person to person trying to get something out of any of them.

Cullen turned to see what she was looking at just as she spotted the News 10 van. 'Shit, someone tipped them off.'

Casey grabbed her phone and hit call. 'I gotta warn Maggie Grace.'

Freezing rain came early afternoon, sheeting down on them. It turned an already difficult search into something torturous.

Spirits had already started to flag, the initial exhilaration dissipating as the hours went by with no additional finds, and the reality of an exhaustive but maybe fruitless search set in.

The epicentre was a little over a mile along Ramona Boulevard from Jon Parker's property; there were fewer houses on this part of the beach, just two or three spaced in the distance, and almost everything in sight seemed drained of colour – the skies, the ocean, the bush. It screamed of hopelessness.

The numbers had swelled, Casey long ago losing track, and now there were personnel, cars and equipment scattered all along the roadway. A fire-department truck had been brought in with a crane arm attached, now extended out twenty feet over the brush, the officer in its cradle afforded a bird's eye view to direct the crews on the ground, but being hammered by the wind and rain. A drone operator dispatched from Harrison was due to show up anytime.

She came off the phone to Billy D; he'd called to tell her he'd run down surveillance footage from three traffic cams – two from the causeway lift bridge and one from a News 10 webcam on the island's eastern bridge. The first piece of good news in what felt like a week. Before she could put her cell away, it started ringing again.

As she answered, she heard Cullen's phone ringing too, him reaching to take it.

'Casey Wray.' She watched Cullen as she answered.

'Detective, this is Ellis Sandford. You should know there's a man outside Jon Parker's house right now trying to get inside. He's shouting all kinds of abuse, and I think he's armed. You need to do something.'

Cullen came off the phone and signalled for her to wrap it up. She mouthed 'Jon Parker?' and he nodded, both of them scrambling for the car at the same time. 'Okay, Mr Sandford, I'm on my way right now, I'm close by. Stay inside your house and stay on the line.'

She jumped into the car, Cullen with the engine running already. 'Mr Sandford, describe the man you can see for me.' They took off, Cullen jamming the horn to try to part the crowd.

'He's ... he's white, young, early twenties maybe. He's—' Sandford broke off, a scramble on the line, saying something inaudible. Then he came back. 'He's trying to smash the window, where are you for Christ's sake?'

'We're ninety seconds away. Is Jon Parker at home?' They got clear of the search personnel and Cullen sped up along Ramona Boulevard.

'Yes. I think so, yes.'

'Okay. I'm gonna get off the line now, stay calm and don't go outside.'

She hit disconnect and peered through the rain, the ocean battering the beach alongside her, the grey water merging with the sky at the horizon. The Stadlers' house came into view ahead.

'Dispatch called me,' Cullen said, explaining how he'd known. 'They had two calls at the same time.'

Casey braced herself against the dash. 'Sandford says the guy's armed.'

'Then let's hope he doesn't wanna get dead today.'

They raced by the Stadler property, then Mrs Dunning's and the Van Heusens'. Parker's place came into view, a car on the street out front, left at an angle as if ditched abruptly, the drivers' door open. As they came close, they could make out the man on Parker's front lawn, hammering at his window.

Tommy Grace.

'Jesus Christ,' Cullen said, seeing it. 'What the fuck's he doing?'

Cullen braked hard and they jumped out, Casey closest, drawing her weapon. 'TOMMY.'

Grace whipped around, his coat hitching to reveal a revolver tucked into his jeans. 'This the motherfucker, right?' He was bug-eyed, spit flying as he said it.

Cullen had his weapon drawn too. 'On your knees, hands behind your head, Tommy. Right now.'

He didn't budge. 'Why're you protecting him? He knows what happened to my sister, get his ass out here.'

Casey aimed her gun at him, greasy raindrops bursting on the metal. 'We know you're armed. We can talk, but only when we get you away from here. Don't be stupid today.'

He glanced towards the pistol in his waistband. 'This? This is just to make him tell me what he knows.' He turned around and hammered on the window with both fists. 'Get out here, motherfucker, I seen you in there—'

Cullen moved then, grabbing Tommy's arm to twist behind him and dragging him facedown into the mud. Casey covered him until Cullen got the cuffs on, then she holstered her own weapon and grabbed the gun from Tommy's pants, unloading it. Tommy kept mouthing off as Cullen stood him up, trying to break free of his grip, but it was half-hearted.

Casey went over to the porch and rang the doorbell, rainwater trickling down her face and the back of her neck. 'Mr Parker, it's Casey Wray, you can come on out.' She rubbed water out of her eyes with the back of her hand.

Cullen read Tommy his rights and muscled him into the car. Ellis Sandford appeared on his porch down the street and Casey motioned for him to go back inside. She knocked on the door again. 'Mr Parker?'

She heard the door being unlocked on the other side, and

then Jon Parker opened up. Pale, shaken. 'What the hell is going on?'

'Are you okay? Did he get to you?'

'What? No. I'm fine, I'm fine.'

'Do you know that man, Jon?'

'He said "his sister". I don't know ... So he's her brother?'

'You've never met him before?'

'No.'

'Have you been in contact with her family? Do you know how he came to be here?'

'Of course not. I don't know her family, didn't even know she had a brother.' He pulled the door open wider. 'You must've told him about me. Is that it?'

She was already shaking her head. 'Absolutely not.'

'You're sure? Because it feels a hell of a lot like you're more interested in screwing with me than anything else.'

'That's categorically not the case. We'll speak to him now, and I'd like you to come down to the precinct for me.'

'Now?'

'When the uniform officers arrive. They can drive you.'

He stared at her, saying nothing. 'I'll think about it.' He slammed the door in her face.

Casey heard her phone go off. She answered as she walked back to the car. In the distance, a cruiser was coming in hot, lights flashing. 'Casey Wray.'

'Detective, it's Greta Van Heusen.'

Jerry's wife, with the newsreader smile. She stopped in Parker's yard and looked around for her, sick of the sensation that they were all watching her every time she set foot in this neighbourhood, judging her unseen from their beach houses. 'If this is about the disturbance, it's taken care of—'

'I know, I saw, but it's not that. Well, it's related to that, but ... What I wanted to tell you is the car. The one that's on the street right now, the man's car.'

'Ma'am?'

'It's the same one I saw come by Jon's house on that first morning. Right after you left.'

A passing comment she just barely remembered. 'Are you certain?'

'Absolutely. It's the same man. I remember ... Everything that morning was so vivid.'

She saw Frank Kidman and his partner in the cruiser as it parked up, Cullen already going over to debrief them. She held a hand up to acknowledge them and went to her own car. 'Okay, thank you Mrs Van Heusen, I appreciate it.'

She cut the call and stopped dead, trying to put it together. How could Tommy have known to show up at Jon Parker's house so soon that first morning? That was before they'd even contacted Tommy or Maggie.

She carried on to the car and opened the passenger door, expecting to find Tommy Grace raging in the backseat.

She was way off.

His head was bowed, his neck veins popping – but from anguish, not anger. He looked up when he realised she was there, tears spilling down his face.

'This is all my fucking fault.'


# CHAPTER 11

Casey placed a Diet Coke bottle in front of Tommy Grace. He didn't react. He was slumped deep into his chair in the interrogation room, staring straight ahead at something only he could see on the bare wall in front of him. He'd been that way since they put him there, as if the tears he shed in the car had drained him of everything. His right arm was cuffed to a loop in the middle of the table.

His clothes were sodden and streaked with mud, his face spattered too, even his hair. The muscles in his cheeks were taut, his bones so sharp it was like they could rupture the skin.

Casey sat down opposite, Cullen at the table already. 'Time for some answers, Tommy.'

He kept his gaze on a spot between them.

'I understand you've waived your right to an attorney?'

'Got nothing to hide.'

'Okay. Let's start with why you went to the property at 218 Ramona Villas today.'

He showed no sign he'd heard her.

Cullen reached over and twisted the top off the Coke, set it down again. 'Take a drink, have a think about how you can help your sister.'

Casey waited, but he still didn't respond. 'Tommy?'

He pushed the bottle away across the tabletop. 'Talk to Jon Parker.'

'We're talking to everyone—'

'Tina was at his house, right?' Tommy said. 'On the night.'

'I can't comment on an ongoing—'

'You asked him how he knew Tina yet?'

She sensed Cullen's impatience beside her but kept her eyes on Tommy. 'His story's they hooked up in a bar. If you know otherwise, tell me.'

He let his head roll back, then studied the walls either side of him.

'Have you ever visited that property before today, Tommy?'

He looked at her when she said it.

'Because we had a report that you were seen there on the morning of Tina's disappearance.'

'Motherfucker's the one, and you protecting him. Should be his ass in this chair.'

'Give us a reason to put him there. Talk to us.'

He lurched forward suddenly, and Cullen jumped to his feet. But Tommy was only doubling over to bury his face between his arms on the tabletop.

Casey pushed her chair back to give him space. 'I can see you're hurting, Tommy, and it's because there's something you want to get off your chest. Whatever it is, it's not too late.'

He spoke without lifting his head. 'I can't.' The words muffled. 'I can't, it'll kill her.'

Cullen looked at her, mouthed, 'What?'

Casey leaned over her knees. 'In the car, Tommy, you said to me, "It's all my fault." What does that mean?'

He was grinding his face into his forearms now, twisting his head side to side, unclear if it was an attempt at denial.

'Tommy?'

Then he was still. His breathing shallow but steady. He sat up, slowly crossed his arms and fixed his eyes on the back wall again.

'Talk to us, Tommy,' Cullen said.

Casey watched him, letting a minute go by in silence.

'You think this is helping Tina, Tommy?' she said, finally.

But still he didn't move or speak, didn't even make eye contact. His posture went beyond defiance, as if he was all by himself in there.

Casey glanced at Cullen and tipped her head to signal they

should let him stew. He nodded and stood up. 'We'll be back, Tommy. What you did today wasn't smart, but you can still help your sister if you talk to us. Think about that.'

They went out into the corridor and followed it around to the office.

Cullen punched his fist into his palm in frustration. 'Felt like he was working up to a confession before he shut down.'

Casey was heading for her desk, but she saw Carletti waving her over.

She stopped and grabbed Cullen's arm. 'See where Billy's at with the traffic-cam footage. Start with the window from 10.30pm to 11.30pm the night Tina disappeared, we're looking for Tommy Grace's Honda, and anyone else travelling onto the beaches. If we're lucky we'll pick up Tina on her way there, but assuming we're not, cross-reference against vehicles coming off post-4am. Also: see about a warrant for Jon Parker's telephone records for the last seven days – I wanna know who he was talking to. And tell Jill to get a dump from the cell tower on Ramona Beach. Let's see if we can't figure out who the hell was out there that night.'

'You expecting Tommy to be one of them?'

'I don't know.'

'He's talking guilty as fuck. What if it was his car in the bushes?'

Carletti hung out his doorway and called over to her. 'Big? Come on.'

Casey looked at him and signalled frantically she was coming. She sensed Cullen was thinking along the same lines as her – Tommy gives his sister a ride to her boyfriend's house, and sticks around to ferry her home safe. But then what? He gets mad and kills her because she overstayed? Even if it was his car, motive felt a long way off. 'One step at a time. I better go.'

Casey cut across the floor to Carletti's. 'Boss?'

He dropped into his chair. The flatscreen on the wall was showing News 10's rolling coverage of the search along Ramona Boulevard. A reporter was talking over footage of HCPD crews picking at roadside undergrowth, a scraggly group of onlookers in the background, toughing out the rain. 'This is where I'm getting my information.'

She looked down. 'Sorry, we just brought Tina Grace's brother in, he was outside Jon Parker's house with a gun...'

Carletti waved it off. 'I'm not pissed at you.' His eyes were locked on the screen, moving with the pictures. 'They've drafted manpower from all over the county, and I haven't even had a phone call.'

'This might not be the news you want, then, but McTeague collared me this morning and told me I was reporting direct to him on Tina Grace.'

The expected outburst didn't come, Ray keeping his eyes on the TV.

'I told him I'd have to clear it with you,' she said.

'Son of a bitch is playing games.'

'What do you want me to do?'

'Nothing.' He watched a few seconds longer; the newsreader in the studio said, 'And we understand reports of a fourth body have proved unfounded – so far?' He broke off to look at her. 'If McTeague's telling you that, it's coming direct from the chief. It's not your problem. Work the case – leave the politics to me.'

'Okay...'

'What've we got out there?'

'You mean bottom line?'

'Yeah. Gut feeling.'

She looked around the walls, thinking. 'I don't know. I'm reserving judgement. See what the ME says once they've examined the body.'

'They already showed a tweet from someone claims they're a local, saying there's been rumours about a serial killer in the area for years. That no one could get the cops to take them seriously.'

'That's bullshit.'

'They're gonna go to town on that angle anyway.'

'Always gonna happen.'

'Maybe, but unless and until it's proven not to be the case, the scrutiny will be through the roof. So you need to protect yourself.'

She came forward and perched on the chair on the other side of the desk. 'What does that mean?'

The reporter on screen talked about 'challenging conditions hampering the search'. Ray picked up a pen and tapped it on his pad – click-click-click. 'Just make sure everything's nailed down. Like you always do, but times a thousand. When this goes sideways, with the media attention, they'll be looking for someone to take a fall. I can guarantee McTeague's thinking that way already.'

'What do you mean "when"? We've barely started.'

'We?'

Casey frowned. 'I mean in the wider sense.'

'Three bodies in the middle of nowhere. Been there Christ knows how long. No witnesses...'

'There's a chance—'

'Get real, Big. Why do you think they sent McTeague in on day one?'

'Because it's high profile. Special Investigations always—'

Carletti was already shaking his head, his tongue curled around his front teeth. 'Damage control.'

'Come on...'

'This is the chief getting his boy in place to shape the narrative. From the start. If the body count tops out at three, and *if* it turns out they've been in there for a time, or they're not connected, then the media loses interest quickly, the pressure goes away and everyone moves on. Then McTeague can step back again quietly and let Lyman work it or backburner it. But you see what they're worried about?'

'More bodies.'

'Yes.' He fixed her with a look, teasing out the silence. 'But specifically Tina Grace. If she's the next one we pull outta there, then this is live, and this is happening right now. A real lead, on a current serial killer. And the media aren't going to let that go. So then the brass has gotta show they were serious about solving it, such as by having their heavy hitter on the ground from day one. And if McTeague *can't* solve it...' he raised his eyebrows at her, as good as pointing a finger '...the brass will want someone to blame.'

Casey looked away, taking a breath before she faced him again. 'If this is supposed to be a pep talk, I'm here to tell you it sucks ass.'

Ray closed his eyes. 'When did I ever need to give *you* a pep talk?'

'Then what is this? What are you telling me?'

'Exactly what I said: cover your back. Whatever you have to do. If this is as bad as it could be, and they can't catch the guy fast, they're gonna drag through everything you did the last couple days, looking for anything you missed.' He put on his impression of Chief Hanrahan's brogue. "Well, unfortunately mistakes were made right at the start of the investigation, which cost us valuable time in catching the perpetrator responsible for these heinous crimes. The mistakes were those of an individual officer, who will be dealt with through the appropriate departmental processes..."'

She stared at him, his eyes tired but hard, hedging over whether there was some deeper meaning he was trying to pass on.

'What's with the brother?' he said. 'A gun?'

It took her a second to catch up, still mulling his warning. 'He's fixated on Parker. I can't tell if he's just putting two and two together, or he knows more than he's telling.'

'Such as?'

'If he gave his sister a ride that night.'

Carletti crossed his arms. 'That would jump him to the front of the suspects line. So is this him trying to point the finger at the guy next to him?'

'Maybe, but it's just a hunch for now. We're looking at the traffic cams, that might tell us something or nothing. But he's saying some weird shit and we can place him at Parker's house the morning after, before we contacted the family, so...'

Carletti nodded, eyes drifting back to the TV. The newsreader asked the reporter, 'How has HCPD responded to claims it's the work of a serial killer?'

'Keep going,' Ray said. 'God willing, she's alive somewhere. You get to bring your girl home, and this whole thing is McTeague and Lyman's problem.'

Across the office, Cullen was huddling with Billy D at his desk. Casey went over and peered between them, black-and-white footage of the causeway on his screen. At first she thought it was paused, but then saw movement at the edges – the water just in shot, rippling in the moonlight. 'Where we at?'

Billy tapped the legal pad in front of him, a list of a half-dozen registrations noted down. 'Forty minutes and that's everything so far.'

'That's a good thing. Less to eliminate against the vehicles coming off the island.'

'I ran the plates anyway, just in case. Nothing's jumping off the page.'

Cullen looked around at her. 'We started at ten, to leave ourselves a cushion, so this is ten-forty on the night of. No sign of Tina yet. Or Tommy.'

A Dodge truck approached the screen, Billy pausing the footage to look closer. The camera was positioned facing southbound traffic on the causeway, coming from the mainland. Although the image was grainy black and white, it was clear enough to make out the driver's face. In this case, a woman with dark wavy hair, at least twenty years too old to be Tina Grace. Billy ran it on again.

'Keep at it, Bill. Come get us right away if Tommy Grace shows up.'

'About him,' Cullen said, 'the gun we took off Tommy is registered in his name, purchased legally.'

'Doesn't matter, we can dangle a threatening-behaviour charge over him.'

Cullen grimaced. 'Frank Kidman sent word, Jon Parker refused to come in. Says he doesn't want to press charges.' He bit his lip looking at her.

Casey turned her head towards the interrogation room. 'Tommy doesn't know that yet.'

Tommy Grace drained the last of the Coke and crushed the plastic bottle as he put it down. It toppled over and came to a rest on its side. He kept his eyes on it, jaw set tight, but avoiding Casey's stare.

'What were you doing in Ramona Villas on the morning Tina disappeared, Tommy?'

'Looking for her.'

'Okay. So you knew where she'd gone the night before?'

He didn't answer, flicking the mangled bottle so it rocked side to side on the tabletop. Cullen grabbed it and tossed it into the trashcan in the corner without taking his eyes off him.

Casey tapped the table, gentle, getting his attention back. 'Tommy?'

'She told me.'

'All right. Because you said to us you didn't speak to Tina the night she disappeared...'

'I thought you meant after. She told me earlier on that's what she was doing, and you already knew it. I'm not about to waste your time telling you shit you already know.'

'You need to let us decide what's important, Tommy. How did she sound about it?'

'What?'

Casey counted the options off on her fingers. 'Was she excited, nervous, afraid—'

'She texted me.' He said it flat.

Cullen slipped his hands off the table and slapped the metal chair legs beneath him in frustration.

Casey ignored the distraction, eyes on Tommy. 'Did you give her a ride?'

He wrinkled his face, the idea ridiculous. 'No.'

'What's with that expression? You didn't approve of her seeing Jon Parker?'

He hung his head and exhaled hard. 'Jesus Christ...'

Casey waited, Cullen glancing at her for a cue. But Tommy was muttering into his own chest, shaking his head. She'd seen this look before, a guilty man lashing out at anyone and anything, fighting the need to unburden himself.

'Tommy, where were you the night Tina disappeared?'

He rubbed his face with both hands, then sat up, reinvigorated. 'Out. My boys'll tell you that.'

'We'll need their names, then.'

'What the fuck you accusing me of?'

'What did you mean earlier when you said "it'll kill her"?'

'What?'

'I asked you if there's something you wanted to tell us...'

'I never said that.'

'You did, Tommy. And before that, you said "this is all my fault". So if something happened, maybe by accident...'

'Fuck you.'

'Were you on Ramona Beach the night she disappeared?'

He pointed at her chest, reaching across the table. 'I said, fuck you.'

Cullen held his palm up to block it. 'Settle down.'

Casey pushed. 'We'll get a list of all the cell phones active on the beach that night, so we'll know soon enough. If you gave her a ride and something went wrong, if you were worried about her – there's all kinds of legitimate reasons—'

'No. Fucking no.'

'If she can still be helped, if she's still alive—'

Tommy exploded out of his chair. 'Fuck you. Fuck your bullshit.' He leaned across and slapped Cullen's hand away.

Cullen jumped up but Casey grabbed his arm. He was shaking with anger.

A knock at the door made all three of them look over, snapping the moment like glass breaking. Another knock, urgent. Then Billy D cracked it open. 'Got something you need to see.'

## CHAPTER 12

The image was frozen on Billy's screen. It showed a black Ford Escape, a man behind the wheel. There was a woman in the seat next to him, slumped against the passenger window, her eyes closed. The top part of the windshield was tinted, obscuring part of her face, the rest hard to make out in the shadows. But she was wearing a thin black coat, and what Casey could see looked for all the world like Tina Grace.

'Can we make it any clearer?'

Billy tapped his mouse to move it on a frame, but only the SUV's flank was visible, the side windows darkened. He backed it up two frames, only the front of the vehicle in shot. 'They must've been hauling ass,' Cullen said. Billy took it back to the original. 'This is the best one. That's her, right?' he said, looking at Casey.

Casey bent close. Hard to be sure, but the hair, the face. The outfit ... 'I think so.'

'The driver anyone we know?' Billy asked.

Cullen shook his head the same time as Casey. The man's

face was in shadow too, but from what was visible, he had dark thinning hair worn in a side part, glasses, an oversized leather jacket on. She looked at the timestamp on the screen – 4.31am.

'I ran the plate,' Billy said. 'It's registered to a Michael Patrick Bell, forty-two years old, white male, address on the west side.' He toggled to a different window on his PC, showing Michael Bell's ID and photo. The man in the picture had a moustache, no glasses, but a similar cinder-block head. 'Pretty sure that's him behind the wheel. Big news is he's got a jacket for promoting prostitution – he was sentenced to five months' jail time in fifteen.'

'Oh shit.' Casey scanned the details on screen. She looked round at Cullen. 'Playboy Jon Parker *has girls coming to his house all the time?*'

'Knew that motherfucker was lying.'

Casey patted Billy on the shoulder. 'Great job. Print that off for me, would you?'

He handed her a sheet of paper. 'Already done.'

She took it, smiling at him. 'We'll make a detective out of you yet, Bill.' She started walking, memorising the address on Bell's licence, Cullen in step.

'Explains some things if Tina Grace was selling herself,' Cullen said.

'Uh-huh.' How she could afford the apartment when she wasn't working. Why Jon Parker was so evasive. She swung by Carletti's office, plastered the printout to the glass partition so he could see it and leaned around the doorjamb. 'New suspect. Got this guy on video, driving what looks a lot like Tina Grace off the beach that night. We're gonna go talk to him now.'

Ray looked up from his keyboard. 'Who is he?'

'Michael Patrick Bell, has priors for pimping.'

'Pimping? She's a working girl?'

'Let's see.' She slipped around the doorway to stand just inside the office. 'What we talked about before, should I notify McTeague now on this, or...?'

Carletti cocked his head, thinking. 'No. See what your guy has to say first. Where's he live?'

'On the west side, Delaney Boulevard.'

'Okay. Go get him.'

She nodded, backing out.

Cullen scratched his nose as they walked down the stairs to the parking lot.

'What?'

'What Ray said about McTeague ... you sure that's the right play?'

'He made his call. Last I checked he was still our boss.'

He said nothing to that, retreating into himself the way he did when he disagreed about something but didn't want the fight.

She jabbed him on the shoulder playfully. 'Quit worrying. It's my ass they'll fire first, right?'

Michael Patrick Bell's address was a narrow A-frame house off the western end of Delaney Boulevard. Three steps led them onto a low porch, fronted by a railing with two broken balusters – half gone, like they'd been kicked out.

No doorbell. Casey banged on the door, looking around for the Ford Escape they'd seen on the camera. There were cars parked up and down the street, but none of them the one they wanted to see. She rapped again, Cullen pulling a sliver of flaking paint from the doorframe.

Still no answer. Casey backtracked down the steps and picked her way through the weeds running around the side of the house, her hand on her holster. A low gate sealed off the backyard, a padlocked chain strung through a makeshift hole in the wood and around the gatepost, loose enough that there was a gap to see through.

'Anything?' Cullen said.

The backyard was as overgrown as the passage they were standing in. A homemade barbecue pit was only just keeping its head above the grass. The acute angle meant she couldn't see the back door, but there were no signs of movement. 'Nuh-uh.' She rattled the gate to see if it brought anyone out, but the place was dead.

They went back around to the front, Casey looking up and down the street. The houses around them were a similar design but a mishmash of reds, blues and greys. Nothing like the uniform white of Ramona Beach. Casey flicked one finger out to point at the neighbouring property. 'Let's see what they can tell us.'

A man in a Carhartt ball cap and matching shirt opened the door, holding a jar of strawberry jelly. Casey glanced at it as she introduced herself.

'Fixing a snack,' the man said, by way of explanation. 'What can I do for you?'

Casey held up the printout of Bell's ID. 'We're looking for this man, you know him?'

The man nodded. 'Yeah, he lived next door awhile.'

'Lived? Not anymore?'

The man shook his head. 'Haven't seen him in weeks. Maybe longer than that.'

'You know where we could find him?'

He shrugged. 'I never even spoke to him once.'

'Anyone along the block that knows him better?' Casey gestured to the other houses.

'Couldn't tell you. Sorry.'

She thanked him and moved off. They tried two more houses across the street, but came away with scraps; Bell was the type kept to himself, only one of the residents even knew his name, and none of them knew where he'd gone to. The house was a rental but no one could provide them with the owners' details. Bell lived alone, came and went at all hours of the day and night, no regular schedule – indicative, to Casey's mind, that he'd gone back to his old habits. No details of family or friends they could try.

They went back to the car, Casey dialling Billy D.

'What's up, Big?'

'We struck out on Michael Bell, looks like he moved on a while ago. See what else you can dig up on him – and find out who arrested him back in fifteen. If it was patrol, get dispatch to put the uniform in touch with me ASAP. I need KAs, hangouts, place of work, any way I can locate him.'

'On it. You need anything else?'

'Yeah, get a uniform posted to watch Jon Parker's house. Tell them to stay on him like glue.'

She hung up and slipped into the passenger seat.

Cullen watched as she put her belt on. 'We're not gonna bring him in yet?'

She rubbed her eyes, the sky the deep purple of a fresh bruise. 'I want one more run to see what we get out of Tommy first. Then it's Parker.'

A radio update from the scene said the body count was holding steady at three. Additional units had arrived from Harrison during the afternoon to help with the search, both human and canine, a nod to the bleak weather forecast; a winter storm The Weather Channel had christened Daisy was due to blow in overnight and forecasted to dump enough snow to bring the whole thing to a halt.

Cullen parked the car at the precinct and they jumped out, the wind already picking up and knifing through her. Casey hurried across the lot, hunching deeper into her overcoat until she made it inside.

Maggie Grace stood up as she came through the doors, her soaking-wet coat tumbling off her lap to the waiting-area floor. She zeroed on Casey. 'What did he do?'

'Mrs Grace, I'm sorry but I can't—'

'That dumbass got you wasting time on his account instead of Tina's, so I absolutely got the right to know what for.'

'I promise you, no time's been lost looking for Tina. There are multiple officers working the case.'

'Why're you talking to me like this? When you called me before, you talked to me like a person. Now you sound like one of those goddamn automatic voices when you call the bank.'

Casey glanced at the floor. 'Tommy was causing a disturbance outside a private residence.'

'He went to that guy Parker's house, didn't he?'

Casey stepped closer. 'How did Tommy know where he lived?'

Maggie ignored the question, hearing only the confirmation she wanted. 'Dammit, I told him not to, he was talking about beating the crap outta him. Did he hit him?'

'No, no one was hurt. But how did he know about Jon Parker, Maggie?'

She shrugged. 'You told me his name. You asked me about him, that first time.'

'Did you ever hear Tommy speak about him before that though?'

'No. Never. Who is he? How's he know Tina?'

Casey looked down, trying to take the heat out of the moment. 'Look, if you can convince Tommy to leave this to us, it'll help everyone.'

Maggie looked away, covering her mouth with her hands. Then she dropped them to her sides, defeated. 'He hasn't listened to me in years. He's a goddamn hothead, I can't get through to him when he gets like this. What happens to him now?' She looked at Cullen, then back at Casey, as if she was weighing who'd give the more favourable answer.

'That's still to be decided. But look, there's something we could use your help with.' Casey turned to Cullen, lowered her voice. 'Speak to Billy and get a closeup shot from the traffic cam for Mrs Grace to ID.'

Maggie grabbed the last word out of the air. 'ID? You found her? Oh shit, is she—'

'We've got footage of a woman we believe to be Tina from the night she disappeared. I'd like for you to take a look to confirm it.'

'Is she alive?'

Casey held her stare, the pleading in her eyes. 'I can't say one way or another. It's just a glimpse...'

Her eyes widened, hope flushing out the desperation. 'There's a chance, though? As long as there's a chance.'

Casey sat down opposite Tommy and unlocked his cuffs. He looked at her without a word, hesitant to take his hand away at first, then rubbing his wrist when he finally did so. Cullen stood in the corner with his arms folded, the way Casey had asked him to. Tommy seemed to spark off him, the kid a wrecking ball running on testosterone and angst, so having him take a back seat seemed only sensible.

'Jon Parker has decided not to press charges,' Casey said. 'Problem for you is we can still file for disorderly conduct, and I'm pretty sure I can find a way to bring a weapons charge. In the circumstance, I'd rather have your co-operation, but it's your call.'

'I swear to Christ I ain't had nothing to do with Tina going missing. It's that motherfucker on the beach—'

Casey held her hand up and he fell silent. She set down the picture of Michael Patrick Bell and turned it around to face him. 'Do you know this man?'

Tommy put a finger on it and brought it closer. He looked at it a few seconds and shook his head. 'Who is he?'

'Someone we need to talk to. You're sure?'

He looked again, his expression blank. 'Yeah.'

'Tommy, I need to ask you something about Tina.' She brought the photo towards her and filed it away again while she took a breath. 'To your knowledge, has she ever been a sex worker?'

He looked her dead in the eye, his lips coming apart slowly, his thoughts spinning almost loud enough to hear.

'Tommy?'

When he spoke at last, he said, 'Where'd you get that from?'

It was the most composed she'd heard him, the effort painted on his face.

'Is that a yes?' Casey said.

He kept his eyes on hers, flicking from one to the other.

She stood up to break it off, paced to the back of the room to reset the dynamic. 'Think about it this way: if Jon Parker's lying about being in a relationship with Tina, it gives a lot more weight to the idea he knows something about what happened to her.'

Tommy swiped his hand back and forth over the tabletop. 'Motherfucker has to know.' He said it into his own chest.

Casey came forward again and gripped the back of her chair. 'Tell me, Tommy. It's taken you too long already.'

He closed his eyes, pressed one knuckle into his lips. 'You can't say shit about this to my mom.'

A promise she couldn't keep, so she let it float by without touching it. 'Go on.'

He kept his eyes shut, trying to hold out, but the boulder was already rolling downhill, freeing him as it did. 'I told her not to do it, right? Told her I'd kick her ass if she started up again, but she ain't never listened to anyone except herself in her whole life.'

Casey gripped the chair back tighter, hearing means, motive... 'Keep going.'

But he fell silent, so she threw a prompt – get him back onto his favourite subject to rev him up again. 'Was Jon Parker a client?'

He nodded, eyes on the floor. 'What else he gonna be?'

'Did she use a pimp?'

He shook his head. 'She's not like that. Selling it on the street and all. It's all cell phones now. Tinder, shit like that. She called herself an escort.'

'You said she was starting up again?'

'She quit it for, like, two years.'

The number tweaked a memory – Brian Walton telling her he and Tina had just celebrated their two-year anniversary. Did she quit because of him? To hide it? If he'd found out suddenly... 'Because she got together with Brian Walton?'

He shrugged.

'Did Brian know about it?'

'Fuck, no.'

'You're sure?'

'Pretty sure.'

Casey wrote down Walton's name and circled it. 'And you obviously didn't approve.'

He looked up. 'No fucking way. But that didn't mean shit to her.'

'Did that cause friction between you?'

'Fuck does that mean – friction?'

'Did it cause arguments? Did you ever try to prevent her doing what she was doing?'

He pointed at her. 'Motherfucker, you still trying to turn this round on me? Is that what you asking, did I ever whup her for selling her ass?' He stood up. 'You ain't filing charges, I can walk outta here anytime I want, right?' He started towards the door.

Cullen pushed himself off the wall. 'Sit your ass back down, Tommy.'

'Shut the fuck up, fat man. You stand in the back like the boss woman told you.'

Cullen cocked his head.

'Oh, you supposed to be the badass? Gonna scare me now?'

Casey stepped into his eyeline. 'Him? He's here to protect

you, Tommy. Make sure I don't hand you the ass-kicking you're so desperate to find.'

He started to laugh but tailed off when he saw them both staring him down. He blew out a breath and grabbed his crotch. 'Fuck this...'

'If I can't get answers from you, you go to jail and there's only one other person I can ask,' Casey said.

He stayed rooted to the spot, his jacket slung over his arm. 'It'll kill her.'

The same line he'd used earlier. The meaning illuminated now. 'Why?'

He broke into an involuntary smile, disbelief. '*Why*, she says. My mom's a drunk, already got a broken heart, and the detective lady stands there and asks why it'd be bad for her to find out her only daughter been selling her ass like a ho. And her son let it happen.' He bent at the waist to yell in her face. 'Why. The. Fuck. You. Think?'

Casey put her hands on her hips, watching him with no expression. 'You through?'

'Fuck you.'

'You can be as obnoxious to me as you want, Tommy, but you're the one kept all this from us. You could've told us this at the start, and it would've bought your sister time. Because that's her most precious commodity now. You asked me about the stats, so you know we're way past twenty-four hours already, no contact or ransom demand, and that's bad. So I'm giving you the chance now: lay it all on the table. Help me to find her while there's still a chance.'

'I told you everything.'

'Did it make you mad when she told you she was going to Jon Parker's house?'

'Hell yes, I already told you that.'

'Did you go after her?'

'No, I was with my crew. How many times—'

'Did she always tell you when she was going on a job?'

'No. I didn't wanna know shit about it.'

'Then why this time?'

He shrugged again but turned his head to look to the door this time.

Getting closer now... 'Tommy?'

'The fuck do I know?'

'So she just texts you out of the blue to tell you she's got a "date"? To taunt you?'

He kept his gaze fixed in place. The muscles around his mouth contracted and tensed.

'Why did you say this is all your fault, Tommy?'

His neck and head were trembling now.

'Why did she text you? Why...' It came to her then, the realisation sudden – the same thing in every family: 'She wanted something, right? What did she want from you, Tommy?'

His head bucked back and forth, tears forming in his eyes, and he bent at the waist and then at the knees until he was doubled over in a crouch. He said something too quietly to hear.

'I can't hear you, Tommy. Say it—'

'She wanted a ride. She asked me to give her a ride.'

Casey looked at Cullen, feeling her heart short circuit as the scales fell away from her eyes. The kid was eaten up by guilt – but not the way she thought.

She went over to stand in front of him. He swiped his sleeve over his eyes, still in a crouch. She gave him a minute, then bent down, mirroring his pose. 'Did you agree to take her?'

He shook his head.

'I need to hear you say it, please. For the tape.'

'No.'

'Okay. So do you know what arrangements she made instead?'

He looked up, first at Cullen, then at Casey. 'I don't know.'

'Were you on the beaches that night, Tommy? Did you go to check on her?'

'No. Swear to God. If I could go back now, I'd pick her up before she could go and drive her round in circles till morning.'

Casey looked up at Cullen, see if he had anything left to ask. He gave a slight shake of the head, then came over and stuck his hand out to help Tommy up.

To her surprise, he took it.

Casey handed him a cup of water and waited for him to take a sip, but he just held it in his hand and stared into it.

'Is it unusual for Tina to ask you for a ride that way?'

He ran his tongue around his cheek, then nodded. 'She knows I don't want nothing to do with it.'

'So why this time?'

His expression – he was already disengaging again. 'Don't know. Look, I know you don't believe me, but I don't know shit about how she carries on. She knows I know, she knows it pisses me off, and she knows I don't wanna hear about it. I couldn't believe she sent me that message.'

Casey nodded at him, 'Okay, Tommy.'

He looked at her, his arms hanging limp by his sides, all the piss and vinegar gone, and a husk left behind. 'You can't tell my mom. I meant what I said, it'd kill her to know. Please.'

# CHAPTER 13

The omens were bad from the start, Jon Parker's lawyer showing up at the precinct even before he did.

Casey met the uniforms bringing Parker in at the main entrance, Clarence Mickelroff with him throughout the process as he was booked. She led him straight to an interview room, where Cullen was already set up. Parker dropped into a chair with a huff and crossed his legs.

'Detectives, this is unnecessary and overkill,' Mickelroff said. 'My client has been co-operative throughout your investigation.' It was two or three years since Casey had last dealt with him, but he was well known around the place, a top-dollar attorney who'd made his name in two high-profile miscarriage-of-justice cases that'd garnered their own TV shows.

'Your client's here on an obstruction charge, Clarence. It's precisely because he hasn't co-operated that he's in that chair.' Casey sat down. 'Mr Parker, you told us you were in a casual relationship with Tina Grace, correct?'

'I never said we were in a relationship. I told you she's not my girlfriend.'

'Your exact words were, "We're casual, you know", and when I asked you how long you'd been seeing each other, *casually*, you said, "Maybe, like a month". That sounds very much like a casual relationship to me.'

Mickelroff looked up from his notes. 'Detective?'

'Were you aware Tina Grace engaged in sex work?' Casey said.

Parker glanced at Mickelroff before he answered. 'No.'

'And you still contend you met her in a bar?'

He looked at Mickelroff again, who held his hand up to signal he was taking over. 'Detective, I fail to see the relevance of any of this to—'

'No, you don't, Clarence. Don't play dumb, it's not a good look on you.' She turned to Parker again. 'We know Tina Grace worked as an escort, she visited your property and vanished, and now there's bodies turning up a mile from where you live. There's two ways this goes now, and this is your last chance to avoid the one that ends up with you in a cell.'

Mickelroff scoffed. 'I'm yet to hear the nature of the obstruction my client is accused of.'

'We've established Tina Grace came to Mr Parker's property for the purposes of engaging in prostitution. That's lie number one—'

'You have evidence my client agreed to pay the woman in exchange for sex?'

'We have a witness who can testify as to why Tina was visiting Mr Parker's property.'

'My client has already stated he was unaware of her background.'

'So you never discussed a fee?'

'No,' Parker said.

'Detective Wray, we both know it's not unusual for girls in that line of work to demand payment only after engaging in sexual activities. If that was her ultimate plan, my client can't be blamed for her dishonest intentions.'

'So your story is you met Tina in a bar, hooked up a few times, but she hadn't asked for money yet?'

Mickelroff put his pen down. 'Look, let's stop dancing around it. My client met this woman on Tinder. He was embarrassed to admit it when he spoke to you and the other officers, and he is very sorry for that. But that's the extent of the inaccuracy here. Everything else my client told you stands, particularly this young woman last being seen heading away from my client's house, after he made multiple attempts to help her and shortly before he dialled 911 because he was concerned for her safety. I'm certain you'll have corroborated as much with the various eyewitnesses by now.'

'Yeah, let's talk about that,' Casey said to Parker. 'We have a report you were arguing with Tina and pointing for her to head on down the road, that last time you caught up to her. What did you say?' Keeping back the existence of the Stadler video, seeing if he'd trap himself in a lie.

Cullen glanced at Mickelroff, then said, 'I don't remember exactly. Just ... "Get a cab and go home".'

Casey took Michael Patrick Bell's picture out of her file and set it in front of Parker. 'Do you recognise this man, Jon?'

Parker looked at it and up again. 'No.'

'How did Tina reach your property the night you arranged to meet?'

'I told you this, we didn't talk about it. A cab, I guess.'

Cullen spoke for the first time. 'Have you used prostitutes in the past, Jon?'

Mickelroff laughed, adjusting his tie pin. 'This is a fishing trip. Don't answer that.'

Casey sat forward, tapping the image. 'This man has a record for pimping. We can place him on Ramona Beach the night she disappeared, and we can connect him directly to Tina. We know you have girls coming over regularly, your neighbours couldn't wait to tell us. So as soon as we can link him to you, your whole story falls apart. If all you're hiding is that you're a habitual user of prostitutes, tell us now and we can start over.

Mickelroff gathered his papers. 'We're through here.'

Casey held her hand up. 'The morning we first came to your property – what time did you leave that day?'

'I don't remember.'

Casey glanced at her notes. 'We left you at 9.55am. Was it right after, or later on?'

'I honestly don't remember.'

'You were golfing at Sentona Hills that day, right? What was your tee time? I guess we can check with them easy enough.'

'Why on earth would you want to, Detective?' Mickelroff said.

'Tommy Grace visited your house after we left that day. Did you speak to him?'

'This is the brother?' Mickelroff asked.

'Yes.'

'The one who threatened my client at his own home?'

Casey ignored him. 'Did you speak to him that morning, Jon?'

'I never saw him before the time I had to call you to arrest him. I guess I was out.'

'Quite a troubled young man, from what I can tell. I hope he's grateful my client decided not to press charges.' Mickelroff zipped his case and Parker stood up on cue.

Casey did the same, eyes locked on Parker. 'Your story's coming apart, Jon. Clarence will get you to dig yourself deeper because that's how he earns his money. Telling us the truth is the only way you can help yourself now.'

Parker waited while Mickelroff put his coat on, then followed him out of the room.

They stood in a holding area to the side of the precinct reception, waiting for the booking sergeant to bring Tommy through. Maggie was standing next to Casey, Cullen a little way apart as if he didn't know what to say to her. Casey read her differently: Maggie was through with talk and just needed to know someone was by her side.

Showing her the still from the causeway cam had been tough, Maggie conflicted as hell when she held it in her hands. Hope and dread hitting her all at once. She'd stared at it for only a second or two before she said, 'It's Tina.'

She'd reeled off a list of questions after that, so fast she'd obviously been thinking them up since she first heard they had a sighting of Tina. Casey kicked herself for that dumb piece of deduction – what else would a distraught mom be thinking about? Casey had been able to answer some of them – the image was captured more than forty-eight hours ago, they hadn't located the vehicle or its driver yet, there were no further video captures that they'd found so far – but she couldn't give her the only two answers she'd really wanted: Where was Tina? Was she alive or dead?

Casey had showed her Michael Bell's picture separately, but Maggie didn't recognise him. That was enough to convince her not to bring up Tina's side hustle – at least for now. Acquiescing to Tommy's pleas even though she didn't feel she owed him anything after all his bullshit.

He came through the doors and dropped his eyes to the floor when Maggie glared at him. The uniform led him to the desk to sign the release paperwork, and Casey slid over to Cullen. 'Stay with her for me, huh? I gotta talk to Tommy a minute.'

He looked at Casey, his expression silently asking *What for?* but he didn't press it when she moved over to the desk.

The sergeant pointed to where Tommy had to sign and then looked at Casey. 'He's all yours. If you want him.'

She waited for the man to slip away before she came around to face Tommy.

'I'm free to go, right?'

Casey nodded. 'But you need to quit playing games with me.'

'Huh?'

'You should've told me everything from the start. That's the way you help your sister.'

Tommy didn't react.

'You could've put us on to Jon Parker hours earlier...'

'I didn't know—'

'Can it. You were seen outside his place right after we were that first morning. You knew where to look and you said nothing.'

'I swear to you, I didn't know. I told you the truth just now, I was looking for Tina on the island, I knew she went there but I didn't know who for. When I saw the patrol cops go by, I followed them. Then I saw you pull up.'

'You could've told us about Tina's work.'

'And then what?' He turned away, frustrated. 'Tell me you'd be looking for her if I told you the truth.'

She inched closer, getting up in his face. 'What?'

'Tell me you wouldna written her off as another white-trash whore gone missing. You couldn't get out of that fucker's place fast enough that first time.'

Maggie Grace called out to them. 'Hey, detective? What's going on, can we go?'

Casey turned back to him. 'You could've told us everything from the start. You tell us the truth and we'd have had a whole lot more questions to ask that morning.'

'I come tell you she's a...' He closed his eyes and opened them again, speaking even more quietly this time. 'I tell you she's an escort, you don't waste even one second looking for her ass. You know that.'

'There are better ways to get what you wanted.'

'Like what?'

'Work with us. Be truthful.'

'I told you everything now.'

'For her sake I hope so.'

She nodded to the doors and brushed past him to say goodbye to Maggie.

'Hey, look ... I'm sorry.'

She stopped, standing side-by-side with him now, but facing opposite directions.

'Seriously,' Tommy said. 'I wanted to tell you but I thought it was the best thing for Tina. But...'

'But?'

He breathed in through his nose. 'If I'd known what you was about back then, maybe I wouldn't have kept it quiet. Wouldn't have needed to.'

Casey looked at him a second, then carried on walking. But the compliment gave her a little lift, in its own way strangely heartfelt.

## CHAPTER 14

'So what are you saying? You like Bell for it?' Carletti swirled his glass of Bushmills, looking at Cullen and then Casey in turn. He had one foot on his desk, his chair angled to face the TV on the wall. The screen showed the press corps waiting for the briefing to start. Coming live from somewhere in the depths of Harrison HQ; standing room only, enough reporters crammed into the small room to fill the chairs provided twice over. All eyes on the small stage at the front, waiting for Chief Hanrahan to show.

Cullen shook his head. 'Bell's the priority right now, but it's still Parker for me.'

'You've been around Tommy Grace too long,' Casey said.

Cullen sniggered and ran his finger around the rim of his tumbler. 'He lied right off the bat. You can't discount that.'

'About his relationship with the girl?' Carletti said.

'Yeah. And that bullshit he was embarrassed? No fucking way.' Cullen gestured with his glass as he spoke, always more expressive with liquor inside him. 'No sale.'

'I'm with you,' Casey said, 'but it doesn't change the fact Tina left the scene with Michael Patrick Bell.'

'What about the Stadler woman's video?' Cullen said. 'Parker was pointing her right in his direction.'

'Sure he was. Maybe he really did want her gone.' Casey shrugged, indicating she was playing devil's advocate.

Carletti swivelled his head watching them go back and forth.

'We don't even know she's alive from the traffic cam,' Cullen said.

'She had to be when she got in. Who hands over a corpse and expects some other guy to just drive off with it?'

'If she overdosed on something, he might not have even known.' Cullen sat up. 'Could be she was alive when he put her in the car and then she went downhill.'

'We checked the hospitals,' Casey said.

'Then Bell panicked and dumped her somewhere, and it's on

both of them.' He glanced at Ray and then back to Casey. 'Since when did you jump to Parker's team anyway?'

'I didn't. I'm just playing both sides.'

Carletti held his hand up. 'Wait, do we even have a positive ID on the cam footage yet?'

'Yeah, Maggie Grace confirmed it's Tina,' Casey said.

He breathed out through his nose. 'The way I see it, we can't even be sure there's a crime here. Aside from the hooking, I mean. But if Bell's her pimp...'

'Tommy Grace was adamant she doesn't use a pimp.'

He slipped his foot off the desk and righted his chair. 'Sure, but she was right there in the guy's car. And didn't the brother also say he doesn't know about her business...?' He scooped up the bottle and poured Cullen a refill, then a double measure for himself. Then he motioned to the spare glass. 'You sure you don't want?'

Casey shook her head. 'I've got more I want to do after.'

Carletti gave her a disapproving smile and poured anyway. '*If* he's her pimp, he's got more reason to keep her alive than most anyone. She's money to him.' There was movement on the TV screen, the chief taking to the rostrum, and Carletti put his foot up on the desk and reclined again. 'An OD I could more likely believe – if it turns out she's not connected to the others.'

'And if she is?' Casey said. 'Does that make Parker more or less likely to be our guy?'

Cullen went to answer, but on screen Chief Hanrahan had started talking, and Carletti shot a finger out to cut him off, jacking the volume with the remote. Hanrahan had run HCPD for two years, and the media ate up his blarney-talking beat-cop-made-good act, so he was naturally the centre of attention; but Captain McTeague was in the shot as well, standing behind him to his right. Casey caught herself wondering again what caused the heat between him and Ray – if it was personal, or went as high as Hanrahan. McTeague outranked Ray, but he wasn't his commanding officer, so any dismissal would have to come from Hanrahan; but Ray still had his command, a fact she took as a positive sign for his prospects. There was a joke around the department, that when the chief spoke, McTeague's lips moved, but Casey had never bought into it; looking at him now, dark eyes staring hard at the back wall, he looked closer to an attack dog than a lapdog. But maybe the chief still had control of his leash.

'Good evening, thank you for your patience. I'll necessarily keep this short, I'm sure you can appreciate the operational reasons for that.'

Casey watched the chief as he got going. Everyone on the job had a story about him; Brian Hanrahan was first-generation Irish, a hint of it lingering in his accent. His family had arrived in the fifties and those that'd heard him tell the story first hand said he made out like they'd come from dirt – as good as clinging to the side of a steamer across the Atlantic. The truth was more prosaic – his old man had been a dentist who made out well enough once they landed Stateside to wind up with his own practice. It wasn't like anyone could ever call the chief on it, so Hanrahan could spin his history any way he liked, without fear of being asked why he'd felt the need to bullshit. The going theory was that a rags-to-riches story, exemplifying the American Dream, had been his way of gaining acceptance as he came up through the ranks. Cullen had confidently told her that last part when Hanrahan was first made chief two years earlier, and it'd made her wonder how the hell Dave Cullen could claim insight into the workings of the boss man's mind.

'As you're aware, last night K9 units discovered human remains in scrubland between Ramona Boulevard and Ocean Road, in the Ramona Beach vicinity. This morning, two additional finds were made in the same proximity. The distance between the three is less than one mile.

'HCPD have, this evening, identified one of the deceased, and we are in the process of trying to contact the family. No further information will be made public until they've been notified...'

Casey sat up. 'Shit, they've got a name?' She looked at Ray, opening her hands.

'First I'm hearing. I told you they cut me out of this one.'

She pulled her phone out, not sure why. 'They can't ... Jesus Christ, they gotta share that with us.' She unlocked the screen, still thinking who she could ask. The only answer she could come up with was on the TV, standing right behind the chief. 'I gotta call McTeague.' She voiced the thought without thinking, Carletti shooting her an accusing look, like she was trying to go around him. He turned back to the screen before she could defend herself.

'...Investigations into the identity of the other two deceased are ongoing. A full search of the area is also ongoing, and upwards of fifty HCPD personnel have been involved in some capacity already. As any of you who've been on the scene will know, the terrain and the sheer size of the area in question makes for an exceptionally challenging set of circumstances, and we're also mindful of the impending storm forecast. The wellbeing of the officers involved in carrying out the search is a priority, so we will be continually monitoring the conditions, with a view to maintaining operations for as long as is safely possible.'

'Waste of time,' Ray said. 'Excuses – like it's gonna stop them hammering us when they have to suspend everything tomorrow.'

'I'd like to take this opportunity to address a couple matters. First of all I want to stress that we are still evaluating every facet of this situation, and any reports otherwise – assigning motives or causes of death or anything else – are just conjecture. We are aware of local reports claiming these deaths are linked, and that they could be the work of a serial murderer, but we have not made any determination to that effect. Simply put, that is pure speculation at this stage. What I do want to do is to reassure residents of Ramona Beach and the surrounding communities that there is no cause for alarm, and to ask that if anybody has any information pertaining to this situation – no matter how insignificant it may seem to you – to contact HCPD. A dedicated hotline is now operational, and the number is on your screen. We'd particularly like to speak to anyone who might've seen a vehicle loitering along Ramona Boulevard, especially at night. Get in touch, we'll take it from there.' He adjusted the mic. 'I'll take a couple questions at this time.'

He picked out Andy Shafer from the *Herald-Dispatch*, his usual go-to when he wanted a softball. Shafer asked for more details about the identities of the deceased. 'I won't release anything more on that right now, Andy.' He pointed again. 'Yes?'

He gave non-answers to two more reporters, enough to show he wasn't shutting the media down, then turned to go. The pack continued shouting questions, and one caught Casey's ear: 'Chief, is this connected to the young woman who disappeared from Ramona Beach two nights ago?'

Hanrahan didn't look back, walking off the podium flanked by McTeague and a suit from the county executive's office.

Cullen made a clicking sound with his tongue, eyes on Carletti who was still watching the screen. It flicked back to a newsreader in-studio and he used the remote to mute him.

Cullen drank off the last of his whiskey, set his glass down next to Casey's, untouched. 'I should get home.'

Carletti wheeled around and winked at him. 'Better use some mouthwash before you do.'

He laughed, but it was forced. 'Luisa's not like that, she understands.'

'She does? So how come you were bitching at me last week when she wouldn't let you go drinking on payday?' Carletti said.

'I wasn't bitching.' Cullen smiled, shot a half-glance at Casey. His cheeks went red. 'That was just me feeling sorry for myself.'

'Sure.' Carletti looked at him through his eyebrows. 'We all know who's in charge over there. Good job too, seeing how she's the brains.'

'Only reason she doesn't like me going drinking is because you're such a degenerate.'

Carletti pointed his thumbs at himself in mock indignation. 'Me? How dare you speak of me in such a fashion. I'll bust your ass back down to patrol, son.' He was fighting off a laugh as he said it.

'What was that supposed to be?' Casey said. 'Like, a British accent?'

Carletti tipped his chair. 'Yeah. Makes me sound more authoritative, huh?'

Casey made a *what are you smoking?* face.

'This guy...' Cullen jangled his keys. 'Anyway – tomorrow, bright and early.'

Casey held her hand up to wave him off.

'Not thirsty?' Ray said when he was gone.

'Nah, I just wanna keep a clear head.'

He saluted her with a tip of his glass. 'I bet you were conscientious even as a kid.'

She smiled, looking down. 'My mom was that way. Comes from her.'

'She did a good job. You miss her, huh?'

His eyes already had that shine to them. Usually she liked it when the drink brought out his paternal side, but right now, sober, all she could think about was how fast she could get back to her work.

He misread her hesitation. 'Sorry, dumb question. Of course you do.'

'No, it's ... Yeah, sure.' She pushed her hair behind her ear. 'Listen, what I said earlier, about calling McTeague – I didn't mean anything by it.'

He tilted his head, frowning. 'Come on, Big. I know you better than that.'

She stood up, flattening her jacket. 'Okay then. So we're good?'

He gave her the thumbs-up. 'Keep doing what you're doing, kid. We'll all be answering to you one day.'

She looked down to hide the goofball smile spreading across her face, the one that broke out when pride and embarrassment and recognition met. 'Now I know you're drunk.'

'I mean it. I'm proud of you, and I'll tell you something else for free: Mrs Wray was too.'

He'd met Angela Wray multiple times, and he'd stood

behind Casey at her funeral three years ago – a favour Casey had asked and Ray had agreed to without hesitation. The fact he still referred to her as Mrs Wray was a mark of respect that went a long way. 'Well, maybe. She had bad judgement. That's why she liked you.'

He laughed as she walked out. But even hearing it didn't stop her feeling unsettled; the nagging sense she'd dug herself into a hole with the McTeague line, and then kept digging. She closed her eyes and took a breath. Then she took out her phone and dialled his number, using the bad adrenaline for courage before it wore off.

It went straight to voicemail so she left a message asking him to call her, then sent him a text as well. She dropped her cell next to her keyboard, looking at it like she couldn't quite believe what she'd done. Demanding answers from Robbie McTeague – hard to imagine even a week ago.

A few minutes later, Ray came out of his office with his coat and bag, heading for the stairs. He stopped by the edge of her desk. 'I want you out of here before that storm hits, hear me?'

She smiled up at him. 'Sure thing.'

'I mean it. You're tired, you're stretched, I don't want you driving home in that weather.'

She nodded. 'I swear.'

He kept looking at her, like he was checking for truthfulness, then tapped the edge of her desk. 'Okay. Until tomorrow.'

She watched him go and went back to her screen. She ran a check on Michael Patrick Bell, but there was nothing extra on the system beyond the information Billy had already dug up. She switched to Google and searched the name, but it came back with dozens of results, so she switched to image search instead and scrolled through four pages of results, but his face wasn't among them. She tried Facebook, Twitter and even

Instagram, but there was no trace of him there either. Unsurprising for a forty-something ex-con. But seeing the Instagram logo made her think about Tinder. She'd never used it herself – her love life had been on life support so long it'd take more than an app to resuscitate it – and she made a note to speak to one of the cybercrime techs tomorrow about getting a look at Tina's account.

Her cell phone rang. She reached for it, expecting McTeague, but hesitated when she saw instead it was a blocked number. She looked around the empty office, her ringtone shrill in the silence.

She stood up gripping her cell, checking the doorway into the office, feeling dumb when there was no one there. Still she felt acutely vulnerable, logic giving way to fear at the thought whoever was targeting her knew when she was alone. She pressed *Accept* and answered without saying anything.

Silence. Then the sound of someone breathing. The rage welled up in her chest—

'Hello?' It was a woman's voice. Hesitant, uncertain.

'Hello? Who's this?'

'I'm looking for ... I need to speak to Casey Wray, is that you?'

'Yeah, this is Casey, who am I speaking to?'

'My name's Tina Grace.'

Casey turned around on the spot, reaching for something to say.

'*Hello?*'

'Yeah, hi, I'm here. Tina ... Tina, where are you right now?'

'You've been looking for me, right?'

'Yeah, I ... How did you get this number?'

'Look, I just wanted to tell you that I'm okay.' She spoke

quickly, in a monotone, like she'd been practising what she would say. 'I'm safe and I'm sorry for worrying people, but I had to get away.'

'Get away? Why? From what?'

'I don't wanna get into it.'

'Have you ... have you contacted your family?'

'No. I wanted to ask you to talk to my mom for me. I can't ... If I call her, she'll try and get me to come back and I can't deal with it.'

'Tina, are you in danger? Is someone threatening you? If you are, I can help you. I'll come pick you up myself, right now, if you need help.'

'No, no, I'm okay. I'm out now, I'm okay.'

Casey picked up a pen and wrote down the time and date of the call on her pad – redundant, but something to do with her hands. 'Okay, I get that, but ... with the call you made, the circumstances – it would really help me to know why you disappeared that way. And also to confirm you're safe. If you would meet with me, or just stop by any police department...'

'I don't need any help, I just want to be left alone. I called you because I thought you'd listen and you could explain to my mom.'

'I really think she'd appreciate hearing from you direct. If you can't call her, can you send her a text or even an email?'

She went quiet, just her breathing on the line. In the background, the rush of traffic – but faint, like she was outdoors but distant from the street.

'Tina?'

'I have to go.'

'Listen, hold on. I need to confirm who I'm talking to. Can you tell me your mom's name?'

'What?'

'I need to know you are who you say you are.'

She sighed, but she sounded exhausted rather than irritated. 'Margaret Grace.'

'Do you have any other family?'

'You know I do.'

'I need you to work with me on this.'

Another sigh. Then, quieter: 'My brother.'

'Uh-huh...?'

'Tommy. My brother is Tommy.'

'Okay. And what about the night you left – were you with anyone?'

'I was with a man.'

'Uh-huh, what's his name?'

'Jon Parker.'

'What were you wearing?'

'What the hell?'

'Please.'

'Like, a black top and a short black skirt. They're in the garbage now.'

Casey scrambled for something else only Tina would know. 'My last question. What's on the living-room wall in your apartment?'

'My TV?'

'Anything else?'

'This is crazy ... My pictures you mean? The collage? That thing's so ugly, I meant to trash it years ago.'

Casey breathed in slow, the lines on her pad blurring as she tried to process it all. It seemed too good to be true. 'What happened, Tina? Why'd you run?'

'I don't...' Her voice was shaky, the emotions she was

bottling up starting to fight their way out. 'Please, I can't talk about it.'

'Why not? What are you scared of?'

She was quiet a second. When she spoke again, she didn't answer the question. 'My mom, is she...? How's she doing?'

'She's worried. Really worried. I know it would make a big difference if you would just—'

'I can't.'

'Give me something. Help me understand what happened to you?'

'I gotta go. Talk to my mom for me. Please.'

The line went dead.

Halfway home, Casey realised she'd made a mistake.

The freezing rain that'd been falling all day had been replaced by snow, pelting the car as she drove. Straight after the call from the woman claiming to be Tina Grace, she'd contacted her cell provider to request a trace, texting Cullen to update him while she was on hold. She'd been bounced around three advisors before finally reaching a supervisor who said she'd look into it and to call back in the morning. By the time Casey had everything wrapped up, she'd lost another forty-five minutes, and Storm Daisy was closing in.

The conditions on the expressway were blizzard-like, visibility cut to almost nothing. Traffic moved at a stop-start crawl, the WFKA reporter on the radio talking about multiple wrecks due to the conditions. Cullen must've picked up her message about the call because he texted back, *Holy shit...*

The jam meant it was past 11pm by the time Casey made it

back to Rockport Gables. Turning onto her street, the wind was driving the snow with such ferocity that she couldn't make out the end of the block, her bungalow just beyond.

In her head, she was still tussling with the call. She so badly wanted to believe it was her; that in defiance of the odds and all expectations, Tina Grace had made it off the beaches in the dead of night and fled. If she had, it left any number of questions to answer, but at least it would mean the young woman Casey saw in her mind – vibrant, optimistic, determined – was still alive, and not a corpse waiting for them in the waterlogged fringes of Black Reed Bay. A ghost, brought back from the dead...

Casey slammed on the brakes. The car stopped just in time. Right in front of her a downed power line was blocking the street. The pole itself was at a forty-five-degree angle, but the tangle of lines it supported hung almost to ground level. Casey screwed her eyes shut, seeing her bed speeding off into the distance. 'Goddammit.'

When she opened them again, a pair of high beams lit up her rearview. Two blinding spots in the mirror, approaching slowly. Casey flicked on her emergency lights; as she turned around to look, her cell phone rang, startling her.

A blocked number again. She grabbed it up, thinking Tina. 'Hello?'

Silence. She glanced in the mirror again, the headlights coming closer still. 'Hello? Tina?' She reached out, found the button to lock the doors.

A rustling sound came down the line, then the sound of someone breathing. Heavy, a man.

'Who the fuck is this?'

The breathing continued. Then a voice. 'Tina Grace is dead.'

Distorted, as before, but guttural and measured. 'Tina Grace is DEAD.'

The headlights pulled up right behind her, some make of pickup – big, close, penning her in. Casey turned all the way around in her seat, could only make out the driver's silhouette.

His hand to his ear, as if he was holding a phone.

She popped the console and pulled her gun from its holster. 'I'm getting real sick of this shit. Answer me, motherfucker, who are you?'

Dead silence. Then the screaming started. One voice, then ten, then a thousand. Louder than before, or at least it felt that way, trapped in the dark, alone in the storm. Casey hit disconnect and stuffed the cell in her pocket, shakes rattling her whole body. It rang again immediately, the sound tearing through the car. She didn't answer, checked back again, the driver behind still holding his hand to his ear. She threw her door open and stepped out into the maelstrom.

The snow was hard and icy, biting at her face and eyes. The wind was kicking up powder off the ground as fast as it brought more down, so much that the truck, its headlights, were the only thing in Casey's world now. She aimed at the driver's side as she inched towards it. 'POLICE.' The storm snatched the word and dragged it away as soon as it left her mouth. She could feel her phone vibrating in her pocket again.

The driver didn't move. She inched closer, the pickup's engine growling at her. 'POLICE.' Futile, no way he could hear her even if—

His door opened.

Casey was eight feet away. She inched around in an arc, until she could just make out his face in profile. White male, thirty to fifty, wearing a baseball cap.

'POLICE. HANDS ON THE WHEEL.'

The man complied, the rest of him a statue as he slowly turned his head to look at her. His eyes flicked between the gun and Casey. Gaunt, shellshocked. 'Ma'am, what the hell?'

'Who are you?'

'Kurt Sorversen.'

'Where's your cell phone?'

He nodded his head, a tiny movement. 'On the seat. You want it, it's all yours...'

'Who're you calling?'

'The cops,' he said, bewildered. 'About the power line.'

'Pass it to me. Using one hand only.'

He reached over without breaking eye contact, as if she might shoot as soon as he did. Eventually his fingers searched it out and he held it out to her.

Casey snatched it from his hand, brought it up so she could see the screen and the man at the same time.

911.

She lowered her weapon. *Shit.*

'Ma'am? What'd I do?'


## CHAPTER 15


Storm Daisy punched above her weight.

Downgraded overnight from a three ('major') to a two ('significant') on the NESIS scale, she nevertheless dumped four inches of snow on Rockport by dawn. Although the worst was over, it was still falling as Casey drove to the precinct – if falling was the right word for the horizontal drifts coming at her windshield. She had the radio tuned to WFKA, and the storm and its impact sucked up most all the airtime; reports were coming in of power outages all over town, county-wide travel disruption, and two deaths attributed to the conditions already. The deaths aside, none of it was news to Casey. The county executive's office had issued an advisory for people to stay home unless travel was absolutely necessary. The search on Ramona Beach would be stood down until further notice, no question.

The last she saw of Kurt Sorversen, he was pulling a three-point turn to get away from her as fast as the storm would allow. She'd sent him off with an apology, rating it fifty-fifty whether he'd make a complaint against her. She'd hung around until patrol showed up to secure the area around the downed power line, then taken a three-block detour to get back home, finally crawling through the door at midnight. The power was out, but she was too beat to care. She'd burrowed under the comforter fully clothed, her holster in reach on the bedside table.

Now she was the first to her desk this morning, the office cold even with the heat cranked up. Even before she sat down, she dialled her mobile carrier to follow up on the trace on Tina's call. The supervisor from the night before had promised to expedite the request, and it turned out she was good to her word. Casey went to the coffee machine while she was on hold, and the music cut out just as her coffee dispensed. An advisor took her reference number and, after another wait, came back with answers. The call had been made from a payphone seven hundred miles away in Knoxville, Tennessee, from an address that Google Maps revealed to be on the edge of downtown – 'That's as much as I can tell you right now, Detective. Hope it's some help.'

She'd spent all night agonising about fucking phone calls. Too keyed up to sleep, she teethed on who was targeting her, and why. Plenty of high-profile serial killers taunted the cops and their victims' families – Zodiac, BTK, more – and now she had to consider that was the case here too. She explained to the advisor about the calls, requesting an urgent trace on their origin too. The woman promised to come back to her as soon as she could.

When she finished with the phone company, Casey's thoughts turned to Maggie Grace again, and whether or not to tell her about the caller purporting to be her daughter. What was worse, false hope, or none? It seemed unthinkable someone would impersonate Tina, but the job had shown her the worst depths of the human condition, and there were some fucked-up humans out there. The fact the woman had referred to her mother as 'Margaret' was a red flag; news reports about the case referred to her by her formal name, but Casey had never heard anyone in real life call her anything but Maggie. But it was the Knoxville element made her the most doubtful; Tina Grace had no known connections to the area, or to Tennessee at all, and even allowing for the circumstances of her disappearance, it seemed an unlikely place for a woman who'd barely left Rockport to suddenly show up.

Casey opened an email from Billy D, reporting back on the contents of Tina's email account. She skimmed through it: no activity since she'd gone missing, nothing in her inbox that pertained to the case. He'd been through her sent and deleted items, found the same heap of nothing – not even a mention of her escort work. He'd made one additional comment at the bottom:

> 'Only thing that stood out was that she was in contact
> with the father – did you know that? Understood he was

off the scene? But there's a thread that started with him emailing her, looks like out of the blue, and she replied a couple times over a few months last year. I've attached the email chain I'm talking about. B.'

Casey opened the attachment and read through it. The dad was a Nathan Grace, seemed like he was living in the Houston area nowadays. His first email to Tina was short, hesitant – an apology for not contacting her before now, a brief explanation that he'd given up alcohol and with encouragement from his counsellor was trying to right some past wrongs – one of them being walking out on his family. In his words:

> 'I'm not trying to barge back into your life, and I have no expectations of your response, but I wanted you to know I'm not the man I was all them years ago, and I'd like the chance to get to know the woman my daughter became, even if it's just over email.'

Tina hadn't responded for four weeks, but when she had, it was to say that she was glad to know he was doing okay, and that maybe they could talk some time. They'd exchanged a couple more replies after that – Tina telling him a little about Tommy and Maggie, about her job at Bronsons, her apartment, him talking about his work on the ship canal, how he'd joined a local church and that was what prompted him to make changes in his life. After that, the conversation had apparently petered out.

Casey tapped out an email to Nathan Grace, supplying her contact details and explaining that Tina was missing, and asking him to get in touch urgently.

Her desk line rang and she grabbed it. 'Casey Wray.'

'Wray, it's Robbie McTeague.'

The first time she'd spoken to him on the phone, his voice deeper and quieter than in person. 'Captain.'

'You left me a message last night.'

'Yeah, I watched the chief's briefing on the TV. We've got an ID on one of the bodies?'

'Correct.'

'Who is she?'

'We're keeping that information close for now.'

'I get that, but...'

'But?'

'I can't give you what you need if I can only see half the picture.'

'I understand that, Detective. You'll be brought into the loop in due course.'

'Sir, with respect, you wanted to know if the cases are connected. I need to know to be able to answer that.'

'Lyman and his guys are on it. It's not your missing girl, and that's your only concern. Where are you with that anyway?'

She switched ears, trying to regroup. 'We've established Tina Grace left the beaches that night and we're trying to trace the driver of the vehicle she was in.'

'I told you everything comes through me, why am I just now hearing about this?'

'I called you last night.'

He grunted, unimpressed. 'Cute. Was she alive?'

'Unknown. We picked her up on a traffic cam, she's in the front passenger seat with her eyes shut.'

'Who's the driver?'

'Michael Patrick Bell, white male, forty-two. Did a stretch for pimping.'

He was silent a moment, digesting the information. 'Your girl's a sex worker?'

'According to her brother, yes, sir.'

He said something under his breath, agitated now, and she made a leap she should have made sooner.

'Your vic was a sex worker too?'

He paused before he answered. 'Yeah. To the surprise of no one.'

'So can I get her name now?'

'It's a connection or a coincidence, not a pattern so far. If we establish a link to your girl, you'll be first to know.' He spoke away from the receiver, trying to catch someone's attention, then came back on the line. 'Do we know Bell? His name come up before now?'

'No, sir.'

'You talked to him yet?'

'We went by his address, but according to his neighbours he moved out weeks ago. I've got a request in with patrol for information on his whereabouts, KAs, family etc.'

'I'll talk to them, you'll get a call in the next ten minutes. I want to know when you've found him, and you don't talk to him without me in the room. Understood?'

'Yes, sir. One other thing.'

'Go.'

'Last night I had a call from a woman claiming to be my misper. Tina Grace.'

He stopped mid-breath. 'Genuine?'

'Unknown. But she did answer some personal questions correctly...'

'Did you trace it?'

'I spoke with the carrier already – they can only tell me it came from Knoxville.'

'As in, Tennessee?' There was an incredulous note in his voice as he said it, and Casey suddenly felt embarrassed for not sounding more cynical in telling him.

'Yeah. I've put a request in with Knoxville PD for any video covering the immediate area around the payphone, but even if there is some, it's anyone's guess if she'll show up in it.'

'Does the woman have any connections there?'

'None that we know of, sir. Her mom says she's barely ever left Rockport.'

An uncomfortable silence stretched. Then: 'Until I hear something more compelling, I'm not buying it. Carry on as before. If it was her, she's a possible witness. But Bell's the last link in the chain that we know of, I want him found as a priority.'

'Yes, sir.'

'Anything else?'

She stared hard at the wall, her vision slipping out of focus. 'No, sir.'

'Stay by your phone.'

Whatever else McTeague was, he was good to his word: the call came in less than eight.

'Casey Wray.'

'Yeah, Wray, this is Cal Morton over at the Second. My sergeant told me to call you about Mike Bell?'

'Hey, thanks.'

'What'd he do? Sarge said he heard the request came down from Captain McTeague himself?'

'Yeah, I'm working on something tangential to the captain's case, feels weird to have some pull for once.'

Morton didn't laugh, missing the sarcasm. 'I don't get that. Bell's your definition of small time.'

'You arrested him a few years back?'

'Yeah, but we just brought him in. He got swept up in a bust on this "modelling" agency that was a front for hookers. They had a glossy website to make the thing look legit to lure the dopes in. Boys, girls, straight, queer, anything and everything. Bell was a driver for them – take them to and from, wait around while they were with the johns.'

'Wait, so he wasn't a pimp in his own right?'

'Him? Nah. When we grabbed him he was sitting in his car, playing online poker on his phone.'

Casey scribbled notes and questions as fast as she could, her hand not keeping up with her brain. 'What was the name of the agency?'

'Executive Elite Talent. Corny as hell.'

'Did they shut it down?'

'I guess. Figure two more opened up by the end of the day though.' Morton coughed up a small laugh, like it was all hopeless.

'I mean did they get the people at the top? Who was running it?'

'I'd have to go back to the file, I don't remember the names off the top of my head.'

'Could you look it up for me? I wouldn't ask but it's important.'

'Yeah, sure, I'll get them to you.'

Her brain was running so far ahead she started to thank him to get him off the line.

'Hold up, I thought you wanted to know how to find Bell?'

'Wait, sorry, yeah. You know where he is?'

'Nah, he dropped outta sight when he got out. But he had an on-off girlfriend lived in Cooperton, you could start there.'

'You have the address?'

'1245 West Fortieth Street. Elena A-S-I-M-O-V-I-C.'

'Thanks, Morton, I owe you a beer.'

'You and everyone else.'

Cullen pushed his way through the doors, brushing snow off the shoulders of his overcoat. Casey jumped out of her seat, signalling for him to turn around. 'Don't take that off, we're outta here.'


# CHAPTER 16


'So what did she say?' Cullen said as they pulled out of the precinct. 'Last night?'

Casey recounted the call from the woman purporting to be Tina Grace.

'Damn,' Cullen said when she'd finished. 'How did she get your number?'

'Tina?'

'Yeah.'

'That another way of saying you think it was bogus?'

'No, I'm just thinking out loud.' He was quiet a moment, something more coming. 'But Knoxville...'

'I know, I know, I got the same from McTeague this morning.'

'You gotta admit it sounds weird.' Cullen braked, pulling up at a red light in heavy traffic.

'Sure. But she knew what was on the apartment wall...'

'Not exactly conclusive – there's a picture of it on her Insta.'

Casey looked over at him. 'There is?'

He was already nodding.

'She said her mom's name was Margaret too,' Casey said quietly, despondency creeping into her voice.

Cullen opened his hands on the wheel. 'And like I say, how'd she get your number?'

'It's on the misper appeal page on the website.'

'So she runs all the way to Knoxville and then decides to Google her own case?'

'Sure, maybe. Maybe she's still in touch with one of her friends. They could've told her.'

'Or the boyfriend? Brian?'

'Can't see it,' Casey said. 'I think he's the victim he acts like – but I'd still like to know if he found out about her side hustle.'

'Why, what's the scenario there? Ex-con Bell takes her home innocently and then Brian Walton just happens to show up and kill her the same night?'

'No, not that. Just that if she was freaking out because Walton had found out what she was doing somehow, maybe that's what set the table for the whole thing. She's panicking about him knowing, maybe takes too much of something to ride it out ... And then Bell – or Jon Parker – came on too strong trying to calm her down. We've seen that kinda shit before.'

Cullen grimaced, closing one eye. 'I just don't buy her being afraid of someone like Brian Walton. Not if she's running with people like Bell.'

'I know.'

The lights changed and they started moving again at last.

'Well, anyway,' Casey said, 'I emailed Ray before you got in this morning, see if there's anything we can do on the Knoxville end.' She looked at Cullen sidelong, his eyebrows raised, betraying his scepticism. 'We gotta try, right?'

The ride should've taken twenty-five minutes but it was nearly double that in the conditions. The snow had given way to sleet and the wind dropped some, and it meant all but the busiest streets were coated in a slick grey slush.

Elena Asimovic's address was the bottom level of a townhouse on a street of mismatched buildings; different heights and designs, some set further back from the kerb, the whole jumble only held together by the tangle of power lines strung haphazard between them. There was a large food mart opposite, the view from Asimovic's house of its windowless brown flank. Like looking out on a prison. They circled the block to check for Bell's Ford Escape, but came up empty.

The sidewalk had been shovelled, but not the steps leading up to the door, and they picked their way up them, Casey feeling the cold seeping through her boots. Cullen rang the bell and they heard a lazy chime from inside, as if the battery was dying.

A man opened up. Casey tensed, reaching for her holster until she realised it wasn't Bell. The man was short but heavyset, hair clipped to the skull to mask the fact he was balding. A scraggly goatee covered his mouth, flecks of grey hairs among the red. Casey felt her adrenaline taper off at the prospect of another false start. 'Detectives Wray and Cullen, sir, we're looking for Elena Asimovic?'

'Yeah?'

Casey squinted at him, spoke slower. 'Does she live here?'

He didn't answer at first, and suddenly there was hope again. 'Yeah, but ... Yeah.'

'She home?' Cullen said.

'What you want her for?'

'We'll discuss that with her.'

He ran his hand over his head and glanced behind as a woman came down the stairs and stopped in the hallway. Casey looked past the man and called over his shoulder. 'Elena Asimovic?'

She tilted her head slightly, started coming towards them. She was petite with mousey-brown hair that she wore in a loose ponytail, a mole above her right eye. She joined the man on the doorstep, him slipping his arm around her waist. 'Yes?'

'HCPD, ma'am, we're trying to locate Michael Patrick Bell, we were told you might be able to help?'

'We broke up a long time ago. I don't see him anymore.'

Her accent was pure Rockport, and Casey felt like an idiot for assuming she'd be foreign just because of the name. 'I understand that, ma'am. But could you point us in the right direction? Family, close friends, colleagues?'

Asimovic rolled her lips over her teeth, thinking about it, then shook her head – hesitant at first, then more certain. 'He's from Florida, and whatever family he had were down there. He never really spoke about them. Not to me, anyway.'

'Okay, something else, maybe. He have any friends? A favourite bar?'

She shook her head again, not even thinking about it this time. 'He's been out of my life a long time.'

'I understand that, ma'am, but even a name from back then would help. If you're worried about getting him in trouble...'

'He never needed my help doing that.'

Casey pulled a sad smile – *I hear ya*. She looked at Cullen and back at Asimovic. 'Look, if we can just talk to him, it would really help us out. We're urgently trying to find a missing young woman. Are you sure there's nothing...'

'I'm sure.'

'What about a telephone number?'

'That piece of shit? I deleted it. Here.' She held out her cell phone. 'Check it if you want.'

Casey nodded slowly. 'That's not necessary.' She turned to the man. 'Can I have your name please, sir?'

'Brent Hatcher.'

'You have some ID?'

He took a wallet out of his back pocket and produced his licence.

Casey examined it and gave it back. Then she took out her business card and offered it to Asimovic. She didn't reach for it, so Casey pressed it gently into her hand. 'Please, just have a think. Call me on that number anytime.'

Brent Hatcher was watching them as they climbed back into the car, but Asimovic kept her eyes on the card in her fingers.

Cullen made a U-turn and Casey looked up at Asimovic's door as they passed it on the way out.

'You think she's scared of him?' Cullen said.

'Who? The boyfriend or Bell?'

'The boyfriend.'

'I don't know.' She took a last look back and then faced front, rubbing her hands for warmth.

'Seemed like she was keeping something back.'

'Yeah. Maybe old Brent's got a thing about her ex – or he's just a dumbass who's watched too many cop shows. She might open up when she's not around him.'

'You wanna stick around?'

She shook her head. 'The uniform from the Second is supposed to be coming back to me with the names of who Bell worked for.' She'd brought Cullen up to speed on Morton's call on the way over. Mention of it now made her check her phone. No messages. 'See if he comes up with the goods and if it helps any, and if not, we'll take another pass at Asimovic – try and get her on her own.'

'You ever think we could be wasting our time here? Y'know, if last night *was* genuine...'

'Trying not to. Anyway, McTeague says we push on, so I guess we push the fuck on.'

'McTeague? What does Ray say about that?'

'He doesn't know yet.'

He chuckled and glanced over at her, bobbing his head in mock bravado. 'Badass Big, gone rogue.'

She pulled a face, catching a glimpse of herself in the wing mirror. 'Gimme a break. Ray already thinks I've gone over to the other team.'

Cullen leaned over the wheel as he edged out at an intersection. 'It's not you he's mad at.'

'I know.'

'You notice how much he's drinking?'

Casey kept her eyes forward, steam billowing from a vent down the street. 'No. Can't say I have.'

'Come on, every night...? And hey, I'm not making any judgements – I would be too, with McTeague hanging a goddamn internal investigation on me.'

'He told you about that?'

'It came up.'

Casey chewed her thumbnail, a question mark suddenly appearing over her status as Ray's *consigliere*. 'What did you say?'

He did a double-take glancing at her. 'It's unreal, right? The fucking "Crackhead from Crimea" goes after a cop and the worst that happens to him, he gets his head bounced off the ground?'

'You were there, Ray's actions were "justified and proportionate", right?' She made air quotes around the words.

Cullen looked over at her before he answered. 'Sure. Of course.' He was quiet a second and then he scratched his nose.

She kept staring at him, waiting.

'What?' He looked over again. 'Zoltan Kuresev is the worst kind of lowlife, he should be on his knees every night thanking God it was Ray in the parking lot that day. Another cop might've killed him – you know it and I know it.'

He didn't say anything more after that, and Casey was too stung to probe any further, afraid she'd give herself away if she did. Ray had been specific in telling her not to talk to the others about the internal, so it hurt to learn she wasn't his only confidant – but she'd be damned before she'd let it show. It was a trait she'd had to develop to get by in the department, but one she now considered a weakness – forever prioritising appearing strong over her real feelings. In the early years, anything else would've seen her tagged as 'too emotional' for the bureau – code for 'too female'.

They drove in silence, only broken a few minutes later when Casey's phone rang. The call was long distance, an area code she didn't recognise.

'Casey Wray.'

'Miss Wray, this is Nathan Grace, you emailed me about my daughter Tina.'

'Mr Grace.' She glanced at Cullen, who shot her a *this should be interesting* look back. 'Yeah, yes, thank you for giving me a call.'

'You said Tina's missing? When did this happen?'

'She was last seen four days ago, sir. I know this is distressing news, I'm sorry to be the one to have to break it to you.'

'That's ... I mean y'all have any idea where she could've went?'

'Right now we really don't, sir, but we're following every lead we can.'

'What does Maggie say?'

'Mrs Grace is co-operating with the investigation, everyone's doing everything they can. One of the things she did was give us access to Tina's email account, and we saw that you made contact with her...'

'Yeah, I ... I made some changes in my life last year, that was a part of the process.'

'So I understand. What I wanted to know is if Tina had contacted you at all this week?'

'No. I haven't heard from her since ... I can't remember when she last emailed me, last year sometime.'

'We have your email correspondence. It seemed to kinda peter out. You didn't agree to speak on the telephone or anything like that?'

'No, we didn't get that far. I mean, I appreciated her even answering me in the first place, I wasn't about to push it and ask to talk to her. They told me you gotta take this stuff real slow; my counsellor said to let Tina set the pace she was comfortable with. She never suggested getting on the phone, so I didn't either. And then, I guess the conversation just fizzled. We went back and forth some about her life and my life, and then she either ran out of things to say or she lost interest. I can't blame her. I thought maybe I'd give it some time and then kick it up again. I guess...' He didn't finish the thought, a heavy regret palpable even from halfway across the country.

'Mr Grace, so I understand, did you try to make contact with Maggie Grace or your son Tommy?'

He took a deep breath before he answered. 'No, I did not.' Another breath. 'I know how that sounds with Tommy, but it's just ... It's what I said, they told me to take it one step at a time. It took a lot to work up the courage to email Tina, I wanted to see how that would've went first, take it from there but, when she was lukewarm ... It's tough, right? And don't get me wrong, I'm not asking for nobody's sympathy, I brought this on myself and I don't deserve nothing, I just ... Trying to make it right, that's all.'

'Sure, I get that. I was just surprised, because Mrs Grace told us at the outset there was no chance Tina would've got in contact with you.'

'I guess Tina never told her. Me and Maggie ... She's a good woman, a really good woman. But she can be fiercer than hell, and...' He huffed down the line, steadying himself. 'Honestly, I was worried she'd tell Tina not to talk to me if she found out, so I wasn't about to encourage it.'

'Okay. I understand.'

'So, I mean, what happens now? Y'all must have some idea where to look?'

'As I said at the outset, we're doing all we can, and I'll make sure you're notified if there are any significant breakthroughs. In the meantime, if you think of anything might be helpful, you know how to contact me.'

'Yeah, I do. I'm sorry I can't give you something more to go on. Is Tommy ... How's he doing?'

'He's okay, Mr Grace.'

'Yeah.' A pause, the sense he wanted advice she wasn't about to give. 'Yeah, okay. Thank you.'

Casey hung up and stared at the blank screen, the feeling like she could've said more, but it would've been out of turn. *Call your damn son.*

Cullen snapped her out of it. 'What'd he say?'

She gave him the headlines from the conversation.

'You look like something's bugging you?'

'Not really. He sounds like a guy just woke up on the wrong side of middle age and realised he's fucked his life up. No alarm bells. I'll have Houston PD check him out anyway.'

Cullen nodded, eyes on the traffic that was snarling as they came into downtown. Their progress slowed until they finally ground to a halt at the 2nd Street intersection, penned in between a UPS truck and a tanker. 'Try not to let this stuff get to you, huh?'

Casey looked down, a nod without conviction.

'I mean it,' Cullen said. 'You can only do what you can do. It's the hope that kills you.'

'I know,' Casey said, 'You're right.' Then she lifted her head again. 'But go back to what we were saying before; if the call was real, maybe there's someone in her circle knows where she is. Or at least knows she's still alive.'

'Okay. Maybe ... but there's no one giving me that impression yet.'

'Then we talk to all of them. I'll do it in my own damn time if I have to. We work on finding Bell at the same time.'

Cullen stuck his bottom lip out in approval. 'Goddamn, I love it when you get decisive.'

Casey looked over at him. 'You feed Shauna this morning?'

'Yeah, why?'

She pointed. 'You got milk on your shirt.'

## CHAPTER 17

As soon as Casey got to her desk, Jill Hart came over, papers in her hand. 'Phone records for you, Big. Jon Parker's calls for the last seven days, cell and home line. And the dump from the Ramona cell tower is here too, every number that pinged it in our timeframe. I've marked out the ones we can identify.'

'Nice work, thanks.' Casey scanned Parker's list, passing the other one to Cullen. 'The only call he made that night was to 911?'

Jill nodded. 'According to this.'

She looked over to Cullen. 'Anything?'

He was still reading as he spoke. 'A couple of the 911 callers, Tina's cell, one registered to a Patrick Ball—'

'Patrick Ball? Is that Bell? Using the world's dumbest fake name?'

'...And one registered to a Kevin Love.'

Casey scoffed but Cullen looked at her blank. 'Kevin Love plays for the Cavs in the NBA,' she said. 'He was an all-star once upon a time, gotta be another fake. What about Tommy Grace, he feature?'

Cullen flipped the page and looked through the rest of the list, but already shaking his head. 'Nope.'

Casey went around next to him, reading over his shoulder. Then she grabbed her phone. 'I got Love, you try Ball.'

She punched the number in, but the line was inactive. She looked up at Cullen and he shook his head. 'Dead.'

'Figures,' Casey said. She looked at Billy. 'Get the addresses for Love and Ball. Chances are they're both fake, but there's a good chance one of them is Bell, and he might just be dumb enough to have used a real address. And if they do turn out to be real people, we need to speak to them ten minutes ago.'

But the day was a bust on every front. Cal Morton, the patrolman who'd arrested Bell in 2015, called back with two names, the men behind the agency he'd worked driving girls for, Executive Elite Talent: Andreas Georgiou had died of pancreatic cancer while he was still in jail, but the other, Hunter Hanwell, was already out. Casey got hold of him, now the proprietor of two vape shops downtown, but he said he couldn't remember anyone called Tina Grace, wouldn't know Michael Patrick Bell if he walked past him, let alone where he was living now, and drew a blank on the name Jon Parker. 'I'm done with all that stuff.'

Cullen drafted in Billy D and Jill to make calls to Tina Grace's friends, working from the lists Brian Walton and Maggie Grace had supplied. They spoke to thirteen people between them, some they'd questioned previously, others for the first time. Eleven women and two men, all of whom denied having any contact with Tina since she'd disappeared.

Moreover, none of them could come up with a reason for why she'd be in Knoxville. Casey and Cullen had debated up front whether to ask questions around Tina's sex work – mindful that it wasn't the kind of side hustle many people would want exposed – but in the end they agreed its relevance trumped potential embarrassment.

Didn't matter.

All thirteen expressed surprise at learning about Tina's sideline, meaning none of them could shed any further light. The name Jon Parker meant nothing. Michael Bell ditto. Girls she escorted with, known associates in the business – no one could give them anything. Tina Grace's double life laid bare, and ever more enigmatic.

In the midst of the trawl, Ray had come by with another strikeout – this time from Knoxville PD. 'I heard back from the lieutenant down there I spoke with earlier. There's no direct video coverage of the payphone Tina Grace – or whoever was impersonating her – called from, and the nearest camera is two hundred yards away – and out of order. There's a food mart in between the two locations, with a surveillance cam in-store, so there is a chance it might've captured her walking past, but only if she approached the payphone from the right direction, was walking on the right side of the street to be visible through the store window ... and on and on. They're gonna send the footage across anyway when they have it.'

'Can we send Knoxville PD her picture and her description at least?'

'Already done.'

She pressed her lips, looking resigned. 'I should've figured. Thanks.'

'They're gonna share both with every precinct, and brief

their patrol units to be on the lookout for anyone that fits. But Case...'

'I know. It's a needle in a haystack.'

He tilted his head. 'My gut says it's a hoax. But if they turn up anything promising, you can go down there to follow it up yourself. Okay?' He patted her shoulder as he moved off.

Casey had tried to stave off her mounting sense of disappointment by chasing up the few leads she had left. She called Houston PD to have them check out Nathan Grace, Tina's father. His records check had already come back clear when she put the call in, Casey explaining the situation and asking if they knew anything about Tina's pops that hadn't made the computer. That came back as a negative, but she managed to persuade the detective on the other end of the line to send a patrol car out to his property anyway, to give him a once-over in person.

Next, Casey spoke with Tina's old boss at Bronsons, the small real-estate company where she'd been employed. He recalled Tina as quiet and hard-working, but prone to tardiness – he'd had to talk to her a couple times about her timekeeping. He reported no unusual or suspicious circumstances around her departure; she'd asked him for a pay rise, one that – in his words – she deserved but he just couldn't give, and two days later she told him she quit. She was popular enough with the other accounting employees, and in the office in general, but not what he'd describe as close to anyone. He wasn't sure if Tina had kept in touch with any of them, but he promised to ask around.

Then she and Cullen had made a second visit to Michael Bell's ex, Elena Asimovic. Cullen had run her and Brent Hatcher through the computer, but neither had priors or wants to their name, so they were on a begging trip anyway – but even that got shot down when there was no one home.

Cal Morton had supplied an additional two KAs of Michael Bell's from back in the day, so they made a try at running them down instead, but the bar where the three men used to go drinking together had shut down in the intervening years, and the trail died there.

And that was the third crash-and-burn in a row; prior to that they'd made visits to the registered addresses for 'Kevin Love' and 'Patrick Ball' – the mystery cell users on Ramona Beach – but it turned out the properties straight up didn't exist.

'What's the chances of two burner phones being active out there in the middle of the night and it's a coincidence?' Cullen said.

'One of them has to be Bell. I'd say fifty-fifty the other is Parker or Tommy – I'd buy either of them.' Casey rubbed her neck on one side. 'I goddamn hope it is, because otherwise we've got a total unknown out there.'

## CHAPTER 18

They were late getting to Cullen's place for dinner. Casey insisted on stopping to buy flowers for Luisa on the way, a small thank-you to add to the two children's books she'd already picked up as gifts for the girls.

Cullen climbed out first, and Casey rubbed her hands over her face to try and drum up some enthusiasm. She loved Luisa and the girls, but her head was in the case, and when she got that way, normal life felt like a distraction. But they were going to the effort of having her over, and the least that deserved was her best attempt at being good company.

Sienna ran into her arms as soon as she came through the door. 'Aunty Big!' She was in Minnie Mouse PJs and her hair was wet.

'Special occasion, so someone gets to stay up a little later than normal,' Luisa said, smiling at Sienna. Casey scooped her up and squeezed her, feeling like a dick for not looking forward to this more. 'When did you get so tall, huh?'

She spun around once and set her down, just as Luisa stepped in with her own hug. 'You look good, girl.'

Casey tilted her head with a frown. 'You can't lie to me, Lu, I'm a cop.' She winked and handed over the flowers. 'These are for you.'

'What? You didn't have to do that, they're beautiful.' Luisa took them with a grin and gave her a glass of wine in exchange. 'Sauvignon. Should be just about cold enough.'

Casey took the glass with an exaggerated show of relief, in that way that says *you're amazing*.

'Shauna's asleep, sorry she couldn't wait up for you guys.'

'Hey, don't worry about it.' She clinked glasses with Luisa and took a sip. 'Something smells good.'

Luisa put her own glass down and moved off again, always in motion. She spoke over her shoulder as she went to the kitchen. 'I figured you guys would be late, and you know how Dave gets when he's cooking in a rush, so I thought I'd throw something together. It's nearly ready, come sit down.'

'Mommy, I want to stay up a bit longer.'

Cullen picked her up and put her on his lap. 'Okay, just a little while, huh?'

Luisa called out from the kitchen. 'You can deal with her when she's cranky in the morning...'

Cullen tickled Sienna. 'You're not gonna be cranky for me, right? Right?'

She was laughing and nodding at the same time.

They sat down at the dining table, and Luisa reappeared with bowls piled with beef and chicken for tacos, then came back again with more bowls of toppings – avocado, lettuce, cheese, jalapenos, more. Casey got up belatedly to help carry stuff, but Luisa insisted she had it covered, making her marvel at the trouble she'd gone to, even with two kids to see to.

Casey wolfed down two tacos, both fully loaded. With an excited Sienna buzzing around the table and then standing on a chair, no one managed to finish a sentence. Casey gave her the book she'd brought, and she insisted on sitting on Casey's lap so she could read it to her while they were eating; Luisa and Cullen found it hilarious watching her trying to balance an impatient four-year-old against not setting a bad example by talking with her mouth full.

When they were done, Cullen picked up Sienna and hoisted her onto his hip. 'Bedtime, little lady.'

'Aww, daddddddyyyy...'

He brought her over to give Luisa and Casey a goodnight hug then took her up the stairs. Casey started stacking the dishes, but Luisa put her hand on her arm. 'You're the guest, sit.' She topped up her glass, then ferried them into the kitchen over Casey's protests.

Alone, Casey took out her cell phone and gazed at her inbox without really reading it, too distracted thinking about the case. Upstairs, she could hear Cullen and Sienna moving about, and then a cell phone ringing and Cullen answering.

Casey went back to her screen, but then came the sound of light footsteps on the stairs, and then Sienna poking her head around the door.

'Aren't you supposed to be in bed?' Casey said with a smile.

'Daddy's talking on the phone.' She rolled her eyes, like it happened all the time. 'I snuck out.'

Casey laughed, the kind of thing she would've done as a kid; her mom used to tell her she'd always fought bedtime, never once allowing herself to admit she was tired. 'How about if Aunty Big tucks you in?'

Sienna nodded, beaming.

Casey picked her up, Sienna wrapping her arms around her neck and laying her head on her shoulder. Those kiddie smells hit her – strawberry shampoo and freshly laundered PJs. All her mom had ever wanted was a grandchild, and it'd caused an unspoken rift between them in her last years, when it became obvious Casey didn't have that same impulse. It wasn't that she didn't want kids of her own, just that she put everything into the job. She barely found time to go to the grocery store; starting a family felt like something other people did.

She carried Sienna into her room and laid her down. From across the hallway, she could hear Cullen talking, his voice hushed as if he didn't want to disturb the kids.

'Okay, time to get some sleep now, huh?' Casey said.

Sienna yawned and said, 'I'm not tired.'

'What's your favourite animal?'

'A unicorn.'

'Huh.' Casey smiled. 'Okay. So I want you to close your eyes and imagine you and Shauna riding the most beautiful unicorns you ever saw, in a magical kingdom where you guys are the princesses. Then tomorrow morning, I want you to draw me a picture of it. Can you do that?'

Sienna lit up, then turned onto her side, snuggling up to her stuffed cat.

'Goodnight.' Casey stood up from her perch on the bed and went to leave the room. But as she came to the door, she caught a fragment of what Cullen was saying: '...and why's it fall on me to take care of it? This isn't just my problem.'

Casey lingered with her hand on the doorknob. His tone wasn't quite panic, but there was a desperation to it that hadn't been there over dinner.

Cullen was quiet again, the other person speaking. Then: 'Why does that sound like a goddamn threat?'

Casey's skin prickled. Secrets in the dark.

Another pause. Then: 'No? I guess we'll see, right?' And then a sound like he tossed the cell on the bed. '*Fuck.*' The expletive spoken to himself, barely audible.

Casey was about to show herself when she heard him go into the bathroom and lock the door.

She came out onto the landing silently. She couldn't hear any movement; she lingered a second and then decided it was best to give him time. She slipped downstairs again.

Luisa was in the kitchen, washing dishes. 'Hey, there you are. I thought you snuck out.'

'Dave's on the phone and Sienna did the sneaking. Figured I'd put her to bed.' She picked up a dishcloth. 'You know who he's talking to?' Casey picked up a dish to dry.

Luisa shook her head. 'Who knows?' She glanced at Casey's empty glass. 'Leave that, huh? He'll be back in a minute, lemme get you a refill.'

'C'mon, it's the least I can do. Thank you for dinner, really.'

Luisa made a *pfft* sound and pushed her refilled glass into her hand. 'Please. It's not often I get grown-up company these days, it's a pleasure. Dave doesn't count.'

Casey leaned on the counter, tiredness bringing on a gentle buzz that one glass of wine wouldn't normally deliver. 'You guys getting any sleep?'

Luisa grimaced. 'Sure. Last Tuesday I think we had a couple hours.' She took a sip from her own glass. 'It's tough because I get pissed at Dave for the hours he puts in, but it's not like he has a choice. And I get it, the job, but when you're tired ... Ah, you know what I mean. You just can't wait to hear that key turn in the lock at the end of the day.'

'I bet.'

'This case you guys are on – he seems pretty hung up on it. She's just a kid, huh?'

'Kinda. She's twenty-four, but ... I dunno, you see what it's done to her family...'

'Must be something about it, because I haven't seen Dave this uptight for a while. Couple years at least. It's bad timing, actually...'

Casey set her glass down, realising Luisa had been edging the conversation towards something more than small talk. 'In what way?'

She glanced over her shoulder towards the kitchen door, as if she was worried about being disturbed. 'The thing is ... Look, you know the job isn't compatible with family life. I know you both look up to Ray Carletti, but it cost him his wife and kids, and Dave can't see the parallels. There's already weeks where the girls don't see him for three or four days at a time.'

Casey opened her hands. 'Lu, I hear you, but you need to talk to him, not—'

'So that's the thing. We've been talking and ... Look, it's taken a while, but he's come around. There are security consultant positions he could walk into—'

'You're talking about him leaving the job?'

Luisa nodded, looking almost guilty. 'He could earn fifty percent more and work less hours. Office hours. I know it's not what you want to hear but...'

Casey looked away, trying to process it.

'The thing is, he's almost there, but the thing that's holding him back is that he feels like he'd be letting you guys down.' She came to stand next to her. 'You, the department, but Ray especially.'

'Ray?'

'Yeah, you know how close they are.'

A little stab of jealousy at hearing it; another knock to her perception of herself as Ray's protégé. Suddenly realising how much of her self-worth she'd attached to that status.

'...And so I was thinking ... if you could just tell him you'd understand, that he'd be doing the right thing – give him that last push. He'd listen to you, Case. It'd make all the difference to him, and I can't tell you what it would do for our family.'

Casey reached for her wine but put it down again. 'I mean ... But there are other ways, right? He could take the sergeant's exam, then he wouldn't need to work so much overtime, and...' She trailed off when she saw Luisa's expression. 'I'm just saying it feels kinda drastic. The other day he was talking about seeing out his twenty. It's only six more years...'

'That's his way of testing the water. When we first started talking about this, he was adamant he'd be in the job for life. It's been a process.'

Casey stared at the wall. 'I don't ... I don't know what to tell you, Lu. If it's what he wants, that's one thing, but if you're asking me to convince him...'

'He knows it's the right move. Deep down. For all of us. I know it wasn't his plan, but kids change things.' Luisa ran her fingers under her eyes, blotting a tear away. 'Anyway, would you just think about it for me? Please?'

Before she could answer, Cullen swept through the kitchen door. 'Fast asleep in record time. I'm winning at this dad shit.' He pointed his empty glass towards Luisa and the last of the Sauvignon. 'What're we talking about?'


# CHAPTER 19

Casey was first to the office again next morning, the snow and ice gone but the thaw leaving the town sodden and brittle.

She did a little circle around their desks, taking her coat off, pausing on Cullen's side to look at the photographs of Shauna and Sienna arranged behind his keyboard. She'd made her excuses at their place soon after Cullen had reappeared the night before, blaming it on too many late nights and early starts. Neither of them were buying it, but she left it for Luisa to deal with.

She hung her coat off her chair and pressed the message button to pick up the voicemail on her phone.

'Yeah, hey, this is Brent Hatcher. Look, uh, you came by my place yesterday to talk to Elena. About Mike Bell? She won't tell you, because she's still scared of that little prick, but I'll give you this for free. He's living at 803 Rose Terrace. She's got nothing to do with him anymore, don't go thinking that. She doesn't know I got this address or that I'm telling you. But he's a piece of shit, so I hope you can go lock him up.' The hang up was abrupt.

Casey was already out of her seat. She threw her coat on and dialled Cullen's cell heading for the exit.

When he answered she didn't even give him time to speak. 'Got a possible address for Michael Bell. Where you at?'

'I'm, uh ... I'm just leaving the house.'

'Shit.' She looked at her watch, trying to calculate the fastest route. 'Stay there, I'll pick you up on the way.' She hung up before he could argue, annoyed that he'd chosen today to be running late.

She went through the doors and started when she walked right into Ray. 'Jesus ... sorry, Boss, I'm in my own little world.'

'Where's the fire?' he said.

'Got a new address for Michael Bell – his ex's new boyfriend came through with it, trying to take him off the scene.'

'Okay ... Where's Dave? You're not going alone?'

'I'm picking him up on the ride over.'

Carletti nodded, going quiet a second as if he was thinking something.

'Look, uh – so you know, McTeague told me not to talk to Bell without him in the room.'

'What?' He shot her a look as he said it, suddenly engaged again, eyes crackling.

'I'm just telling you what he said.'

Carletti closed his eyes, breathing out. 'Look, I'm not ... Who the fuck does he think he is?' He held his hands up. 'You go, find the guy and bring him in. I'll see what I can do about McTeague.'

'Maybe we should pick our battles? I know he's all up in your shit but what would it matter if he sits in?'

'It matters to me. Now go, do your thing.'

It was past eight when Casey grabbed Cullen.

'I could've met you at the precinct,' he said, climbing in the passenger side.

'It's quicker this way.'

'So where we going?'

'803 Rose Terrace. It's past the hospital, you know it?'

He shook his head, staring out his window.

'What kept you this morning?' Casey said, irritation creeping into her voice.

'Don't – Jesus, I've already had Luisa on my back today. We had a fight, that's why I got held up. And now she's pissed at me.'

'About what?'

'Doesn't matter.' But he looked at her as if she already knew.

Casey glanced over, the silence building. 'She talked to me, but you know that already, right?'

He looked at his lap, nodding. 'That's what we were fighting about. I said she had no right to go to you behind my back.'

'She's worried about you, dumbass.'

'Don't take her side.'

'I'm not taking anyone's side. But I can see why she's thinking the way she is.'

'You're telling me I should quit? Is that what you're saying to me?'

'Take it easy, I'm not telling you anything.' She dug her fingers into the steering wheel; a conversation she didn't want to have anyway, and now it was going badly wrong. 'Do you want to quit? I mean, there's days I think...'

'It's not that straightforward.' It seemed like he was about to say something more, but he just kept staring through his window.

They rode in silence, Casey angry at him, angry at Lu for putting her in the middle, angry at herself for getting into it when she didn't need the distraction.

She took the expressway as far as the Rose Terrace exit.

'It was good to see your girls last night,' Casey said. 'Sienna's so grown up.'

Cullen was looking at his cell, brooding. 'Yeah.'

'So I tucked her in, at bedtime. That was cool. She said she snuck out, that you had to take a call?'

Cullen glanced up then, looking surprised. His lips made a shape before he said, 'Cute.' He went back to his screen. 'She didn't tell me that.'

Casey waited for him to offer something more, but he wouldn't even look up.

She followed Rose Terrace looking for the 800 block. It was early enough that the area was still quiet; there was trash scattered across the sidewalks, and boarded-up basement windows on either side. Most of the snow had melted, but a few dirty-brown piles dotted the kerb; a different part of town, but on the same lowly ladder rung as Maggie Grace's neighbourhood.

Finally they came to 803, Casey glancing as they went by without stopping. She spotted a Ford Escape parked a few yards further on and pulled up next to it. The licence plate was Michael Bell's. Cullen saw it at the same time. 'That's our boy.'

Casey set the brake and faced around to survey the house. It was a green clapboard bungalow, a single rotting step leading onto the narrow porch by the front door. There were two windows facing the street, a flimsy drape visible inside one, hanging limp off its rail. She couldn't see anything through the other one.

Cullen still had his eyes on the place when she turned to him. 'Look, if there's ever something you want to talk about, you know I'm here, right?'

'So you can tell me what my wife wants me to do some more?'

'Goddammit, Dave, I'm just trying to help.'

'Then quit taking her side.'

'Not everyone has someone in their life cares about them that way. The way Luisa does.'

'That doesn't mean she's always right.'

'Don't be an asshole—'

He slapped the dash. 'Drop it, Case. Let's just get this done.'

He opened his door and slipped out. He was already halfway across the street when Casey made it out her side.

There was no sign of movement as they approached the bungalow. The front yard was a mess of weeds, cigarette cartons and discarded liquor bottles, its mailbox lying on its side. The neighbouring house had windows boarded up with plywood. A chain-link fence separated the two, a low gate hanging off its hinges blocking access to the rear of Bell's. Casey nodded to it. 'I'll take the back. Thirty seconds.'

She crossed to the gate, ready to jump it, but there was no lock, so she slipped through and along the side passage, slowing up as she approached the back yard. She drew her gun and pressed herself against the wall, then peered around the corner of the bungalow.

The back yard was as overgrown as the front, as if no one had been out there for some time. She crept around the corner in silence, the back door coming into view, still no sign of movement. She pulled out her radio and whispered '*Set*.'

Then, from the front, she heard Cullen knock.

Silence. No sound of movement inside. Another knock, Cullen calling out this time. 'Hello?'

She waited a few seconds longer. Still nothing. Her adrenaline tapering, looking like they'd missed him. Already calculating their next move, his car out front, how long they could hang around waiting for him...

She heard the front door open. Then gunfire...

She pressed herself to the wall and whispered 'Shots fired, 803 Rose Terrace,' into her radio, then reached for the backdoor handle – unlocked. She threw it open, staying out of sight...

No sound.

Her heart exploding. She crouched low, stole a look inside: no one there.

She took a deep breath and stayed low, rounding the doorway. 'POLICE.'

A shot flew above her head.

Ten feet in front of her, a man cowering in a doorway off to the right. She fired twice, dropping him. He hit the floor heavy.

She kept her aim on him. 'POLICE. DROP YOUR WEAPON.'

She could hear her heartbeat. Complete silence apart from the sound of the blood rushing round her body. The image of her mother's face flashed through her mind for some reason. It felt like she was frozen in the crouch for hours. In reality it was maybe a second before she moved off again.

She was in a narrow galley kitchen, countertops either side of her, a stack of dirty plates, a half-smoked blunt in an ashtray. Strong smell of weed and old cooking oil. The shooter was motionless at the other end. She moved towards him, keeping her weapon trained on him but glancing elsewhere. 'Dave?'

As she stepped across the kitchen, the front door came into view ahead of her, at the other end of a short hallway. Through it, she saw Cullen on his back on the porch. 'DAVE?'

No response.

The shooter had blood coming from his chest and his neck. There was a gun in his hand, a stubby revolver, loosely gripped in his fingers. He wasn't moving. She stepped over his legs and ran to Cullen. 'Dave, talk to me...'

There was blood pouring from his forehead and his mouth, the latter smashed and disfigured. Red streams running down his skin and collecting on the rotting porch beneath him, before draining between the planks. He was motionless.

'No, no...'

She reached down, felt for a pulse. Couldn't find one. Tried again. Couldn't find one. Pressing harder, as if she could will it into being.

She pulled her radio and called it in, *officer down* coming from her lips but someone else saying it, no longer in charge of her own body, the sensation like she was watching this play out on a TV. *803 Rose Terrace.*

She swivelled on her knee, thinking she heard a sound behind her. The gunman where she'd left him, no signs of movement.

The dispatcher asked her something as she stood up, but Casey didn't answer. She silenced the radio and moved inside again, gun first.

*Police, is there anyone else in the house?*

Silence.

She moved to the shooter. Michael Patrick Bell – a positive

ID. He was on his side, between the hallway and the living room, a TV playing to an empty room beyond him. She touched his neck but already knew he was gone. Realising too late that the place was a house of death.

As she stood, a stream of rage and hate and violence rose through her chest, feeding an impulse to empty the rest of her clip into him. She might've done it if the urge for self-preservation hadn't taken over.

The two closed doors she'd passed in the hallway: she kicked the first one open – a bedroom, empty. The second: a bathroom, empty. Stank of piss.

Just her. The only one left alive. She wheeled around and ran outside to where Cullen had gone down. She dropped to her knees beside him and draped her jacket over his chest. She touched his cheek, the skin cold. There was a bullet hole in his forehead, a circular wound that was pouring blood. The second shot had caught him in the mouth, his top teeth shattered, his lip cleaved in two.

Tears spilled from her eyes. Trying to say his name but her voice catching in her throat.

She pulled out the radio again. *How long for the paramedics?* She couldn't hear the answer over the roar in her head.

*How long?*

*How fucking long?*

*How...*

## CHAPTER 20

The EMTs arrived shortly after the first uniforms. They took over CPR, cutting her adrift. They went to work double time, but their body language confirmed what she already knew – it was futile. Casey stood against the wall, a few feet back, watching their every movement. She didn't look away, didn't even want to blink, as if he wasn't really gone for as long as she could hold him in her eyes.

Then they stopped. It felt premature, as if there had to be something else to try, some miracle to be worked. Some scream to let loose.

She thought about Luisa and the girls and her whole body shook.

The patrol sergeant took possession of her gun. She didn't know the man, and it felt like an act of judgement. Her hands were smeared with blood – Bell's or Cullen's, or both.

The EMTs guided her to the back of the ambulance and gently asked her to sit down. She couldn't take her eyes off Cullen's body, discarded medical packaging and equipment littered all around him.

Two patrolmen were taping off the scene, and one of them kept glancing over at the corpse as he worked. The third or fourth time she caught him, she yelled at him to put his fucking eyes somewhere else. A paramedic appeared at her side then, trying to usher her inside the ambulance, urging her to take it easy. She refused, because she couldn't see Cullen from there, so they put a foil blanket around her shoulders and gave her a bottle of water.

A different EMT looked her over, even though she told him she was unhurt. He said her pulse and blood pressure were through the roof, but there was no sign of physical injury. The other uniform stood guard.

Ray showed up and found her there, his face completely white. He wrapped her up in his arms without a word passing between them.

Robbie McTeague arrived maybe ten minutes after Ray, bringing two other Special Investigations officers with him. He deployed them to direct the uniforms and came over to the ambulance where Casey was sitting. 'Wray ... Jesus Christ, I'm sorry.'

Carletti made a beeline as soon as he saw him. He stood next to her but said nothing, maybe the first time she'd known him lost for words.

'Are you hurt?' McTeague said.

She shook her head.

'We'll need to get you to the emergency room anyway. There's a counsellor on the way for you to talk to. Chief Hanrahan's aware, he's due here ASAP.' He jutted his bottom jaw out, mouth ajar. 'Is there anyone you need to call? Family, partner?'

She shook her head again.

McTeague glanced at Carletti like he wanted confirmation that was right. He turned back to her. 'I know this is tough, but there will be an investigation. I don't need to tell you not to say anything to anyone until—'

'She did nothing wrong,' Ray said.

'I'm not saying she did. It's standard procedure, you know that. There's a union rep on the way, we can wait for that, but I want you out of here before the media show up.'

'Have you told his family?' Casey said.

'The chief is contacting them.'

'I need to speak to them. His wife – I was with her last night. We had dinner at their place, he's got two girls, they'll—' A sob burst in her throat.

'The chief is taking care of it. There'll be time later.'

They took her clothes into evidence at the emergency room, leaving her in a hospital gown until replacements could be found for her to wear. They tested for the presence of drugs and alcohol in her system, and took a blood sample at the same time. The union rep reiterated that she shouldn't say a word to anyone about what had happened until they could get her a lawyer. She wanted to speak to Ray, but was told it wasn't appropriate; she hadn't seen him since the ambulance took her away. A counsellor came to talk with her, a round-faced woman whose name she forgot as soon as she heard it, but a stranger was the last person she wanted to confide in. The woman assured her that anything she said about the incident was protected under privilege. Standard procedure, all of it. All of it adding to her feeling that she'd done something wrong.

Every time she closed her eyes, she saw the two dead men. Her mind warped her recollection, making it that she was the one who'd shot Cullen, Bell a ghost who'd never really been there. She knew it was a lie, but the vision wouldn't leave her. The smell from inside Bell's bungalow kept coming back to her, blood and weed and piss, the death house a part of her now, its air infecting her. When the counsellor left, she was alone for the first time; she sank to the floor and sobbed.

A lawyer showed up, and made her talk through everything,

start to finish. He made her tell it twice, the first time uninterrupted, the second time peppering her with questions, and more follow-ups when she was through. Everything he asked seemed designed to emphasise her guilt: What were they doing directly before the incident? What was her mindset? Cullen's? How had they decided on their approach? Their tactics? Who had decided who should cover the front and the back?

It went on for hours before he said they were done. The lawyer offered no words of comfort or resolution, saying only that her rep would be in touch. All she wanted to hear was that it wasn't her fault, but he was never about to comment on that. After, the doctor signed her off for discharge, advising her not to be alone if she could help it. She didn't have the strength to admit she had no choice in the matter.

The union rep advised her that she'd have to take a cab home – that procedure meant the department couldn't send a uniform to give her a ride, to preclude the chance of her inadvertently saying something she shouldn't. She felt like they were cutting her adrift.

Back inside the house, she filled a glass of water and set it on the table untouched. She sat on the couch in the dark with her head between her knees. All cried out, the exhaustion was so profound it was physical; not tiredness but an actual pain, as if she'd been used as a punch bag for twelve straight hours.

Then she realised how selfish that sounded. That the pain was a gift, because it meant she was still alive. That she should've been the one to take the front, and if she had...

She picked up the phone and dialled, the call she'd been desperate to make, and the one which terrified her.

Her hands shook as she waited.

'Hello?' Luisa's voice. Ragged, talking through broken glass. The union rep told Casey at the hospital that Chief Hanrahan had informed the family.

'Lu, it's Casey.'

'Case...' A silent pause, as if she was steeling herself. 'Casey...'

'Lu, I'm sorry. I'm so sorry. He...' Her own voice broke, but the words kept spilling out of her. 'I tried to save him. I swear to God, I tried...'

'Case, what ... What the fuck happened?'

She wanted to tell her everything, every last detail. To at least let her have the last few minutes of her husband's life, as horrific as they were. 'I can't ... I'm so sorry, I'm not allowed to talk about it.'

'No, Case, don't do that. The chief said ... Hanrahan wouldn't tell me anything either. The union guy the same. Please...'

'There's an investigation. When it's done, I swear to God, I'll tell you everything you want to know—'

'I don't give a damn about an investigation. My husband's on a slab and no one will tell me why. This is you and me, Case, you have to tell me something.' Casey heard a woman's voice in the background telling her to try and be calm. 'No I will not be fucking calm. I have a right to know. "Killed in the line of duty" – as if that's supposed to be enough.'

Casey paused before she spoke again. 'Lu, is there someone there with you? For support?'

Luisa took a breath, then another, gathering herself. 'My mom.'

'Good, that's good. And ... the girls? How...?'

'Sienna's destroyed. Literally destroyed.'

The words smashed the oxygen out of Casey's lungs. An untapped reservoir of tears opened up.

Luisa spoke away from the phone: 'I'm okay, I'm okay.' Then: 'Casey?'

'I'm here.'

'I'm sorry, I know that you ... I didn't mean to...' She started crying before she could finish the sentence.

'It's okay.'

'Are you hurt? I mean did you get hurt too?'

'No, I...' *I killed him. I killed the guy who did it. I did it for all of us.* 'I got lucky.'

She heard a child start to wail in the background. A rushed whisper in Luisa's ear: 'It's Sienna again...'

'Case, I have to go, Sienna needs me.'

'Okay. If you need anything, at all...'

There was a pause, as if Luisa had thought of something she could do for her, and Casey held her breath.

'Get out of there, Case. The department, get out. Before it takes you too.'

Luisa hung up before she could respond.

The house was quiet and still around her, the darkness a shroud she wanted to smother her.


# CHAPTER 21


They placed Casey on administrative leave pending further evaluation. In the weeks that followed, they sent her to see the counsellor again and called her to headquarters for a formal interview. There was a shit-ton of use-of-force paperwork to complete. Her first time back in the department – a clarification session on her statements – every conversation started with 'I'm sorry' or 'how you doing?' Even Dana Torres, who'd called once a week to check in on her and keep her updated on the investigations, was suddenly hesitant and uncertain. No one said shit to her that she wanted to hear. How could they when she didn't even know what to say to herself?

She spent most of her time at home, an emptiness inside her nothing could touch. They gave her sleeping pills, but all they did was swap insomnia for anxiety. Booze made her lose her shit. She relived it every minute she was awake, and nothing she did could take her out of her own head; no respite from her thoughts. She called Luisa a couple times, leaving messages on her machine, but never got a call back. She spent whole nights saying sorry to Cullen's ghost, and she wanted someone to tell her it wasn't her fault.

After three weeks they cleared her of any wrongdoing. Two eyewitness statements and a cell-phone video of the immediate aftermath of Cullen's killing provided sufficient corroboration of Casey's account. The administrative investigation found they'd acted in accordance with departmental regs and procedures, and the DA concluded there were no criminal charges arising from the incident. The same day as they informed her of the decision, Ray came by to return her service weapon. It nearly broke her.

'The last thing I said, before we went in – I called him an asshole.'

'Case, c'mon, it's the kinda thing happens twenty times a day. It wouldn't have meant anything to him.'

'It's not just ... We had a fight. I was pissed because he got held up, so he went in there all fired up. I should've made him take a second, calm down first. Shit, it should've been me. I should've taken the door.'

'You can't fall into that trap. Michael Bell's the only one to blame for what happened out there. You put that fucker where he belongs.'

Casey drank off the rest of her Bushmills and put her glass on the table, more than half the bottle gone, Ray leading the charge. He had a thousand-yard stare pointed at the wall.

She let herself sink back into the sofa. 'He was thinking about getting out, y'know.'

'Dave?'

She nodded.

'No fucking way.'

'Luisa was encouraging him.'

'So this is coming from her?'

'Uh-huh.'

'And what did he have to say about it?'

'He said it wasn't that straightforward.'

Ray crossed his legs. 'He never would've gone through with it. He lived for the job.'

'He loved his girls too, though. That's what had him thinking.'

Ray shook his head. His eyes were vacant again, and she couldn't tell if he was disagreeing or just disbelieving.

'There was something going on with him, I don't know ... Something wasn't right.'

'What are you talking about?'

'I was at his place the night before, they had me over for dinner. He went to put Sienna to bed, but she snuck down when he took a call, so I took her up myself.'

Ray nodded for her to go on.

'I guess he didn't know I was there, and I heard him talking ... He said something like, "This isn't my problem to take care of, and..." She swallowed, as if she was talking out of turn. 'He said, "Is that a threat?", something like that. He sounded ... When he hung up, he sounded scared.'

Ray stared through her, as if trying to understand what it meant. 'He tell you what it was about?'

She shook her head. 'I never told him what I heard. But he was still kinda rattled the next day. I said to him, right before we went in, I said if he ever wanted to talk to me – about anything – he could. But he ... goddamn, he just blew me off.'

'Hey...' He reached for her, his hand on her shoulder. 'Come on...'

She ran her fingers through her hair, pulling it back. 'I just keep thinking, if I'd kept my damn mouth shut, maybe he wouldna gone in there all riled up, maybe he would've seen it coming, or ... That one percent, you know? Maybe his head was one percent clearer, he could've done something to stop it.'

'That's not it, Case. That's you still trying to blame yourself for something that's not your fault.'

She took a deep breath, blew it out like smoke. 'The counsellor said basically the same.'

He angled himself to face her. 'See? There you go.'

'She told me the anger and guilt are normal. That it's the mind's way of protecting me from even more painful emotions.'

He held his hand up like he was thinking about it, then let

it drop onto his leg again. 'I mean, I'm not a guy for shrinks and stuff, but that kinda makes sense to me.'

'I'm not sure. Feels like they're giving me a pass.'

'Even McTeague knows you did nothing wrong. Whatever else I think of him, he's thorough, and he'd throw you under the bus in a second if he had to.'

Casey rubbed her eyes. 'She said it'll change in time and it's normal to feel numb or detached too, or go the other way and get crazy anxiety. I asked her how long it takes and she said it can be weeks or it can be years.'

'It won't be like that for you. You're too strong.'

'I don't know anymore. These last few years...' She poured a finger of Bushmills but changed her mind and pushed the glass away from her across the table. She'd waited weeks for this conversation, so much she'd bottled inside, and now it felt like it was all coming out wrong. 'I need to stop with this stuff. My head's fucked up as it is.'

'How come you never give yourself any credit?'

'What does that mean?' He looked at her like he was about to speak but she waved her hand to cut him off. 'Wait, shit, no – we don't need to be talking about me.'

'Some days I think if you could see yourself the way the rest see you, your goddamn head would explode.'

She blushed. 'I don't ... Shit, you don't have to say that.' His belief in her had always exceeded her own – and she'd never needed to hear it more than now.

'I don't have to say anything. But one day you're gonna have to accept what people see in you.' Ray checked his watch. 'Anyway, I should go.' He reached for his keys on the armrest.

It was sudden enough to catch her off-guard; a safety blanket being ripped away. 'You sure you should be driving?'

'C'mon, you know me.'

'Yeah, but…' She blushed deeper looking at the bottle, feeling like she'd overstepped.

'I'll be fine.'

She glanced around the room, grasping for something to make him stay. The fear of loneliness as potent as the desire to have him keep telling her she'd done nothing wrong.

She picked up her glass and drank a finger off, hoping it would prompt him to do the same. 'Changed my mind. Another?'

He looked at his whiskey and thought about it, but he shook his head. 'I can't.'

'You know what, you could sleep in the spare room? It's all made up.'

He stood up, overbalancing slightly. Casey jumped up and grabbed his arm to steady him. 'Hey, seriously, you can't get in the car like that.'

'Will you quit worrying?'

'If you got stopped, and it got back to McTeague…'

'Which fucking uniform is gonna dime me to that shitbag? They hate him more than I do.'

'Just stay here tonight,' she said, hearing how frantic she sounded at the thought of losing him. 'It's not you, it's all those crazy people that don't know how to drive.' She faced him, speaking over whatever he started to say. 'Please. If something happened to you as well…'

'Nothing's gonna happen to me.'

'You don't know that. No one does.' Suddenly overcome with the thought, talking her fear into reality. 'I mean, look at Dave.' She clicked her fingers: *as sudden as that.*

'Case, it's not the same thing. I'll be fine.'

'You don't ... You can't know that. Please...'

'Casey, I understand where this is coming from, but—'

She leaned in and kissed him on the lips.

He recoiled as she did. His whole body stiff, staring at her in shock.

She pulled back as fast as she'd done it. She looked at him, feeling like she did when she saw Cullen fall.

'Case...' He took a faltering step back, keeping eye contact like he didn't know what she might do next.

'I'm sorry.' She covered her face. 'I told you, I don't even know what I'm doing right now...'

'I gotta go.' He bunched his keys in his fist and walked.

A further appointment was scheduled with the counsellor two days later, and she cleared Casey to go back to work. She sat cross-legged on her bed that night and wept.

## CHAPTER 22

Michael Patrick Bell's death had broken the case wide open in Casey's absence. McTeague's team carried out searches on his residence and found the burner phone registered to the alias Patrick Ball that'd pinged the Ramona Beach tower the night of Tina's disappearance. The phone had been wiped, but the tech crew got to work and managed to retrieve most of its data.

The deleted internet history included searches for every kind of violent pornography imaginable, with a special predilection for rape fantasies. There were no contacts saved

in the phone, and best they could tell, never had been any –
but when they worked with the provider to reconstruct a call
list, it threw up one number already known to the
investigation: that of Kevin Love – the second burner cell
active on Ramona Beach that night. It was a connection
Casey had suspected, but its confirmation brought them no
closer to knowing who was behind the fake name. An analysis
of the phone's movements immediately after Tina
disappeared, revealed the last ping was on the same Ramona
Beach tower – after that, it went cold. There was nothing to
indicate why Bell had deactivated the cell but not disposed
of it – beyond his misplaced belief that wiping it would
render it useless as evidence.

Or maybe he just knew there was no denying his guilt: the
most vital item recovered from Bell's property was a lone key
to a storage unit. They quickly traced its origin to a facility eight
blocks north of his residence; and on opening it up, they
discovered an evidential treasure trove. DNA analysis matched
items of clothing found inside to the one identified victim from
the Ramona Beach marshlands, who McTeague's team then
named publically as Michelle Montara. Ray told Casey he'd
only found out her identity from a News 10 bulletin, McTeague
keeping it close right to the last minute.

Montara, aged twenty-three and a native of Rockport, had
been reported missing three months earlier by her parents, and
the initial investigation into her disappearance had established,
to the shock of her family and friends, that she'd worked as an
escort intermittently over the preceding four years. There'd
been no open leads into her whereabouts prior to her body
being discovered in the vicinity of Ramona Beach.

Also found in the unit was a purse containing a Jersey City

driver's licence for a twenty-four-year-old woman named as Rhonda Clavert. NCIC had no file on her, Jersey City PD neither – not even a misper report. They finally tracked her family down through Facebook – both parents dead, a sister in Alabama she hadn't spoken to in six years, who thought she was living in Philadelphia and expressed muted surprise upon being notified of Rhonda's violent death. They flew the woman up to Rockport and she provided a DNA sample, which allowed them to confirm her sister's identity as the second of the Ramona Beach victims. She asked for payment for her time, claiming she wanted it so she could get Rhonda's name tattooed on her wrist in remembrance.

They processed dozens of items from the house and the storage unit, but nothing they could link to, or that could identify, the third Ramona vic. Tests conducted by the medical examiner's office indicated she'd been dead longer than the other two, maybe for as long as six months. DNA samples extracted from her remains couldn't be matched to any held in the database, so the skeleton crew still working the investigation were looking at KAs of Montara or Clavert, even though no connection had been established between the women in life.

The searches on Bell's property also turned up a second burner phone; in addition to the cell he'd used the night he took Tina, they found a unit he'd first activated a day later – seemingly a replacement. The same model, set up the same as the first, but this one had been used to make outgoing calls to two known numbers – Maggie Grace's, just once, and Casey's, a handful of times. A simple comparison against Casey's records confirmed it: Bell was behind the threatening phone calls. Amidst all the wreckage he'd left behind, the revelation that the sick fuck had been taunting her and Maggie seemed insignificant; but the sense of relief that came with it was undeniable.

The news Casey wanted most and least came last. Forensic techs picked Bell's Ford Escape apart inch by inch, turning up hair and fibre samples they could match back to Tina Grace and, latterly, Clavert and Montara. None of that was unexpected – they knew Tina had been in the vehicle, so it was no surprise two of the other vics had too. The new information came from the trunk: photographs showed the only item inside at the time the SUV was seized was a dark-purple blanket, laid flat. But when they stripped it all out, both the lining and the blanket tested positive for traces of blood.

Tina's blood.

# CHAPTER 23

Day one back on the job and the return she was dreading. Five weeks since the shooting.

Casey took the stairs to Hanrahan's office on the fourth floor of headquarters, trying to work off some of the adrenaline flooding her body. Dress uniform to see the chief, stiff and scratchy, a formality that made her feel even more out of sorts than she already was. A window at the top of the stairwell offered a view over Harrison, a low-rise town that looked crushed under the weight of heavy grey skies.

She sat in the waiting area outside his office for ten minutes before the secretary showed her in, a tingling feeling in her guts like she'd drunk too much black coffee. Hanrahan was at his desk, the office smaller than she was expecting but decked out pretty much how she'd imagined it: miniature flags next to his

computer – state and Old Glory; glowing front pages framed
and displayed on the walls; photos of his predecessors as chief
in rows behind him; posed shots with the county executive and
assorted members of Congress.

He stood up like it was an effort – a butcher lifting a carcass.
Maybe five-eight, barrel chested and thickset all over, grey hair
combed in strands across his scalp, a drinker's complexion. 'The
cold does me no favours,' he said. 'Thirteen years I walked a
beat and I swear to God I never felt it once. The longer I sit in
this office, the worse it gets. Stand easy, detective.'

A Gaelic edge to his accent even after all these years, hard Ts
and clipped vowels, coming from deep inside his chest, almost
bypassing his mouth. Casey stood facing him.

'I'm sorry about what happened to your partner. Dave
Cullen was an outstanding detective and a stand-up guy. He's
a loss to all of us.'

'Thank you, sir.'

'You put the other son of a bitch in the ground.'

She nodded. 'Sir.'

He grazed his knuckle against his chin, pensive. 'What in
God's name was he thinking?'

'Sir?'

'Michael Patrick Bell, that was his name?'

'Yes, sir. I'd be speculating, but I'd say he panicked, sir. Either
that or he was set on going out in a blaze of glory.'

'And a good man's dead because of it. Is that all we're worth
these days?'

'Sir, I...'

He rubbed his temples, waving off the need for an answer.
'It makes me mad, that's all. The margins are getting thinner all
the time, squeezed by the politicians, and these fucking

tweakers and lunatics who'll pull a trigger easy as they'll blink. You wonder how we're supposed to do the job at all.' He came around the desk now and offered his hand. 'Forgive me, I should've done that sooner. You're a hero in this man's department.' She shook it, and then he folded his arms tight. 'How are you faring?'

It was so unexpected that she almost took a step back. 'I'm, uh ... I'm fine, thank you, sir. They cleared me to come back to work, and that's all I want, really.'

'I understand that, and they're fine sentiments indeed. But I want you to remember something: what you did takes courage. Anger, regret, guilt, those are all normal, but don't ever let them take that fact from you. The memory is a broken camera, remember that; it obscures more than it reveals. Did he say anything when you put him down? After?'

He was jumping around so fast she couldn't find her footing, the questions coming out of nowhere. 'No, sir. Nothing.'

He looked away at that, fixing his gaze on a point on the wall, his jaw muscles flexing and bulging. 'A shame. I'd been comforting myself with the notion he suffered.' Quiet, almost spoken to himself. Then he shifted his gaze again, the trance broken. 'You know David's wife, isn't that right?'

'Yes, sir. Luisa.'

'I spoke to her at length. Not the first time, right after, that was brief – as it should be. But a few days later. I went to see her to pay my respects. And those beautiful girls ... they broke my heart.' He leaned against the desk, shaking his head. 'Broke my fucking heart. Are you close with her?'

'I ... I don't know, sir. She's probably got closer friends than me, but I like to think so. I hope we will continue to be, in light of ... what happened. I've reached out to her a couple times.'

'And has she responded?'

'Not yet, sir. But with everything she's dealing with...'

'Then do me a favour: don't let her slip away. It'll still be raw now, but once things settle down a bit, she's going to come up for air and it'll all hit her all over again. And at the same time, she'll feel cut off from us, and that'll make the hit twice as hard. So just do your best to be there for her, let her know she'll always be a part of the family.'

'Of course, sir.'

He stood up again, those laboured first movements forgotten, now a man who couldn't stay still. 'Thank you, Detective. I get reports about you, you know.' He retraced his steps around the desk, came to a stop in front of his seat. He broke out a half-smile, his mouth a straight line but his eyes twinkling. 'Keep it up, your time is at hand. Dismissed.'

Back down the stairs, glad to be done with it but even less sure than before about why he'd called her in. Sympathies and condolences, that was all as expected. But that parting shot, what was that about? A promise or a threat?

She passed one of Lyman's guys on the stairs, a pat on the shoulder and another 'sorry about your partner' as she did, eyes down and a nod in reply. Into the parking lot, the second meeting now coming into view, maybe the one she was dreading even more. As she pulled out, she noticed Robbie McTeague standing by the entrance watching her go.

Maggie Grace opened the door with the TV remote in her hand, embarrassed when she realised she was still holding it. 'All I do is channel surf. I don't know what else to ... Anyway, hell, sorry. You wanna come inside?'

'Sure.' Casey followed her into the living room, the TV tuned to News 10. Maggie killed the sound.

'You know the department will call you if there's any news,' Casey said, nodding towards the screen. 'I'm back now, *I'll* call.'

Maggie stopped in the middle of the room and turned to look at her. 'You think there's any real chance?'

Casey shifted her weight, and Maggie must've sensed the coming equivocation because she cut in before Casey could speak. 'No, seriously. Level with me.'

'I don't know.' She brought her hands together to stop from fidgeting. 'There's a chance, but I don't want to get your hopes up.'

'Up? They're in the gutter.' She laid the remote on the table. 'You say they'll call but I ain't heard from anyone since they found the blood. It's been – I don't even know, what, four weeks now? Every day another reporter calls me or shows up at the door and it's like they know more than I do about what's happening. The only thing stopping them coming back is they figure out I don't know shit.'

The TV picture changed, and suddenly it was Cullen's headshot on the screen, a report about officer-welfare concerns in the wake of his death. Maggie saw her looking and put her hands to her mouth. 'Shit, I'm sorry. I never even asked...'

'Forget it, you've got enough on your mind. But I promise it'll be better now they let me back in the office. The communication, I mean.'

'They said on the news he had a family, wife and kids?'

Casey nodded. 'They're trying to hang in there.'

'What's worse, a parent loses a kid or a kid loses a parent? Jesus Christ, this world...' She rubbed her face, her eye, pushed her hair back. 'I had this bible-thumper come by and try to tell me it's all part of God's plan, and that we just have to trust Him. Giving me pamphlets. The hell would think I wanna hear that? His plan's for my kid to be running around that way so someone can do this to her?'

'I'm sorry you had to find out that way.'

'That she's walking the street? Shit, I knew. Tommy thinks I'm an idiot, but I knew.'

'Really?' Casey put her hand on her hip. 'How come you didn't say something at the start—'

'No, I mean...' She closed her eyes, frustrated. 'I mean I had a feeling. How else she gonna afford that apartment? And then she quits her job and still she's bringing me groceries and stuff – I knew she didn't have that much money saved, so it had to be something. I figured maybe it was drugs – honestly, that's what I thought it was. I was more worried Tommy had got her into something. I guess ... Look, maybe I just didn't want to know the truth. I got one kid running wild already, my girl was supposed to be the sensible one. Hell, she is the sensible one, she just...' She scratched her arm, a tic in her cheek as if there was more to say, but then she closed her eyes for a few seconds, willing it back down again. 'I don't know how she got her head turned around.'

Casey nodded. 'It's almost always money. Maybe it was the only way she could keep up the payments on her apartment.'

'Yeah, I guess...' Maggie perched on the edge of a chair but stood up again as soon as she did. 'You want a drink? Iced tea or something?'

'No, I'm fine, thanks. I just came to check in on you. How's Tommy?' She glanced towards the hallway, the house silent apart from them.

'He's still charging around like he's gonna find her. I think he's gotta feel like he's doing something, y'know?'

'Uh-huh. He keeping away from Jon Parker though?'

She nodded. 'I appreciate what you did for him on that.'

'Mr Parker decided not to press charges – that's what made the difference. He might not next time. Make sure he gets that.'

'Yeah.' She glanced at the TV, embarrassed again. 'Casey, what happens now?'

Casey ran her hand along her forearm. 'It's too early to say. We're still investigating Michael Bell, and the outcome of that determines what we do next.'

'He killed all them other girls...'

'We don't know that for certain yet.'

'Come on...'

'Like I said, I don't want to get your hopes up. I can't imagine what you're going through, but we just need to take it one day at a time.'

'You promised me at the start you were gonna be straight with me.'

'I am.'

'Then tell me this: why'd he do it? All of them, I mean.'

'I can't answer that.'

'Can't or won't?'

'Can't.'

'She's in there somewhere though, right?'

'Maggie....'

'No, she's in those marshes. She has to be.' She backed away, turning to plant her hands on the table, hanging her head. 'I went by there, to see it. I walked the beach for I don't know how long, trying to work myself up to it, and then I went through one of those tunnels goes under the road, and it stank and it was freezing cold, and I nearly turned around and went back, but I couldn't stop myself.'

'We're still searching...'

'How long for?' She looked over her shoulder. 'I see them saying they got the guy killed them others, the investigation's good as over. You telling me if they don't find her soon, they won't wind it down? There's no guarantee you'll find her, either way.'

The weight of the phone call weeks before pressed down on Casey now. That same shitty choice: false hope or no hope. 'Look, there's something you need to know. I had a call, from a woman claiming to be Tina.'

'What? What the...?'

'This was ... a while ago. Just before my partner...'

Maggie's face was frozen, her mouth open.

Casey went on. 'You have to understand, there's no way of knowing it was definitely her.'

'Why didn't you get her to call me?'

'The caller was insistent ... that she didn't want to talk to you.'

Her face twisted now. 'Why not?'

'She didn't say.'

'Then it wasn't her.'

Casey looked to the side, choosing her words.

'Tina got no reason not to talk to me. None. Goddammit I told you, she was here, the day before...'

'She said it's because she thought you'd be able to convince her to come back.'

'What? Bullshit. It's not her. She knows there's nothing she can't come to me about and I wouldn't help her.'

*But she kept some things back from you.* 'If it was to do with her escort work, someone threatening her – that could explain it. But look, we don't know it was her. There's plenty of cranks and attention-seekers out there.'

'Can't you … couldn't you trace it or something? What about the cell tower thing you did with her phone?'

'We traced it to a payphone in Knoxville. Can you think of any reason why Tina would be there?'

But the look on her face told Casey the answer before she opened her mouth. 'Knoxville? I don't even know where that is. What is it, Tennessee?'

Casey nodded. 'We did everything we could to verify if it could've been her or not, but there was no direct surveillance coverage of the payphone. Knoxville PD checked every other cam in the vicinity anyway, they issued her picture and description to all their patrol units, they made an appeal for any witness sightings, but…' She shook her head. 'Without further contact, there just wasn't anything to go on. And we can't rule out the possibility it was a hoax.'

Maggie was staring at her, wide-eyed. 'Christ, Jesus … This is purgatory. That's what this is. What the hell am I supposed to think now? To feel?'

'Like I said, I don't want to give you false hope. But I don't want you to give up either.' It felt empty saying it, already regretting telling her about the call.

Maggie went across to one of the armchairs and retrieved a glass of clear liquid placed out of sight on its far side. She sat down and took a gulp, then another, her eyes on the TV, but vacant. 'If it was him – if he's the one she was scared of, what is it, Bell? If it was him, she could come back now, right? You took care of him.'

A thought that'd crossed Casey's mind too. No way to know for sure. She wanted to put her arms around Maggie and promise her she'd never stop looking, never stop until she had a resolution – for her, for Tina, for Dave Cullen and Luisa, his death senseless and empty if it left only questions without answers. She wanted to promise her all those things, but they were out of reach, and she'd done enough damage for one day. She locked her eyes open to stop a tear falling as she went to the door. 'I'm sorry. I'll be in touch.'

Nine o'clock that night. A day that'd felt long at 7am and still wouldn't quit.

The venue was Shakey's, the place bursting – condensation on the windows, sweat running down the walls, even though it was barely thirty degrees outside. The sign on the door said *Private Event* but anyone with an ear to the street got the message long before they saw it; tonight was cops only.

The wake.

The formal ceremony took place the same day as the funeral, the department properly represented by Chief Hanrahan and selected senior officers; the county executive was in attendance, and the family honoured with dress uniforms and folded flags. This was the real memorial. Seeing Dave Cullen off on a tide of whiskey and beer.

It was the last thing she felt like doing. But there was no question she'd be there. Anything else was as disrespectful to the living as it was to the dead. They were a family and anyone who carried the badge was part of it; when one of them fell, they all felt it, and the cop wake was as much about reinforcing those bonds as it was marking the passing.

Casey caught looks as soon as she walked in, no two the same, emotions as high as they were conflicted. She was the bereaved partner, the hero who put the cop-killer down – and maybe the one to blame in the first place. Whispers had got back to her about that last one. Didn't matter that both investigations had cleared her conduct, that multiple eyewitnesses saw what happened; there was always going to be someone saying Cullen's bitch partner must've fucked up and got him killed. It took her legs out from under her, a callback to when she'd first made detective; four years of progress, respect, lost in the time it took to pull a trigger. It stung worse because it was the conclusion she'd arrived at first, without the need for anyone else's judgement. The counsellor termed it survivor's guilt, a label she'd heard of before without ever really understanding it – and she still didn't. It could've been her at that door, a fifty-fifty call that she made without thinking and cost Cullen his life. She couldn't live with the idea that fate could be so random; it was easier to keep blaming herself.

Suddenly Dana Torres pushed her way through the crowd and put her arm around Casey's shoulders, handing her a beer with her free hand. She craned her neck to meet Casey's eyes, smiling. 'You earned that, and maybe a couple more. We missed you.' Then she took her arm back, stared down the onlookers and started clapping.

Casey's face started burning up. One by one, more people in the crowd joined in clapping, until it seemed like the whole room was doing it. Casey dipped her head, her eyes filling.

It went on for a few seconds, shoulder slaps raining down,

then Billy D and Jill were in front of her, smiling, taking their turns to wrap her up in a hug. 'It's good to have you back, Big.'

Eventually the applause faded out as the room regained its composure, and a night that was all about appearances started doing its thing again. Casey felt her shoulders drop, a vague release of tension, and then she took a sip from her beer. Someone shouted, 'To Dave Cullen, the best goddamn cop I ever knew.' A cheer went around, drinks raised to the ceiling, and someone cranked the music up.

She picked her way through the crowd, following Dana, more backslaps and handshakes, *sorrys* and *hang toughs*, until finally they reached the table where the group had been sitting before she arrived. Ray was seated on the far side of it, and she met his slight nod and sent one right back.

It was an hour and three beers before they finally spoke. She'd been studious in avoiding him up to that point, the stream of well-wishers and commiserators an easy way to pretend she wasn't. But when the flow dwindled, she saw him at the bar and decided she had to make the first move.

She came to stand by his shoulder. 'I'll take a beer, if you're ordering?'

He half turned to look at her. 'Sure.' He nodded at the Coors in her hand. 'You want the same?'

'Whatever's cold.'

He signalled Hendrix the bartender – so called because of the tie-dye headscarf he wore habitually. He set down the drinks and refused a tip, despite Ray's protestations; the brass and the police benevolent association were covering the tab, and Hendrix saw this as his contribution. Ray swivelled around and passed her the bottle, puffing his chest out as he worked up to it. 'Look, uh, the other night...'

'Yeah, about that.' Casey set her empty on the bar. 'I've been giving it a lot of thought, and I think we should have the wedding in Florida. It's easy enough to get a licence down there, the weather's kinda guaranteed as long as we do it outside of hurricane season, there's plenty of hotels for the guests, and...' She only stopped because the look on his face made her break out in a grin.

He shot her the look a few seconds more, then broke into his own grin. 'You're a dick.'

'Hey, look, I'm sorry. I came over to say I'm sorry, I wanted to break the ice.'

'Making fun of an old man...'

'I'm not, I swear. I didn't want to make a big deal out of it when it was nothing. I screwed up, my head was all over the place. I don't want this to be a thing, I haven't secretly been in love with you all this time, promise.'

'What?' His face had gone dead serious. 'You haven't?'

'Can we pretend it never happened?'

'Well, it's not that easy.'

She stopped smiling. 'It was just a moment of madness kinda thing, y'know? I just lost Dave, I was scared of being alone ... I don't know.'

He looked away, shaking his head. 'I get that, but ... I mean, I just put my apartment up for sale. I figured your place is bigger, we'd have more space if we moved in together there, we could maybe get a dog that way and...'

She slapped him on the chest as his face dissolved. 'Asshole.'

He had to lean back against the bar he was laughing so hard.

He wiped a tear from his eye with the back of his hand, holding his drink. 'You earned that one. We're even.'

She slapped him again, drawing more laughs from Ray because she nearly spilled her beer doing it. She took a drink, and the smile on her face felt like a forgotten sensation. Relief spread through her with the glow from the alcohol.

He clinked his drink lightly against hers. 'So the DA's satisfied Bell was the guy, they're closing the file on all three murders. Congratulations.'

She paused with her beer to her lips, taking it in. 'Doesn't feel like much of a win. We don't even have an ID on the third vic. And Tina Grace is still unaccounted for.'

'I know. You don't have to feel good about it right now – but stow it away, sometime down the road, you can give yourself a pat on the back.'

'That's not the general view though, huh.' She tipped her head to the crowd.

'Meaning what?'

'I heard the whispers. That it's my fault, I must've fucked up somehow, all of it. And for what it's worth, there's nothing anyone can say I haven't already thought myself.'

'That's not the consensus thinking. Straight up. Yeah, okay, there's always gonna be some wiseass who wasn't there who thinks he's an expert on the situation, but they're assholes and they move on to the next thing quick enough. Anyone who matters knows what you did, and more importantly, you know what you did. You were there, don't let your mind screw with you; the memory's like a broken camera, it plays tricks on you.'

The same line Hanrahan had come out with earlier; the same sentiments.

'You put a cop-killer in the ground, and solved a triple

homicide.' He lifted his eyebrows. 'That makes you good police.'

She nodded, her gaze out of focus on the bartop. The words just sitting there in her head, like the proverbial seeds on stony ground.

It was going on eleven when he showed up.

She'd wonder, later, what he'd been doing until that time of night – working, maybe, but she got the feeling he'd timed it to catch her at her most vulnerable; tipsy but not out of it, emotionally drained, physically exhausted. Ray had given a heartfelt eulogy that left Casey and most everyone else that heard it in tears, and the crowd had slowly thinned after that. But more than half the cops were still standing, working on getting fall-down drunk – until McTeague came through the door.

The tradition was that the brass showed up early, stayed for a token drink, then exited to leave the rank and file to it; Chief Hanrahan had been and gone by the time Casey arrived, staying only long enough to offer a few words and make sure the tab was running. So that couldn't explain McTeague's presence, especially this late. The wake was supposed to be a chance for the department to get drunk and shed tears together, without the bosses there to pass judgement. And McTeague was the last cop in Hampstead County anyone wanted passing judgement.

He went to Ray first and Casey watched on, too far away to hear what was said, trying some second-rate lip-reading as she stood with Dana Torres. There wasn't much to see; McTeague went in stern-faced and came away the same, but he shook Ray's hand with a bearing that spoke of how much it cost him to do it. After that he sat down at the bar.

Casey did her best to ignore him. She went back to her conversation with Dana, a roundup of Billy D's most recent hookups, but her drink was empty, and had been for long enough that sensible thoughts like *take your ass home to bed* were starting to assert themselves. She excused herself to go to the bathroom, then made a short tour of the room to say her goodbyes, finding Ray first.

'You doing okay?' he said. He was shiny-eyed and red-faced, gripping a big tumbler of Bushmills like it was a rock.

'Yeah, just beat.' She jutted her chin at the bar. 'What's he doing here?'

McTeague had a full beer in his hand, watching the crowd without looking like he was paying attention.

'Paying his respects.'

'That what he said to you?'

'Not in so many words, but ... pretty much.'

'I don't understand why he has to play these fucking games.'

'Don't let him get to you. He might just be playing it straight tonight.'

Casey stared at the side of McTeague's face, emboldened by the booze. 'Whatever. I gotta get some sleep, I'll see you tomorrow.'

'You gonna be okay getting home?'

She was nodding, already moving off. 'Yeah, I got an Uber coming. No problem.'

She sought out Dana to say goodbye, Jill Hart already home and in bed according to her text message. On her way to the door, she spotted Billy D in conversation with a blonde she didn't know; she left him to it and went outside into the cold.

She walked down the street, moving through shadows and light, the convenience store along the block painting the sidewalk electric blue. She opened the Uber app.

'Wray.'

She stopped, turned. McTeague was a few paces behind her. She hesitated, caught between going to him and waiting.

He came up to her. 'First day back?'

'Yes, Captain.'

He glanced around at the Shakey's sign, orange letters burning bright against the night. 'Tough re-entry.'

'It's been okay.'

'Any word from your girl?'

'No. Nothing since the Knoxville call.'

His mouth curled down. 'You give that any credence now?'

'I don't know. The mother doesn't, but she's hurting.'

He hunched his shoulders tighter in his overcoat. 'You think Bell killed her?'

'Like I said...'

'What about the others?'

Cautious now, a weird question for him to ask. 'It's your investigation, sir.'

'I asked you, Detective.'

She put her hands in her pockets, her four-beer buzz evaporating fast. She let her gaze stray to the Shakey's doorway, worried how it'd look if Ray or one of the others came out now. 'The DA's satisfied Bell was responsible, so I'm not sure what you're asking me. The evidence points that way...'

'How'd you come by Bell's address?'

She looked at him, trying to get a read. It was his team had conducted the review into her actions, and the report was comprehensive; slim-to-no chance he didn't already know all this. Which meant he was leading her. 'An ex-girlfriend of his. Her new partner called me with it.'

'Uh-huh, Elena Asimovic and Brent Hatcher. Where did Hatcher get it from?'

'I didn't ask. Is that the point you're making, sir?'

'He told you she didn't know anything about it, according to your statement. That didn't make you wonder where her boyfriend could've got it from?'

'The information was good, sir. I don't know what else I was—'

'Get off the defensive, Wray. My guys cleared you already, you think I didn't green-light that?'

'Then what—?'

'You're a mystery to me, Detective. I can't figure out if you're a good cop who's oblivious, or you're just complicit.'

Her stomach flipped. 'Complicit in what?'

'So you're going with oblivious?'

A Prius pulled up beside them, the driver leaning across to call out the passenger window. 'Uber?'

Casey held up a finger. 'Just one second. Please.' She turned back to McTeague. 'I honestly don't know what you're talking about, sir. You wanna clue me in, I'll do my best to answer. If there's some evidence I don't know about...'

'Ray Carletti is the dirtiest cop I ever knew. You jump ship now, maybe we can help each other. If you don't, then there's nothing I can do for you.'

He turned and walked off into the darkness.

# CHAPTER 24

Another night awake. Tired to flat-out exhausted. Tossing, turning, pacing; scouring the darkness for what she'd missed.

Still in her head now as she came into the office: Ray C dirty? Fuck the heat between him and McTeague, that wasn't an accusation anyone threw out there lightly. And consider the source: McTeague liked to screw with people. He knew how tight she was with Ray. This was him trying to drive a wedge between them. Why? She thought back to Chief Hanrahan's parting line in his office that morning – *I get reports about you. Your time is at hand.* Was that a pre-runner to this? Everyone knew him and McTeague were tight – had he known this was coming? Or did he in fact send McTeague to deliver the message?

Ray was her boss, mentor, the closest thing to a father figure she'd ever allowed into her life. There was no way he was dirty. There was no one he confided in more than her, no way she wouldn't know. It was his department, his rules, everyone got that – the same as in any family; but just because their loyalty lay with him more than the brass at Harrison, didn't make it a rogue outfit run by a dirty cop. Shit, it used to be the sign of a well-run crew.

*No one he confided in more than her.* That thought wasn't so copper-bottomed anymore. She recalled Cullen bringing up the internal inquiry over the Zoltan Kuresev incident – the one Ray had sworn her to secrecy over; the one she assumed he'd confided about in her alone.

And what about the inquiry itself? Kuresev was a crackhead who'd attacked his arresting officer outside the precinct. Like Cullen had said, he was lucky to get away with a beating –

another cop might've killed him; it didn't come close to marking Ray as dirty. The inquiry was a fig leaf, trumped up because said crackhead was playing the victim card and had found himself an ambulance-chaser dumb enough to take a shot at a payout from HCPD. It was bullshit that would be dismissed, and McTeague knew it.

Wasn't it?

What about the after-hours drinking in the office? An old-school tradition the brass had cracked down on – Ray the holdout. It was considered a serious offence on the upper floors at Harrison, but nowhere else. If that was why McTeague was gunning for him, the man was even more petty than she'd realised.

*Look at what you're doing.*

Doubt. She'd let it go to work already. Dancing to McTeague's tune and letting his music play in her head.

There were papers all over her desk – phone records, files, reports, memos that had been left for her while she was off, no chance to go through it the day before. She set about bringing some order to it all, but her eyes kept wandering to Cullen's desk. It'd been cleared out – the photographs of his girls gone, along with everything else. She'd called Luisa before going to the wake, in part prompted by what the chief had said about the department not abandoning her.

'Did he tell you what we were fighting about, that morning?' Luisa had said.

'Not in so many words, but … I mean it didn't take much to figure it out.'

'Was he still mad at me?'

'No.'

'Of course he was.'

'He was mad at me, Lu. I told him he was stupid for being pissed at you.'

'What did he say about that?'

'That was pretty much the end of it.'

She'd gone quiet at that.

'How are the girls doing?'

A brittle intake of breath before she'd answered. 'I don't think Sienna believes it yet. She's used to not seeing him for days at a time, so she keeps asking where he is and when he's coming back, and I have to go through it all again. She already won't let me out of her sight, so it's starting to hit home. I'm terrified what happens when it does fully. Shauna's too young, but she's not sleeping so good – they pick up on stuff, y'know? Makes everything harder.'

'Can you get some help, is there...?'

'Mom's staying with us, she's been great, and Maureen and Tom are helping out too.' Cullen's parents. 'But there's not ... There's only so much anyone can do. It's never gonna be the same.'

'I saw the chief today. He wanted me to make sure you know you'll always be part of the family. He told me to tell you that – not that I wouldn't have anyway.'

'Family. Huh.'

'I know, it sounds corny but he meant it sincerely.'

'No ... I never thought of it as family, Case. It's different for you, you're in it, but it's just The Job to me. It tore my family up, even before this. It's never been a family, it's the opposite.'

Casey hadn't known what to say to that. It was a perspective she'd never considered – 'the family' from the outside, looking in. Told you're part of it, a different picture in reality. A justification for all those hours of overtime and absent weekends, but what was the payback for Luisa and all the other partners? It brought back Ray's uncharacteristic assessment: *It takes and it takes.* He'd never said the job cost him his marriage, but that was on account of it being self-evident.

Staring at the empty seat opposite now, the sense of loss threatened to overwhelm her. She turned her focus to the mess in front of her again to distract herself. Messages – one in Jill Hart's writing; a woman named Lisa Borden had called in saying she knew Tina Grace and wanted to speak to the detectives investigating. Casey scanned the list of Tina's friends she and Cullen had spoken to, but Borden's name wasn't on it. She picked up her phone and dialled the number.

'Yeah?'

'This is Detective Casey Wray with HCPD, am I speaking to Lisa Borden?'

'Oh yeah, hey. About Tina, right?'

'Yes, ma'am.'

'Look, I don't know if this matters anymore. Y'all shot the guy that killed her, right?'

'A suspect was killed, but we're still investigating her disappearance. You said you knew Tina?'

'Yeah, we ... I guess we worked together.'

'At Bronsons?' Casey rifled the employee list they'd put together for her.

'What? No, we were, uh ... we were with the same agency.'

Casey put the papers down. 'Ma'am? Escort work, you mean?'

'I don't do that anymore, I can't get in trouble, right?'

'No, ma'am, we're not interested in that. What was it you wanted to talk about?'

'I saw about Tina on the news and, I was like, oh my God. I

never ... I mean, we all knew there were risks, but that was like, getting ripped off or maybe getting beat up. But then I remembered this thing Tina told me about.'

'Ma'am?'

'This sounds kinda stupid but I told a couple friends about it, and they said I should call.'

'You did the right thing. Tell me.'

'So Tina and me were cool but not, like, tight – it's not like you'd see the other girls every day. Anyway, I ran into her at the grocery store one time, and we got talking, kinda comparing notes – how many jobs we were getting, how much the agency was taking, always the same stuff. And then at the end she asks me if I've heard about the story going around. I didn't know what she was talking about, so she tells me there's this rumour about a high-end client, real secretive, nobody knew who he was, but whenever a girl went to see him, she disappeared afterwards. Like, literally, if you go on a job to this guy, you're dead.'

Casey's hand fluttered holding her pen. High end, secretive: *Jon Parker.* 'Go on.'

'I kinda laughed it off because it sounded like the sort of crap some of the girls make up to scare off the competition, and Tina kinda laughed too, like she wanted me to think she didn't believe it either, but I don't know...'

'Did she go into any more detail?'

'Not really. I asked her where she heard it, and she was just like, "Oh, you know, people are saying it". But she didn't know anything about who this guy was supposed to be, I guess that's what you're asking. She said no one did, like that was the whole point. But she told me to be careful, just watch out.'

'What about the girls who'd gone missing? Did she tell you anything about them?'

'No, she literally just threw it out there. But I never heard about girls going missing or anything like that, so I just let it go. Kinda think now, like, why would I have heard about it, though? I didn't even know that many girls in the job, and there must be hundreds. And it's not like every girl goes missing makes the news, right?'

'Lisa, when did this conversation take place exactly?'

'Last year. I remember there was Christmas stuff in the store already, but I couldn't tell you exactly when.'

'What about the name of the agency?'

'West Side Talent. They used to promise girls modelling work, that was how they got them in, but most of us knew what we were signing up for. I got out when they started farming girls out for porn. You do what you do to get by, but once they get you on camera, that's forever.'

Casey flipped her notebook to the page with the names of the proprietors of Executive Elite Talent, the agency Michael Bell was busted driving for in 2015. 'Who was in charge?'

A hesitation – her first. 'I don't remember.'

'I can find out easy enough, just help me take a shortcut. I'll keep your name out of it.'

'Honestly, I don't know. I only ever dealt with a woman, Leanne, but she wasn't the boss.'

'Leanne who? Do you have a surname?'

'I never knew it. Just Leanne.'

'Hunter Hanwell?' Casey looked down the page. 'Andreas Georgiou?' Georgiou – dead of pancreatic cancer, late 2016 – so not him. 'Scratch that last one.'

'I don't know those names.'

'What about Michael Patrick Bell?'

'That's the guy you shot, right? The one I was talking about before?'

'Did you ever work with him? Or come across him?'

'No. Never.'

'What about the women? Rhonda Clavert, Michelle Montara...'

'Nope. I thought about that, because of what Tina said. But that guy, Bell – he wasn't a high roller, was he?'

Dirty plates all over the countertops, the floor slick with his blood. 'No.'

'And he killed them, right?'

Casey coughed away from the phone. 'Is there anyone else would know about this? Did you hear it from anyone else at the time?'

'No, only Tina.'

Casey closed her notebook. 'It's helpful to know, thank you. I'll talk to some colleagues that specialise in that area and see if they picked up on anything similar. One more thing – are you in contact with any of the other girls you worked with? So I can speak with them?'

'Detective, I'm sorry but I left all that behind.'

Casey couldn't tell if she was telling the truth or just didn't want to be seen helping the police. She thanked her and put the phone down, thinking she'd call back in a day or two to see if she could squeeze any names out of her after all. She stood up, seeing Jon Parker's face but now cut with doubt. How many of his neighbours would fit the bill of high end and secretive? Ellis Sandford vibed control freak, his nose in everyone's business. And what about Jerry Van Heusen, lived next door to Sandford? Van Heusen was pulling in eight figures a year according to Parker – and he'd admitted himself to being on the street the same time as Tina. As she thought about the names and faces, it started to feel like they were all in it together – protecting each other, a woman's life of no consequence to entitled men of money and status. She walked to the coffee machine and pressed for a black coffee – no milk, a pure jolt needed this morning.

All of them had seen Tina on the street that night, alone in the dark. But it was Michael Bell's car she'd ended up in. She'd seen Bell kill in cold blood first hand; the evidence against him for the others was overwhelming. He had items belonging to two of the victims in his storage unit, and Tina's blood was found in his car. No evidential link to the unidentified third vic had yet been established, but the DA was satisfied Bell was guilty of her murder. Common sense said as much. Motive was lacking, but everything they knew about him painted Bell as a misogynistic sadist, so probably it was no more complicated than that. He'd taunted her with phone calls in the dead of night, for fuck's sake; where was this doubt coming from?

McTeague was part of it – his unprompted questions about how she'd come by Bell's address. Now this new wrinkle was fuelling more doubt. It felt like a pretty standard urban myth, but the chance it was true was hard to dismiss, given the source.

As her coffee dispensed, she saw Ray coming through the office doors, Jill Hart next to him; she was leaning close to listen, a serious look on her face. Casey realised they couldn't see her because of the vending machine, and she watched as Ray talked, feeling jealous, and ridiculous for it, all at once. She touched her cheeks, on fire at the prospect of facing Ray, McTeague's accusation a guilty secret burning inside her. She left her coffee where it stood and followed the corridor to the back stairs.

Something lit up behind Elena Asimovic's eyes when she opened the door to her house, but Casey couldn't get a read on what it was.

'Detective Wray, Miss Asimovic – we spoke before?'

'Yeah.' Leaning on the leading edge of the door like a shield. 'You killed him.'

Casey lifted her chin slightly, defying the statement's directness. 'You're aware of the circumstances of Michael Bell's death?'

'Yeah, I know. Don't get me wrong, I don't care.'

'I understand, it must've come as a shock anyway.'

'How'd you track him down in the end?'

A beat, a breath. Uncertainty on both sides; Casey trying to read if she knew it'd come from her boyfriend, Hatcher, or if she really was in the dark. 'We got a tipoff. I wanted to ask you a few questions about him though.'

'I told you, I haven't seen him in years.'

'This is about your time together. Was he ever violent towards you?'

She shifted her feet, the door closing over a couple inches. 'Mike? No. He was a piece of shit, and I found out after he was sleeping around, but he never hit me.'

'What about his previous partners? Or any history of violence at all?'

'I don't know about the others. He got his ass kicked in a bar fight one time, but that was when he mouthed off to the wrong guy. I don't think he even threw a punch. Had his tooth knocked out.'

'Were the police called?'

She screwed up her face. 'Next day he couldn't even remember what started it. He wouldn't speak to the cops anyhow, wasn't his way.'

'Was this a regular type of thing?'

'No. He had a big mouth when he was drunk but he was a pussy first of all.'

'A pussy how?'

'Just that. I mean he'd run away from a fight every time, but it was more than that, he was always scared.'

'Of what?'

'Honestly? I never knew. It was just how he was.'

'What did he do for work when you were together?'

'He was a driver.'

'Were you aware he was involved in prostitution?'

'Sure. Not at the start, but...' She rubbed a patch of bare wood on the doorframe, her gaze turning distant. 'Look, I made some stupid choices, huh? I was using back then, years and years, but I been clean eighteen months now. I told you he was a piece of crap, I just didn't see it in time.'

'I'm not judging, Elena, I'm just trying to understand what motivated him.'

'Why? He's dead.'

She glanced past her, into the house. 'Is Mr Hatcher home?'

'Brent? What for?'

'Did he have any kind of relationship with Michael Bell?'

'No.'

'Did they ever speak, to your knowledge?'

She touched her lip absently. 'Brent doesn't ... He never knew Mike. He ... I don't understand.'

Another flick of the eyes to glance behind her. 'Is he home?'

'No.'

'Where can I find him?'

'He works at the auto-shop on 33rd. Franklin's.' She stepped back and opened the door all the way now. 'What is this? I know what you're thinking, "the kinda guy she goes for", but Brent's not like Mike, he's straight up. I don't always date assholes. He won't be able to tell you anything about Mike.'

Casey spotted Hatcher as she pulled into the parking lot at Franklin's. He saw her and turned as she got out, mouthing something to himself.

'Mr Hatcher, Detective Wray, you remember me.'

He came out of the bay he was working in, the mechanics either side looking on. 'Yeah, what can I do for you?'

'Where'd you get Michael Patrick Bell's address from, Brent?'

'Friend of a friend.' He wiped the tool he was holding on his overall, looking down as he did.

'Name?'

'I don't know.'

'You don't know your friend's name?'

'No, I don't know the guy's name who gave it to him.'

'Feels like you're ducking me here, Brent.'

He looked to one side, looked back. Said nothing.

'Brent, the name?'

'Malcolm DeWitt. He's my cousin.'

'Not a friend.'

'Same thing. Why's it matter, he's dead ain't he?'

'I'm obsessive. How come your cousin can get an address for a guy you never met, when Elena couldn't?'

He shrugged.

She stepped closer. 'It is too damn cold out here to be playing dumb and dumber with you. If Elena gave you the address, tell me now. If not, you tell me how Malcolm Fuckwit got it, or you tell me where to find him.'

'This is what I get for doing the right thing?'

'This is part of doing the right thing. A continuation of doing the right thing.'

'Jesus Christ...'

'DeWitt's details now, or I tell everyone you're a rat motherfucker. Starting with Elena.'

He half turned away, lifting the tool slowly as he did. 'Shiiit...'

Casey threw her coat back and snapped her hand to her gun.

He dropped the tool like a hot coal, metal clanging on concrete, holding his hands up. 'I wasn't ... Shit, I was just...' A shout came from the repair bays behind him, the other mechanics caught between coming to help and staying rooted to the spot.

Casey was jangling, realising late that he'd just been dragging his heels, not threatening her. She let her coat fall back into place over her sidearm. 'Elena told me she didn't know anything about it, and I believe her. So you tell me what I want to know, or I make sure all your buddies here know you're a snitch.' She made a show of glancing around Franklin's, wrinkling her nose. 'This look like the kind of place to keep a snitch on the payroll for long?'

He brought his hands down slowly. 'Don't do this to me. Please...'

'He's dead, what're you afraid of, Brent?'

He kept shaking his head, like he could wish himself away.

'Brent?'

'I need to get my cell out.' He nodded to his pants pocket, requesting permission.

'Go on.'

He took it out and poked at the screen for a few seconds until he turned it around to show her. He didn't say a word.

Onscreen, an email from what looked like an anonymous account – *aq12yLKke52f49@hotmail.com*. No greeting, no signoff. The text was just a few lines – Michael Bell's address and an instruction to pass this on to HCPD. Underneath it, a photo of Bell outside the bungalow, proving he lived there. Casey had to look away when she recognised it.

'Who sent you this?'

'I don't know.'

Casey stared at him a long second. 'You're telling me this just showed up outta the blue?'

'Exactly that. Then I got this.' He held up another email, this time a picture of Hatcher and Asimovic on their doorstep. The message with it read, 'PASS ON THE FUCKING ADDRESS TODAY OR WE CUT YOUR GIRLS THROAT'. 'Please, I didn't ask for this shit…'

Casey took the phone and checked the message date and time – just a few hours before the shootout at Bell's place. 'When was the first message…' Before she could finish the thought, she'd already scrolled back to look it up herself, seeing it'd been sent the day before that. 'And you're telling me you don't know anything about the sender?'

He shook his head.

'Have they contacted you since? Phone calls, anything?'

'No. But they're watching us, you can see that…'

'I know. That's why you should've told me about this. Day one.'

'I didn't know...' He took a breath, ran his hand over his face. 'Elena told me he was some dipshit scumbag. I didn't know he was gonna go kill a cop. I had no fucking clue it was gonna blow up into this. I figured you'd pick him up and that would be it.'

Casey watched as he spoke, saw a man sweating fear. She held up his cell. 'I'm gonna need to keep this.'

Casey went straight to the cyber techs that'd worked on Michael Bell's phone, mid-morning when she arrived, a tray of takeout coffees in hand as a bribe. Maranda Jessup led the team, a softly spoken MIT graduate who'd spurned Silicon Valley for what she called 'her own startup' – her subtly damning assessment of HCPD's tech setup when she'd joined eleven years before. Now she stood holding Brent Hatcher's cell phone in front of her.

'So someone wanted you to have friend Bell's address real bad, huh?'

'Yeah. And they were impatient about it too. So you know what I'm gonna ask...'

'I do, but I'm probably going to disappoint you.'

'Can we get anything at all from it?'

'Sure. I'll get the IP address of the user and we can subpoena the provider to give us the account holder's information, but the chances it leads us to the sender are next to none. Unless whoever sent this was dumb enough to use their home internet connection, all we'll get are the details of whatever router or wifi network they used. I'll do it anyway, but my guess is if they know enough to set up a dummy account, they'll have known to send it from a public network.'

'Okay, but let's do it anyway.' Casey clasped her fingers together. 'And, uh, any chance I could skip the line on this one?'

Maranda tilted her head, one eyebrow arched. 'You asking me for special treatment, Big?'

Casey shrugged – *you know me* ... 'Any of those other jerks bring you coffee?' she said.

Maranda laughed, taking a cup. 'Sure. I'll get on it now.'

Casey sat at her desk surrounded by lists. Phone records, call logs, Bronsons employees, Tina Grace's friends and associates. The anonymous emails needling her. She thought back to the timeframe in question: who had known they were looking for Michael Bell at the time the emails were sent? Cal Morton, the patrol officer at the Second, the one who'd busted Bell years before, he'd put them on to Elena Asimovic. Bell's neighbours at his old address – she and Cullen had canvassed the surrounding houses trying to track him down. Tommy Grace and Jon Parker – they'd shown Bell's picture to both, and both had denied knowing him. But...

Go back to her original theory: two burner phones active on Ramona Beach on the night of Tina's disappearance. Michael Bell the owner of one of them, under the alias Patrick Ball; his records revealed he'd taken a call that night from the other, registered to the still-unknown Kevin Love. Her hunch had been that Love was either Tommy or Parker – but there was no proof of it. Tommy seemed unlikely with what she knew now.

She picked up Jon Parker's call list for the seven days leading up to Tina's disappearance. She went through it again, looking to see if he'd called either of Michael Bell's cell phones; but neither number showed up. She looked again at the night Tina vanished, when Parker had made just one call, highlighted – to 911. It seemed to throb as she looked at it.

She crosschecked against Michael Bell/Patrick Ball's list, looking for any shared contacts that could link the two men – but there were none. Kevin Love's number was right there on the top page, taunting her; an incoming call received from him at 4.12am – just minutes before Tina Grace dialled 911 and shortly before she ended up in Bell's car. The numbers jumbling before her eyes, the timelines crossing and hazing in her mind, something there, but out of reach.

She searched through the file for the call records from the Kevin Love phone, but the paperwork was missing. She got up and went to Jill Hart's desk. 'Hey, I had a question. The burner phones that pinged the tower on Ramona Beach the night Tina Grace disappeared – how come we never requested a warrant for the other one's records – Kevin Love? Once we knew he spoke to Michael Bell that night?'

Jill looked up, confused. 'I'm not...' She went back to her keyboard, tapped something in. Then she pointed. 'We did, look.'

The email with the records attachment was on the screen. 'I saved it into the file on the system.'

'It never made it into the paper file?'

Jill clicked through to a different screen. 'I think it did, I printed it off myself. Here.' She pointed to the notification on the screen of when it'd been sent to the printer.

Casey put her hands on her hips. 'Okay. Weird that it's not there now. Can you fire another copy off for me please?'

Jill clicked her mouse, and Casey made for the printer room.

There was one sheet waiting for her and she carried it back to her desk, scanning the details as she walked. The last call from the Kevin Love account was made just a few hours after Tina's disappearance, and after that there was nothing – the phone probably deactivated, just like Bell's. She dialled the last number called, another cell phone, but it rang for a minute or two and then cut out. No voicemail to indicate who owned it.

She sat down and kept working through the list – highlighting the call to Michael Bell, then looking for anything else familiar. When she got to the end, she went through them again, this time looking at the locations the calls were made from. Mostly Ramona Beach, a couple from downtown Rockport, a couple from Sentona...

Sentona Hills. The country club where Jon Parker was a member. Where he spent the day golfing after Tina disappeared.

Jon Parker to Michael Patrick Bell.

She looked at the highlighted call – the two men speaking right as Tina was about to vanish.

*If it was him.*

She went back to her timeline of the night – the call made at the same time Tina was outside the Stadlers' property at 214. A connection sparked; she brought up the video Marie Stadler had taken, covering that exact timeframe; Tina Grace's final exchange with Jon Parker as he stabbed the air to send her in the direction of Michael Bell's vehicle. Casey watched it through to the end, the movements familiar, but taking on a new significance. Then she grabbed Parker's log again, searching for the call made right at that time.

Nothing there. Exactly what she wanted. 'Got your ass now, motherfucker.'

She jumped up and turned towards Ray's office. He was hidden behind his monitor, where he'd been all day, and the two hadn't spoken. For Casey, McTeague's bombshell was like a wall between them. The worst part wasn't the knowing so much as the guilt; whether to clue Ray in. She'd been wrestling with it ever since McTeague approached her – but what would she say? McTeague's coming for you? He knew that already. On what grounds? Over what? When? She couldn't answer any of those, meaning any warning she could give was impotent.

But ... McTeague was the one hinting there was more to the Ramona Beach murders than just Michael Patrick Bell – mirroring her own instincts. Why use that to get her attention? Did he sense she couldn't let it go and think he could use that to build a bridge with her? He had to know that even if he did, there was no way she could walk over it if it meant leaving Ray to drown on the other side.

And besides: who the fuck was he to dangle information like that? Her investigation into Tina was still live; if he knew something, he should share it.

She took a deep breath and crossed to Ray's office. He looked up when she stopped in his doorway, tilting his chair back. 'Are we winning?'

'I've got him.'

'Who?'

'Jon Parker. Take a look.' She came around his desk and played Marie Stadler's video, Ray leaning forward when it started.

'This is old, isn't it?' he said. 'Didn't we see this already?'

'Yeah, but look at this...' She let it play out, hitting pause right before it ended.

Ray looked up from the screen, his face blank. 'What am I seeing here?'

She pointed to Jon Parker, walking out of shot with his cell phone to his ear, then laid Parker's cell records on the desk. 'The video is 4.12am. Look at his call list...' She ran her finger down the rows. 'Nothing there. Only his call to 911 nine minutes later. So he's got a second phone he didn't tell us about. And the call he's making is at the *exact* same time as Michael Bell's burner cell received an incoming from the other burner on Ramona Beach that night. Jon Parker is Kevin Love.'

He squinted reading the list, then sat back and looked at the ceiling in silence. 'That's still a leap.'

'It's the only unaccounted-for call that pinged the Ramona tower within a forty-minute window. There's no one else it could be.'

'Son of a bitch.'

She smiled. 'Right?'

Ray brought his chair forward again, nodding. 'Okay. But even if Parker had a second cell, what does it prove?'

'It proves he's a lying piece of shit who knew more about Tina Grace's disappearance than he admitted to. We've got him on tape calling her killer.'

He closed his eyes, nodding. 'I get that, Big, I'm trying to see it from the DA's point of view.'

'We get a search warrant for the cell and it might get us closer to Tina.'

'It's not me you need to convince...'

'I know.'

He studied her a few seconds. 'You okay? You look like you got something else on your mind.'

'It's just...' She hesitated, McTeague on the tip of her tongue.

'It's Cullen, y'know? Doesn't feel right without him still.' The lie came easy because it was true – just not the true answer.

'I know. I feel the same way.' He stood up and faced her, took a gentle grip on her shoulders. 'He thought the world of you, you know that right? He told me, all the time, how much he learned, partnering with you.'

She dropped her gaze to the floor, flushing. 'He never could hold his liquor.'

Ray smiled at the joke, then slowly turned away to pick up the call list. His eyes moved, scanning it, thinking. 'What are the chances he kept the burner cell? Smart money says it's at the bottom of the bay.'

'Bell kept his. And Parker's arrogant enough to think he's outsmarted us...'

Ray nodded. 'The DA's going to have a shitfit if it looks like we're saying they closed the case too soon.'

'If Parker was involved, he needs to go down.'

'Sure, of course – but are we trying to find Tina or trying to nail Parker?'

'It's all the same thing, right?'

'Maybe.'

For the first time, she saw doubt in his eyes when he looked at her. 'Maybe?'

He planted his hands on the desk. 'Look, I'm not denying it looks like Parker's hiding something, there's no question in my mind he's a slimy piece of shit. But the way this plays to me, he used Bell as a driver and he was trying to get her the hell out of there. If there was more to it than that, something to link him to the other vics, you gotta figure McTeague's crew would've turned it up.'

'Okay, what about this?' She took out her phone and

showed him the anonymous emails alerting Brent Hatcher to Bell's whereabouts. 'Somebody went to a lot of trouble to make sure we'd know where Bell was holed up. Does this look like a normal tipoff to you?'

He took the phone and read through them again, then looked up. 'No. It does not.' He kept staring at the screen a few seconds longer, something turning behind his blank expression. 'What's McTeague's take on this?'

'I haven't told him yet.'

He held the phone out for her to take back. 'This one really got to you, huh?'

She met his eyes and nodded.

He breathed out slowly through his nose. 'Let me see if I can get you a warrant without the DA ripping my head off. No promises. And it'll need to be watertight or Parker'll have Clarence Mickelroff get it thrown out.'

She felt a jolt inside, a little electric spark. 'Thanks, boss.'

## CHAPTER 25

Rain was blowing in off the Atlantic as Casey approached the end of the causeway, sweeping across the blacktop in waves and spattering the choppy waters of the bay.

She sped along an empty Ocean Road then made the turning onto Ramona Boulevard, following it to Jon Parker's place. The Atlantic's black waters shadowed her as she drove, the grey sky above just as oppressive.

She went by Parker's house and carried on until she was far enough past that she wouldn't be easily seen. Then she found a place to pull over.

His Lex was on the driveway, and she watched in vain for ten, twenty, thirty minutes, no chance to catch a glimpse of him – what she really wanted, as if she could see him with new eyes now. Time stretched, and she found herself questioning what he was doing; she imagined him inside, satisfied he'd got one over on the dumb bitch cop they sent to try and investigate him, working his phones to line up his next 'date'. Tina Grace long forgotten, as disposable to him as a takeout cup.

Ray's question from earlier resurfaced then: *Is this about Tina, or Parker?* She looked at herself in the rearview, only her eyes visible, doubt making a resurgence. 'You sure you're still objective about this one, Casey? What are you even doing here?'

She shook her head and looked away. Talking to herself the way her mom used to; a habit she used to rib her for, one she swore she'd never slip into herself.

She tried to justify her conclusions. Her theory felt solid, even without the physical evidence: Parker had lied to them from minute one, and he'd always been her leading candidate for the Kevin Love alias. The challenge was discerning what it proved – and more importantly, if it helped her shine a light on Tina Grace's fate. What did Parker say to Bell on that call? An instruction to come pick Tina up, or something worse? Did he know where Bell had taken her? Left her?

Worse was the thought that Tina had known what was coming. Her 911 call – 'He's gonna kill me.' If it *was* Bell gave her the ride there, why would she only then be terrified of him? Casey thought about Tina's rumour – girls disappearing after going to a job with a high-end client. What if it was real, if Parker was that guy, and she'd somehow found out over the course of their date? Was it possible he'd admitted it to her, some kind of sick pride at work? In any other circumstance, it would be easier to imagine Tina high or drunk and falling for her own paranoid urban legend – but with three bodies less than a mile from his property...

A movement at the house made her look up. And then there he was: Playboy Jon Parker, looking tanned and relaxed in fitted navy slacks and immaculate golf shoes, putting his clubs into his car and climbing inside. He gunned the engine and backed the Lex onto the road, pointing it her way. She slid lower in her seat, suddenly afraid he might've spotted her. The Lexus came along the street in her direction, but as he approached, he just kept accelerating and cruised right by.

Casey sat up when he was gone, watching him disappear down Ramona Boulevard. Everything he'd done to avoid scrutiny, all the lies he'd told, the secrets he still held, and he got to just sail on through his perfect life unflustered? Fuck that.

She snatched up her cell, tapped a message to Ray: *How's my warrant looking?*

He replied just before she pulled away: *Trying.*

Her phone rang as she pulled into the precinct parking lot and she grabbed it off the passenger seat, hoping to see Ray's name on the screen. A department number.

'Yeah?'

'Casey, it's Maranda Jessup at tech.'

She took a breath so the disappointment wouldn't creep into her voice. 'Maranda, hey, what've you got for me?'

'Almost exactly what I promised – not much.'

Casey felt her chest deflate again. 'Hit me.'

'The emails you had me look at, giving up your guy Bell's address: the first was sent using a VPN – you know what that is?'

'That's where it reroutes your IP address to hide your location?'

'Bingo – and in this case, it places our sender in the middle of Los Angeles.'

'Any way we can get past the reroutes and figure out where they really were?'

'You know what I'm gonna say...'

'Jeez, you wanna throw a girl a bone here? What about the other email?'

'This one's a little more interesting. The sender dispensed with the VPN this time, I'm thinking maybe they were in a rush, or mobile and didn't have one set up on their device.'

'Okay, so what's that tell us?'

'In itself, nothing. But I can tell you the sender used a public Wifi network in Westport Village.'

Westport – one of the commuter suburbs heading west out of town. In her head she ran through lists of people linked to the case, or to Michael Bell, trying to think of any connection to that area, but drew a blank. It was a relatively prosperous part of town, a million miles from Bell's tumbledown neighbourhood. 'Any info on the user?'

'Nothing, it's an open Wifi network covering the mall. So that narrows it down to an area of something like a half-mile.'

'The mall? So theoretically they could show up on a security camera?'

'Sure, but what are you going to look for? Someone holding a cell phone? And don't forget, it could be someone in the parking lot, in the bathrooms, anywhere.'

'Goddammit.'

'Sorry, Big – I did warn you I wouldn't have good news...'

'A woman of your word,' Casey said, drawing a small laugh. 'Hey, I get it, appreciate the rush job anyway.'

'Sure thing.'

Casey hung up and dropped the cell in her pocket. Every step forward taking her further away.

She went inside and ran up the stairs, a day that'd started out promising turning sour. She remembered the joke Ray used to make about days like this: 'You know what I call 'em, Big? Workdays.'

She went straight over to his office, but there was no sign of him. She turned around, Dana at her desk. 'You know where the lieutenant's at?'

'He's in meetings all afternoon. I've been waiting on him to authorise my vacation time...'

'Vacation?' She patted Dana's chair as she went by. 'Who the hell would wanna get away from this place?'

She dropped into her seat and let her head roll back, the lists and papers she'd been working through earlier still strewn across the desk. The Kevin Love call logs, implicating Parker, right there taunting her, while the son of a bitch golfed. The evidence she needed off limits, until she had the warrant. One last link to Tina Grace, slipping further out of reach with every passing second.

Then she sat up, another route opening up in her mind. A shortcut – but the price was heavy. She grappled with it a moment, the buzz of the office fading out, deciding if she was willing to pay it. Her fingers wrapped around her cell phone. Already knowing she was.

She found McTeague's number and dialled.

# CHAPTER 26

Casey parked in the floodlight's beam, the white light crisp and sharp, cutting through the night. The parking lot was empty aside from her, acres of asphalt standing silent as a graveyard.

Her armpits were damp, even though the meeting was her call, the location too, shocked how readily he'd agreed to all of it. Now McTeague swung into the lot and pulled up beside her, his window already down. Casey lowered hers and let the cold air flood in. 'Captain. Thanks for coming.'

A slight nod. 'You wanna tell me what we're doing out here?'

She took her phone out, the screen glow outlining her face in the wing mirror. 'You were right about me getting Michael Bell's address.' She had the emails sent to Brent Hatcher already on the screen and she passed the phone over to him without further explanation.

'What am…?' He kept reading, the meaning becoming clear. Then he opened his door and got out, passed the phone back to her through the window. 'What do we know about the sender?'

'Almost nothing. The first one was sent through a VPN that places them in Los Angeles. The second was sent from right here.'

He kept his eyes on her a moment longer, then looked around slowly. The mall was lit up even at night, the Ross and Sears signs glowing vivid blue in the darkness. 'Westport Mall? Is there a significance?'

She climbed out of the car so he wasn't looming over her anymore. 'Not that I know of. But it's public, anonymous. Hide in plain sight.'

He riffled his fingers on the car roof, looking around and then at her again. 'You're convinced Bell isn't the end of this.'

'What I care about is what happened to Tina Grace.'

'Not the other vics?'

She folded her arms. 'That's a cheap shot.'

He closed his eyes and dipped his head, a retreat from it. 'What I meant is why are you fixated on her in particular?'

'C'mon, you're telling me you never got an attachment to a case? You sit with the family, you walk them through all the shit...'

He folded his arms and leaned against his car. 'You didn't set this up just to tell me about the address.'

She came a half-step closer to him. 'I've got more, but I want to know what you were hinting at the other night. At Cullen's wake.' Talking to him like this made her lightheaded; out of nowhere, finding herself with sway over Robbie McTeague.

He stared at her a long second, and it felt like he was making a decision in that moment. He pulled out his own cell, slow and deliberate, like he was crossing the Rubicon in his mind. He held up a photograph for her to look at, a crack running down the middle of his screen. 'This is Bell's signature from the rental agreement on the storage unit we pulled the Ramona Beach vics' clothing from.' He swiped to the next photograph. 'Here's a bank sample for comparison.'

They were similar, but not the same – the second more angular, the script tighter and more crowded. Casey took the phone out of his hand to look closer. 'This is ... These are two different people.'

'Yeah.' He waited until she looked away and took it back from her. 'The manager at the storage place has no recollection of seeing Bell before, same for his staff. So what does that tell me?'

'There's no way he could remember everyone comes through there.'

'We found the key to the unit in Bell's residence, but we never lifted his prints or DNA off of it. Bell only moved into that bungalow four weeks before he died, he's moved around plenty, had a history of ditching out on landlords without settling the rent. The storage unit was paid up for the next six months – cash in advance. Does that sound like our guy to you?'

'Jesus.' She pushed her hair back and stuffed her hands back in her pockets. 'Are you saying he was set up?'

'Not yet.'

'Then...?'

'Just that the address was a nice get. The storage unit even better. Full of keepsakes from his vics, all of it. And they both just fell into our laps.'

Her face changed, and he caught it, looking like he wanted to take it back. 'I didn't mean ... I know the price we paid.'

She swiped her hand to blow it off. 'How about we just skip to the part where you tell me what you want from me, Captain.'

'I need to know if I can trust you.'

She held her arms out. 'With what?'

'Carletti.'

Her head dipped at that.

He shifted his weight, his floodlit shadow moving on the ground. Red lights blurring on the freeway in the distance behind him, the engine sounds carrying in the freezing night air. 'You really don't see it with him, do you?'

'See what? You came at me on the second-worst day of my goddamn life with an implication and a bunch of cryptic bullshit...'

'I was sure you were clued in. Not all the way, but I figured he would've given you a piece to keep you quiet.' He straightened up to his full height and took a breath. 'Like Cullen.'

The name shorted every circuit in her head. She didn't say anything, just watched his mouth, not even certain she'd heard right.

'But as hard as I've looked, I can't find your fingerprints on any of it. So are you just smarter than Carletti? Or does he keep you out of it to protect you?'

She was staring at him, everything in overdrive: the lights dazzling, the cold suddenly imperceptible.

He studied her face, his breath fogging in wisps, coming to some conclusion...

'Shit,' he said. 'You really are in the dark?'

'What exactly are you accusing him of?'

'Street rips, trafficking, witness intimidation – Carletti's good for all of it.'

'Bullshit.'

'I know you're close to him, but what I'm telling you is the truth. You know about Zoltan Kuresev?'

Kuresev – the crackhead who'd triggered McTeague's inquiry with his brutality suit against Ray. 'Of course. He took a kick at Cullen, and the lieutenant handed him his ass. The suit is horseshit, and so's your inquiry – departmental failings is bull and you know it.'

'Kuresev weighs a buck-thirty soaking wet. He's got no history of violence. He's gonna start kicking Dave Cullen in front of a building full of cops?'

The one doubt she'd always had about the incident now blowing up large enough to project on the fucking sky. 'So what's your version?'

'Zoltan Kuresev is only about the next fix, which is why he

was dumb enough to burglarise Ray Carletti's house in the first place – even though he didn't know it was Carletti's. One of the things he took was a duffel containing eight pounds of marijuana that Ray ripped from Alfonso Duarte's crew. Ray had Kuresev brought in so he could beat on him until he gave up where he had it stashed. He smashed his head into the ground as a warning to the street not to fuck with him.'

She turned her face away from him so he wouldn't see her reaction. 'Half the guys we bring in try some version of that story. Except we don't fall for it.'

'In this case it's true. I've got two witnesses who saw Dave Cullen recover the dope from Kuresev's flop.'

Her whole body was starting to spin. 'They're lying.'

'Look, I know you don't want to believe it about either of them, but I've been doing this a long time. You think I'd say this if I wasn't sure? If I didn't have the evidence? It was Cullen picked up Kuresev for Ray in the first place. Then he sent him to go get his dope back. Ray wasn't in that parking lot by coincidence, it was all planned.'

She stuffed her hands into her pockets and made herself look at him again. 'You're a real piece of shit, you know that? Why're you bringing Dave into this? Because he can't defend himself?'

'I'm not doing anything to him. Cullen made his choices. They both did.'

'If there was anything to this – *anything* – you'd have moved on him by now. Everyone knows you hate Carletti.'

'Because I've always known he's dirty. But the proof's only coming out now.'

'Then why haven't you taken him down?'

'It's not that simple.'

She stared into him, looking for the rest of it. 'Don't tell me this is about protecting the department, some shit like that.'

'There's what we know, what we can prove, and what we'll allow to come to light. You know they're three different things.'

'Then why are you telling me this? What do you want from me?'

He leaned against his car. 'Kuresev's attorney is playing it smart. He's holding the dope angle back from the media because he's using it as leverage. He knows it's got more value as a threat than out in the open. If it goes to trial, no court's gonna want to order a fat settlement to a perp with a sheet like Kuresev, so his strategy is to get HCPD to pay more now to keep everything under wraps.'

'You're still not saying what you want from me.'

'Kuresev's gonna get his money because he's the thin end of the wedge when it comes to Carletti and corruption in the department. What we know about is bad enough, what's keeping the chief and the county executive awake at night is what we don't know. So Kuresev gets paid to go away quietly, and it's my job to figure out the extent of what else there is.'

'You want me to inform for you.'

'I've been watching you a long time. I think you're a good cop, and I think you know which way's up.'

She stepped back from him, running up against the car, her eyes slipping out of focus as she tried to take it in. 'I don't know anything about any of this. Assuming this isn't bullshit, how am I supposed to get anything from him?'

'Cullen's gone now. Carletti's gonna need someone he can trust. You think of anyone else fits the bill better?'

She thought about the cosy conversation with Jill Hart a few days before. Jealousy and paranoia at the time. Now...? 'What about my case? Bell and Tina Grace?'

'You keep working it. Something you need, you speak to me.'

'I need access to your files on the other vics. And whatever else you've got on Bell.'

'The files are no problem. On Bell, what you've seen is all I've got.' McTeague ran the back of his hand over his mouth. 'But why don't you tell me about the warrant you want.'

Casey squared up to him, trying not to show how shocked she was that he already knew. 'Why're you letting the DA conclude the investigation if you're not convinced Bell's the killer?"

'I have questions, that's all. And it's not me *letting* them do anything, that's the DA's call.'

'Come on, everyone knows you're their guy inside the department.'

'What if I am? It's a one-way street.'

'You're telling me you've got no sway? Come the fuck on. Someone over there tipped you off about my warrant.'

'Maybe. Sometimes.' He pushed himself off his car. 'But there's not a DA alive would turn down a slam dunk like Bell. Unless I've got something concrete to offer them, they're satisfied he's their guy and they're taking the easy win.'

'And you're okay with that?'

'No. That's why I'm giving you the ball. You brought me here to show me those emails because you've got suspicions the same as I do. That gives us common cause. You said you've got more, so I'm asking you: what else have you got?'

She studied his expression – genuine. She was amazed at how they were talking almost like equals. A month before she'd have laughed at the idea. There was a rush came with the feeling, an urge to impress to cement the dynamic. 'Jon Parker called Bell on a burner cell right before Tina disappeared. He's behind the Kevin Love alias; he knew Bell and he lied.'

He didn't react. Disappointment needled her gut, but she pressed ahead anyway, detailing how the call records matched with the Stadler video.

'It's not enough.'

'For what?'

'A judge. Your search warrant.'

'You don't know that. Ray's working on it, but...'

'But he hasn't got the pull with the judges, and the DA won't help him because they don't want him screwing with their closure.'

They stared at each other, Casey not knowing what to say. She let her hands drop to her sides, deflated. An illusion, that's all it was; thinking she had sway over McTeague – until she showed him her cards and he dismissed them as nothing.

She reached behind herself and popped the car door.

'You're leaving?' McTeague said.

'I just gave you what I've got and you took a piss on it. I think we're through.'

'I'm not saying it can't be done,' he said. 'You'll get your warrant if I push it.'

She stopped, halfway turned around, the deal he was touting suddenly coming clear. 'So that's what it comes down to? I have to snitch for you just to be able to do my job properly?'

'It's not a tradeoff. I'm making it easier for you to do the right thing. Besides, you didn't even ask me what you get out of it yet.'

'What do you mean? The warrant – I get my warrant.'

A pained smile. 'Jesus Christ, if your naivety thing is an act, you're good.'

'I swear to God, talk straight to me or I'm gone.'

'You're the first cop I ever fitted for a rat jacket that didn't ask for a raise. If a warrant's all you want for snitching, you got it, but you should charge a higher price.'

She held her hands up, exasperated. 'I thought it was about good cops and bad cops, "knowing which way's up".'

'The two aren't mutually exclusive.' He reached around and held her door for her. 'When Carletti's gone, I'll see you get his command.'

She slid into her seat. 'I don't play your games. Just get me the warrant.' She thought about what Ray's reaction would be when he found out she'd gone over his head, to McTeague of all people, her stomach churning. 'It's the right thing to do.'

## CHAPTER 27

The cell phone ringing on the nightstand woke her, and straightaway it was all back in front of her, as clear as a TV being turned on in the dark. Carletti. Cullen. Dope. Running through her head most of the night, past 4am the last time she'd looked at the clock. All of it still there now, the flow uninterrupted, as if she'd never slept at all.

Something felt wrong – the bedroom lighter than her usual wakeup. She grabbed the phone as she looked at the clock through blurry eyes, curse words spilling out when she saw she'd overslept. She felt wired and groggy at the same time, McTeague's rat jacket crushing her chest before she'd even put it on.

She answered the phone and just like that, he was in her ear again.

'Captain?'

'Where are you?'

'Just about to leave the house.'

'Your warrant's good to go.'

'That's ...Thanks.'

'I'll meet you at Parker's place.'

'I'll be there.' She cut the call, already making for the shower.

She rolled up to Parker's just before nine, sunlight breaking through the clouds overhead in pinprick shafts. The wind had dropped, enough that she could hear the ocean washing over the beach beneath the dunes. Across the street, the bare groundsel trees and spike grass barely moved in the breeze, standing silent and serene, no hint of the carnage they'd concealed just a mile along the road. As she stepped out of the car, she saw McTeague coming down Ramona Boulevard and felt a weird sense of relief that she'd made it before him.

He parked behind her, and she waited for him at the bottom of the driveway. 'Don't you sleep?' she said as he came over.

'Best time to catch a judge is first thing.' He looked at the house, squinting in the dappled sunlight. 'There a chance Parker gets violent?'

She shook her head. 'It'd be out of character if he did.'

'Okay. Let's go.'

Casey went first up the path and banged on the door. 'It's Casey Wray from HCPD, Mr Parker. Open up.'

No answer came. She knocked again, harder.

No response.

Casey tilted her head at the Lexus on the driveway. 'His car's here. Lemme check around back.'

She skirted the side of the house, the sound of the ocean growing louder as she went. At the end of the back yard, the marram grass lining the top of the dunes swayed and danced. A charged quiet, jazzing her inside like a ten-shot coffee.

She came around to the rear and went to the French doors. She peered through the glass, cupping her hands around her eyes to see inside.

'Shit.' She pulled her gun. 'CAPTAIN.'

She tried the door handle and it came open, and she pushed through the doorway, gun first.

Jon Parker was slumped across the couch and its armrest at a drunken angle, gunshot wounds to his head and chest. 'No, no...' Casey moved towards him. 'POLICE, IS THERE ANYBODY IN THE HOUSE?'

McTeague came through the doors behind her, his sidearm drawn.

Casey holstered her gun and reached down to check for a pulse. She glanced back at McTeague. 'Nothing.' She drew her pistol again and crept across the living room to check the kitchen, then toed open the bathroom door – empty. She tried the door to the garage – locked.

McTeague started edging up the staircase. Breathing fast, she stationed herself on the bottom step to cover the ground floor while he checked the bedrooms, his footsteps moving slowly above her. After a few seconds he called down. 'Clear.'

Casey pulled her cell and dialled 911.

## CHAPTER 28

He'd been shot at close range, once in the chest, once in the head. There was no sign of forced entry, no sign of a struggle. The bedrooms, closets and furniture were undisturbed, nothing to indicate a burglary gone bad or any other motive.

'Someone he knew,' McTeague said. They were walking back to the cars. A brief scan of the front and back of the house had offered up no footprints, no clue to where the killer had come from or gone to, no physical evidence.

'He's been dead a few hours at least,' Casey said. 'That puts us in the middle of the night. Either he let them in, or they had a key.'

'We know of anyone who might have a key to his place?'

She shook her head. 'But I wouldn't rule out a fuckbuddy. Or a cleaner, something like that.' She pointed to Ellis Sandford's house. 'This guy's in everyone's business, we should try him first.'

She started towards Sandford's place, but McTeague touched her shoulder to turn her back around.

'This stinks,' he said. 'The timing, all of it.'

'That's what I've been saying all along.'

He was nodding as she moved off again across the grass.

Sandford answered as soon as she knocked. The first patrol cars came down the road behind them, and McTeague peeled off to intercept them. Sandford spotted them before Casey could speak, his face becoming a question mark.

'Mr Sandford, I'm sorry to disturb you but there was an incident at Mr Parker's home last night, I wanted to see if you saw or heard anything?'

'I don't ... What kind of incident?'

'I'm afraid Jon Parker is dead, sir.'

'Dead? How?'

'I can't get into the details right now but it looks likely we'll be treating this as a homicide. So anything you can tell me will be extremely valuable.'

He stepped to one side, bracing himself against the doorframe. 'No, I ... I didn't see anything. Or hear anything. Not a thing.' His eyes were hollow in disbelief.

'Did you see Mr Parker last night or talk to him at all?'

'No. I noticed him pull up in the evening but ... No, I didn't speak to him yesterday.'

'Do you happen to know if he has any family – next of kin, someone we can contact?'

'He's got a sister in Boston, that's about all I know. I don't have her details, she's never been to visit, to my knowledge. His parents passed some years ago.' His eyes strayed to the scene at Parker's house.

Two uniforms were setting up a perimeter, drawing some of the other residents out onto the street; Casey picked out Greta Van Heusen and Marie Stadler standing together, their gazes alternating between the scene and where she stood. McTeague had collared the other two uniforms and was directing them where to start canvassing. She had a feeling it would be futile; if Sandford hadn't seen anything, the chances anyone else had felt slim.

'I appreciate your help, Mr Sandford. Here's my card again if anything comes back to you.'

He took it, his eyes locked on Parker's house now, unblinking. 'I don't understand what's happening to this place. It's like it's cursed.'

They stood by McTeague's car as the CSIs went to work inside and out. Her phone buzzed again and she looked down – a voicemail from Ray. The second call of his she'd dodged that morning.

Uniform were going door to door, but none of the residents so far had reported seeing or hearing anything. Greta Van Heusen confirmed her husband Jerry had left for work at 5.30am as normal; Casey got hold of him on his cell phone, but he said he hadn't noticed anything or anyone unusual at that time. The general reaction in the neighbourhood seemed to match Ellis Sandford's – shock coupled with a feeling that something was deeply wrong on Ramona Beach.

Casey called Billy D at the office.

'Hey, Big, heard the news – that's some crazy shit.'

'Yeah. Listen—'

'Lieutenant Ray's trying to get hold of you, did you know? He seems kinda pissed.'

Casey blanched. She glanced around to make sure McTeague was out of earshot. 'Yeah, I know. I must've forgot his birthday or something. Listen, Bill, I need you to co-ordinate with Maranda Jessup at tech. I want everything we can get from Jon Parker's electronics, as fast as we can get it.'

There was a pause, Billy scrabbling for a pen. 'Okay, sure. Anything in particular you want me to prioritise?'

She turned around, watching McTeague across the street and then the scene behind him, tapping her hand against her thigh. 'We won't know until we look. Make sure everything comes to you and me as soon as we have it, we'll divide it up so we can work through it faster. I want to know who he spoke to, who he met with, anything and everything. He was golfing yesterday afternoon, so I'll talk to the staff at Sentona Hills, and uniform are canvassing this end, so we'll see what the neighbours know, if anything. You get me everything else.'

'No problem.'

'Thanks, Bill.'

'You want me to get the boss on the line?'

'No. Tell him I'll call him soon as I can.'

She cut the call, McTeague waiting for her expectantly.

'What are we dealing with here?' he said when she came over.

She looked at her feet, not wanting to admit she was at a loss. 'If it's someone he knew, we'll get them. Phone records, messages, emails – we pull them all and they'll lead us there.'

'I mean big picture. That's what's bothering me.'

'Yeah.'

'Someone wanted us to find Bell, and now this guy's dead too. I don't buy coincidence here, so I'm starting to think someone's covering their tracks.'

'Then you *are* calling Bell a setup.'

He looked to the side, one eye closed against the sunlight. 'I'm still not there yet, but there's more here that we're not seeing. Is there anything else we can do to find the sender on those emails?'

'Maranda at tech says not.'

He grimaced. 'Of course not.'

'But about that: there were only a few people knew we were looking for Bell as a suspect at the time the emails were sent.' She tilted her head toward the house. 'Parker was one of them.'

'You think Parker sent them?'

'He's the only one with an established link to Bell – through the call on the burner phones.'

'What's the motive for capping Parker then?'

'Maybe this is a revenge thing. Parker dropped the dime on Bell, and this is someone coming for payback?'

He thought about it a moment, nodding. 'That could fly. If Parker was the real killer, he'd have every reason to point us at Bell. He'd have the means to pay off a storage locker in advance, and fill it with evidence. You liked Parker for the murders before you got to Bell, right?'

'He lied to us from the get-go. Mickelroff tried to explain it away as him being embarrassed when we brought him in, but I was never totally convinced.'

He bulged his cheek with his tongue. 'Okay. Keep that thought between us for now.'

'Look, there's one other suspect we need to rule out. Tommy Grace.'

'Tina's brother?'

'Yeah. I honestly don't buy him as a killer, but he came around here before trying to get at Parker. And he was carrying.'

'Jesus Christ. As if that family needs any more shit. Go talk to him, I'll take care of this.'

'Okay.' She took her phone out. 'I'll call Maranda Jessup on the way and tell her to clear the decks. I want to know what we can get from Parker's devices ASAP.'

McTeague called after her as she went to the car. She turned around. 'Yeah?'

'Watch yourself when you talk to Tommy Grace, Big. Be sure this family's not a blind spot for you.'

Casey rang the bell expecting Maggie Grace to answer, but it was Tommy himself who came to the door.

'Detective?'

'I need to talk to you, Tommy.'

'Shit. Is it Tina?'

'No, I'm not here about Tina. Where were you last night? Between 10pm and 9am?'

'I been here all night. Why?'

'Is there anyone who can corroborate that?'

'Why? What for?'

'Answer my question, please.'

'Ain't no one here with me if that's what you want to know. Mom went out yesterday and she never came home.'

'Do you have any idea where she's at?'

'Some bar or other. It's what she does now, since you all forgot about her.'

Casey closed her eyes, Tommy's line only a flesh wound, but flashing a glimpse of a new set of bad possibilities. 'So you were home alone the whole time?'

'I was sleeping, yeah. You gonna tell me what's going on?'

'Jon Parker was murdered last night.'

He stared at her, saying nothing. Then his eyes narrowed. 'You accusing me?'

'No. I'm trying to eliminate you actually.'

'Why would I kill his ass?'

'After what you did before? You really need me to answer that?'

'That was then. Things changed, he didn't do it, right?'

'Just think for a minute, Tommy. Did anyone see you at home last night, anyone call you on the landline, anything at all?'

'Landline got disconnected 'cus mom stopped paying the bills.' He ran his knuckle under his nose. 'Ain't no one came by here last night. My car's in the shop getting fixed, so tell me how I'm supposed to get out to the beach to shoot him?'

'Where's your gun, Tommy?'

'Inside.'

'When was the last time you fired it?'

'I never fired it.'

'Never? Not even at the range, nothing like that?'

'The fuck am I gonna do at a range? Hang out with all the cops and Republicans? It's for protection, I'm not some NRA freak.'

'Okay. Then I'd like you to come with me to the station to run some tests, see if we can't eliminate you right now.'

'Are you arresting me?'

'I could, but I'm asking you to come voluntarily.'

'I got nothing to hide but I ain't coming to the station. No way.'

'How'd you know he was shot, Tommy?'

'It's what you said.'

'I said murdered.'

He jerked his hand out by his hip. 'Shit, it was just words, how else he gonna get killed?'

'If you've got nothing to hide, come with me now and let's get this cleared up.'

He stepped back from the doorway, looking off to one side, his neck pulsing where it was twisted. Then he held his hands out, as if she was going to cuff him. 'Fuck it. I told you, this is nothing to do with me.'

Casey gave him a look and pointed to the car instead. She took her cell phone out, looking for Maggie Grace's number, a sense of dread surging. 'When's the last time you heard from your mom?'

Vander Halpin, scene manager at Parker's house, gave Casey the first debrief that afternoon. McTeague was already on the line when she dialled in, an unexpected presence, the feeling like he was shadowing everything she did.

None of what they heard was encouraging. Parker had been shot at close range with a .38 – a detail that tweaked Casey because it was the same calibre as Tommy's pistol. There was no obvious sign of defensive wounds, nothing to indicate Parker had tried to stop his assailant or even got his hands up trying to protect himself when the first shot was fired. Given he was facing his killer at close quarters, it reinforced Casey's assumption that his assailant must've been known to him.

Halpin advised that they'd recovered various hair and fibre samples, along with a multitude of fingerprints, all of which were being processed. Casey undercut his budding optimism when she brought up Parker's reputation as a womaniser, and the fact that any number of people could've been through the house. Aside from the samples, they'd found one partial footprint, likely a man's, from the grass outside the French doors. It was pointed away from the house, suggesting – if it was the assailant's – that that was the point of exit. Which would only confirm what she suspected from the doors being unlocked when they got there. Halpin's team had taken a cast for comparison.

A search of the property yielded one laptop, an iPad and a single cell phone – Parker's personal iPhone, registered under his own name and address. No sign of a burner – but for Casey that didn't prove anything one way or another; the last call from the Kevin Love cell was made in the hours after Tina's disappearance; she always feared the subsequent lack of activity was a sign it'd been ditched, so its absence didn't eliminate Parker as its owner. But the chance of finding out what happened to Tina felt more remote than ever. Halpin finished up saying they'd passed everything to the tech team to get to work on.

Better news came when Casey got off the call: residue tests on Tommy and his pistol came back negative. The gun hadn't been fired in some time, and more importantly was in such a state of disrepair that if it had been fired, it likely would've come apart at the seams. Tommy the half-assed tough guy – but true to his word at least. Casey delivered the news to him, and his comeback wasn't much of a surprise: 'Told you it wasn't me.'

'Yeah, you did. Look, I can't reach your mom, I've called her a couple times and she's not picking up. Were you serious when you said this is normal for her now?'

His face softened, signs of concern creeping in. 'Not the booze, but being gone this long is. She stayed out one night last week, but she showed up the next morning. She'd been drinking the whole time, I had to put her ass to bed.'

'Do you know where she'd been? Specifically?'

'A couple neighbourhood bars. I tried them already. She was at one of them last night until late, but she hasn't been by today.'

'What about friends? Is there anyplace she might be at?'

He flared his nostrils, thinking. 'I can try some people.'

'Do that and get back to me. I'd like to know as soon as she turns up.'

'What, you care again now? Is that it?'

'I never stopped caring.'

'That's why you pulled me in here on this bullshit.'

Casey stepped back from him, suddenly exhausted. 'You're your own worst enemy, Tommy. Just call me soon as you hear something.'

Maranda Jessup came through with her preliminary report at the end of the day. Casey caught the call at her desk.

'We managed to get into Parker's iPhone – the dummy had all his codes and passwords noted down on a pad in his desk. He had two email accounts set up on it; one of them's a Hotmail, but it's not the one your emails came from. The laptop only shows those two accounts too, same with the iPad, but of course that doesn't rule out the dummy account being his. But, also to note, I can't see anything to indicate he's ever set up VPN software on any of the three devices. He could have another laptop or something he used, but that's just guesswork, and I'd rate it unlikely; he doesn't seem to be the most tech-savvy guy and it doesn't look like he's ever cleared out his browsing history.'

'Any red flags in there?'

'No. He was a regular on various porn sites, but garden-variety stuff. Aside from that, it's a pretty small roster of sites he visited – Yahoo and the *New York Times* for news, ESPN, NBA.com; Twitter and Instagram too – although it looks like he was a lurker who used them to check out girls. He's got a Facebook profile, that'll take a bit longer to go through – he was conversing-with-slash-hassling a bunch of women over Messenger, but there's nothing obviously alarming in there, not even dick pics or anything. It's mostly him flirting and trying to set up dates.'

'With escorts?'

'Doesn't seem that way, but I'll need to look at it longer. It's hard to tell sometimes when it's done online.'

'What about a Tinder account?'

'I haven't got to it yet. Your guy was a real dog, huh?'

'Can you bump that up your list? I'd like to know the content of his conversations with Tina Grace.'

'Sure. In fact, hold on a minute...' The line went quiet, and Casey's eyes strayed to Ray's office again – empty all afternoon. 'Okay, I'm in his account, but there's no sign of Tina Grace in here. Did she use an alias?'

'Not that we're aware. You're certain?'

'Certain as I can be...'

Casey had written Tina's name on her pad and now traced a cross through it. 'Huh. Does her name appear anywhere else in his stuff?'

'Not that I've seen yet. I'll go through everything in closer detail, but I wanted to give you a snapshot now. Anything else you want me to look for specifically?'

'Yeah, any mention of, or contact with, Michael Patrick Bell, aka Patrick Ball.'

'No problem.' She paused. 'I'm looking at his contacts now. He's not listed, at least not under those names. Let me have the numbers you've got for him?'

Casey read out the numbers for Bell's burner phones.

'Thanks.' Another pause. 'Nope, they're not saved anywhere on this handset.'

'Dammit.' She propped her head up on the desk with her fist. 'Listen, can I get a look at his stuff myself?'

'Sure, soon as we're done. But in the meantime I've sent you some goodies to start with – I've run off a dump of all his text messages and Facebook Messenger chats, that should be in your inbox now. Something to get you started.'

'Amazing. Thank you.'

'Don't thank me. There's a shitload.'

The words blurred in front of her eyes. Sheets and sheets of Parker's messages she'd printed out, less than a quarter of the way through and so far none of them relevant. Chats with various women, ranging from courtly to sleazy, locker-room talk with some of his buddies, all interspersed with endless automated messages: notifications from his bank, his cellular provider, tee times from Sentona Hills – on and on. She kept stopping, tiredness making her concentration fritz, her cell phone the easy distraction. Checking, waiting, for word from Tommy Grace.

She'd called him twice, Maggie still AWOL. She checked her Recents, the last time more than two hours ago, thought about trying him again...

The phone lit up in her hands: *Ray calling*.

She still hadn't spoken to him that day. She took a breath before she hit Accept.

'Hey, boss, listen I'm sorry—'

'Casey, where are you?' He was out of breath, angsty.

'I'm at my desk.'

'Okay stay there, I'm coming up now.'

He hung up.

Casey looked around, the office sparse, wondering what

the hell was coming her way. She glanced at the doors, a flash thought to try to duck out. But that would only prolong it; she couldn't dodge him forever, and if he was going to chew her out for going over his head, better to get it over with.

She watched the doors, her heart rate climbing until it jumped when he burst through them.

Casey stood up as he rushed over. 'Boss, sorry, I know you're mad at me—'

'What?' He stopped dead in front of Cullen's desk. 'Forget about that, something you need to see.' He passed her a printout. 'I don't want you to worry about this, we're gonna take care of it...'

It was an email, sent to the precinct's general enquiries account. Before she could even get to the body of the text, her eye was drawn to the images underneath it. Two pictures of her house, taken from the street. The first showed just the front, evening shadows creeping across the lawn the only indication of when it was taken.

The second was a night-time shot taken from further away. It showed her at her door, probably unlocking it, her back to the camera.

She read the email's text:

> 'JOHN PARKER NOT THE END OF IT. BITCH CASEY WRAY THE NEXT TO DIE. GET YOUR SHIT STRAIGHT, YOU'RE NEXT. GET YOU ANY TIME, WILL NOT SEE IT COMING.'

Casey glanced up at him, then looked down to read it again. 'This is...' The sender was aq12yLKke52f49@hotmail.com – the same dummy account that'd directed them to Michael Bell's address. 'This is bullshit. We've got someone scared, bring it the fuck on.'

'Yeah, I know. But, look, it kills me to say this, but there's more. You know Rick Santana over at the Third? Vice dick?'

'Yeah, kinda.' She knew the name, didn't know the guy personally.

'One of his CIs came to him, looking for a payday for street chatter about someone putting a hit on a cop. Ricky called me earlier because the name the CI heard was Casey Wray.'

Her chest tightened. She manufactured a shrug. 'It's a common name.'

That brought a rictus grin to his face. 'You're such a wiseass.'

'Fuck it. Gimme the CI's name and lemme go shake it out of him. I've been looking for the asshole behind this email address anyway, maybe now we get some answers.'

'C'mon, you know how this works. Ricky already dropped the CI on his head, but the guy swore on his kid's life he didn't know who was behind it. He just heard about "Some guy was looking to kill the bitch".'

Casey handed the printout back to him. 'Some motherfucker wants to take a shot at me, let him try. He just better hope I don't see him coming.'

'Case … it's not that straightforward. After what happened to Dave, there's heightened sensitivity around officer safety. I know you're not gonna want to hear this, but I gotta bench you for a little while…'

She started to protest but he threw his hands up.

'It's just for a few days while we get this taken care of. And before you say anything, the second we figure out who this is, you will be right there taking the door so you can let him know what you think of his bullshit.' He tilted the paper in his hand so it stood upright between them.

'You cannot ... There is no way you're sending me home because of this.'

'Not home. That's clearly compromised. You book yourself into a hotel someplace no one will find you.'

'You're actually gonna bow to this? This is what they want, have me taken off the investigation. It's an empty threat.'

'We don't know it's empty. And the word has come down on this, it went all the way up to the chief and back.'

'Hanrahan? Are you fucking kidding me?'

'With what happened, there's no way they're taking a chance on this. I'd love to tell you it's rooted only in concern for your wellbeing, and I'm not saying it's not, but he's also imagining headlines that say, 'Department fails to protect hero cop'. You get that, right?'

'So what about the Parker investigation? And Tina Grace?'

'I'm giving the Parker thing to Billy – he's up to speed on it and he's ready to step up. And he's got you a phone call away for anything he needs.'

A thought crashed her head – Cullen gone, McTeague's words about Carletti needing someone else he can trust, Ray sliding Billy right into that spot.

She stared at him, saw the same face she'd been looking at for four years, the wrinkles around the corners of his eyes that made it look like he was always about to break out a smile, and she just couldn't believe it. She knew him, knew how he worked and how he thought, and she couldn't reconcile it with McTeague's version of the man. She felt a protective urge well up in her chest, so much so that she almost blurted it all out right then.

'What?' Ray said.

She blinked, snapped to. 'What about Tina?'

'You'll be back in a couple of days most likely, maybe a week. Nothing's gonna change in that time and you can stay in touch with the family...'

'Her mom's gone off the reservation.'

'What do you mean?'

She walked him through what she knew from Tommy.

He put his hands on his hips and sighed. 'Are they in touch with Victim Services?'

'They were, Maggie blew it off after a couple sessions. She's an addict, Ray, she needs proper help.'

'Put them back together when she shows up, they might be able to support her to get into a programme. You can go figure out where she's at – you're not under house arrest. Just stay away from your place and the Parker thing, and don't take any chances. Meanwhile we've got plainclothes watching your place 24/7, the tech guys working on the email, and every cop in town is leaning on their CIs for info on who's talking up a hit. One way or another, we find this son of a bitch.'

Casey looked him over and saw it was the end of the road. She took a breath, reloading for one last protest, but Ray beat her to the punch.

'I know what you did with McTeague. I don't like it, but I understand why you did it, because I know what this one means to you. We'll talk about it later.' He shot her a look that said he meant it. 'Now get going, I'll walk you out.'

# CHAPTER 29

The motel was next to a twenty-four-hour Laundromat on Creighton Avenue, in the shadow of an elevated stretch of the expressway, Casey swerving the big chains for somewhere sleazier but more anonymous. A metal staircase led up from the rear parking lot to an open balcony, five rooms spaced evenly along it, doorways recessed into the concrete. A squat brown building with a sloping red roof, she'd already forgotten the place's name – something generic like The Expressway Inn. No one in the department knew where she was, not even Ray – at his insistence. 'Just watch your ass,' was his parting shot as he'd packed her into her car.

Off-white walls, mismatched wooden chairs; a short breakfast bar separated a kitchenette from the rest of the room, a black faux-marble surface studded with fake quartz, the whole thing flimsy and cheap. But the bed was large and new enough, the sheets tired but clean. She'd seen worse flops the department used, and more to the point, smelled worse.

She searched the cupboards for a glass and filled it with bottled water from the refrigerator. Then she perched on the lone barstool and called McTeague.

He didn't answer, and she set her phone down on the countertop, feeling all the hours catching up to her. Still no word from Tommy or Maggie, no resolution to anything. And underneath the tiredness and the grime and the uncertainty, no matter how hard she tried not to acknowledge it: fear – pressing against the base of her spine, as cold and sharp as the tip of a blade.

Her phone rang, McTeague calling her back, and she snatched it up.

'Captain—'

'I heard what happened. Where are you?'

'At a motel.'

'Okay. I've got people looking into this, we're gonna get it taken care of.'

'Seriously? It's bullshit, it's someone getting desperate.'

'Maybe, but the information's solid, I had it checked out. So we be careful. The chief wants you to know your safety is his number-one concern right now.'

'Yeah, the lieutenant told me as much.'

'I understand that tone of voice, but I can promise you he's sincere.'

'Then tell him I appreciate it.'

'Did Maggie Grace show up?'

'Not yet. You want someone to worry about, there's your woman.'

'Is there a chance she had something to do with Parker? I know her boy's story checked out, but the same motive works for her.'

Casey remembered Maggie telling her she'd walked the beach in desperation and taken the underpass through to where Tina disappeared – all of it on Parker's doorstep. 'Can't see it. She's torn up and angry and scared, but she's the type turns it inward. She'd be more likely to do something to herself than anyone else. Besides, it seems like Tommy had shifted his anger to Bell, doesn't sound like they were blaming Parker anymore. She'd take her cue from him.'

'What did you get from Parker's electronics?'

'Nothing yet. Which is about what I expected now we know he wasn't sending those emails. Maranda's crew are still combing them, she's sent me his call logs and text messages, but it's all vanilla, what I've seen so far.'

'Okay. I want you to keep a hand on the wheel with this.'

'Sure thing. Billy Drocker's picking up the file, but I'm supposed to be consulting in the background.'

'So he's Ray's guy now?'

Jibing with her own thought, but somehow uglier to hear it outside her own head. 'We're all Ray's guys, remember?'

He grunted, not clear if it was in agreement or disapproval. 'When this is past, you're gonna have to choose a side.'

'Are you absolutely sure about what you told me? I know the lieutenant, we've spent more hours sharing a bottle than I could even count, and he's an open book when he's half in the bag. Not one time did he even hint at the kind of shit you're accusing him of.'

'Yeah. I'm sure.' The line crackled as he breathed out, weary-sounding. 'There anything you need?'

'A decent night's sleep?'

'Look after yourself.'

When he was gone, she leaned against the countertop, holding the glass of water to her forehead. Wondering if it was possible she didn't hate him anymore.

Maranda Jessup sent another batch of goodies from Jon Parker's devices – emails, phone records – and Casey worked through them into the night.

The motel room was quiet at 11pm, but not silent – traffic noises from the expressway a kind of white noise for her to work to. The street out front led to the on-ramp a block away, and every big rig that went by rattled the walls and the windows, the vibrations rising up through the floor, just frequent enough to break her concentration every time she found a groove. Unfamiliar surroundings. Twice she drifted to the front door to check the spyhole, seeing nothing on the other side except the amber glare from the parking-lot lights, the bleak expanse of asphalt beneath them deserted apart from a handful of cars. She kept her gun in reach as she worked on the bartop.

Her phone buzzed – the noise startling her. She saw Tommy's name on the message and grabbed it up: *Mom showed up. She in a bad way. Can u talk to her?*

Casey texted back: *I'm on my way over.*

Tommy was waiting in the doorway when she pulled up. He looked pale and shook in the porch light, gesturing Casey inside with his finger by his hip.

'Where's she been?'

He stopped in the hallway in front of her and leaned against the wall, rubbing his face. 'Different bars all of yesterday, says she can't remember after that.'

'Is she still drunk?'

'She's sobering up slowly and she's making sense at least. She keeps crying to herself, I didn't ... Look, I'm sorry and all for calling you. I didn't know what to do.'

'It's okay, really it is. Before I go in there, does she know about Jon Parker?'

He puffed out his cheeks, shaking his head. 'I don't know. She hasn't said anything about it.'

Casey nodded and peered around him into the living room, Maggie just out of sight but the sound of sobbing audible. She looked to Tommy again, and he nodded his permission for her to go in.

The smell was potent – stale booze and old cigarette smoke, like a dive bar that'd been closed up all night. Maggie was slumped in the corner of the sofa, dressed in jeans and a sweater that was stained down the right arm. Casey went around in front of her, slipping down into a crouch so they'd be at the same level.

Maggie made eye contact and broke it again right away, focusing on nothing. Her cheeks were wet.

Casey reached out and took her hand softly. Out of the corner of her eye, she saw Tommy hovering in the doorway and she half turned her head to him. 'How about a coffee for your mom?'

Tommy nodded, slowly at first and then faster, taking the hint. He slipped away into the kitchen.

'What happened?' Casey said.

'I don't ... I don't even know.' She still wouldn't look at her.

'Where did you spend last night?'

She checked Tommy wasn't at the doorway and spoke again in a lower voice. 'Some guy's house. He bought me a drink, then another ... I can't even remember. I was already hammered. I woke up this morning and I didn't have the first fucking clue where I was, so I got out of there and...' She pressed her fist into the sofa cushion. 'Shit, I was on my way home, I just wanted to take a shower and go to bed. But the hangover was a monster and I was starting to get real bad anxiety and hating on myself and I just wanted to fast forward through it all. So I went and got another drink.'

Casey looked around, choosing her words. 'When was your last one?'

She shrugged she didn't know. 'Sometime this afternoon. Turned out I was right by the causeway, so I took a cab to the beaches again and just walked. Miles and miles. I don't even know where I started out.'

'You were on the beaches? What time was this?'

'Few hours ago, I guess.'

Casey felt her neck prickle. 'What about yesterday?'

Maggie wrinkled her face in confusion. 'Yesterday? No, I told you, I was drinking.'

'The whole time? Is there a chance you went to the beaches yesterday?'

'No, I don't ... I don't think so.'

Casey slipped her hand loose of Maggie's. 'Did you take anything else? Yesterday or today?'

'No, nothing. I even quit taking Xanax a few days ago, it was making me feel like my head was wrapped in a blanket.' She pushed her hair back with her hands. 'I'm so fucking tired, Case. I can't keep on feeling like this all the time.'

'Why'd you stop taking the meds? You can't just quit, you gotta talk to the doctors before you do something like that. That might be what set you off.'

Maggie pressed her lips together, staring at the wall.

Casey let her stare a minute, regrouping. When she started to speak again, the words caught in her throat. 'Maggie ... have you ever talked to anyone about your drinking?'

She didn't answer.

'Let me hook you up with Victim Services again. They can help you cope, make sure you get the right kind of help.'

'"The right kind"? You think I never tried AA before?'

'Okay, but there are alternatives—'

'Case, I am what I am.'

She glared at Casey as she said it, but the words dripped with self-loathing.

'Sorry,' Casey said. 'I'm not here to lecture you.'

'I know. Forget it.' Maggie rolled her head back, fighting a yawn. 'I'm sorry Tommy got you involved.'

'I asked him to tell me when you showed up again. And I'm glad he did.' Casey stood up. 'Can you remember which bar you were in last night?'

'O'Hennessey's.'

'You happen to know what time you left there?'

She looked up at Casey. 'I told you, I can't remember. Why's it matter?'

Casey spoke softly. 'What about the guy you left with?'

'What about him?' An edge to her voice now.

'Can you tell me his name?'

'What is this? You sound like you're questioning me. I know I been a jackass but I'm a grown-ass woman.'

'It's not ... Settle down a minute, okay? Maybe you didn't see the news: Jon Parker was murdered last night.'

She didn't react at first, and Casey thought she'd blanked on the name. But in fact she was still processing it. 'What the fuck?'

'Yeah, we're still trying to figure out what's going on. So ... it'd be worthwhile if you could remember the name of the guy you were with.'

'Are you saying ... Wait, am I a suspect?'

Casey let her silence answer for her.

'I didn't even go to the beaches until today,' Maggie said. 'I didn't go to his house, I just wanted—' She couldn't get the words out. 'I wanted to be near her. I just wanted to be near her. But I couldn't face going by that house again, Case, I swear to God...'

'You said yourself you can't remember everything. So we just need to be sure. I'll talk to the people at O'Hennessey's, but you can help me to help you.'

'Jesus Christ, I didn't ...Why would I do that? Y'all said it was that other piece of shit. Bell. Casey, I didn't, I couldn't kill someone. Even because of Tina.'

'I hear you. But I'm not in charge of the case directly right now, and I want to make sure there's no room for doubt.'

Her expression softened. 'What do you mean you're not in charge of the case?'

'It's just a temporary thing. Besides, it means I can concentrate on Tina. So think for me and see if you can come up with a name. Or a street address, even.'

'The bartender might know.' She covered her face to mask her embarrassment. 'If you're gonna talk to them anyway, could you...?'

Casey nodded. 'I'll ask. But see if you can remember for me. Get some sleep. I'll talk to you tomorrow.'

She looked like she was crashing as Casey left the room.

Tommy came out of the kitchen to catch her before she went out the door. 'Hey, uh, Detective – thanks.'

'Sure. Just look out for her tomorrow, okay? She might land hard.'

'Got it. And Detective? With Tina ... I know she's not coming back, but, I mean is there any chance she gets found?' He twisted his head to indicate Maggie in the living room. 'It'd kill her, but being able to bury her, say goodbye properly ... I think it could help.'

Casey bit down on her bottom lip before she spoke. 'I don't want to give you false hope. Parker and Bell were the last two people to see Tina, as far as we know. With both of them gone

... It's real tough. But as long as there's a rock to turn over, I'll keep going. I promise you that.'

## CHAPTER 30

Back at the motel room, turning over not one rock but hundreds.

She'd been working an hour already since she got back. Going through his phone records, the only item that caught her interest was a call Parker made at 1pm to his big-money attorney, Clarence Mickelroff, approximately fourteen hours before he was killed. In itself it meant nothing, but she couldn't think what reason Parker would've had to contact Mickelroff at that point – he'd been cleared of any involvement in the Ramona Beach murders by then. Next she'd turned to Parker's emails and messages, working through them chronologically. She hadn't realised she was drifting off until her phone buzzed with a text message, jolting her awake with a start. It was from Tommy – a one-liner to say Maggie was asleep in bed.

She let out a breath, a feeling as if she'd been holding it for forty-eight hours straight.

Nothing from Ray, nothing from McTeague. Past 1am, too late for further updates tonight; the isolation like a prison sentence. She laid the phone down and went back to her laptop, her vision still blurry from sleep. The email she had open was from Parker to himself. No subject, just a four-digit code in the message body, and then the automatic tag saying 'sent from my iPhone'. Nothing else. She stared at the four numbers, thinking about what they could relate to. Some kind of banking or PIN code was the first thought that came to her.

She looked at the date and time of the mail – sent the last day he was alive, at 1.33pm. A half-hour after the call to Mickelroff. She thought back to what he would've been doing at that time: right around when he left for Sentona Hills to play golf, Casey there to see him drive away. Was this some kind of booking or payment confirmation code maybe? That didn't feel right, she would've seen others the same. She looked away from the screen and rubbed her eyes.

A call to his lawyer, an email to himself, then a drive to his club to make his tee time. Where was his head at when this was happening?

She got up to make coffee, but her cell buzzed again and she grabbed it up, expecting a follow-up from Tommy:

*BITCH CASEY WRAY NEXT TO DIE*

She dropped it like a hot stone, the skin on her face going taut.

She eased her gun out of its holster, quietly, as if they were in the room with her, the message whispered into her ear. She went to the door and checked the spyhole, but the balcony and the parking lot were empty. She tested the catch to make sure it was locked. Crossing to the window, she nudged a gap in the drapes and checked the street. A black Prius cruised by without slowing; the sidewalks were empty.

She stood there in silence, listening, waiting for the sound of a footstep on the staircase outside, a shoe scraping on the balcony. Only the muted traffic sounds from the expressway came back to her.

Then her cell buzzed again. Kept buzzing. She snatched it up, a blocked number calling. She pressed Accept but didn't say anything.

She heard a man breathing, soft but ragged, like a rake pulled across gravel. She swallowed, waiting...

One woman screamed. Then ten, then a thousand...

'Who is this? Who the fuck is this?'

The screaming intensified.

'You can't...' She screwed her eyes shut. Michael Bell was dead. She put the bullets in him herself.

The screaming reached a crescendo then stopped just as suddenly as it started. Then a return to the sound of the man breathing.

'Who the fuck is this?'

He fell silent. No sound at all. She looked at the screen to check it was still connected, her hand trembling. The call timer ticked away the seconds.

She put it back to her ear. 'Whoever you are—'

'Tina Grace is dead.' The voice distorted, mechanical, the same as the call to her house and during the storm.

'How do you know that?'

'Tina Grace is dead.'

'Tell me—'

'Bitch Casey Wray next to die.'

'Fuck you.'

'Gonna kill you. We know where you are. Gonna kill you.'

'I said fuck you, mother—'

The call cut out.

Casey stood frozen in the middle of the room. She let the phone slip from her fingers onto the bed and covered her face.

# CHAPTER 31

She woke with a start, her head on the desk, hair splayed over her forearms and onto her laptop. 5.37am, the smell of stale coffee from the cup next to her; the lights on, still dark outside the window. Her shoulders and neck were numb, her mind on fire – the call churning again as soon as she opened her eyes.

Michael Bell was dead, but the screams were the same – she was certain of that much. Thinking back now, she wasn't even sure if the call was live or pre-recorded like before. It brought to mind McTeague's evidence – the signature slip from the storage rental, paid up months in advance, the implication that someone set up Bell to take the fall. But her best suspect for that had been Jon Parker – now he was dead too. In the middle of the night, it'd felt like Bell was coming for her from his fucking grave; removed from the initial shock, daylight made the reality somehow worse: a direct threat on her life from a total unknown. Impossible to see coming.

She'd worked through the night, too spooked to close her eyes by choice. At some point she must've crashed, two hours of dreamless sleep that she was paying for now, the pain shifting from her neck and shoulders and into her head. She'd finished with Parker's messages and gone back to his call list, working through it one number at a time, using Google as a reverse directory to identify each recipient. The search engine provided answers on destinations for some of them – a broker's office, the clubhouse at Sentona Hills, a pizza delivery place – but some were personal numbers that Google didn't have listed, so she waited until 7am and then started dialling them herself. He'd made his last call at 6.33pm the evening before he was killed; she tapped the number into her phone and hit dial, but it was dead. She went to move on to the next one but then stopped.

The number was already there on her call log, half a screen down in the Recents listings, indicating she'd called it previously. She looked at it again, didn't recognise it as one she knew. She tapped the information icon and it showed that she'd dialled the same number two days ago.

She stood up, went across the room to the window. On Creighton Avenue, traffic was already building up at the intersection down the block. The muffled sound of a radio blaring from one of the vehicles below. Scanning the sidewalks again as she tried to place having made the old call.

Almost forty-eight hours ago; it felt like a month. She remembered being in the office that morning, the timing shortly before she'd driven out to Parker's place, after she figured out he was—

It came to her then. When she'd found the Kevin Love call list missing from the paper file and had to ask Jilly to print out another copy for her. Casey had tried calling the last number listed when she collected the printout, on the off chance someone picked up – when she was still trying to figure out who was behind the alias. The number had just kept ringing and she'd moved on.

She tried to figure the significance. The last number Jon Parker had called, hours before his death. Probably the last person he ever spoke to, aside from his killer. Unless the recipient was one and the same.

She brought up the rest of Parker's calls and ran a search for the number. It didn't feature. The last person he'd ever called, and it was the only time he'd done so – at least from his own cell. But it was also the last number he'd called from his Kevin

Love burner, right before it went dark, weeks before. A number that wasn't saved in his personal contacts. She switched over to the call list from Michael Bell's burner, cross-checking it for contacts with the same number.

It cropped up a handful of times. She went through them line by line. Various instances, including...

Including two calls in the half-hour after Tina Grace disappeared. Bell calling the unknown party right after he took Tina. For what purpose? To tell them he'd got her? For instructions?

She studied Bell's list again, this time concentrating on the most recent calls. Right at the top, the last call Bell took on the phone, an incoming from the same number. The date and time: a half-hour before she and Cullen had rolled up at his property to try and arrest him.

Two dead men. In contact with one mystery number at every crucial point in her timeline.

More than that: in contact shortly before both of them were killed.

She called Billy D but got his voicemail. 'Call me the second you get this.'

Casey made the run to Clarence Mickelroff's office downtown in twenty minutes. She messaged Ray on the way to update him on the new threat overnight. She kept her text as dry as possible, trying to downplay the threat, but he couldn't miss the significance of someone using Bell's playbook, and even as she tried to shrug it off, she had to admit to herself: she was scared.

His reply was almost instant: *Fuck. Putting in a priority request with your provider now. We'll find this asshole. Stay safe.*

It was before eight and Mickelroff's receptionist wasn't at her desk yet, so she pushed through the double doors, the glass still slick with whatever cleaning products they used on them, and went along the corridor until she saw his name on the corner office. She peered inside, saw him already working, knocked once and went in. Mickelroff straightened in his chair – controlled, despite the surprise.

'Good morning, counsellor. Sorry to barge in, but I could really use a minute of your time.' She held up the takeout coffee she'd brought along as a peace offering.

He looked at her, surprise moving to bemusement, before he set his face to impassive again. 'I should say "make an appointment", but I'm curious enough about what you want to disengage my better judgement.' He held his hand up to refuse the coffee she offered. 'I quit caffeine.'

Casey set it down on her side of his desk anyway. 'Jon Parker called you the afternoon before he was killed, and I would just love to know what you talked about.'

'I don't recall.'

'This was two days ago.'

Mickelroff waved his fingers. 'I speak to clients all the time.' He raised his eyebrows, almost a dare. 'Unless you had something specific to jog my memory?'

'I'm not on a fishing trip, here, I'm just trying to figure out who offed your client. Did he mention being threatened by anyone, was he scared of something? Anyone he'd gotten into an argument with?'

'Don't you think I'd have called you by now if he did?'

'Come on, Clarence, we don't have to pretend to like each other to help each other out.'

'I'm ambivalent about your department and its practices, detective, but I have no issue with you personally. You and your colleagues went after him very hard – for a crime he was absolved of any involvement in. You can't blame him for wondering if he'd heard the last of you.'

'That's your story?'

'Unless you have a better one...?'

Casey turned her gaze to the ceiling. 'Did he mention planning to meet anyone that day? Anyone he'd talked to?'

'No. None of it. It was a very limited conversation.'

Casey shifted her weight, her righteous confidence ebbing away; in its place, a feeling like she was grasping. 'Did Parker ever talk to you about having a second phone?'

Mickelroff steepled his fingers above his lap. 'This came up earlier in the investigation, as I recall. I believe he told you not.'

'But what did he say to you privately?'

'The same thing.'

'So he was lying to you too.'

He cocked his head to one side as he shrugged, his eyes closed. 'All my clients lie. To a greater or lesser extent.' He must've sensed her frustration because he'd laid his arms on the armrests as if he was finished but then carried on. 'Look, for what it's worth, Jon Parker struck me as someone I wouldn't want my daughter dating, but not as a bad guy. Not a lot shocks me these days, but hearing about his murder most definitely did. As to his state of mind, he seemed reasonably upbeat again, which was his default setting. Certainly nothing to indicate what was about to happen to him.' He picked up his pen and glanced at his blotter to signal the conversation was coming to a close.

'Let me show you something.' She took out her phone and held up the four-digit code Parker had emailed to himself. 'Does this mean anything at all to you?'

Mickelroff leaned over the desk to look then shook his head. 'Nothing.'

'Parker sent this to himself not long after calling you. In that context, can you think of anything it might relate to?'

He looked one more time, then shook his head again. 'Not a thing.'

Casey tapped the top of the chair she'd been leaning on, acknowledging her thanks, and started to back off towards the door. Then she paused. 'I know he didn't meet Tina Grace on Tinder. I know he had a second phone registered to a dummy name, and I know he was calling Michael Bell on it right after he left her on the street. Tina's still out there, dead or alive, and her family are desperate to know the truth. So if he said anything to you about what happened to her...'

'I can assure you he didn't.'

'He's dead, Clarence. Anything he might've told you ... You don't have to protect him now...'

'Detective Wray, I'm sorry. I'd help you if I could.'

Casey dipped her head, nodding to her own feet as if it was what she expected to hear all along. 'Just reflect on your conversations with him and if something comes to mind, give me a call. Okay?'

Mickelroff met her eyes as she opened the door, saying nothing.

Billy was calling as she walked out of the building onto the street. Casey hit Accept and cut across his 'Hey—'

'Bill, listen, I've got something: Jon Parker made a call a few hours before he was killed to a number that's now dead. He called the same number from his Kevin Love burner phone right before it went dark, the night Tina Grace disappeared. You getting this?'

'Uh-huh.' He drew it out, sounding like he was reaching for a pen. 'Shoot.'

'Okay. Michael Bell made two calls to the same number within a half-hour of snatching Tina Grace – and whoever owns that phone called Bell a half-hour before Dave and me got to his place that morning.'

'Damn, Big, you been working all night?'

'Feels like longer. I'm gonna hit you with it now, take this down.' She set her phone to speaker so she could bring the number up on screen and call it out to him. When he read it back to her correctly, she put the phone to her ear again. 'Okay, good. I want everything we can get on that cell phone. With the pattern so far, my guess is it'll be another burner registered to a fake name and address, but we get the call records, text records, ownership records, all of it, and we see if we can trace it back to the real user somehow. Eventually we gotta get to the bottom of this fucking barrel. You get all that?'

'Yeah. I'm on it now. Hey, Big, the lieutenant told us about last night. You doing okay?'

She glanced both ways along the sidewalk. 'Never better. Something else: Parker emailed himself a four-digit code the day he died – you get to that email yet?'

'Not yet, we're still working through his stuff.'

'Okay. There's no explanation for what it is, just the digits. I don't know what it means, so just keep it in mind, it might become relevant. Last thing...'

'Shoot.'

'Maggie Grace went on a forty-eight-hour bender and ended up at the beach near Jon Parker's house yesterday afternoon. She's claiming she went home with a guy picked her up in the bar the night before, I'll check that out. I'm sure it's nothing, but I wanted to let you know.'

'Thanks, Big.'

'You find anything on Tina Grace in his stuff?'

'Nothing. You'll be the first to know.' He exhaled, a hint at the strain he was under as he drew it out. 'This cell number ... That's gotta go beyond coincidence. What's the connection here?'

'I don't know. But whoever's on that number knows more about all this shit than we do.'

## CHAPTER 32

The driveway from the front gate to the main building at Sentona Hills ran for more than a mile and a half.

The road tracked alongside one of the club's three golf courses, green fairways that looked waterlogged after all the snow and rain. A light drizzle was coming down, no deterrent to the groups of golfers sheltering under oversized Callaway umbrellas. On the other side of her, a fence ran parallel the length of the drive, a group of walnut-coloured horses huddled far off in the pasture.

Casey parked at the front entrance and badged her way through the main reception, taking directions to the clubhouse.

It was set in its own part of the complex, a low and wide Spanish-colonial style building with whitewashed walls and terracotta shingles on the roof. She went inside and found a twenty-something woman with a high-wattage smile behind the desk, made to look older than her years by the club's dowdy burgundy uniform. Casey showed her badge. 'Ma'am, I'm detective Casey Wray from HCPD. I wanted to ask about one of your members, Jon Parker. You might've seen on the news, he was murdered a couple days back?'

'Mr Parker? My God, I had no idea. He was here all the time, what happened?'

'We're still figuring that out. We believe this was the last place he visited before he died. I'd like to know who he played with, whether he spoke to anyone else around the club, if he showed any signs of agitation or distress, anything along those lines. Were you working that day?'

'Yeah, I was here. In fact, I remember seeing him come through when he finished up. He's kind of a charmer. Or he thinks he is, anyway—' She stopped herself, spreading her fingers on the counter. 'Sorry, that probably sounds kinda harsh.'

'Did you talk to him?'

'No. I mean, like, I think I said "All set?" or something as he passed through, but he didn't stop to talk.'

'Who did he play with?'

She frowned, trying to remember. 'I'd have to check the computer...' She tapped something into the terminal under the counter. 'Okay, he played with the Knutsons and Mr Hagimura.'

'Are they regular playing partners?'

'I don't think so. At busy times we just group players

together into foursomes so that we can accommodate as many members as possible.'

'I'm gonna need contact numbers for those individuals, please.'

'I'm sorry, I don't think I can give that information out. But I could call them and ask if they'd be willing to speak to you?'

Casey stretched her neck to one side and the other, trying not to get worked up. 'Okay, sure. If you could call them now, I'd appreciate it.'

The woman picked up the desk phone and started to dial.

Casey took the list of Parker's calls out of her bag and studied it again while she waited. Aside from the crucial call to the unknown party at 6.33pm, his last three calls were all to Sentona Hills – two of them placed right around the time she was watching his house, waiting for her warrant. The thought of it made her sick now; the lines she'd crossed, the friendship she'd betrayed to get it, Parker already dead before it could do her any good. She showed the list to the woman. 'These are calls Jon Parker made the day he died. Did you take any of these?'

The woman started to shake her head but then cut herself off to speak into the handset. But it turned out she was connected to a voicemail, and she left a message with Casey's details. She hung up and cradled the phone against her shoulder. 'I wasn't on shift then, that would've been my colleague Andrea. She's off right now, did you want me to get her to call you?'

Casey breathed out through her nose, frustrated at getting pinballed around. She ran her finger down the list, trying to decide the likelihood of there being anything of worth in the Sentona Hills calls. Came down on the side of being thorough. 'Yeah. Yes please.'

The woman smiled and said 'Sure,' as she started dialling another of Parker's playing partners.

Casey came away from Sentona Hills with nothing to show for the morning's work. Fighting the sense that she was holding on to the case by the last fraying threads, and they were about to come away.

One of Parker's golfing buddies called her back within a half-hour – Harold Knutson, a retired surgeon in his sixties who'd played with Parker along with his wife, Claire. But he had nothing useful to tell; he'd never met Parker before that day and said there was nothing that came to mind as remarkable. 'We mostly spoke about the Jets and the Knicks, how terrible they both are this year.'

She thanked Knutson and called Billy, but he was still waiting for the provider to get back to him with an ID for the mystery number Parker and Bell had been talking to. 'The request is in, and I told them it's a rush job.'

'Call them every hour. Let me know soon as you hear. What about my new fan from last night?'

'Still chasing that too. Hold on ... Big, the lieutenant wants to speak to you.' There was a rustling sound as he passed the handset over.

'Case? What's happening?' Ray's voice.

'Chasing down some loose ends on Jon Parker. Don't worry, I only went by Sentona Hills.'

'Okay. Listen, I put a call in to the chief, he wants to put additional precautions in place to make sure you're safe.'

She switched ears. 'Like what?'

'He wants you out of harm's way. Out of the state if possible. Take a long drive and hole up somewhere until this blows over. The department will cover the bill.'

'What? I can't just leave.'

'It's what the chief wants. And ... I agree with him.'

'Tina's still missing. No way.'

'Case, it's an order.'

'For how long? What if we don't find this creep?'

'One thing at a time. Just get clear for now, huh?'

She rested her head on the steering wheel, trying to visualise it. Running, hiding, who knew how long for? It felt so wrong.

Slowly, she sat upright again. 'I gotta go.'

She was parked outside O'Hennessey's. She went inside and, after a few tries, managed to find a bartender who remembered Maggie Grace being there two days before. 'Yeah, she was here late afternoon and most of the night. She kept alternating between Millers and Jacks.'

'Can you tell me what time she left?'

The man leaned on the bartop. 'Uh ... had to be around midnight. I get off then, but I always end up hanging around for a time, and she was out of here before I was.'

'Did she leave with anyone?'

He shook his head. 'Nope.'

The hairs on Casey's arm prickled. 'Did you see if she took a cab, anything like that?'

'She went out the door, that was that.' He shrugged.

'Anyone she spoke to while she was here?'

'I honestly don't remember. She's been by here a handful of times. I've seen her talking to guys before, but I couldn't tell you about the other night. It was pretty busy.'

Casey patted the bartop, her mind already out the door.

It was late afternoon when the cell provider came through with the information. Casey was back at the motel, trawling through more of Parker's data when Billy called to tell her.

'Got it, Big. The number's registered to a Jeffrey Lewkins, 10345 West Spruce Street. And there's more.'

Casey scribbled it down as he spoke. 'Hit me.'

'The call you took last night came from the same number. The network just confirmed it.'

She was already out of her chair. 'I'm rolling.'

'Case, hold up ... The lieutenant says no. He's standing over me right now. Here...'

She grabbed her coat as Ray came on the line. 'Hey, it's me. I thought I told you to take a vacation?'

'I'm still packing.'

'Goddammit ... Look, wherever you are, hang tight. We don't know who this guy is or what he's about.'

'You said I could be there to take the door.'

'Sure, but ... that was before I spoke to the chief.'

'This guy – Jesus Christ, he talked to Bell and Parker right before they died, he talked to Bell right after he took Tina ... It all goes through him.'

'I get all that. But if this is the psycho that's been threatening you, the risk of you showing up on his doorstep is too great. He could see you coming.'

'Like Dave, you mean.'

'Case, don't. I didn't mean it like...'

'I deserve a chance to be there.'

'We've got a cruiser two minutes away. Billy and Jill are leaving now. A little caution doesn't hurt here. It might not even be his cell. For all we know he's some poor schmo who's had his address appropriated.'

Her phone beeped in her ear, someone else trying to get through to her. She glanced at the screen – Tommy Grace.

Ray was still talking when she put it back to her ear. '...and they've sent over the phone's records too – Bell and Parker are on the call list multiple times. I'll email it to you now, see if there's anything jumps out at you.'

'Okay—' Her phone beeped in her ear again – Tommy trying a second time. 'Dammit ... Tommy Grace is trying to wear out my line.'

'Go deal with that, there's nothing you can do right now. I'll call you again as soon as it's done.'

Casey stood up and smacked the table in frustration. Then she grabbed up her phone again and pressed to call Tommy back.

He answered, didn't give her a chance to speak. 'Mom's gone again. She was supposed to go to an AA meet but she never showed up.'

'Tommy, slow down.' A flutter in her chest; Maggie had actually listened to her. 'Okay, so how long—'

'She took my gun.'

Casey froze. 'What for?'

'I don't know what the hell she's thinking. She was talking earlier about ... shit, I don't even know. Like, "It should be me, it should be me".'

"Where is she?'

'I called O'Hennessey's and the other places she's been drinking, but she ain't been by this time. I'm guessing the beaches again. She's losing her mind, she keeps talking about seeing Tina there in her dreams.'

'When's the last time you talked to her?'

'This morning. Before I left. About an hour ago I got a message from one of the women she knew from AA before, checking if Mom's okay because she said Mom called her to find out when they hold the meetings now, and she'd promised her she was gonna come along. But she never showed up. I didn't think much about it until I got home and saw the gun was gone ... Shit, you gotta do something.'

Casey scrabbled for her car keys. 'Where would she go, Tommy? Where exactly, I mean?'

'The beach, around where Tina went. She goes through the Fourth Street underpass. She keeps talking crazy about Tina walking that stretch of the beach, waiting for someone to find her. That only she can see her, shit like that.'

'I'm going now. Stay by the phone, call me straightaway if you hear from her.'

## CHAPTER 33

Casey hit eighty going across the causeway. Her thoughts kept crossing and washing back over each other.

Maggie prowling the beaches with a gun. Her alibi blown apart by the bartender. Still no sense to why she'd have killed Jon Parker – not anymore, at least.

But that was assuming a rational mind. Tommy's description – and what she'd seen with her own eyes – was a woman coming apart; ditching her meds abruptly, grief, booze; AA a desperate recognition she needed help, but attendance, in the end, too great a hurdle. It was a lethal combination for someone under unrelenting strain. She'd seen it before, mental defences worn away until the person that was left no longer resembled who they'd been before. Unpredictable, to themselves most of all. Capable of anything.

Her phone rang. She expected it to be Ray with an update, but it was McTeague's name showing on the screen. She hit the button on the steering wheel to answer it on speaker. 'Captain?'

'Wray, we need to talk. Where are you?'

'Maggie Grace has gone AWOL, sounds like she's armed. I'm on the causeway.'

'What? Where is she?'

'Best guess is she's on the beaches by Jon Parker's. Tommy Grace called me. She might be a threat to herself.'

'Goddammit. Where is Tommy Grace right now?'

'He's at home, I told him to wait by the phone. Why?'

'Have you got backup?'

'I don't have time...'

'I'll meet you there.'

Casey stopped where the access tunnel let out and scanned the beach in the dusk, breathing hard. She brought her hands to her mouth, made a funnel. 'MAGGIE?'

She twisted the other way and called again, already moving off, straining her eyes in the gloom. The sun was well below the horizon, inverting the colours overhead – white clouds rendered black against a deep violet sky, like an image in negative. There was no wind, the scene static if not for the waves curling up the beach. No one else in sight.

She started running again, calling out, 'MAGGIE?'

Her feet sank into the sand as she went, dragging her down. Casey pushed on, calling out and recognising the desperation in her own voice. She made a one-eighty, checking behind her in case she'd missed something. Just before she turned back, she caught a glimpse of a figure emerging from the same tunnel she'd come through. McTeague.

Another fifty yards, her muscles protesting now, trying to slow her to a jog. She scanned left to right, right to left...

There, in the ocean. Maggie, barely visible, standing waist-deep and facing the horizon. Casey angled her path towards her, only seeing as she came closer that her right arm was bent to her head. Holding the gun.

Casey ran into the water, crashing through the low waves, tasting salt on her lips. 'Maggie, hold on...'

She startled at hearing Casey's voice. The gun was touching her temple. Her hair was lank from the spray, wavy strands grazing her shoulders, soaking her denim shirt. She was shivering. 'Maggie, Jesus Christ, don't...' Casey waded closer until the water was around her thighs, and then stopped. 'Just don't.'

They stared at each other. The ocean was calm, but a bigger wave came in, knocking Maggie off balance, her gun arm flailing for a second as she caught her footing. Casey tensed, fearing it'd go off by accident; the chaos that would ensue. She glanced back for McTeague, saw him jogging across the beach, halfway to their position already. An added urgency because she knew how he'd assess the scene: potential suicide-by-cop.

'Maggie, please. You do this and Tommy will be dead inside six months. You're all he's got left. He can't lose you too.'

Maggie's lips moved, no sound at first. 'I didn't ... This isn't what I meant for...'

'I know. I know why you're here.'

'You don't...'

'You're mad as hell, you want to make the pain go away. I understand that. You want justice.'

Maggie shook her head once. 'That's not it.'

Casey waited for her to finish, but she already had. Casey reached out her hand. 'Come talk to me then. Tell me. Just put that down first.'

The shout came from behind her. 'Detective Wray?'

She turned, McTeague at the water's edge, his hand on his sidearm in its holster. She patted the air down. 'I got this.'

McTeague was looking past her. 'You need to put that down and come on out, Mrs Grace.'

She held her arm up for him to stop. 'Robbie, I said I got this. Just...' She faced Maggie again. 'Think about what I said. About Tommy. You know I'm right.'

'He'd be better off without me.'

'That's not ... Maggie, believe me, that's never true. I'm so sorry for everything but this isn't the answer.'

Maggie twisted the gun, and Casey sensed McTeague twitch behind her. 'Robbie, no. NO.' Glancing back, he'd drawn his weapon but it was still by his side.

'Don't lose your judgement, Big.'

'It's a cry for help, goddammit.'

He wouldn't look at her, his eyes locked on Maggie. Watchful. Casey thinking he was right and wrong, all at once. Running out of time.

She held her arms out wide – *I'm on your side* – and started moving closer again, taking measured steps. 'Maggie, talk to me. We can figure this out. Things don't feel any better, you can come back and finish this tomorrow, but you don't get that option the other way around.' They were five feet apart now. 'Just talk. Please...'

'DETECTIVE...'

Maggie waded deeper into the ocean and threw her free

hand out. Casey called after her. 'Stop...' The water was lapping Maggie's chest now, her eyes filled with tears. She brought the hand back hesitantly, like she was abandoning her last defence, and pushed the hair off her forehead.

Casey held her breath, paralysed by the sense it was now or never, but the decision wasn't hers.

'I came here...' Maggie swayed with the waves, her eyes like she was a million miles away, seeing things too painful for any mother to bear. 'Why couldn't he just kill me? I came here because I want him to kill me.'

Saying the words was enough to break the dam. She gripped her face, her body wracked with sobs. She brought the gun down, let it disappear below the water, and Casey rushed over to take it, Maggie offering no resistance. Casey wrapped her arms around her, pulling her close.

'Why couldn't he just kill me, Case? That's all I want.'

'No you don't. You don't.'

'It's all ... This is on me. It's all on me..'

'Maggie, no. You feel that way because it's a mom's instinct, but you can't—'

'I know what I mean, Casey. She's dead because of me.'

Casey went still. 'What?'

'It's my fault. I killed her.'

Casey gripped her as hard as she could, starting to shiver, the cold water registering for the first time. 'Maggie, what are you saying to me right now? '

'The hooking. She did it for me. For the money.'

'Why?'

'To put me through rehab. She wanted me to get sober, but she couldn't afford it, so...' She trailed off, her mouth locked open in a silent wail.

Casey could only look on, starting to see it.

The wail found its escape as a shriek and then a gasp for breath, Maggie almost panting before she spoke again. 'She started hooking to help me get sober. And I still couldn't do it. Everything she's done for me...' She buried her face in Casey's shoulder. Casey held her as she shook, too stunned to know what to say. 'I shoulda finished this the other day,' Maggie said. 'I made it all the way out here and ... That's what I shoulda done.'

Casey turned her eyes to the beach, whispering, 'It's not your fault.'

But it had no effect, Maggie's words a form of self-harm, cutting deep. Her failure, the wound salted with guilt.

She started to guide her out of the water, making for the sand. McTeague was standing ankle deep, his gun holstered again, his arm outstretched. He took off his suit jacket as they drew near and wrapped it around them both. 'Let's get her to the car.' Then, to Maggie: 'Mrs Grace, have you taken anything today?'

Maggie shook her head, her steps stilted and hesitant, tears pouring from her eyes still.

McTeague looked over but said nothing. Casey held his stare as they inched up the beach, waiting for his reprimand, but he kept his silence.

They crossed the sand slowly, angling towards the underpass, Maggie's arm draped around her shoulder. As they approached the entrance, Casey looked up at the graffiti sprayed above the tunnel mouth:

*You live in my* ♥

Words Maggie could've written for Tina, but she didn't even seem to notice them. Someone else's requiem for someone else's pain.

## CHAPTER 34

McTeague guided Maggie into the backseat of his car, pulling a blanket from the trunk to wrap around her while Casey called the medics.

When she got off the phone, she saw there was a voicemail waiting. She dialled to pick it up, Ray's voice in her ear. 'We picked up Jeffrey Lewkins at his property. He's denying ever owning a burner phone and all knowledge of its existence. We've brought him in, but he doesn't look promising to me – looks like identity theft. I'll let you know as soon as there's more.'

She went over to McTeague. Maggie was sitting sideways, half in and half out the car, doubled over, a bottle of water dangling from one hand.

'She say anything more?'

He shook his head. 'How long until the medics show up?'

'Fifteen minutes. They said to get her warmed up and watch for signs of shock.'

'Did you tell them you're not a rookie?'

Casey shrugged, *You know what they're like*. 'Thanks. For back there.'

He nodded, looking at the ground and then past her towards the dark ocean. 'You took a risk.'

'She's only a danger to herself.'

'You don't know that for sure. I warned you you've got a blind spot where this family's concerned.'

'What does that mean? She was never about to turn the gun on us.'

He tipped his head to signal they should step a few paces away from the car. Casey followed him, a bad feeling coming over her like a cloak. With Maggie out of earshot, he said, 'Not her, the son. Lab results came back, one of the hair samples taken from Parker's house comes from Tommy Grace. There's a fingerprint from the French doors that's his too. On the inside.'

Casey glanced at Maggie. 'He can't ... He went there, the time he tried to get at Parker. We arrested him. He could've—'

'Was he inside the house?'

Casey looked away, reeling. 'No.'

'I know you don't want it to be him.'

'It's not about what I want, but I just don't see it. The residue tests were clear, the gun was a negative.'

'The residue tests aren't conclusive. He could have access to another weapon.'

'But he was there before. The morning after Tina disappeared, his car was seen outside. Parker denied it, but...'

'But what? Do we know if he was inside the house at that time?'

She shook her head.

'I'm finding it hard to believe Parker would invite him in to wander around, leaving contact samples.'

Casey put her hands on her hips and nodded reluctantly. 'If he was involved...' She glanced towards Maggie. 'Christ knows what it'll do to her.'

McTeague worked his jaw side to side. 'I sent patrol to pick him up. I'll talk to him when I get back.' He folded his arms and faced her head on. 'You holding up okay?'

'Me? Sure. They picked up a suspect for the threat against me, but it doesn't sound like he's the guy. No link to Bell or Parker yet.'

He nodded his head twice. 'The chief wanted me to check you found somewhere safe. He's taking this personally.'

'I got a place.'

He stared at her like he was assessing if she was telling the truth. 'We're gonna take care of this.' He moved off towards his car, ending the conversation in a way that felt like an admonishment.

Casey stood in the gloom, a sense of emptiness gnawing inside her. No closer to finding Tina than she had been on day one. Maggie Grace trying to take her own life. Tommy Grace a murder suspect. Cullen dead, Bell and Parker taking their secrets to the grave. Jeffrey Lewkin looking like a dead end for the mystery burner. Overcome by feelings of loss and fatigue, and the desperate senselessness of all of it. She looked over at McTeague; his allegations against Ray and Cullen, the thought that even when this was done, there was more pain to come. She wanted to crawl into a hole and stay there.

Her cell started ringing. She was sick of it and for a second she was going to ignore it, her motivation bottoming out. But she took it out anyway and looked at the screen – the call originating from Sentona Hills.

'Detective Casey Wray.'

'Hi, this is Andrea Bartle calling from Sentona Hills – you spoke to my colleague earlier today? She asked me to give you a call?'

It took Casey a second to place the name – the woman who'd fielded Jon Parker's calls there the day he died. 'Okay, right – yeah, thanks for getting back to me.'

'Hey that's no problem. It's like I said to the other officer earlier, we're happy to help any way we can.'

'Other ... Sorry, what other officer?'

'The one that called earlier on. He was asking about the lockers too, same as Mr Parker.'

'Wait ... I'm sorry, you've lost me. Can we back up here?'

'Sure, the officer that called earlier was asking about whether Mr Parker kept a locker here. I told him the same I was going to tell you, that was what Mr Parker was enquiring about on the day he died. I thought it was a coincidence but I never even gave it a thought until—'

'Jon Parker called you to ask about using a locker?' Her mind accelerating hard again, a piece falling into place.

'Yeah, that's right. He said he was going straight from the club to the airport for some kind of business trip, and he wanted to know if he could leave some items in the lockers while he was away or whether they were emptied out regularly. I told him they do check them, like, once a week, but we could arrange for maintenance to leave his alone.'

The four-digit number Parker emailed himself. Not a PIN code... 'So did he leave something in a locker?'

'Yeah. He's been a member here a long time so we try to—'

'Which locker please?'

'Number 271. We were happy to accommodate, but after what happened, it never even crossed my mind. We should've got maintenance to open it up.'

'It hasn't been opened?'

'No.'

Casey's pulse hit red. 'Keep it that way. Close that locker room off, don't let anyone inside.' She glanced at her watch. She waved to try to get McTeague's attention but he was crouched in front of Maggie. 'Ma'am you said another cop called about this?' Ice water down her spine, everything shifting and changing-

'Yeah, not too long ago. Actually, he wanted to know the locker number too.'

'What was his name?'

'Lemme see, I was just looking for it ... Yeah, Captain McTeague.'

Casey stared over the roof of her own car, her vision tunnelling. Something he'd kept from her? Something he was holding over her? How did he even know...?

'Detective?'

'I'll be there inside a half hour. Don't go anywhere.'

She hung up and called out to McTeague. 'Hey ... uh, I gotta go. Stay with her until the EMTs arrive.'

He stood up, looking startled, started to ask where she was going.

She gunned the engine and took off.

Speeding through the darkness to Sentona Hills. Pushing the car hard along the highway, still ten minutes out. Trying to make sense of it all. Putting herself in Parker's shoes that last day.

Casey figures out his burner phone link to Michael Patrick Bell, inching closer to proving his involvement. But Parker didn't know that yet, her search warrant still pending at the time. Meanwhile, he's at home, enquiring about stowing something in the lockers at Sentona Hills and calling Clarence Mickelroff for some kind of reassurance. Clarence tells him he's safe. Unless...

Unless there was something in the house that could prove his involvement. Some piece of evidence he'd been dumb enough to hold on to – and which he now feared Casey hadn't given up on. The storage unit rented in Michael Bell's name was full of mementos, so someone had been collecting. What if it was Parker all along? Casey was still prowling, maybe he sensed she was a threat, that she was intending to come back with a search warrant – or maybe Mickelroff got a tipoff and warned him. Another leap followed from it: what if Parker spotted her outside his house that day? She was sure she'd stayed out of sight, but if she'd screwed up and he'd seen her, that would explain why he felt he had to make his move. He'd have known it was too risky to make a trip somewhere just to ditch whatever it was – but Sentona Hills to play golf? That wouldn't raise anyone's suspicions. The four-digit number he'd sent to himself: a locker code for something important enough to keep but dangerous enough to hide.

Her headlights ran ahead of her on the blacktop, like her thoughts. Why was McTeague calling Sentona Hills without telling her? How did he even know to make the call or to ask about lockers? She thought back over everything she'd told him, but it couldn't have come from her – she hadn't even made the connection herself then. And why would he keep it from her anyway? Driving breakneck with this terrifying feeling like she was being played.

# CHAPTER 35

The Sentona Hills sign was lit amber under spotlights, like a beacon guiding her in. Casey turned onto the long driveway leading up to the complex, the lights from the main building the only ones visible on the horizon in front of her, the dark fairways and pastures all around threatening to swallow her up.

She pulled into the parking lot, and the scene she found there made her hit the brake. Slow-motion chaos all around. Employees and club members alike were streaming from the building, sharing a dazed look. Cell-phone screens bobbed in the darkness like searchlights, people milling in all directions. Casey lowered her window and could just make out the screeching alarm coming from inside the building. She pulled her car over to the side and ditched it.

The staff members in their burgundy uniforms were easy enough to pick out. She buttonholed the nearest one, a woman pressing a finger to her ear, straining to hear something through her earpiece.

Casey whipped her badge out. 'Ma'am, what's going on?'

The woman glanced over, distracted. 'Fire alarm.'

Casey looked at the sprawling building, no outward sign of smoke or flames. 'Is this a drill?'

The woman glanced again, noting the badge this time before she answered. 'No. An alarm was tripped in one of the locker rooms, we're evacuating as a precaution. The fire department are on their way.'

Casey scanned the crowd, a throng moving and shifting like starlings, some milling around waiting, others heading for their cars. High beams backlit the swirl of tailpipe fumes, creating a surreal atmosphere. Car horns blared as too many tried to get out of the lot at the same time, civility breaking down as the noise level ratcheted up.

Her phone was ringing in her pocket – McTeague. She put it back in her coat and pushed her way through the crowd towards the building, speeding up as she came closer. At the front entrance, a man in burgundy tried to stop her going inside. She badged him out of the way. 'Where are the men's lockers?'

'What?'

'Lockers. Male changing rooms. Where are they?'

'Well there are three sets of changing rooms, but you can't go in there right now.'

'271. I need number 271.'

He stared at her in disbelief, something in her face making him jump to. He pointed. 'Down that corridor, then take the second left. Next to the gym. But, ma'am...'

She ran inside, pausing for a beat as she turned into the corridor he'd indicated. The alarm was piercing there, reverberating off the walls and tiled floors. But there was no smell of smoke.

She moved off again, running down the corridor and making the left, brass signs on the wall confirming the way. The changing room was in front of her, and she ran through the door.

The place was a mess, wet towels spilling off the benches to the floor, a scatter of coats left behind on their hooks, even a pair of shoes abandoned in one corner. It smelled of sweat and deodorant. She looked around, couldn't see any lockers, so she moved past the benches, rounding a corner where it gave way to a larger area, a wall of varnished teak lockers in front of her-

She froze when she saw him.

'Boss?'

Ray spun around at hearing her voice. He was in front of an open locker, a Ziploc bag in his hand, containing something

she couldn't make out. He looked like he was seeing a ghost. He lowered his hands to his sides and straightened up, like someone who knew they seemed tense and had to make an effort to appear casual. 'Case, you made it.'

'Made it?'

'Yeah, Billy told me about the code in the emails, we were knocking it around and Dana figured out maybe it was a locker combination.'

'Dana put that together?'

'Yeah.' He tried for a smile, only half his mouth obeying. 'She remembered you said Parker went to Sentona Hills that day, and...'

'They said ... I talked to someone here, they said it was McTeague called about it.'

'McTeague?' He screwed his face up. 'They must've got that wrong.' He set whatever he was holding down in the locker again, shifting slightly so he was blocking her view.

Casey felt like she was rooted to the spot. On the wall next to her, she noticed the fire alarm had been tripped. She pointed to the open locker door. 'So what's inside?'

He glanced behind himself like he'd forgotten it was there. 'It's a cell phone. Guess maybe it's Parker's burner – the dumbass kept it after all.'

'Okay, perfect. Let's get it processed. I'll call the office.' She brought her phone out of her pocket and made to dial.

'Case, hold on. You sure you want to play it that way? I mean, the techs get hold of it, could take days to get any answers, and that's if they don't screw it up or miss something. If there's a clue relating to Tina on here, don't you wanna get that right away? We could just take it back to the department right now, power it up...'

The alarm was wailing, burrowing all the way into her brain. Ray's smile forced, everything about the scene a half-turn off – like bum notes in a familiar piece of music. 'No, Maranda's crew are good, I think she should have it first. She'll get it done fast. Why'd you set off the alarm?'

'I had to clear the place out.'

'Why?'

'Just a precaution.'

Casey tried to peer around him into the open locker. 'What else is in there?'

Ray glanced behind himself again, his gaze lingering this time. He turned back to her and didn't say anything at first, his tongue curled over his bottom lip. Then he put his hands on his hips. 'Tapes.' He let out a small laugh, his chest deflating. 'The fucker kept tapes.'

There was regret in his voice. Just a hollow echo to his words, but unmissable. Knowing too, a desperately wrong feeling now, the room suddenly stifling, like trying to breathe in a sauna. 'You sound like you know something about them?'

He turned his eyes to the floor. 'Put your cell phone away, Case.'

'Why?'

'Please. For me.'

She slipped it into her pants pocket, letting her hand rest there. Her wrist grazing her holster.

He looked her in the eyes again, shaking his head. 'I'm so fucking tired. I wish you knew.' He came forward a few steps and sat down on one of the benches, resting his elbows on his knees, head in his hands.

'You wanna tell me what's going on here?'

He pulled his hands through his hair, gripping two fistfuls.

The he looked up sharply. 'I know McTeague's been talking shit about me. What's he told you?'

She took a step closer. 'He said you're dirty.'

'I know that. Specifically.'

'He said you had eight pounds of stolen dope in your house. That Zoltan Kuresev robbed you for it and that's why you beat his ass.'

He stuck his bottom lip out. 'You believe him?'

'Boss, if you've got something you wanna get off your chest...'

'He painted me as some kind of kingpin then?'

'Something like that.'

He shook his head, the crooked smile back. 'Son of a bitch doesn't even know he's being played.'

He looked away, and she snuck another glance at the locker. 'What does that mean?'

'It's that Lee Harvey Oswald line: *I'm a patsy*. But it's true.'

Her legs were trembling. All her focus not to let it show. 'Jesus Christ, whatever you're trying to say.'

'Hanrahan. It's on Hanrahan, all of it.'

'The chief? What?'

'McTeague thinks I'm the kingpin because that's what Hanrahan's fed him, and he's so far up the chief's ass, he can't see what's in front of his face.' He ran his hand over his mouth. 'Hanrahan's been running schemes for years, and one of them is pimping hookers to his rich buddies – there's a whole little club of the fuckers that came together through this place. High end, discreet, big money. Jon Parker was one of them. I mean, that's not even the half of it, but it's where it all came apart.'

All she could do was stare at him.

'Hanrahan's smart, he runs everything through front companies and cutouts and lowlifes he can extort or threaten.

He has other cops at the top of the chain, his guys, and he makes sure the right people get their cut. I don't know for sure the county executive's office is on the list, but you can't tell me someone there doesn't have their hand out. Point is, Hanrahan kept himself insulated. Except that when he was building everything up, he went through a period of fucking his own girls – he used to call it "testing the merchandise". But the higher he went in the department, the more paranoid he got about it, and by the time he was made chief, the girls he'd been with back in the day started disappearing...'

Casey stared at him, her eyes watering and blurring, trying to recognise the man sitting on the bench in front of her. Every point of connection with him, every emotional connection to him, severing.

'He knew none of his johns would spill because he had dirt on all of them, and they're rich so they're all invested in keeping quiet. But the girls ... you know what they're like. He's just some fat old guy with a funny accent to most of them, but he never knew if one might remember him, and then start talking ... so he decided the risk was too great. So one by one...' He shook his head, like the thought of it made him sick. 'But there was one girl from a couple of years back he couldn't track down, like she'd slipped off the radar. And it just sent him over the edge. He's in too deep to stop, but there's this one loose end he can't tie off – it made his paranoia ten times worse. And then Tina Grace walked into Jon Parker's place.'

Casey wanted to throw up.

'Seems like she'd fallen in with one of Hanrahan's front companies when she first got in the game, and that's where he came into contact with her, and then one thing led to another. He wasn't a crazy back then, so he wouldn't even have noticed or cared when she quit and went straight, she was nothing to him. But by the time she showed up at Parker's, right under his nose, she was this holy fucking grail Hanrahan's been killing himself trying to find.'

'Parker didn't realise at first who she was, but after they get high, she starts telling him she's in on this huge fucking secret. How there's this rumour about working girls disappearing, but it's not a rumour, it's true, and she knows who's behind it, but he'd never believe her if she told him. Parker puts two and two together at this point, but instead of doing any of the smart things he could've done, he drops Hanrahan's name before she even gets the chance – I guess to impress her or something. Tina must've realised she'd opened up to the wrong guy, and she panicked.'

He stood up, walked to a locker and leaned his head against it. 'And that's when he called me.'

Casey gripped her Glock tight, as if it was stopping her from falling. Her throat dry, the noise and the heat crushing her, fucking Godzilla rampaging around her skull.

He stood up again, earnest now. 'Case, you gotta understand, I had no choice. Hanrahan's had me on a choke chain forever. You honestly buy me for some dirty cop mastermind? Fuck that, you know me, I'm too lazy for that shit. All I wanted to do was bust heads and drink whiskey. I took a few short cuts when I was starting out, and Hanrahan got wise to it, and it was like he was taking me under his wing. I swear to God, he talked to me like everyone did it. What's it hurt if some scumbag dealer gets his money taken? I mean, that's how it started – take their cash, everyone gets a taste, no harm, no foul. But then it becomes, "Well, how about we take some of their dope too? Just so it doesn't jam up the evidence locker. And then why don't we take a few bucks from the defence lawyer to screw up the case, so their boy gets off clean? Then it's fair on everyone." I know that look, it sounds stupid saying it now, but that's how they get you – one bite at a time. And by the time I figured out the scale of what Hanrahan had going on, he had me.'

Casey stared at him, the words she was hearing coming from a stranger's mouth. Alien, incomprehensible. 'Go back to the part about having no choice.' She took a breath to stop her voice faltering. 'Please, Ray, whatever you say next, please don't say you killed her...'

He threw his hands out. 'No, no way. I swear to you.'

It was an exhale in a hurricane, but somehow she still felt relieved.

'So?'

'I told you Hanrahan uses cops to keep it all going. Keeps him above it all and enforces loyalty. Parker had my number, so when Tina started flipping out, he called me.'

'The other burner, connecting Parker and Bell. It was yours.'

He dipped his head and dug his fingers into the back of his neck.

'You fucking called me. You ... My God, "Bitch Casey Wray, next to die" – that came out of your fucking mouth.'

'It was never real, it was just to get you off the case. Why d'you think the chief was so desperate to put some distance between you and Rockport?'

She stood there, looking at him, her whole world spinning. 'So what did you say to Bell when he took Tina?' Casey said. 'Kill her?'

'I didn't ... I never said those words. I told Bell to take care of it. I didn't think...'

Casey pulled her gun. 'You motherfucker. You son of a bitch.'

'I'm sorry, Casey. Truly.'

She realised then her eyes were tearing up. She had the gun aimed at his chest but she could barely see him.

'After that, Hanrahan saw an opportunity and decided to pin all of them on Bell. I didn't even know he'd kept those goddamn mementos. I knew he was crazy but I had no idea he was that sick. I mean, mentally sick. But worse than that – he needs to be put down. You know the only thing he was worried about after Tina? The fact that he never kept anything from the very first girl; that's why there was nothing in the storage place from that other vic they found at the beach. He only started with the keepsakes after her.'

Her legs were rubber now, barely able to hold her up, even as she felt weightless. As insubstantial as a flame.

'What I should've known is that you wouldn't let it go. When you got close, Parker panicked and started trying to threaten me to get you to back off. Tells me he's still got his burner, all the contacts listed properly in it, and tapes of all the times we spoke – I mean, fuck, he had conversations going back years. Me arranging burner phones, setting up dates, naming names – Hanrahan, all of it. And he just drops it on me, like a fucking bomb. I didn't know what the fuck to do, had no idea where he would've kept them stashed, so...'

'So you killed him.'

He looked at her, big eyes pleading for understanding.

The alarm cut out and left them in silence. So sudden it was deafening. Filling the space between them like a black hole.

'Did Dave know?'

He shook his head, eager to grab anything that might

ameliorate. 'The Kuresev stuff was his breaking point. He never had the stomach for it, that's why he wanted to quit the department. He was smart about that, he saw it all for what it was. Where it led.'

'What happened to Tina Grace?'

'I don't know. I swear.'

'Don't lie to me...'

'Case—'

'Don't you fucking lie to me...'

'You think I'm gonna ask Bell that question? Fuck, no.'

'Who does know? Hanrahan?'

He looked at her with dead eyes, like she was being dumb. 'Deniability is his religion.'

'There must be ... Someone has to know. Bell must've talked—'

'She's gone, Case. Hanrahan's paranoid and obsessed, she never stood a chance. He even sent a guy down to Knoxville on a wild-goose chase after you got that hoax call, just to make sure – and that was after Bell swore to me again he'd taken care of it. Some poor bastard spent two days tearing the place up, knowing he was chasing a ghost.'

Casey took a step to the side, fighting to keep the Glock steady. 'I can't believe this. I can't believe I'm listening to this.'

He opened his hands. 'I'm sorry. I never wanted this to touch you.'

That lit a fire inside her. 'Why the fuck didn't you talk to me? All the hours, all the advice, all the ... Fuck, why didn't you say something?'

'It wasn't for you, Case. You're a good cop.'

'Don't fucking patronise me. I would've helped you out of it, you could've ... Shit, there were other ways. It's on you. It's all on you. Tina Grace could've walked out of there ... Holy shit, all the times...' She couldn't finish the sentence, choking on her own words, poison in her mouth. Just the sight of him nauseating her. 'You motherfucker.'

He had his head dipped. When he looked up, his eyes were damp. 'I'm sorry.' His voice a cracked whisper.

'McTeague checked out the threat against me, he told me it was serious.'

'I had to make it look real. I planted the story, but you were never in danger, I swear. I never would've let anything happen to you...'

She motioned with the gun, harnessing her anger to find composure. 'Get away from the locker. Turn around, hands behind your head.'

He stared at her, unmoving. Then he slipped his hand down by his side.

'What the fuck are you doing?' Casey said.

He was still again. 'C'mon, Big. That's not how this goes now.'

She cocked her head. 'What, you're gonna kill me after all?'

He shook his head like she was being ridiculous. 'I was a dead man the minute you walked in this room. This way, at least I get to decide.'

'Don't give me that shit.'

'I'm not on a sympathy trip, it's a statement of fact. Because you could never let me walk out of here with this phone ... could you?'

She didn't answer.

'I swear, I'd be gone forever. Just disappear. I just need this phone and the tapes and a few hours...'

She shook her head slowly.

He closed his eyes and smiled. 'That's what I thought. So...'

'If this is true, you've got the golden ticket. Flip on Hanrahan and the others.'

'Flip on Hanrahan? I wouldn't see the week out.'

'There's protection.'

He turned his mouth down, rueful. 'You know that wouldn't work. And if I end up in jail, I wouldn't last the day. So now you gotta help me out.' His hand moved again, slowly unclipping his holster.

'No fucking way.'

'Please.'

'You pull that gun and I'm gonna shoot you. Don't make me do that.'

He nodded. 'One last favour.'

'Ray, please...'

He hesitated, fingers hovering. 'I need you to be strong here, Case.'

Shaking. Tears streaming. 'Ray...'

He nodded again, certain. 'You cannot allow me to draw my weapon, Detective.'

Sobbing, shaking her head.

'Just, please, tell my boys I was a good man once.'

He drew his sidearm and raised it at her.

She shot him twice.

# CHAPTER 36

*Eight Days Later*

The rain that'd hammered Rockport for a week stopped that

morning. Sitting on a bench on the south shore, the skies over Black Reed Bay were still heavy grey, the threat of more to come, but for now it was just good to be outside. Cold, damp air in her lungs, deep breaths to remind her she was still alive.

There were times in the last week Casey could've believed otherwise.

A stream of offices that all looked the same. Grey carpets and beige walls, trying to answer their questions when all she had was questions herself.

At first it was Internal Affairs, but as soon as the outline of it came into view, the Feds swooped in. The same questions again and then again, regurgitating the little she knew, her feet barely touching the floor, part of her still in that locker room across from Carletti. A part she might never get back; unsure she even wanted it.

Hanrahan had taken the first off-ramp he could. Three days after Carletti's death, he'd been found in his office with a single gunshot wound to the head. Already, there were whispers around the department that someone else had pulled the trigger, but the people saying that didn't know the full story. Jon Parker's locker had turned out to be a danger only to Carletti; the tapes he'd made sounded incriminating and made clear Ray's involvement, but they were vague enough that a good defence attorney might've been able to get him off the hook. What the conspiracy theorists didn't know – because it hadn't been made public – was that Ray had left his own confession. A full detailing, recorded on video on his iPhone, of everything he knew about Hanrahan, backed up with names, dates, banking records and surveillance photos. Turned out Ray had been building his own case against the chief, maybe his own insurance policy. An irony if that was so; not enough to save him, but enough to take Hanrahan down too. Hanrahan must've got word of its existence, because he was dead within twelve hours of the scope of Ray's testimony becoming known.

She was looking out over the bay. The beaches were a smudge on the horizon, the flat expanse of black water a million miles wide under pregnant skies. With everything they'd come to signify to her, she'd have been happy to see all the barrier islands cut loose to drift into the Atlantic.

She spotted McTeague coming along the sidewalk towards her and tensed reflexively. He sat down heavily next to her, gazing out over the water without speaking at first. He looked older than the last time she'd seen him, shortly after Sentona Hills. Always burdened, now he had the bearing of a man crippled by it.

'How you feeling?' he said finally.

'Fried.'

He nodded.

'Like I want to sleep for a month but I can't even sit still,' she said.

'Yeah.' He rubbed his face, the least assured she'd ever seen him. 'Yeah, I get that way.'

A cyclist dismounted a short way along from them, and McTeague eyed him. Only when he moved on did he speak again. 'The Feds finished with you for now?'

She blew out her cheeks. 'Who knows? Some days they call me in, some days they don't. You?'

He shook his head. 'It's not gonna be over anytime soon.'

She turned to look at him, understanding his implication. 'They don't believe you didn't know.'

'Would you?'

She looked away, thinking about it. 'Yeah, I would. But only because I talked to Ray Carletti every day the last four years and never saw it.' She laughed once, a small and sad sound, shaking her head at herself. 'So maybe I'm not the character witness you need.'

He looked along the bench at her. 'For whatever it's worth, I never saw it either, I swear. With Hanrahan I mean. And that's on me; I was so fucking focused on Carletti, and he knew it and just kept stoking it. Blinded my goddamn self.'

'They'll believe you in the end. The evidence will speak for itself.'

He flicked his hand to wave it away. 'Doesn't matter. I already decided to hand in my badge.'

She studied her fingers, white with cold, cradled in her lap. 'Not the kind of decision you should make now. It's hard not to doubt yourself, but that might change.'

'I don't want it to. I missed it and I'll live with that, but not with a badge. I lost the right to that.'

She turned to him sharply. 'The implication being I did too?'

'No. Not for a second. You never let Carletti manipulate you the way I let Hanrahan.'

She thought about that. The years she'd spent looking at Ray as a father figure, the department a surrogate family. If she'd not been so single-minded in seeking acceptance, maybe she'd have seen him for what he was; seen through the cracks in the facade he presented to the world. They were there, and she'd missed them, and it hurt to admit that; but the longer she'd dwelt on it, the more that thinking felt like victim-blaming. 'It's on them, no one else. I'm not here to try to change your mind, but the department's going to need good cops when all this is done. If it even survives.'

'It'll survive. It'll just be unrecognisable. But it's got good cops already.' He stared at the side of her face. 'Before I go I'm gonna make sure you get Ray's command.'

She didn't reply to that, and for a minute they sat in silence, watching the seabirds dip and swoop over the water. She was thinking about getting up to leave when he spoke again. 'Took real guts to pull that trigger.'

She kept watching the birds, carefree and free. A place she'd left behind and couldn't imagine getting back to. 'I didn't have a choice.'

'You know that's not true. And not everyone could've made that choice.'

'I don't regret it, if you're trying to reassure me.'

He studied her, like he was checking for signs she meant it.

She folded her arms around herself, the wind picking up and biting. 'Ray called Michael Patrick Bell right before Dave and I got to his place that morning.'

He nodded along. 'Son of a bitch was warning him.'

She looked at him and shook her head. 'That's what I thought at first too. But it was Ray sent the tipoff with his address in the first place.' Searches of Ray's personal items had revealed as much; he'd been smart enough to use a VPN, but not to erase all traces of the anonymous Hotmail account he'd set up. 'He wanted us to find Bell. So the only reason he was calling him that morning was to tell him to take care of another problem. He sent us into a fucking ambush.'

McTeague hung his head.

She was nowhere close to processing that particular revelation. Of all the things that'd come to light in the wake of Carletti's death – that it was him who'd tipped off Jon Parker that Casey was on to his burner phone, him who'd slow-walked her application for the search warrant – everything else was a distant second to knowing he'd tried to have her killed. That he'd succeeded in having Cullen killed – afraid of what he might reveal if he went through with his threat to quit the department. 'I feel like I never really knew him at all. Stupid, gullible...'

'Jesus Christ.'

'Yeah. So no regrets. None.' She stood up, her heart swelling again with as much pain as she could take for one day. 'But I'll tell you what scares me: I nearly didn't do it. I knew what he wanted me to do, and I thought he was bluffing. I didn't think in a million years he'd have killed me. Even with everything he'd just told me, I trusted him with my own life, because I thought I meant something to him. So you wanna talk about doubting your judgement? Mine nearly got me killed. And I have to live with that.'

He was looking up at her from the bench, as if he couldn't believe what he was hearing. As if she had something more to say that might make some sense of it all. Finally, he said, 'You weren't the only one he fooled.'

For a second she worried he was going to ask about Cullen – the one name Ray had kept out of his video confession. At first Casey had assumed it was out of loyalty, carried through to the grave, but later she decided it was his way of paying a debt. He'd sent his friend to die to ensure his silence; the least he could do was see that Luisa and the girls wouldn't be deprived of his pension. Casey saw no reason to tell Luisa the truth, nor IA or the Feds. Dave's failings were his own, not his wife's, and much less his kids'; they'd have to grow up without their dad, at least let them think he'd been a hero.

She stared at McTeague, waiting, the look in his eyes like he knew exactly what she was thinking. He said nothing.

'Live and learn, I guess.' She lifted her eyebrows and shrugged as she said it, as if the levity in her words was real. As if she believed it. As if that was all it took to draw a line under the most personal betrayal imaginable.

## CHAPTER 37

She was at home, on her sofa when the call came. There was a rerun of *Seinfeld* on the TV, Casey flipping between that and Facebook on her phone, when the screen changed.

A number she didn't know. Something that made her hesitate from answering after everything.

'Casey Wray.'

'Detective?'

A voice she'd heard before, couldn't immediately place. 'Who is this?'

'Detective, it's Tina Grace.'

Casey went cold. It came back in a rush, the same voice as last time. 'Look, whoever the fuck you are—'

'It's me, I swear. Let me explain—'

'Fuck off, okay? I'm gonna find you, and I am gonna bust your ass—'

'On my 911 call I said I was in Barton Beach by mistake. I didn't know where I was.'

Casey stopped dead. The 911 call had never been made public.

'Are you there?'

'I'm here. How is this ... How the fuck is this possible?'

'I need to talk to you. I saw on the news he's dead.'

Casey hesitated. 'Who?'

'Hanrahan.'

'This is ... You're really screwing with me, girl. Who the fuck are you?'

'I know this is fucked up, and I know I'm probably in a shitload of trouble, but I never thought I'd be able to come back. That's why I told you I was okay and that you didn't have to look for me anymore. And then ... He's really dead?'

Casey shut the TV off and tossed the remote along the couch. 'I don't understand what's going on. Why are you doing this?'

'Would you believe me if I called you with FaceTime?'

Too stunned to say anything. Before she could answer, the beeping sound in her ear told her another call was coming through. She brought the cell down to look and saw it was a FaceTime from the same number. She hit Accept.

And then Tina Grace's face was in front of her. Trembling, taking a faltering breath. The first hint of a nervous smile.

'What in the hell?'

'I can explain. Honestly. But I just needed to hear it from you. He really killed himself?'

She screwed her eyes shut and opened them again, Tina still there. 'Chief Hanrahan shot himself in the head.'

Tina dipped her head forward and covered her face. She wouldn't look up again at first, her breaths coming short and stunted. 'Oh my God.'

'Tina ... Jesus Christ, what happened to you? I can't believe this. Where are you?'

'Houston.'

Houston – a bell ringing in her mind. 'Houston? Are you ... Did you look up your dad or something?'

Tina nodded. 'It's what I told you last time, I had to get away.

I'd emailed him a couple times, so I figured ... I mean, he nearly shit when I showed up here. I'm really sorry he lied to you guys, it was my fault. I begged him not to tell you on the phone, please don't blame him. Houston PD came by and asked about me and he lied for me to them too. Please, he can't get in trouble because of me.'

She shook her head to herself, hangdog Nathan Grace deserving an Oscar for his acting. Any anger she felt was quickly swallowed by joy. 'It's ... It's not important right now. You're alive. Jesus Christ, I'm so happy...'

'I know I've put you all through hell, but ... I mean, you get it now, right? Why I had to do it?'

The chief of police trying to have her killed; and somehow, against all the odds, she'd escaped. Fooled them all. 'Yeah. I get it. Have you called your mom yet?'

'I had to be certain first. But if he's gone ... I'm safe, right?'

Casey struggled with what to say to that. The fallout was still in progress – four other cops under investigation for suspected links to Hanrahan's operation – and no guarantee that was all of them. A chance there were more like Carletti, so far undetected. 'Call your mom, talk it over with her. You have to decide what's right for you.'

'I want to come home.'

Tina came through the Arrivals gate and flung her arms around Casey.

At first Casey was still too stunned to react. Right up to the moment she saw her, she had doubts about all of it. Doubted

Tina would show up, doubted she wouldn't have second thoughts, even doubted it wasn't some extended psychosis.

And then there she was. In the flesh. As real as Casey's own hands and feet.

She was just as slight as in her photographs, but she'd cut her hair and dyed it blonde. She had a small bag with her that didn't look enough for a trip to the grocery store, let alone someone who'd disappeared herself. Casey took it off her and led her to the car.

When they came outside, Tina looked across at her. 'I honestly thought I'd never be able to come back.'

'I don't ... I don't even know where to start. I have so many questions. I'm sorry for what you've been through. All of it.'

'My mom told me you saved her life. A bunch of times.'

'She's exaggerating.'

Tina shook her head. 'She told me you never gave up. That even when she had, you wouldn't.'

Casey looked away, her cheeks firing red.

'Seriously. Thank you.'

Casey told her there was no pressure to talk, but it all came out on the ride to Maggie's house. It felt like Tina had never been able to tell the whole story before, and once she started, it became catharsis.

She spoke about meeting Hanrahan for the first time, three years before. Back then just another client, calling himself Max, but one the bosses at Executive Elite Talent would fall over themselves to accommodate. Only realising much later who he really was when she saw him on News 10 after he was made chief. The little thrill she got at first from their shared secret; remembering how naive she was at the time, shocked to find a cop would go with an escort.

In time she pretty much forgot about him. The job was easy and lucrative, but she didn't like the work or the people it brought her into contact with, especially at the agency. She'd put aside enough to get Maggie started in rehab, and she began to think about getting out. Then the story went round about girls going missing after seeing this secret high-roller client, and it scared her enough to give her the final nudge. She quit Executive Elite and eventually got the job at Bronsons, and for a long time she didn't give much thought to her old life.

But boredom and impatience crept in over time, and eventually the lure of the money became too much – and more so as Maggie's drinking got worse again. The job had changed since she left, Tinder and the other social-media platforms making it easier for girls to get work, everything done online. Compared to the cheap-ass wages and limited advancement prospects at Bronsons, the hours and the convenience – and the new-found control – made it seem like a better option, so she joined a new agency: West Side Talent. The only complication was that now she had a boyfriend, and she hated sneaking around behind Brian Walton's back.

But that story she'd heard – girls disappearing – hadn't gone away. And now she was back and it kept creeping closer to home. She'd met Michelle Montara during her first stint in the business, at a party Executive Elite Talent had thrown for some of their exclusive clients. She remembered her only because she'd seen her being led off to a separate apartment, and caught a glimpse of her waiting date: Max, as she knew him then. Now, two years later, the word was she was one of the missing girls.

Then she'd heard a rumour Rhonda Clavert was another, and she started to get really fucking scared.

'You knew them both?' Casey said.

'Michelle didn't work for Executive Elite, they brought her in just for that party, I guess. And Rhonda ... She was only with the agency five minutes. She wasn't really cut out for it, you could see that, so I tried to look after her some. She told me they'd made her go with this guy who was, like, rough with her, who kinda forced her to do stuff she wasn't comfortable with, and when she talked to the office about it, they told her not to bring it up ever again. So she asked me about it and she told me it was this guy Max. She quit pretty soon after. Thing is, he'd done the same with me – like, after the first time we had sex, he waited and then he made me go again. Usually you get in and get out, but he acted like he could do whatever he wanted. He was into choking, all that kind of kink shit, and I didn't know what I was supposed to do. I was still so green back then, I ... Shit, I didn't have a clue what I was doing.'

'So anyway, after Rhonda talked to me, I started asking some of the others about this Max guy, because I figured someone should say something. Like, I didn't wanna be the troublemaker or nothing, but I didn't want this guy taking liberties, especially with girls like Rhonda. But most of the girls didn't know who I was talking about – I figured out after they probably only sent a few of us his way. So before I quit, I went to the bosses about him. Soon as I started talking they shut me down. I didn't give a fuck back by that point, I just wanted to get out. I didn't figure out who he really was until later – and then I just couldn't believe it.'

Casey stared at the road ahead, raging in her own head. She made a mental note to track down all the bosses and make them pay. Along with anyone else associated with Executive Elite Talent. And all the others. 'Tina ... Jesus Christ. I'm sorry.'

'I should've done something back then. But who the fuck would've believed me, right? I mean the goddamn chief of police?'

Casey nodded her head and they rode in silence for a few seconds. Then she glanced across at her again. 'Can I ask, what happened after you left Jon Parker's house?'

Tina stared at her hands, holding the silence a few seconds more, thinking about her answer. 'So you know I went knocking on the other houses along the beach. None of those fuckers would help me. I got to the last one and the road was just pitch-black after that, so I turned back. Then I saw him coming towards me and I told him to just stay the fuck away from me.'

'You mean Parker?'

'Yeah. He was all like, "My driver's waiting for you up the street, will you get the fuck outta here." I was shit scared, so when I saw the guy and the car down there, I called 911, because I thought Parker was just trying to get me off the street so he could deal with me out of sight. But then the goddamn driver guy came from nowhere and took my cell outta my hands. I had no fucking idea he was, like, in with them. They sent him to pick me up but I thought he was just a driver.

'You gotta understand, as soon as Parker said Hanrahan's name, back in the house, I could see it in his eyes: he knew who I was, or, like, what I knew. And I mean it was obvious he was gonna do something – he went into the bathroom with his cell phone and I could hear him talking to someone. It was four in the fucking morning, who does that? So I went through his pants and took two hundred bucks, and I was gonna run right away, but he came out before I could split, so I tried to act like everything was fine until he left me alone long enough to get out. I know you'd probably say I shoulda waited for the police, but I was freaking out like crazy, so when he said "There's the car, get in," it felt like a trap. It was a trap.'

'So then how did you get away from Bell?'

'He thought I was out of it. Like passed out. He took a call when we were driving and I could tell the other guy was trying to convince him of something, so after that I knew he was supposed to be getting rid of me. He stopped the car outside this house, I guess his place, and he went to get something from the trunk, so I grabbed my cell and when he came back I hit him with the door. He punched me in the mouth as I got out, but then a car crossed the intersection along the block and it distracted him long enough for me to take off. I swear I didn't stop running for, like, fifteen blocks. After that I honestly thought the whole fucking world was coming for me, so I took the first bus out of town. That got me as far as Knoxville, and then I realised I was, like, halfway to Houston already, so I just kept going.'

They pulled up outside Maggie's house, Casey still trying to come to terms with what she was hearing. Through the noise in her head, one question came through strongest.

'Did, uh ... Tina, did you know there was a third victim we found out there? We couldn't put an ID on her.'

Tina nodded. 'I don't know who she was.'

'Maybe once we've got you settled, maybe in time, you can tell me some names we could start with.'

Tina didn't respond right away, and Casey backtracked a little. 'Not right now, we can get to this once we've got you the help you need.'

'It's not that. It's just...'

Casey glanced at her but kept quiet.

'I have no idea how many girls he was with,' Tina said. 'But there had to be others. I can't believe it was just four of us. So...'

So there were more bodies waiting to be found. Buried, or lying in the half-light; abandoned, forgotten, destroyed, each wasted life a tragedy, the whole almost too sad to contemplate. Tina Grace a survivor, a small mercy to be thankful for. The thought Casey clung to as she saw Maggie throw the door open and come running across the yard.

Tina jumped out of the car and ran straight into her outstretched arms, into an embrace so fierce it toppled them both to the grass. Maggie laughing hard, tears in her eyes. She'd called Casey the day before, to tell her she hadn't touched alcohol since that day on the beach, and that she'd made an AA meet four days running. Casey waved to her, but Maggie was wrapped too tight around Tina to see.

Then Tommy was in the doorway. Carletti's confession had cleared him over Jon Parker's murder, but not before he'd admitted to being inside Parker's house that first morning. After Casey and Cullen had driven away, Tommy had knocked on the door and forced his way inside, punching Jon Parker in the face as he tried to glean information on his sister's whereabouts – leaving him with the black eye Parker later claimed was from a boxing workout. At some point as Tommy charged around the house, he'd left his fingerprint on the French doors.

Now Tommy ran over and dropped to his knees beside the two women on the grass. He hesitated just long enough to glance at Casey, sending a slight nod her way before he threw himself down on top of them to be part of it.

Casey smiled and looked away, stuck on thoughts of lives lost and lives saved, and how fine the line between the two could be. A line she'd walk as long as she wore a badge, even knowing they could never beat the darkness into retreat. But every victory was a light that stayed on, a beacon in that darkness; a reminder that there was hope to be found, even in a treacherous world.

# AFTERWORD

This novel is a work of fiction. It is inspired, however, by the terrible crimes that have been attributed to the unidentified murderer known as The Long Island Serial Killer.

Between December 2010 and April 2011, ten sets of remains were discovered in and around the remote Gilgo Beach area of Long Island. Police at the time stated they believed a single killer was responsible for all ten deaths. Additional finds since have raised the possibility of as many as sixteen victims – and that multiple killers have used the area as a dumping ground. In 2011, the Suffolk County DA made the chilling statement that, 'It is clear that the area in and around Gilgo Beach has been used to discard human remains for some period of time.'

The characters featured in this book are fictional, so as not to sensationalise or dishonour the memory of the victims and their families. It is my sincere hope they will one day soon see justice done.

# ACKNOWLEDGEMENTS

Every novel is only as good as the team behind it, and I am lucky to have the most amazing team helping me bring these books to life. My sincere thanks to:

My incredible publisher, Karen Sullivan, who always sees the best in my work and then manages to make it even better. Also to Cole Sullivan, West Camel, Liz Barnsley, Victoria Goldman, Anne Cater and all the team at Orenda Books, as well as Sophie Goodfellow at FMCM.

Jane Gregory, Stephanie Glencross and Mary Jones at David Higham, for all their support and hard work bringing my books to readers.

Mark Swan, who makes the best covers in the business – every time.

Superintendent James Mackay, for patiently sharing his incredible knowledge of US policing; any errors that remain are mine and mine alone.

Jeremy Preston at Surrey County Libraries, for being a brilliant supporter of my work, and a passionate champion of books, authors and reading.

Beverley Fox and the team at Weybridge Library, for all their support and encouragement, and for thrusting my work into the hands of so many new readers.

Ellie Mae, for suggesting the title of this book.

Steve Andrews, for keeping me in curries and red wine.

Camilla Davey, for being such a generous supporter of my books (and for introducing me to people as 'a famous author'!).

Janet, Chris and Ruby, for keeping us (partially, in my case) sane through lockdown.

To my family, for always supporting me to spend more time staring blankly at an empty page.

And most of all, the readers, bloggers, booksellers and book lovers who've read and enjoyed my work, and helped spread the word. All my gratitude.